A HEARTBEAT AWAY

She didn't need to ask what Luke was talking about. It was obvious that he was lost in a memory, and not a pleasant one at that. There was pain and grief etched in the depths of his eyes. Ignoring her own pain, she slid over closer to the edge of the bed and reached out to him. He hesitated only a heartbeat before pulling her onto his lap, burying his face in her hair. She closed her eyes and held on to him for dear life.

The storm seemed to gather new strength, but it might only have been the one brewing in her bedroom. Cora knew the instant the flavor of their embrace changed. Luke nuzzled her neck, sending spicy shivers of heat dancing through her. Waves of dizziness, which had nothing at all to do with the bump on her head, made her crazy for his kiss. They'd come so close on other occasions, but this time she wasn't going to let either one of them run scared.

BOOK YOUR PLACE ON OUR WEBSITE AND MAKE THE READING CONNECTION!

We've created a customized website just for our very special readers, where you can get the inside scoop on everything that's going on with Zebra, Pinnacle and Kensington books.

When you come online, you'll have the exciting opportunity to:

- View covers of upcoming books
- Read sample chapters
- Learn about our future publishing schedule (listed by publication month *and author*)
- Find out when your favorite authors will be visiting a city near you
- Search for and order backlist books from our online catalog
- Check out author bios and background information
- Send e-mail to your favorite authors
- Meet the Kensington staff online
- Join us in weekly chats with authors, readers and other guests
- Get writing guidelines
- AND MUCH MORE!

Visit our website at
http://www.kensingtonbooks.com

THE OUTLAW GROOM

PAT PRITCHARD

ZEBRA BOOKS
Kensington Publishing Corp.
http://www.kensingtonbooks.com

ZEBRA BOOKS are published by

Kensington Publishing Corp.
850 Third Avenue
New York, NY 10022

All Kensington titles, imprints and distributed lines are available at special quantity discounts for bulk purchases for sales promotion, premiums, fund-raising, educational or institutional use.

Special book excerpts or customized printings can also be created to fit specific needs. For details, write or phone the office of the Kensington Special Sales Manager: Kensington Publishing Corp., 850 Third Avenue, New York, NY 10022. Attn. Special Sales Department. Phone: 1-800-221-2647.

Zebra and the Z logo Reg. U.S. Pat. & TM Off.

First Printing: January 2005
10 9 8 7 6 5 4 3 2 1

Printed in the United States of America

CHAPTER 1

Luke's world had narrowed down to one small room with no windows and a single door. His companions were nothing to brag about, but the sound of their scuttling along in the corners and crevices kept him from feeling completely alone.

Sitting with his back against the wall, he pulled a threadbare blanket up around his shoulders to ward off the cold and the ever-present stench of men living in fear and despair. His feet itched to be pacing the short distance from one wall to the other and back again, but tonight he refused to give those outside the satisfaction. That didn't mean he could sleep or that the minutes weren't passing slowly enough to drive him mad.

Over and over, he reminded himself that eventually morning would come. The warden might control every aspect of his prisoners' lives, but not even he could hold back the dawn. Luke glared at the door, knowing in an hour or two at the most someone would walk through it to freedom. It had happened before, but this time it was supposed to be his turn.

If there was a God in heaven . . .

If they weren't lying to him . . .

Damn it to hell, would the minutes never end?

He swiped at his face with the back of his hand, the

need for sleep and maybe a few tears burning in his eyes. For the hundredth time since the lights went out, he let his plans for the next few days play out in his mind, each time adding more details. With the few dollars they'd give him on the way out, he'd get a room at a cheap hotel and then pay whatever it cost to take a bath hot enough to scald the smell of prison off his skin.

If there was enough money left, he'd buy a hot meal, a good cigar, and some cheap whiskey, and then maybe find a pretty woman to look at. He didn't know what such things cost anymore, but he was sure that he didn't have enough money to buy a night's pleasure in a whore's arms. But he could look for free, so that would have to be enough.

His brother Jack had promised to catch up with him in the next day or so. The two of them would celebrate their reunion and Luke's freedom before riding away from Kansas, never to look back. They'd head directly for Missouri and the small farm that had been their childhood home. Clenching his fists, he swore once he was back in the Ozarks, he'd never leave again.

The shriek of rusty metal door hinges cut through the silence. Luke cocked his head, listening for the telltale sound of rattling keys and the shuffle of a guard's approaching footsteps. At first, the sounds were so faint that he thought his feverish mind had imagined them. But no, someone—make that several someones—was coming his way. He sat up straighter, throwing the blanket to the side.

He couldn't help how he looked or how he smelled, but damned if he would let them see how scared he was that this was all a dream and tomorrow he'd wake up back in this cell again. The footsteps stopped right outside his cell door.

"Well, Johnny Reb, seems like this is your lucky day."

The sound of the key turning in the lock was the sweetest thing Luke had ever heard. He waited for the door to swing open before standing up. He hated the weakness that had him reaching for the bars in the cell wall for support, but he'd make it out on his own two feet or die trying. To his surprise, as soon as he staggered through the door, new energy flowed through his veins.

It hadn't been a dream after all. For the first time in almost five years, he was going to smell fresh air and walk free in the sunshine.

The sun poured through the window and right into her face. Still not quite awake, Cora instinctively rooted deeper into the covers trying to avoid the inevitable. The bright morning light chased her across the bed until she had no choice but to surrender or fall off onto the floor. Tossing the quilt aside, she sat up and glared at the unadorned window.

"By this time next week you'll have curtains."

She crawled out of bed and slipped her wrapper on over her flannel nightgown. A pair of wool socks helped ward off the morning chill until the stove could take over the job. Although she needed to pay a call on the privy out back, she took the time to coax a handful of kindling and a pine knot into catching fire before going outside. By the time she returned, the stove would be hot enough to heat up last night's coffee and to fry up some bacon and eggs.

Outside the air still had quite a nip to it, but spring had definitely settled in to stay. She was due in town in just over an hour, so she didn't have time to dawdle. Even so, she paused long enough to look around the rough ground that would eventually be her front yard. In her mind's eye, she could envision a row of rose bushes climbing along a fence that had yet to be built. Just beyond the future flowers, she'd plant her first vegetable garden. Visions of beans and squash pleased her greatly.

A lot of hard work lay between her and the reality of her dreams, and she was anxious to get started. She'd waited a long, long time to have a home of her own, a life of her own away from the eagle eyes of her sole relative. Aunt Henrietta, although not pleased with Cora's choice of locations, had actually helped her niece set up housekeeping. It was one of life's contradictions that Cora felt closer to her elderly aunt now than she did when she lived with the woman.

She reached for the skillet that Henrietta had insisted on giving to her. It would have taken Cora months, perhaps years, to season a new one to this one's prime condition. Every time she used it, she thought of her aunt, making her wonder if that had been the reason behind the unexpected gift.

As she waited for the bacon to start sizzling, Cora looked around her tidy kitchen, her eyes sliding right past the big oak table with its six matching chairs. Not for the first time, she regretted buying it. It fit the room, it was well made, but it was lonely to sit at all by herself.

Why hadn't someone warned her that living alone was a two-edged sword? She loved the freedom to make all of her own decisions—what to eat, when to get up, when to go to bed. But on the other hand, she had no one to read with, no one to talk to, no one to hold her during the long hours of the night.

She dished up her breakfast and pulled a chair over near the window. The room faced west across gently rolling fields all the way to the hills in the distance. She liked knowing the view would change as the seasons passed. Right now the woods were green with bright splashes of white blossoms from the dogwoods scattered under the taller trees. Come fall, the hills would be ablaze with color—fiery red, bright orange, and pure yellows. Even winter would have its own stark beauty.

An image filled her mind—of her sitting by that same window in a time forty years distant, still alone. She shook her head to clear it, wishing she could rid herself of the dark mood that had plagued her for the past few days.

"Cora Lawford, you sure are feeling sorry for yourself. Why, look at this fine morning and be grateful for what you have!" She'd also taken up talking to herself since moving into her house. Was that another symptom of impending spinsterhood?

Ignoring that nasty little voice in her head, she picked up her plate and set it by the sink, deciding the few dishes could wait until after dinner. It was hardly worth the effort to wash one plate and a skillet. Well aware that she was letting time get away from her, she hurried into her bedroom to get dressed.

Ten minutes later, she set off toward town at a brisk walk. She lived only a mile or so outside of Lee's Mill along a narrow road. The new schoolhouse where she would start work in the fall was not quite two miles farther out on the far side of an abandoned farm. Her lack of close neighbors was the main reason that Aunt Henrietta didn't like Cora's new home. Each time she said so, she sniffed in disapproval and announced that it wasn't proper for a single woman to be living so far out on her own. Cora knew it was only her way of saying she worried about her only niece's well-being.

But other than the occasional bout of loneliness, Cora loved the small house she'd had built. Most days she was happy, but lately it seemed as if all of her friends were busy getting married and having babies. Lucy Mulroney, the storekeeper in town, had just given birth to a beautiful baby boy. Then at church last Sunday, Melinda Hayes, the pastor's wife, had confirmed she was expecting by the end of the year.

And Cora didn't even have a beau.

Had it been only last year when the three of them had founded the Luminary Society, a group dedicated to the education of women in Lee's Mill? Perhaps it was because they'd accomplished so much in such a short time that it seemed as if the Society had been around far longer than it really had been.

Immediately Josie Hughes came to mind, one of the first women to join and one of their biggest successes. When Josie had approached the Society, she could neither read nor write. In a very short time, she'd learned enough that Lucy had hired her to work part-time in her store. Of course, now that Josie was happily married to Mitch Hughes, she was too busy out on their farm to come into town more than one or two days a month.

Cora was pleased for her friends; truly she was. She just wished that they could spare a little more time for her. Maybe it was selfish of her to feel that way, but she couldn't help herself. Rather than continue to dwell on such negative thoughts, she hurried her steps. Lucy wouldn't complain if Cora was late opening the store for her, but Cora prided herself on being both a good friend and reliable.

She had been helping Lucy in the Thomas Mercantile off and on for some time. But now that Lucy had a new baby to care for, Cora had volunteered to work extra hours to give her friend more time at home with her young family. Her motives weren't entirely selfless. Working in the store gave her the opportunity to meet and visit with people from all walks of life. In Cora's opinion, Aunt Henrietta had been far too particular about the type of person she allowed Cora to associate with. From behind the counter in the store, she'd had long conversations with miners, farmhands, and even a couple of women who worked at The River Lady.

Henrietta would be horrified if she knew. Cora smiled at the thought.

Just past the last bend in the road the trees thinned out enough that she could see the first few houses along the River Road. The store was located a few blocks ahead near the center of town. Cora deliberately avoided going past her aunt's house for fear Henrietta would call out to her. She couldn't afford to waste any more time if she were to get to the store on time. Feeling a little guilty for avoiding her aunt, she promised herself that she would stop for a quick visit on her way home.

And perhaps get an invitation to dinner. It would be nice to have a hot meal after a long day at the store without cooking it herself. She lifted her skirts as she climbed the steps up to the sidewalk. Two older women, both friends of Henrietta's, came out of the hotel just as she passed by.

"Morning, Cora. Does your aunt know you're out and about so early this morning?"

"I don't know. I haven't spoken to her in a few days."

"Well, we're on our way to her house for a Bible reading. Perhaps you'd like to join us."

As if she hadn't spent far too much time in their company doing exactly that. There was no telling how many hours she'd wasted listening to these same women criticize everyone in town under the guise of religion. She resented their nosiness, and, knowing that every word would be reported to her aunt, she answered politely anyway.

"I'm sorry, ladies. As much as I'd love nothing more than to be a part of your group, I'm afraid I promised Lucy Mulroney I would open the store for her. She'd like to stay home with her new baby this morning." She swept her skirts to the side as she moved past them. She wasn't at all sure her attempt at smiling was very successful. "So if you'll excuse me, I don't want to be late."

She left the women clucking behind her like the two old hens that they were. The image brought a genuine smile to Cora's face that lasted until she reached the newspaper office. She opened the door and stepped inside. The smell of ink and cigar smoke hung heavily in the air. Will, the typesetter, ignored her as she walked past him into Cade Mulroney's office.

Her friend's husband sat at his desk, hunched over a pile of papers and murmuring under his breath. He looked up as she crossed the threshold into his office.

"Cora, good morning," he said, rising to his feet. "I figured you'd be along about now."

She glanced at the clock on the wall behind him and was relieved to see that she was right on time. "Lucy said you'd have the key to the store."

"That I do." He patted his pockets and frowned. "I know she gave it to me this morning. Where could it be?" He started shuffling through the stacks of papers scattered over his desk.

She noticed his jacket was hanging on a peg by the door. "Did you leave it in your coat pocket?"

"Lord, I hope so. I'd hate to tell Lucy I've lost another one." He gave Cora a conspiratorial wink. "Last time she threatened to hang it on a chain around my neck."

Cora could just see Lucy doing exactly that. Cade towered over his wife, but Lucy could stand toe to toe with the devil himself when necessary. As editor of the town's only newspaper, Cade was a man to be reckoned with in Lee's Mill. Despite his formidable reputation, he obviously adored his wife and family. Cora liked him immensely.

He slipped his hand into the pocket of his jacket and immediately pulled out the missing key with a triumphant smile. When Cora held out her hand for it, he shook his head. "Sorry, but I'm under strict orders to unlock the door and make sure everything is safe and sound before leaving you there alone."

"Would you have to do that for Lucy?" Cora asked, her hands on her hips, ready to do battle.

He held up his hands in surrender. "No, but with the new baby and everything, Lucy feels the need to mother everyone in sight. You won't believe this, but I swear it's the truth—last night at dinner, she actually offered to cut up my meat for me."

Cora laughed, as he had intended her to. "All right, you can escort me to the store."

She might not like it, but she'd let him. Sometimes her friends forgot that Cora was no longer the young girl who'd been taken in by her aunt after the death of her parents. She was constantly having to remind people that she was now an adult.

Cade led the way out of his office. He stopped beside his employee long enough to give Will a stern look. "I'll only be gone a few minutes. Be here when I get back."

The typesetter managed to look hurt and guilty at the same time. "I wasn't planning on going anywhere."

Cade gave a long-suffering sigh as he ushered Cora outside. "I swear, if I so much as turn my back, he's over at The River Lady. I've never known anyone who likes being in a saloon more than that man does."

Cora hid a smile. She knew his frustration was very real. According to Lucy, Will lost all ability to read and write as soon as he had a beer or two under his belt. Cade had enough to do to get the paper published without having to chain his sole employee to his desk. Of course, that didn't keep the whole situation from being most entertaining for others to watch.

They didn't have far to walk, since the store was next door to the newspaper office. Cade unlocked the door and then stood back to let Cora walk through the door first. She appreciated the gesture. It was his way of letting her know that she was perfectly capable of checking the store out herself.

"I'll go on back to work." He kept glancing back toward his office, no doubt convinced that Will was about to bolt for freedom. "Lucy said she'd like you to come by for lunch unless you have other plans."

"That will be fine. If you see her, tell Lucy I'll be over around one o'clock. I owe your daughter a game of chess, and I couldn't possibly resist a chance to hold that handsome son of yours."

"He is good-looking, isn't he?" Cade was understandably proud of his family. His daughter was from a previous marriage, a decidedly unhappy one. But Mary had blossomed under the combined attention of an adoring father and a loving stepmother. She took her new role as a big sister very seriously.

Cora loved to spend time with the Mulroney family. Mary had claimed her as an honorary aunt because neither of Mary's parents had any siblings. Since Cora herself had only one relative left, she appreciated the attachment even if it was due to friendship rather than blood.

Now that she had the store to herself, she set about following Lucy's routine for opening up for business. She took a fresh apron off the hook in the storeroom and tied it on over her dress. After checking the till, she turned the sign in the front window and unlocked the door. Once she had everything in place to handle the first customers of the day, she picked up the broom and went outside to sweep away the dust that had accumulated since yesterday.

She'd no sooner gotten into a steady rhythm than Melinda Hayes joined her on the porch.

"Good morning, Cora."

As usual, Melinda looked serenely happy, and she had every reason to be. After all, not only was she married to a wonderful man, but the pair would be new parents by the end of the year. Once again, Cora fought down a nasty little surge of jealousy as she set the broom aside long enough to hug her friend.

"Did you stop by just to say hello, or do you have some shopping to do?"

"Both, really," Melinda said with a smile. "I wanted to see how you were settling in out there by yourself."

Interesting. Evidently Henrietta wasn't the only one who worried about Cora's living so far out of town. "I'm doing very well. After I get home, I plan to spend the evening laying out plans for my first gardens."

Melinda, a gardening enthusiast herself, perked up at that. "I'll check my own garden to see what kind of cuttings I can give you. And don't forget to mention that you will be needing plants at the next Society meeting. I'll bet a lot of members will be able to give you starts from their own gardens. That will help get you off to a good beginning."

Cora should have thought of that herself. With donations, her limited budget would stretch a lot further. "I will. Thank you for suggesting it."

Melinda linked her arm through Cora's and tugged her toward the door. "I'm also here to buy some new fabric. I'm going to be needing a new wardrobe in the next few months." She blushed as she placed her hand on her still-narrow waist. "I want to get an early start on sewing."

Once inside, the two women headed straight for the counter where Lucy displayed all the latest fabrics and pattern books. It didn't take long for Melinda to make her selections. Cora cut the required lengths of fabric while Melinda picked out the matching trims.

When they were finished, Cora wrapped the items up in brown paper and secured it with string. Then she totaled up the cost for her friend. "Do you want to pay now or put it on your account?"

Melinda picked up her package and hugged it close. "On the account for now. Be sure and tell Lucy, though, that Daniel will stop by later in the week to take care of what we owe."

After Melinda left, Cora neatly recorded the purchases in the ledger and made a note about when Pastor Hayes would make payment. With that out of the way, she looked around for what she needed to do next. The shelves were fairly well stocked, but the ones in the back could use straightening. She pulled out the feather duster and headed in that direction. No sooner had she cleared off the top shelf than the bell in the front of the store chimed, announcing the arrival of another customer.

She climbed down off the crate she'd been using for a stool and hurried back to the counter. After wiping her hands on her apron and patting her hair to make sure it was still tidy, she stood ready to greet her next customers.

Two men—both strangers to her—paused just inside the door. They seemed in no hurry to approach the counter. Although at first she thought they were familiarizing themselves with the layout of a store that was new to them, she had an uneasy suspicion that they were checking to make sure they were alone in the store. With her.

Just that quickly she went from being industrious storekeeper to vulnerable woman. She fought the urge either to duck behind the counter before they came any closer or to slip out the back door of the store. As a matter of pride, she stood her ground as the two men spoke quietly. Finally, one of them disappeared behind a tall shelf piled high with hardware, while the other one walked straight toward her.

Her pulse raced when he reached the counter. He pushed his hat back farther on his head, revealing reddish brown hair and a pair of laughing brown eyes that invited her to smile back at him.

She managed a small one as she asked, "Good morning, sir. Can I help you find something in particular?"

He leaned against the counter. "Well, my brother and I just came in to pick up some supplies, but it's a real pleasure to have found a pretty woman instead." A pair of dimples accompanied the sly smile he gave her.

Cora might not have all that much experience with men, but she knew enough to recognize flirting when she heard it and to be a little bit flattered. Besides, she suspected that it came as naturally to this man as breathing. She chose to concentrate on the reason for their visit.

"Do you have a list of what you want?" she asked, as

her eyes slid past him, trying to gauge the location of the other brother. He was still lurking somewhere near the front of the store where he could keep an eye on the street outside. She shivered despite the warmth of the day.

"Please call me Jack." He pulled a piece of paper from his shirt pocket and dropped it on the counter.

Cora flattened out his list and read it over. "I don't think I've seen either of you around Lee's Mill before. Are you and your brother new to town?" If she found out their names, she could check them out with the sheriff or even Cade. Between the two of them, they knew almost everyone in the area.

He glanced back toward the front of the store before answering, as if unsure how much his brother would want him to say. "We've been gone a long time, but actually we grew up on a farm just north of here."

"Really? Where exactly?" she asked with what she hoped sounded like neighborly interest. All the while, visions of the old abandoned farm that lay between her house and the new school filled her mind.

Another voice joined the conversation as the other brother finally made an appearance. "Like he said, north of here."

Jack almost snapped to attention. "Ma'am, may I present my brother Luke?"

"Ma'am." Luke acknowledged the introduction with a barely perceptible nod. "Come on, Jack, let's pick up what we need and get out of here."

At least she now knew their first names. Jack followed his brother over toward the canned goods and started pulling things down off the shelf. While they made their selections, she took the opportunity to study the two men. There seemed to be as many similarities as there were differences. Both were an inch, maybe two, under six feet tall, although Jack was considerably heavier than his brother.

Based on build alone, she would have picked Jack as the elder of the two. But something in the way that he deferred to Luke made her think Jack was used to being the follower in their relationship. His easy smile and friendly nature were definitely appealing, but it was the other brother who intrigued her.

At first she thought he had a more slender build than Jack, but from the way his clothes hung loosely from his shoulders, Luke looked as if he'd recently lost weight. Compared to his brother, Luke's coloring was washed out and pale. Was he sickly?

Maybe he'd . . . She stopped midthought when she realized that she'd been caught staring. Slowly, Luke had turned in her direction, trapping her with the sheer power of his gaze alone. His eyes were ice-blue, but they left her feeling anything but cold. An unfamiliar warmth flooded her senses to settle somewhere deep inside her as she stood helpless to look away.

Son of a bitch, the last thing he needed right now was to have some big-eyed female storekeeper watching his every move. She all but reeked of innocence, the kind he hadn't seen in five long years. If she had any menfolk around, they should have known enough to keep her locked away from the likes of him. What could they be thinking of by leaving her to tend the store by herself?

She'd clearly been enjoying the way Jack flirted with her, but then Jack had always had a way with women. Their own mother, God rest her soul, had never hesitated to take the strap to Luke for every transgression. But all Jack had to do was shuffle his feet and look sorry, and she'd forgive him almost anything. Ma had sure enough loved them both, but Jack was something special.

Luke checked on his brother's progress in gathering the supplies they'd need to set up housekeeping. Jack had stopped by the family cabin on his way to Kansas to meet up with Luke. He said the roof was in sorry condition, which meant that everything inside the house was probably worth little more than the effort it would take to break it up into kindling.

When they'd started for home, Luke had figured on having to rebuild with little or no money. That hadn't bothered Luke as much as it had Jack. Even if they had to camp out for the next six months, it was a hell of a lot better than living behind bars.

The two of them had picked up a few days' work here and there along the way back from Kansas. Mostly it had netted them only enough to get a hot meal and enough beans and bacon to travel on a few more days. To Luke's surprise, once they were back in Missouri, Jack had confessed to having some money stashed away in a bank in Springfield. He hadn't been particularly forthcoming about how he'd come by the money in the first place, but Luke wasn't going to press the issue. Neither of them was much inclined to talk about how he'd spent his time since the war.

For now, the two of them were going to get enough supplies to keep them warm and fed until they could make the cabin livable.

He deliberately broke off eye contact with the young woman and walked behind a counter of hand tools, finding it more comfortable to have a pile of hardware and shelving between them. Maybe it would have been easier if he'd had enough money to pay for an evening's pleasure with a whore. After a five-year drought, it was just his damned bad luck that the first woman he met up with was the last kind of woman a decent man would mess around with.

Not that his body was listening to his conscience. The second he'd laid eyes on her, certain portions of his anatomy had started screaming out their need. He'd managed to ignore them so far, but if she kept staring at him . . . damn, he needed to get out of there, and soon.

Shirts, he needed a couple more shirts. That at least would take him back to the front of the store and away from those eyes. Jack could deal with the rest of the supply list by himself. Once Luke reached the neatly stacked piles of ready-made clothing, he stood staring down at the array of colors, unable to make a decision. Or even remember why he was there in the first place.

The soft sweep of a woman's skirts trailing across the floor in his direction had Luke bracing himself to face the woman again. Damn, if she didn't keep her distance, he wouldn't be responsible for the consequences. She'd find out right soon what happened to decent women who insisted on parading more than the dry goods in front of the wrong man. And he was definitely the wrong man.

"Can I help you find something?"

He spun around, ready to tear into her but good, only to find himself face-to-face with a very pretty woman with a small baby sleeping in her arms. He managed to fight his temper back under control. With quiet dignity, she stood her ground, patiently waiting for him to quit acting the fool.

Manners only dimly remembered from his childhood had him snatching his hat off his head as he struggled to say something intelligent. She saved him the trouble.

"If you're looking for a good-quality shirt that will hold up to hard work, I'd suggest this style." She shifted the baby slightly to free up one hand so she could tug a couple of shirts out of the pile. "These should be about the right size for you, if you don't mind them both being blue. Otherwise, a new shipment should come in about a week."

He barely glanced at the shirts. "Thank you, ma'am. They'll do fine."

"If you're sure."

"I'm sure."

She tilted her head to one side as if to study his face better. "I don't believe we've met before. I'm Lucy Mulroney. This is my store."

"Luke Gibson, ma'am. That's my brother Jack at the counter." Her last name struck a chord. "You wouldn't be related to a Cade Mulroney by any chance?"

"He's my husband. Do you know him?"

"From the war. He was a fine officer." He meant it, too. Unlike some of the men Luke had served under, Cade hadn't made a habit of wasting his men's lives unnecessarily.

Lucy rewarded his comment with a smile that could teach the sun a thing or two about spreading warmth. Just then, the baby stirred a bit in its sleep, drawing her attention away from Luke. Damned if he couldn't have stood there all day watching her coo over the little scrap of humanity in her arms. It had been a long time since he had seen something so normal, so peaceful.

Jack broke up the moment. "Hey, Luke. We have everything we need. Are you ready to pay up and go?"

Luke offered Lucy a quick smile. He was surprised to find out that he remembered how to go about it.

"Seems that we're about done here. Tell your husband I said hello."

"You should tell him yourself. He's right next door at the newspaper office. I know he'd enjoy seeing you."

"Maybe next time I'm in town."

"So you're going to stay in the area? He'll be pleased to hear that."

"Our family farm is just outside of town."

"Luke, are you coming?"

He wanted to tell his brother to shut up, but it was hardly Jack's fault that Luke would rather talk to Lucy Mulroney than face her assistant again. Reluctantly, he headed back toward the counter with Lucy following along behind. Jack had several burlap bags sitting on the floor at his feet. Luke tossed the shirts on the counter. "Add these to the total."

Lucy hovered close by, but it was the younger woman who spoke. "Do you want to set up an account with us or pay for everything now?"

"We'll pay cash."

If Mrs. Mulroney noticed the snarl in his voice, she gave no sign of it. Her assistant quickly added the cost of the shirts to the list she'd made in the ledger. Ignoring Luke, she offered a bright smile to Jack as she counted out his change.

"Thank you for coming in today, Jack."

She pointedly ignored Luke, which should have pleased him. Instead, it made him want to punch something. Like his brother, for instance.

Jack gave both women another one of his heart-fluttering smiles. "I'll have to make a habit of stopping by, especially now that I know where to find the two prettiest women in Lee's Mill."

Lucy rolled her eyes at the blatant flattery, but her

friend seemed to soak it up. Luke knew he should warn her that flirting came to Jack as easily as breathing and wasn't to be taken seriously, but that was her problem and not his. Definitely not his. But it would be a miracle if he got out of the store without laying into his brother with both fists. Rather than risk it, he grabbed the closest sack to keep his hands busy and started for the door without another word.

From now on, Jack could buy all their supplies. Luke had enough to do in just rebuilding his life.

CHAPTER 2

The sun beat down from directly overhead, its heat intensified by the muggy humidity. Sweat and dust mixed in equal parts on his skin, making it itch like crazy as he crawled down across the roof. He'd been swinging a hammer for close to three hours replacing missing shingles and patching holes. It was time for a break. There was great pleasure in being able to make even that small decision for himself.

He sat down on the edge of the roof and swung his legs down over the side. Judging the distance to the ground, he decided he'd rather jump than trust his life to the rickety ladder he'd found under a pile of junk in the barn. He hit the ground with a bone-jarring jolt, but otherwise intact. Unbuttoning his shirt, he headed for the well and a drink to flush the dust from his throat. A couple of quick pumps on the handle produced a steady stream of cool, clear Missouri spring water. He drank his fill and then poured the rest over his head and chest, using his shirt as a towel to dry off.

He had to laugh. His poor mother had spent a hell of a lot of time and energy just to give him a passing acquaintance with soap and water. As a boy, he'd fought against the whole idea of cleanliness. There'd been more important things to do with his time—fishing, hunting, frog gigging. It's a wonder that she ever got him to sit still long enough to learn how to read and write, much less anything else he'd regarded as a waste of time.

But since getting out of prison, he'd spent a fair amount of time scrubbing his skin until it screamed for relief. He knew it was all in his mind, but every so often, he caught a whiff of prison stench in the air, especially at night. Sometimes he wondered if he'd ever leave that hell behind him completely. Probably not, but he'd settle for learning to live with the memory if the nightmares would go away.

He suspected Jack was getting damned tired of hearing him whimper in his sleep.

Speaking of his brother, he wondered where the hell he was. As far as Luke could tell, Jack hadn't been home since he rode out around noon the day before. Evidently he had friends in the area he'd gone to visit. Luke had nothing against Jack's spending time with them. But if they were going to make a go of the farm again, it was going to take both of them to get it back in shape.

Right now, he was concentrating on making the house livable. Another hour or two on the roof and at least they'd be dry. A good coat of whitewash would improve the looks of the outside, but that could wait for a while. In the next few days, he needed to get a garden planted. If all went well, by mid- to late summer they'd have fresh vegetables to eat clear through fall. A second planting later on in the summer would give them squash, turnips, and potatoes that would last them through winter. He'd like to produce enough of their own food to keep from having to buy so much.

It had been three days since he and Jack had stopped in at the mercantile in town, but the memory of that big-eyed girl who had waited on them hadn't faded one bit. He filled another ladle of water and drank it down, as if that would clear the image from his mind along with the dryness in his throat.

He had no business thinking about her at all. She reeked of innocence, the kind he hadn't seen since before the war. The men of Lee's Mill must be blind if they weren't lined up around the block just to look at her. If he hadn't found so much to keep himself busy since coming home, he would have been fighting to be the one leading the charge.

The sound of a horse approaching had him edging back toward the house and the rifle he'd left leaning against the side of the porch. So far, he'd had no call to feel threatened since he'd come home, but old habits died hard. Even his pa used to keep the shotgun within reach, saying a wise man was never too trusting.

He didn't recognize the horse that was just then coming into sight, but the rider looked familiar. It had been damned near eight years since he'd last laid eyes on Cade Mulroney, but the man hadn't changed all that much. A little grayer, maybe, and he sure looked better fed, but it was Cade all right. Luke set the gun back down and walked out to greet his guest.

"Luke Gibson, you old son of a gun, how are you doing?" Cade dismounted and started right for him, limping a bit as he walked.

"Not as well as you are. I hear tell that you've got a new wife and family." Luke held out his hand, but that wasn't enough for his old commanding officer. He got caught up in a hug that threatened to crack a few ribs. "I met your wife and son. She's far too beautiful for the likes of you."

Cade laughed as they separated. "That's true enough, but don't go telling Lucy that. I've finally got her convinced that she's lucky to have me."

Luke turned serious. "She seems like a real nice lady, sir. Congratulations on the birth of your son."

"Thank you, but call me Cade. The war's been over a long time now. I'd rather be your friend than your commanding officer."

If they were going to renew their friendship, Luke wanted it to be based on bedrock. He didn't give a damn what most people thought of him, but Cade Mulroney was a different matter. "You might not feel that way if you knew where I've been the past five years."

Cade didn't hesitate. "I'm willing to listen over a cup of coffee."

"Come on inside. I'll make a new pot." Luke led the way toward the house. They stepped around a fresh-cut pile of wood and a heap of trash that Luke had been meaning to burn. "Sorry about the mess, but the place has been vacant for the better part of ten years. What the leaks in the roof didn't ruin, the four-legged trespassers did."

"I've seen worse." Cade neatly avoided a stack of shingles that Luke had left just inside the door. He pulled up an empty crate and sat down at the wobbly table that was the only piece of furniture in the room.

Luke busied himself putting the coffee on to boil. "Hope you like it strong."

"Sure do. You'd think I'd have drunk my fill since the fighting ended, but those years of drinking boiled peanuts and sweet potato skins left their mark. Sometimes the only way I know the war is finally over is to drink real coffee."

It felt good to talk with someone who had fought on the same side—the losing side—of the war. Those years had left them all changed, but at least Cade might come close to understanding what had happened to Luke.

"So spit it out, man. There isn't much I haven't heard. You won't shock me."

Luke stared out the small window in the back of the cabin, not wanting to see the respect die in Cade's eyes as he told him the sordid details of his past. He drew what strength he could from the familiar sight of his boyhood haunts before starting.

"I'm not sure where to begin . . ."

Cade watched his friend, trying to find the youth he'd known in the hard-eyed man standing in front of him. The war hadn't been easy on any of them, but it had been worse for some. He'd bet Luke was one of them. "Start after we lost track of each other. I pretty much know what happened up to that point."

Luke still wouldn't look at him. "I didn't want to leave Missouri when most of the regulars pulled out. I guess this farm isn't much by some folks' standards, but it was enough to support a family. When Pa was killed, Ma needed my help to keep food on the table." His words coasted to a stop as the memories pulled him back into the past.

"If they had left us alone, I would have been content to be a farmer."

Cade didn't have to ask who "they" were. It didn't matter. In Missouri, it was neighbor against neighbor, friend against friend. Being neutral had been all but impossible.

"I rode with Quantrill for a while even though my heart wasn't in it." He turned bleak eyes toward Cade. "But those Yankees kept coming and coming. Nothing and nobody was safe from them."

Cade had heard all about how bad it had gotten by the end. By then, he'd already been a prisoner of war and out of the fighting. The whispers from the past had his leg aching. He'd lost men in battle, and he'd lost men to disease and neglect in the prison. Both haunted his dreams.

"We might not have been part of the great Confederate Army, but we were fighting the war all the same. When the last shot was fired, most of us were plenty willing to lay down our arms and go home. They just wouldn't let us."

Bitterness rolled off of Luke's words in waves. Suddenly, Cade wasn't all that sure he wanted to hear where the story was going to end. But if his friend needed to tell him, he could sure as hell listen.

"There was a kid that rode with us—although none of us were really ever young again after the first shots were fired and the dying started. No matter how bad it got or how hungry we were, though, Freddy could make us laugh. He'd crack a joke or something and things didn't seem so bad." Luke's eyes closed as he drew a shuddering breath. "We were told to report in and surrender. Because we were with the irregulars, it was up to the local Union commander to decide what to do with us. Well, he decided that Freddy was a traitor and had him shot."

Cade already knew what Luke was about to say, so he said it for him. "You shot the Yankee."

"Yeah, I sure enough did, and I don't regret it for one second. Freddy shouldn't have died. Not like that."

"What happened next?"

"A sympathetic judge thought he did me a favor. Instead of hanging me on the spot, he sent me to prison for five years." He went back to staring out the window. "In Kansas."

Missouri and Kansas shared a common border, but there had been hard feelings on both sides long before the fighting had started anywhere else. Cade was willing to bet that at least some of the guards would have taken great delight in making the life of an ex-Confederate from Missouri a living hell.

Luke stood stone still, as if waiting for Cade to pass judgment on him. As if he had the right—he had his own invisible scars left from those years. He couldn't offer words of comfort, but he could tell Luke he was welcome back in Lee's Mill.

"So when do you want to come to dinner? Lucy told me not to take no for an answer."

The abrupt change in topics left Luke floundering for a few seconds. Finally, he gave Cade a wry smile. "You name the night, and I'll be there."

"How about Sunday dinner? We get home from church around noon, so come any time after that."

"You sure Mrs. Mulroney won't mind?"

"You'll find out soon enough that Lucy doesn't push easily. If she said to invite you, she wants you there." Cade stood up. "I'd better get back to town. The newspaper doesn't write itself."

The coffee chose that moment to boil over, sending rivulets spitting and dancing all over the stove. Cursing, Luke lunged across the small room and, using a handy rag, yanked the pot off the heat. "Damn, I'm always doing that. You sure you won't stay for a cup?"

"No, I really do need to be going. If you come into town before Sunday, be sure to stop in and say hello. I keep a bottle of the good stuff in my desk for friends."

"Thanks for stopping by, Cade. Maybe next time you'll get to meet my brother Jack."

Cade had wondered where Jack was, but he didn't want to ask. "Bring him to dinner with you."

"I may do just that."

"I'm thinking about closing the store and opening a saloon for all the women in town. What do you think?"

Cora managed to drag her eyes away from the window long enough to answer. "Whatever you want to do is fine with me. Let me know if you need my help."

The sound of her two friends laughing abruptly brought Cora's attention back to where it belonged. "All right, what did I just agree to?" She put her hands on her hips and gave Lucy and Melinda a stern look.

It didn't work. They exchanged glances and started laughing again. At least Lucy had the decency to answer. "I said I was thinking about closing the store down and opening a saloon for women. You agreed to help."

Cora rolled her eyes. "All right, you two, I'm sorry. I don't know where my mind has been lately. I can't seem to concentrate on anything."

Lucy gave her a knowing smile as she patted her son on the back. "Did this all start the other day when the Gibson brothers rode into town?"

"No, it didn't." She wasn't lying. It had only gotten worse after meeting them. "I just have a lot on my mind, what with the new house and a new job starting in a couple of months."

"Well, if you're sure . . ."

Her cheeks stained bright red, Cora ignored her

meddlesome friend's comment. Instead she held out her arms to take the baby. Settling young Roy against her shoulder, she walked the length of the store and back, crooning little nonsense songs.

Melinda Hayes, the minister's wife, smoothly changed the subject. "So, Lucy, why don't you show me that new fabric that came in? I think I've got enough clothes to last through my confinement, but I need to make a few more things for the baby." She shot Cora a sympathetic look over her shoulder as Lucy led the way over to the corner where the fabrics were displayed.

Cora nuzzled Roy's neck and kissed his cheek. She inhaled deeply of the sweet baby smell and hugged the little boy up close. Normally, she didn't mind a bit of teasing, so she didn't know why it bothered her so much this time. Honesty forced her to admit, at least to herself, that she had been watching for another glimpse of the Gibsons. Or at least one of them.

Things would have been simpler if the one had been Jack, the flirt. She suspected that any woman still breathing would have been treated to his smile and teasing banter. His face was easy on the eyes, and it didn't hurt to look as long as her heart was safe. No, it wasn't him that had her heart racing every time someone rode by the store.

She realized that once again she'd come to a stop by the front window, staring out at the street as if wishing would make Luke Gibson appear. Feeling foolish, she forced herself to join her two friends as they tried to pick which fabrics would make the softest clothing for a baby. Not that she had any need for such information personally, but it would help to know if any customers asked for her opinion.

Her interest in the subject lasted all of about two

minutes. When she yawned for the second time, Lucy looked up from the fabric she was cutting and smiled.

"Do you want me to take Roy, so you can go? It's time for his nap anyway."

"No, you go ahead with what you're doing. I'll go put him down for his nap on my way out."

Cade had made a second cradle for the baby so Lucy could keep it at the store. Cora eased the little boy down off her shoulder and onto his back. He stirred restlessly for a few seconds before settling back into a sound sleep. She covered him with a light-weight blanket and tiptoed away.

She felt a little guilty leaving Lucy and Melinda. But they were so engrossed in what they were doing, they hardly noticed when she slipped out the front door with her basket of supplies that she'd purchased. Once she was outside, she automatically started the long walk home. She hadn't gone more than a quarter of a mile when a familiar figure rode into sight.

Mitch Hughes, the former sheriff, pulled up a short distance away and waited for her to get closer. He had resigned his office to take up farming full-time once he got married, but he still occasionally helped out Jake, the new sheriff. Mitch was one of Cora's favorite people.

"Morning, Miss Cora."

"Good morning, Mr. Hughes. How is Mrs. Hughes?"

"Josie is just fine, thank you. I'll be sure to tell her you were asking about her." He swung down out of the saddle. "Mind if I walk with you a spell?"

"Not at all. I'd be glad for the company."

Cora knew Mitch rarely did something without a good reason. He fell into step beside her, shorten-ing his long strides to match her shorter ones. They walked along in companionable silence for a few minutes. Finally, she prodded him into telling her what was on his mind.

"If you've got something to say, Mitch, go ahead and spit it out. I'm pretty used to people poking their noses in my business." She softened her words with a smile.

Mitch offered her one of his rare smiles in return. "I can't help but worry about you living out here all by yourself."

"Well, I'm not alone anymore. Jack and Luke Gibson have moved back onto their family farm. That should reassure you some."

His mouth took on a decidedly grim set. "I wish it did."

"Lucy mentioned that Cade knows Luke from the war. They served together." It was one of the few facts that she'd been able to garner about the man. She only wished she knew why it was so important to her to find out more.

"I know they did. Cade seems to think Luke Gibson is all right, but there have been complaints about riders moving through the area, especially at night."

She hadn't heard that. "Do you think the Gibsons are involved with them?"

"No, but keep your eyes open. At the first sign of trouble, you let me or the sheriff know."

"I will. It might make you feel better to know that I did have Bud Keller out to install stout locks on my doors and windows. I also keep a loaded rifle handy."

"Do you know how to use it?" The corner of his mouth kicked up in a quick smile.

"Cade showed me how when I bought it. We've been target shooting several times. He said it would work against all kinds of varmints—especially the two-legged kind." And she prayed she'd never have to find that out for a fact.

"Well, it sounds like you have things under control." He mounted up. "Josie said to tell you that she'll be in for the next meeting of the Luminary Society. I'm supposed to stop by and tell Lucy that Josie knows it's her turn to bring the cookies."

"I'm glad to hear that she's coming. I don't get to see nearly enough of her these days, or you either, for that matter." An idea occurred to her. "How about the two of you coming to my house for dinner a week from Sunday? I'd be pleased to have you."

"I'll have to check with Josie, but I'm sure she'd love to come." He turned his horse back toward town. "Keep your eyes open and lock your doors."

She sassed him with a mock salute. "Yes, sir. I will, sir."

"I could go tell your aunt the same things I just told you."

His expression warned her that his threat was only half in jest. He knew her Aunt Henrietta would be right out to try to drag Cora back to the safety of her house in town. The woman had almost succeeded in smothering Cora during the years she'd been forced to live under the same roof with her. There was no way she would go back to living that way.

"I promise I'll keep a sharp eye out, Mitch. If I notice anything, you'll be the first one to know."

"None of us like you walking out here all the time."

"Well, that's about to change. I have the stable owner looking for a gentle horse for me. I'll need one for certain before school starts in the fall."

Apparently that was enough to satisfy him because he touched the brim of his hat in salute before riding off. She watched him disappear around a bend in the road before resuming her walk. Although she liked Mitch and knew his concern for her was genuine, she wished he'd kept his mouth shut about the unknown riders.

Ever since the war had ended, bands of restless men had ridden through the area. Most had been harmless as they moved on west, leaving their homes and the memories of the war behind. But others had taken to committing lawless acts: robbing banks, stagecoaches, even trains. The very thought had her hurrying her steps the last short distance to her house.

Once inside, she locked the door. It was a good long while before her hands stopped shaking.

"Where are you going this time?" Luke knew he sounded more like a worried parent than an older brother. Jack's interest in hard work had lasted all of two days before he'd started disappearing.

"I already told you. I'm going to see my friends." Jack gave the cinch on his saddle another yank. "I'll be back sometime tomorrow."

Luke knew better than to try to talk Jack into staying. The last time he'd tried that, Jack had stayed away even longer. "All right. I'd like some help clearing the back pasture, but it can wait until tomorrow."

Feeling frustrated and not knowing what to do about it, Luke watched Jack disappear down the overgrown path that led back to the road. They'd already missed out on so much time in their lives, time when they could have become friends as well as brothers. Maybe it was too late for that, but he hoped like hell it wasn't. Jack was all he had left in the world besides what was left of the farm.

He looked around the place, seeing it for what it

could be rather than what it was. All his good memories were tied to this Missouri farm—was it too much to want to build some new ones? But there was so damned much to be done. The list went on and on: plowing, weeding, painting, fence mending—all of it far easier for two to accomplish than just one man working alone. It made him tired thinking about it.

They were also in need of supplies, the one chore Jack probably would have taken care of. He would jump at any chance to flirt with a pretty woman. Luke tried telling himself that Cade wouldn't appreciate Jack's bothering his wife, but he rarely lied to himself. The truth was that he couldn't stand to see that other woman—the one with big, innocent eyes—listening to Jack's insincerity and believing every word.

He could hold off another day, maybe two, before going into town, but he was damned sick and tired of beans three times a day. He also wanted to find out who might have a few chickens for sale and maybe a milk cow. Cade had told him to stop by any time he was in town. As newspaper editor, he probably knew everyone within fifty miles of Lee's Mill. Surely he'd be able to point Luke in the right direction.

His decision made, he headed for the house to clean up a bit. Maybe he'd stay in town long enough to have dinner. It would be a real pleasure to eat someone else's cooking for a change.

An hour later, he rode into Lee's Mill. This time he took the opportunity to look around, noting the changes since he'd last seen it. Before he'd been sent to prison, his visits home had been erratic, especially once he'd started riding with the irregulars. Even then, the town had been growing. Now he hardly recognized the place. The hotel and bank were the same. So was The River Lady, at least on the outside. Maybe later he'd check out the inside.

But the church was new, and so was Cade's newspaper office. His eyes slid past the store and back again, noting that it was so new that the walls hadn't had time to weather. He wondered what had happened to the original Thomas Mercantile.

Maybe if he stopped in to see Cade first he could find out who was working at the store. If it was Lucy Mulroney, he'd head on over and get his supplies. If not, well, he'd have to think about it. Maybe he could drop the list off and pick up the supplies later, when it was safe.

For now, he'd stop off at Cade's. After tying his horse at the closest hitching rail, he walked up to the newspaper office door only to find it locked, with a note tacked on the wall announcing that Cade was gone for the next couple of hours. Damn. He yanked his hat off his head and dusted it against his leg in frustration.

He supposed he could come back later, but that was a coward's way. He pulled out the list he'd brought with him and studied it. Even if he dragged his heels, it shouldn't take more than a few minutes to gather up the things he needed. Feeling more as if he were riding into battle than going shopping, he marched down the sidewalk to the Thomas Mercantile and walked in.

The brass bell overhead chimed out his arrival. He closed the door and waited to see who was behind the counter, but only silence greeted him. Finally, he heard the faint sound of footsteps overhead. Taking advantage of the temporary reprieve, he began yanking things off the shelves as fast as he could find them. In no time at all, he had a substantial pile sitting on the counter. He was about to go back for another load when he heard the creak of the stairs.

Deciding he could do without the rest, he waited at the counter to see who was coming. He got his answer soon enough.

"Hello? I'm sorry if I kept you waiting. I was . . ." Cora paused in her descent. "Mr. Gibson."

She stared at him as if not quite sure she wanted to come any closer. Belatedly remembering his manners, he tipped his hat in a token effort to be polite. "I helped myself to what I needed." He waited to see if she'd actually come close enough to total his purchases or if she'd break and run.

Evidently she was made of sterner stuff than she looked because she immediately started for the counter. "I am sorry I wasn't here to help you, but Cade's daughter Mary and I were in the middle of a game of chess."

Now that was a surprise. None of the women he used to know would have had the slightest interest in the game. Had things changed that much in five years? Curiosity made him ask, "Who won?"

Another voice joined the conversation. "I did, but I think she let me."

The two adults turned to face the young girl coming down the stairs. Her dark hair and striking silver-gray eyes marked her as Cade's daughter. He guessed her age at about eight or so, but she carried herself with more dignity than he would have expected in someone so young.

Cora protested the implication that she would cheat, even if it was to lose. "Now, young lady, I did not. You captured my queen all on your own."

The look Mary gave Cora said all too clearly how much she believed that one. She turned her attention to Luke. "I'm Mary Mulroney." She came the rest of the way down the stairs to stop right in front of him.

"I'm Luke Gibson, Mary Mulroney." He squatted down to her eye level. "I've known your papa for a long time."

She tilted her head to the side. "I heard them talking about you." She scrunched up her face as she tried to think what had been said.

He tried not to wince when he thought of all the bad things she could have overheard. Cora had come out from behind the counter to stand guard beside the little girl. Did she really think he'd do something to harm a child?

Mary's expressive face lit up as she remembered. "I know. You're coming to dinner on Sunday!"

"Why, that's right, Miss Mary. Your pa stopped by my farm to invite me. I'm looking forward to it." He stood back up. "I hear that your ma is a fine cook."

"She is," Mary agreed. Then she dropped her voice to a whisper. "Only she'll make you eat your vegetables, even if you're full."

"Well, thank you for the warning. I'll make sure I'm plenty hungry when I come." He met Cora's gaze over Mary's head. Her eyes were dancing with laughter.

The moment of shared amusement passed, and it was back to business. Cora touched Mary on the shoulder. "Time for you to go pick up the chessboard, young lady. You've got chores to do."

"Bye, Mr. Luke."

"Bye, Miss Mary." He watched as Mary skipped off and disappeared back up the stairs. When she was out of sight, he slowly turned to face Cora. "Cade will have his hands full when she gets older. She's going to be a beauty."

"You're right. She will be, but more important, she'll have a mind of her own."

Characteristics that Cora shared, but he wasn't about to say so. Hell, he didn't even want to think it. "Look, can we get on with this? I need to get back."

He knew he sounded gruff, but once again he found himself needing to get away before he did something stupid, like tell the woman just how beautiful she was.

Cora managed not to flinch at the sudden change that came over Luke. She immediately began to record his purchases, hoping he wouldn't notice how her hand trembled as she wrote. As if sensing that he was making her nervous, he walked away from the counter without a word. She made herself write down two more items before she allowed herself a quick peek to see what had caught his attention.

To her surprise, he was standing in front of a shelf of books that Lucy kept on hand for the members of the Luminary Society to read. Part of their goal when they formed the society was to encourage the women of Lee's Mill to read all types of literature. Since they relied on donations, they had a rather odd collection of books to choose from.

Luke ran his finger along the titles, stopping every so often to take one of the books off the shelf to look through it before carefully putting it back. She came out from behind the counter after she finished with his order. Evidently he was so engrossed in the books that he didn't realize that she was so close because he jumped when she spoke, almost dropping a book.

"I didn't mean to startle you, Mr. Gibson, but I thought you might like to know that those books are here for people to borrow." She corrected herself. "I should say that we have them for the members of the Luminary Society to use, but we don't mind if someone else borrows them as long as we get them back."

She could see the flicker of temptation in his eyes, but then he shook his head.

"No thanks. Maybe some other time." He shoved the book back where it belonged. "How much do I owe?"

"Do you want to pay cash or charge your purchases?"

"Cash."

"Fine." She could talk in one-word answers, too.

When she showed him the total in the ledger, he practically shoved the money at her, as if he couldn't wait to get away. While she made change, she tried to make conversation. Maybe he wouldn't be in such a hurry to leave if she could think of something to say. Her tongue remained firmly tied until he was almost to the door.

Finally, she managed to blurt out, "I guess I'll be seeing you again soon, Mr. Gibson."

He stopped midstride to glare back over his shoulder. "How do you figure?"

"Well, first of all, I own the place next to yours, so we're bound to run into each other once in a while." She let him digest that particular bit of bad news before delivering the killing blow. "But mainly because Lucy invited me to Sunday dinner, too."

Whatever he had to say in response was lost in the sound of the door slamming on his way out. She had a strong suspicion that it was just as well that she didn't understand his one-word comment.

It took every bit of resolve she could muster to keep from rushing to the window to watch his retreat. What had she done to make him dislike her so? It would have been nice to think he was abrupt and cold with everyone, but she knew better. She hadn't missed how polite he'd been to Lucy the first time he came into the store. And he couldn't have been more kind to Mary. Not everyone had the knack of making a young child feel at ease.

So it was only she who made him act that way. The idea hurt her feelings, although she didn't understand why it should. After all, she'd only met him twice, a total of maybe twenty minutes. On the other hand, she'd done nothing to offend him as far as she could tell.

She walked over to the small mirror that Lucy had hung on the wall and studied her appearance. Her dress was nothing fancy, but she thought the dark green looked good with her dark hair and eyes. She'd taken care to braid her hair neatly. If there was something about her that offended, she couldn't begin to guess what it was.

A movement outside the window warned her in time that she was about to get company. She hurried back to the counter and tried to look busy as the door opened. She was relieved that it was Lucy returning to take over the store.

"We're back." Lucy removed her hat and hurried back to the storeroom to put on her apron. "How did everything go?"

Cora kept her head bowed over the ledger as she totaled the figures. "Fine. It was busy earlier, but it's been pretty quiet for the past hour since Roy went down for his nap. Mary and I even managed to fit in a game of chess."

All too innocently, Lucy asked, "Was that Luke Gibson I saw riding out of town?"

"Probably. He was in here a short time ago for

supplies." Cora took pride in how disinterested she sounded. If only her pulse would quit racing, everything would be fine. "Mary tells me that Luke, um, Mr. Gibson, is also coming to dinner on Sunday."

She should have known better than to try to fool Lucy. Her friend arched an eyebrow. "Luke, is it? I wasn't aware the two of you were on a first-name basis."

"We're not. I only meant to make it clear which Mr. Gibson I meant. After all, there are two."

"Ah, well, I see." Lucy picked up her feather duster and started cleaning.

And she probably did see far more than Cora wanted her to, but any further protests would only serve to convince Lucy that she was on to something. Far better to change the subject.

"Is there anything else you want me to do before I leave?"

"No, I should be fine. Don't forget the fabric you ordered."

"Thanks for reminding me." Cora escaped into the storeroom. She hung up her apron before putting on her hat and shawl. Picking up the bundle of fabric she'd picked out for curtains, she looked around to make sure she hadn't forgotten anything important.

"Well, if you don't need me, I'd better be going. Aunt Henrietta wants me to stop by before I go home. With luck, she won't keep me too long because she doesn't want me walking alone once the sun goes down. I'd like to get home while the light is good enough to get started on my curtains."

Lucy gave her a bright smile. "That's such nice fabric you chose. It will make up nicely, I think. Let me know if you need any help. Tell Henrietta hello for me."

"I will, if you'll tell Mary that I look forward to

our next game. By the way, she's catching on to the fact that we've been helping her win. She doesn't appreciate it."

"Well, she doesn't like losing either. We'll just have to get trickier."

"Good luck with that. She's too smart to be fooled for long."

Lucy beamed with maternal pride as Cora waved good-bye. Mary wasn't her daughter by blood, but she was in all the ways that really mattered.

CHAPTER 3

The river murmured and rumbled over the rocks in its path, making it hard to listen for unwelcome visitors. Judging from the moon's position in the sky, it had to be past midnight, and Jack had been standing guard for damn near five hours. If someone didn't relieve him soon, he was going to lie down on the rocks and go to sleep.

Three short whistles followed by a long one warned him that his relief was approaching. Even though the signal was correct, he kept his finger on the trigger of his rifle; it didn't pay to get careless. Fortunately, the moonlight was bright enough for him to recognize Baxter long before he got close.

Jack's hand trembled slightly as he lowered the rifle and let the outlaw leader make his final approach. Why was Baxter himself coming out to the river? Normally, it would have been one of the others who got stuck with standing guard during the late hours. Was something wrong?

Baxter grinned at Jack, his teeth gleaming whitely in the night, as if he knew exactly what Jack had been thinking. The man had a quicksilver personality, swinging from laughter to murderous fury in the blink of an eye. Or in the wisp of time it took a man to die.

"Evening, Jack. Any problems?" Baxter stopped short of the pool of shadows where Jack had been standing watch.

"No, sir, it's been quiet." He was proud of how calm he sounded as he stepped out of the cluster of trees and scrub brush to stand before the acknowledged leader of the gang.

"That's good, boy." Baxter turned his back toward Jack, a clear signal that the older man believed Jack was no threat. While he stood watching the river, Baxter took out the makings to roll himself a cigarette. He offered the small bag to Jack when he was finished.

It took Jack a little longer to make his, but at least he didn't spill the tobacco. Baxter struck a match to light his cigarette and then held the flame out for Jack to use.

"Thanks."

For several minutes they stood in silence as the river slipped past them. Jack exhaled, sending a blue-gray cloud of smoke drifting away on the breeze as he waited for Baxter to come to the point. He obviously had something on his mind, but Jack was in no hurry to hear what it was. Finally, Baxter took a deep draw off his smoke and flicked the butt out into the river.

"We need to be riding soon." Baxter stretched his arms as if to relieve some stiffness. "By the beginning of next week at the latest."

Jack held his breath. If Baxter and the others were to go riding, it meant that they were getting low on both supplies and money. Since none of them were inclined to look for honest work, that could only mean that Baxter had another type of job in mind. So far, they'd let Jack hang around with them, but he'd yet to be invited along on one of their rides. The money they'd given him was his pay for standing guard and running errands for the others.

But now his pulse raced along, sweeping away the last vestiges of weariness. He felt as if the ground had opened up in front of him, and the slightest breeze would send him toppling over the edge.

"How are things at the farm?" Baxter rocked forward on his toes and back as he stared down at the river. "Are you and your brother getting along all right?"

Jack hesitated before answering, still unsure what Baxter wanted him to say. What did the man really want to know?

"The farm needs work." That seemed safe enough to say.

"So"—Baxter turned to face him—"why are you here?"

The question hung there between them. Finally, the outlaw kicked at a rock and walked away without waiting for Jack to answer. When he was little more than another shadow along the river, his voice came floating back.

"When you know the answer, come see me."

A few minutes later a man known only as Coop came wandering out to relieve Jack. Instead of finding a quiet spot to lay out his bedroll, Jack found himself saddling his gelding. When he had his gear stowed in his saddlebags, he led the horse out of camp. No one questioned his middle-of-the-night departure. He wasn't the first man with a reason to disappear into the darkness; it was doubtful that he'd be the last. For everyone's safety, there were guards posted at intervals all along the winding trail to the outlaw camp. If Baxter wanted him stopped—or dead—he wouldn't have made it as far as the first turn. Even so, he itched as if someone had a rifle aimed dead center at his back.

It took longer than he would have liked to put some distance between himself and the group back at the river. Besides, he wasn't sure what he was running from or running toward. For now, he needed to get away from Baxter and the others so he could think clearly what he wanted from them. But if he threw his lot in with them, he'd be crossing a line that would change his life forever. It was one thing to live by the gun when it was clear who the enemy was. Things were different now.

Once he reached the road, he had to choose a direction. It was too late to head for town. That left the only other place he could go and feel welcome: the farm, overgrown with weeds as it was. It was rocky, too, not unlike his relationship with Luke. He found it hard to remember beyond the war years when he looked up to his older brother as he had tagged along behind him. The two of them had explored every square inch of the family farm and the river beyond. He closed his eyes as he remembered how excited he'd been the first time he'd caught fish for the family dinner.

Looking back, a couple of bluegills and a small-mouth bass probably hadn't been worth the effort to clean them, but Luke had done so without complaint. Jack had almost danced his way home, anxious to present their mother with his offering for their evening meal. She had immediately changed her plans for supper, instead serving up fried fish, cornbread, and fresh greens from the garden. Even Pa had claimed it to be one of the finest meals he'd ever had.

But that was back before the war had destroyed their family. Pa had died early on. Ma had hung on to the farm for the sake of her boys, as she struggled to keep food on the table and the Yankees away from the door. Luke had joined up with the Confederates but then rode with the irregulars because it gave him more opportunity to help out at home.

Then their mother died, worn out from too much work and too much worry. Despite Luke's protests, Jack had picked up Pa's rifle and joined up. From that point on, the two of them had fought, not just the war but each other. Neither of them had been willing to back down an inch—Jack no longer willing to tag along at Luke's heels, Luke unable to see his brother as an adult despite his youth. The five years Luke had spent in prison had only served to put more distance between them.

Lost in thought, Jack almost missed the overgrown path that led to the farm. Fortunately, his horse knew the scent of home and protested. Jack shook off the ghosts of his past and let his horse carry them to the makeshift corral by the barn.

Before his foot touched the ground, Luke came out of the shadows, a rifle cradled in his arms. No doubt he'd been out walking again, unable to sleep. He'd spent a good part of most nights out under the stars. Jack figured it had to do with the time Luke had spent in prison. So far, he'd been unwilling to talk about what he'd been through behind bars. Jack wasn't sure he wanted to know.

"Kind of late to be coming home." Luke leaned against the fence and watched as Jack unsaddled his horse.

"I don't answer to you." They'd been over this before. There was no more heat left in the argument, but they couldn't seem to move past it.

"Be ready to dig stumps come sunup." Luke walked away, no doubt to seek his bedroll.

Jack thought about arguing, but there was no point. He'd get up when he damn well felt like it. And if Luke pushed him too hard, he'd ride out and never look back.

Sunday morning dawned clear and warm. Luke had already been up for an hour before the sun made its appearance over the hills. He'd dragged a couple of old stumps up on the porch to use as a seat and a table. Leaning against the house, he sat with his legs propped up on the railing, content to enjoy the dawning of the day. Streaks of pink and gold painted the horizon as they stretched out and faded in the light of the sun. Sorry the show was over, he drank the last of his coffee and tossed the dregs out on the ground. There were chores to be done, and he'd better get started.

Jack was home, but he was damned near useless when it came to getting any serious work done. Granted, he had helped dig out some stumps a couple of days before, and he had a better head for carpentry than Luke did. But getting him to turn a willing hand to work was tricky at best. No matter how carefully Luke approached Jack, fireworks were sure to explode.

But he had bigger problems to worry about than his prickly younger brother. Today was the day he'd been both looking forward to and dreading all week. What could he have been thinking of to accept an invitation to Cade Mulroney's house for Sunday dinner? He had no business sitting down to eat with decent folks. Not yet. He wasn't ready.

Cade already knew the worst about Luke and had issued the invitation anyway. But how would his wife feel about having a convicted murderer sharing a meal with her children? It was too late to worry about that. Either she'd let him in the house or she wouldn't. And what of her other guest?

Rather than think about Cora, he picked up the bucket and headed for the well. A couple of quick pumps on the handle had a steady stream of water flowing. It took several trips to fill the trough with enough water to last until evening. Until he could afford a load of hay, the horses would have to make do with grazing in the pasture. At least the grass was plentiful since the fields had lain fallow for years.

Next year, though, that would change. He closed his eyes and imagined a field of tall corn growing in neat rows. Ears of corn weren't much to build a man's dreams on, but the idea was enough to help him see past all the work that still needed to be done.

He looked around to see what else he could do to keep himself busy until it was time to clean up for his trip into town. Back when he was a boy, Sunday morning had always been the start of a lazy day. There hadn't been a real preacher in Lee's Mill in those days, but Pa would read from the Bible while Ma fried up chicken with gravy and biscuits and mashed potatoes. He and Jack had chafed under their father's stern lectures on the proper behavior on the Sabbath.

Fortunately, Pa had understood the restless hearts of boys and would set them free to wander the hills as soon as the noonday meal was over. Other than caring for the animals, there were no chores on Sundays. In his own way, he'd taught them to love the land that fed and sheltered them. They'd gotten down on their knees and given thanks to God for his gifts.

Luke had quit talking to God a long time ago.

Glancing back at the cabin, he wondered if Jack shared the same fond memories of their boyhood. With a five-year difference in their ages, it was hard to know. The war had forced both of them to grow up before their time. He had his own demons to fight, but Jack had a lot of anger in him, too. It got in the way of finding some peace between them.

He needed something to keep his hands and mind busy until it was time to get cleaned up before riding into town. He wished he had borrowed a book at the store, but he hadn't wanted to be beholden to anyone, especially that big-eyed girl. For about the hundredth time in the past three days, his eyes were drawn to the south, looking for the plume of smoke that announced their neighbor was at home.

Damn, why did she have to live so close?

He didn't want anything to do with her, and now he had to ride past her place every time he went into Lee's Mill. Worse yet, he kept finding and discarding excuses for doing just that. He had no business even thinking such things. He deliberately turned due north and walked out to the pasture where he and Jack had been pulling stumps.

After making two turns around the pasture, he gave up all pretense of doing anything constructive and headed back for the house. Jack was just heading into the privy as Luke rounded the corner of the barn. Luke knew better than to approach him until Jack had had time to drink some coffee. Figuring to help that process along, he poured them each a cup and carried them out onto the porch.

If Jack was surprised to find Luke waiting for him, he didn't complain. He grabbed the coffee as soon as he saw it and sank down on the other stump to sip it down.

"I'm going into town to have Sunday dinner with

Cade Mulroney and his family. He said to invite you along, if you were of a mind to come." Luke kept his voice carefully neutral, especially since he wasn't all that sure he wanted Jack to say yes. Not with Cora Lawford among the invited guests. The afternoon was going to be stressful enough without having to watch his younger brother charm all the women at the table with so little effort.

"Thank him for thinking of me, but I think I'll stick close to home today." Jack took another long drink of coffee. "I thought I might try my luck at the river. See if I can catch us some fish for supper."

"That sounds good." Luke watched Jack out of the corner of his eye. "Think one of us could manage to make some cornbread to go with the fish?"

Jack flashed him a genuine smile. "I'm willing to give it a try. Besides, if it doesn't turn out, we can always use it to shore up the porch."

"In that case, make a double batch. The chicken coop could use some help standing upright."

The shared laughter felt damned good. Luke was almost afraid to say anything else for fear he'd spoil the moment. The silence spun out between them as he struggled to think of a safe subject for conversation. Then it was too late, as Jack drank the last of his coffee and disappeared back into the cabin.

Luke tugged at his collar and cursed. He knew the shirt fit just fine; it was the afternoon stretching out ahead that had him feeling choked. At least he'd passed the first hurdle. He'd been worried that he'd run into his neighbor on the way to their mutual destination. About the time he passed by her house, it dawned on him that she had probably left hours earlier for church. Why was it that relief felt suspiciously like disappointment?

He took a moment to study her home. The house wasn't huge, but it was a damned sight bigger than the cabin he and Jack shared. The place was so new that the lumber hadn't even begun to fade. What had possessed a single woman to buy a place so far out of town? There had to be vacant lots closer in where she'd be safer.

Not that it was any of his damned business. Jerking on the reins, he turned his horse back toward town. For the moment he tried to concentrate on how beautiful the day was. Of course, any day he didn't spend in prison was beautiful, no matter what the weather. He shivered despite the bright sun. He'd lost so much of his life huddled behind iron bars.

But he was determined not to dwell on what couldn't be changed. Even the huge amount of work it would take to restore the farm didn't bother him. With each task he accomplished came the knowledge that he'd taken another step in rebuilding his life. And while he could deal with stubborn tree stumps and sagging porches, he wasn't at all sure he was ready for people.

But he was about to find out. The road widened out as it led into town. Luke turned left before reaching Front Street, following the directions Cade had given him. He wished he'd walked; it would have taken him longer to get there, and the exercise might have burned off some tension. It didn't take any time at all to find the neat house tucked in behind the newspaper office.

A riot of bright-colored flowers grew in window boxes and around the porch, giving the place a bright, cheery look. Luke tried to imagine someone planting flowers around the cabin. Although his mother used to have a couple of rosebushes that she'd fussed with, somehow he couldn't quite see either him or Jack wasting much time with flowers. That was definitely a woman's touch, and the likelihood of either of them bringing home a wife was pretty slim.

Wishing he could give in to the temptation to turn tail and run, he dismounted and tied his horse to the fence that surrounded the front yard. If he weren't so short on money, he would have put the horse up at the stable for a few hours.

The front door opened before he could walk through the gate. He was relieved to see it was Cade coming to greet him. He had his infant son tucked in the crook of his arm. Stepping off the porch, he waved Luke on in.

"Luke, I'm glad you could make it!" He carefully shifted his son so he could carry him one-handed and held his other hand out to Luke.

Luke shook his friend's hand before taking the time to admire the baby. Once again, he was struck by the sweet innocence of the sleeping child. He couldn't resist reaching out with his finger to stroke the infant's tiny hand.

"He's something, isn't he?"

Luke knew Cade wasn't bragging. Both of them had seen far too much death and senseless destruction to ever take for granted something as precious as new life.

"Would you like to hold him?"

Before he could answer, Cade thrust his son into Luke's arms. Terror like he hadn't felt in years paralyzed him on the spot. Had Cade lost his mind, entrusting Luke with something so fragile? He would have glared at his friend, but he was afraid to take his eyes off the tiny burden in his arms.

"His name is Roy."

The baby stirred and then sleepily blinked his eyes open. When he caught sight of Luke, his eyes almost crossed in an effort to focus on his face. Luke waited for little Roy to realize that he was being held by a total stranger and scream in terror. Instead, he blew a couple of spit bubbles and then smiled.

"He smiled at me!" Luke risked a quick glance at Cade to see if he'd taken note of the miracle.

The proud papa grinned. "Every time he does that, it makes me feel like I own the whole damned world."

A feminine voice entered the conversation. "If you keep cursing like that around him, his first word is going to be a shameful one." Lucy walked up to her husband and shook her finger in Cade's face. "And it won't be *his* mouth I wash out with soap."

Cade grabbed her hand and kissed it. "I'll try to do better, but I won't promise."

Lucy pulled her hand free from her husband's grasp with a smile that she shared with Luke. "Welcome, Mr. Gibson. I'm pleased you were able to join us for dinner."

"Thank you for inviting me, Mrs. Mulroney."

Evidently Roy had finally realized that his mother was close by. He screwed up his face in a fierce scowl and threatened to cry. That was enough to send Luke into full panic. He thrust Roy at his mother, glad to be relieved of the responsibility.

She accepted the burden of her son with a serene smile. "Come on inside. I must warn you, though, that Mary is hoping that you play chess. She says she's tired of playing against me and Cora. Something about us letting her win."

"I'm pretty rusty, but I used to play with my pa." He tagged along behind Lucy with Cade.

As soon as they stepped inside, he drew an appreciative breath. "Fried chicken and apple pie?"

"Right on both counts, Mr. Gibson. This is your lucky day, because Cora Lawford insisted on baking the pie. I'm afraid I cannot compete with her when it comes to pastries."

"I'm sure you're exaggerating. I took one look at Cade the other day and knew someone has been feeding him right."

"Well, thank you for that, but one bite of Cora's pie will convince you."

Cora picked that moment to walk into the room. "Lucy, you know very well that you're one of the best cooks in Lee's Mill."

It felt as if all the air in the room had disappeared. Was it possible that each time he saw her she was prettier? He hoped his body's immediate reaction wasn't as noticeable as he feared.

"Hello, Mr. Gibson. I'm pleased you decided to come."

Which meant she thought he wouldn't. It was nice to know that she thought he was a coward.

Lucy seemed to pick up on the underlying tension. She shot her friend a questioning look before saying, "Let me put Roy down in his cradle and then we'll eat. Cade, you and Mr. Gibson can go wash up."

Luke was relieved to follow his friend out of the room. Of course, they had to pass right by Cora on their way. He kept his eyes focused directly on Cade's back, refusing to acknowledge her presence. Damn, he'd never realized that temptation smelled like cinnamon and apples.

***

Cora stood her ground, fighting the urge to back away from Luke Gibson as he stalked past her as if she were just another picture on the wall. Well, she wasn't here because of him. After all, she was Lucy's guest and, as such, she had every right to be there. If Luke Gibson didn't like it, well, that was too bad.

"Cora, would you let Mary know I'm about to serve dinner?"

Grateful for an excuse to disappear for a moment, she hurried upstairs to Mary's room. She found her little friend busy hosting a dinner party for her dolls.

"Well, Mistress Mary, I don't mean to intrude.However, your presence is requested downstairs." She dropped into a curtsy. It wasn't the first time that Cora had pretended to be a lady's maid, one of Mary's favorite games.

Mary rose to her feet with as much dignity as an eight-year-old could muster. "Thank you, Miss Lawford. Please tell Mrs. Mulroney that I will join her shortly."

"Yes, ma'am. I will relay the message."

She backed out of the room, with head bowed. Then, with a wicked giggle, she charged back into the room to grab Mary and twirl her around. When both of them were breathless with laughter, they collapsed on the bed.

"Come on, you little minx, we'd better hurry. We don't want to miss out on your mother's fried chicken."

"Can't we start with the pie? I promise to eat my vegetables." Mary accompanied that statement with a shudder.

Cora pretended to consider the idea. "No, I don't think so."

"Why not?"

"Your mother won't approve, especially with company for dinner. Mr. Gibson just arrived."

Mary's disappointment immediately disappeared. "Did anyone ask if he could play chess?"

"I don't know."

Mary was on her feet and heading for the door before Cora could answer, leaving her no choice but to follow along in the little girl's wake. She wished she were the one with a good excuse to talk to Luke Gibson. Instead, she found herself in the questionable position of listening in on a child's conversation just to glean one more fact about the man.

And she'd had the nerve to tease Melinda when she first fell in love with her future husband.

Not that she was in love with Luke Gibson, not by a long shot. She wasn't even sure if she liked him. No, her interest stemmed from the fact that he was her nearest neighbor. Mitch Hughes, her friend and the former sheriff, had warned her to be careful, hadn't he? It seemed only sensible to learn as much as she could about Luke and his brother.

Right now he was allowing Mary to lead him to the table while she explained that she needed a new chess partner. Cora followed along behind, wishing she had the charm of a little girl.

Once everyone was arranged around the table to Lucy's satisfaction, she asked her husband to say grace. Cora dutifully bowed her head, but not before she peeked to see how Luke responded. An expression close to pain flitted across his features. He quickly bowed his head, but Cora suspected he did so more to hide what he was thinking rather than out of any sense of piety.

Why would a simple table prayer hurt? Then the moment was gone as Cade's amen was echoed around the table. For several minutes, everyone was kept busy passing bowls and platters heaped with food.

Cora, a frequent guest of the Mulroney household, was not at all surprised by the number and variety of dishes to choose from. If she was going to have room for the pie, she knew to keep her portions small. Luke, on the other hand, was busy piling his plate high with every new offering. She caught Lucy's eye and shared a private smile; after all, there was no greater compliment to the cook than a hardy appetite.

When the last platter had been passed, Luke complimented Lucy on her meal. "I haven't tasted cooking this good since my mother died."

"Thank you for saying so." Lucy gave him a quick smile while she added a sizable serving of green beans to Mary's plate. "And tell me, Mr. Gibson, did your mother make you eat your vegetables before you could have pie?"

Mary turned her wide eyes in his direction, no doubt hoping he could save her from such a horrid fate. Cora knew before he even opened his mouth that he was going to back Lucy's play.

"Yes, ma'am, she did." He then winked at Mary, who slumped dejectedly in her seat, no doubt resigned to her fate. "But I learned early on that if I served myself, I ended up with a lot fewer vegetables on my plate."

Cora hid a smile as the adults all watched Mary mulling over that piece of advice. There wasn't a doubt in her mind that the next time the vegetables were passed, Mary would see to her own servings.

She also noticed that so far, Luke hadn't even so much as glanced in her direction. Considering the table wasn't all that big, it had to be a deliberate choice on his part. Well, that didn't mean she had to ignore him.

"So, Mr. Gibson, how is your brother Jack? We were hoping that he would come with you."

"He had to stay home and get some work done." He glanced at Lucy. "He asked me to thank you for including him in your invitation."

It wasn't much of an answer, but Cora drew some satisfaction from the way his jaw tensed and that he still refused to look in her direction.

"Well, be sure to tell him how disappointed I—I mean, we—were. Perhaps he'll be able to come next time."

This time a pair of ice-blue eyes glanced in her direction. She fought the urge to shiver after he looked back at his plate. The reasons behind her interest in him weren't clear, even to her. But if he weren't so intent on ignoring her, perhaps she wouldn't feel so compelled to keep poking and prodding at him. For the moment, she bit back the urge to say anything more to him.

Luke and Cade carried most of the conversation, discussing what crops brought the highest prices. Cora wasn't much interested in corn or wheat, but she enjoyed listening to the two of them. Even Mary seemed content to sit quietly while the men moved on to job possibilities.

"What did you have in mind?"

"Something temporary, I hope. Jack and I had enough to pay the taxes on the property, but we're going need some start-up cash." Luke helped himself to another piece of chicken. "I plan to spend this season clearing the fields where they've gotten overgrown. But come next spring, we'll need seed and such to really start farming."

"I guess I'd ask down at the mill first." Cade balanced his chair on its back two legs as he gave the matter some further thought. "Do you remember Bud Keller?"

Luke's eyebrows drew together in a thoughtful expression. "I think so. Seems to me that he and Pa knew each other. Had a passel of children, although I guess they'd all be grown up now."

Cade nodded. "Anyway, Bud does a lot of the building around Lee's Mill and White's Ferry, too. Mostly he and his boys do the work, but sometimes he hires on extra help when he has a big project or several going at once."

"I'll make a point to talk to him if I can track him down."

Cora latched on to the chance to contribute to the conversation. "He promised to stop by my place tomorrow or the next day to talk about putting up a fence for me. If you'd like, I can tell him that you'd like to speak to him."

"No, thanks. I'll do my own job hunting." Luke pushed his plate back from the edge of the table. "Mrs. Mulroney, that was a right fine meal. Thank you."

"I hope you saved room for some of Cora's pie and coffee."

Cora, still smarting from his rejection of her offer, half expected him to find some excuse not to have dessert just because she'd been the one to bake the pie. Rather than wait around to be insulted even further, she picked up her plate and started clearing the table. To her surprise, he proved her wrong.

"I always have room for pie. And enough time for a quick game of chess, Miss Mary, if you promise to go easy on me. It's been a long time since I've played."

Mary immediately leapt to her feet, ready to lead the charge to the chessboard. She was brought up short by a sharp look from her mother. "May I be excused?" The words came out in an exasperated rush. Manners clearly had no place in her life when they interfered with a game of chess.

Lucy shooed her out of the room. "Go on; you're excused." To Luke, she added, "I hope you know what you're letting yourself in for. Cade, you go on along with them. I'll serve the pie and coffee in a few minutes."

Lucy picked up a load of dishes and followed Cora out to the kitchen. It took them several more trips to get everything. While Cora rolled her sleeves up and filled the sink with hot water, Lucy scraped the dishes and stacked them for washing. She had a few questions for her younger friend.

After checking to make sure that the others were out of hearing, she dove right in. "So what's going on between you and Luke Gibson?"

Cora sputtered, "Nothing is going on. How could you ask something like that?"

Lucy noticed she was scrubbing a plate hard enough to take the finish off. Nothing, indeed. "I had to ask because every time you talk to him, it's like watching a pair of cats hissing and spitting at each other."

Cora closed her eyes for a few seconds, no doubt wondering if she could get by pretending she didn't understand. But Lucy was her best friend and knew her too well.

"Talk to me, Cora. I've never seen you this upset about a man."

Cora drew a shuddering breath and let it out. "I don't know. It's been that way since that first day that he and Jack came into the store." She slipped a stack of plates into the water.

"If he weren't so nice to the rest of you, I'd think he was just a difficult person. There must be something wrong with me." Her eyes blinked several times, as if fighting back tears.

Lucy clucked her tongue and shook her head. "Cora Lawford, you're smarter than that. There's nothing wrong with you." She slipped her arm around Cora's shoulders and gave her a quick squeeze. "If he's not smart enough to figure that out, well, then the man's a complete fool."

"He sure wasn't happy to find out that I own the place next to his. You can't even see his house from mine."

Lucy took the single plate that Cora had been scrubbing and handed her another one to work out her frustrations on. The truth was that she suspected that Luke found Cora all too attractive and was fighting it tooth and nail. Considering what Lucy knew of his past, she was relieved. He'd had a rough way to go for a good long time. According to her husband, Luke needed to rebuild his life even more than his farm. Cade had told her as much of Luke's story as he felt he could, but that didn't give her the right to share it with Cora. Not without Luke's permission.

"Give him some time, Cora. He and his brother have a long way to go to make their farm into a home again."

"That's no excuse," Cora complained as she reached for another stack of dishes. "Look at my place. I have to put in a garden, plant the yard, and put up a fence."

"But you have the money to do most of that, not to mention you have a job starting in a couple of months." Lucy wiped her hands on her apron. "And you have a solid group of friends who love and care about you."

She cut the pie and dished it up while she gave Cora a chance to think that over. After she had three pieces of pie, a glass of milk, and two cups of coffee arranged on a tray, she carried it to the other room.

She set the tray down on the table beside the sofa. Cade was the only one who paid the slightest bit of attention to her. Mary was too busy considering her next move while Luke looked on with intense interest. The chessboard sat between them on a low table.

"Check!" Mary crowed with glee. "And mate."

Lucy hid a smile at the look of complete shock on their guest's face. Evidently the threat to his king had come out of nowhere. His eyes narrowed in concentration while he searched in vain for a safe haven from her daughter's relentless onslaught. Finally, he tipped his king over in surrender.

"Mary Mulroney, you have your father's gift for leading your men in battle."

He smiled at the little girl, who grinned back at him. For once Mary wasn't complaining that someone had allowed her to win. She immediately started to set the board up for another game.

"Can we play again?"

Lucy decided that their guest could use some rescuing. "Not now, Mary. Why don't you move the game out of the way for now? Mr. Gibson would probably like a chance to eat his pie and drink his coffee while it is still hot."

He gave her a grateful look. "I will want a rematch, but not until I have a chance to practice some. She's deadly. Cade, you have taught her well."

Cade chuckled. "I didn't teach her. Lucy and Cora did."

"Or didn't you think that women were capable

of such things?" Cora had slipped into the room unnoticed.

Luke kept his eyes firmly on Lucy, not acknowledging Cora's presence by even a quick glance. "Well, then, my compliments, Mrs. Mulroney. You did a fine job."

Then he quickly took a bite of the pie to avoid having to say more. *The poor fool*, Lucy thought. If he wanted Cora to leave him alone, he was certainly going about it the wrong way. The more he ignored her, the harder Cora would work to get his attention. Lucy felt a faint stir of pity for the poor man. He shouldn't forget that Cora had taught Mary how to play chess. She understood strategy and pursuit of a goal.

For the next few minutes, conversation was sporadic as they all finished their pie. When both of the men had finished off a second piece each, Luke stood up, obviously ready to take his leave.

"I had better get back to the farm. I want to thank you again for inviting me to your home, Mrs. Mulroney." He retrieved his hat from a hook on the wall near the door. "I can't remember when I've had cooking that good."

She accepted the compliment as sincere, especially knowing where he'd spent the past five years. "I have a basket for you to take with you. Since your brother couldn't come with you, I thought maybe you'd like to take some of the dinner to him."

"That would be right kind of you, Mrs. Mulroney. I know Jack will appreciate it."

"Cora, would you get the basket I left on the table for me?"

Luke's eyes watched her leave the room, telling Lucy she'd been right in her suspicions. Cora's interest in Luke wasn't completely one-sided. She wasn't sure which of the two was in for the roughest ride. Her only hope was that her young friend didn't get hurt. For all her stubbornness and intelligence, Cora's feelings were pretty fragile.

"Here is the basket, Mr. Gibson."

Cora practically shoved the basket at him. If it weren't for his quick reflexes, the bundle of food could have ended up splattered on Lucy's best braided rug. Once he had a good grip on the basket, Luke practically bolted out the door. Apparently oblivious to the undercurrents, Cade followed after him.

"We'll do this again soon, Luke."

"I'd like that." He paused on the porch. "Do you think that Mrs. Samuels would mind me stopping by to ask about buying chickens today?"

"I wouldn't think so. If she doesn't have any to spare, let me know, and I'll ask around some more."

By then Mary, Lucy, and Cora had joined them outside.

"Well, thanks again." Then he smiled down at Mary. "I'll be wanting another game, Miss Mary. Next time I won't underestimate my opponent."

The smile died away as he nodded toward Cora. "Miss Lawford."

Cora was back in the house, the door slamming closed behind her, before he'd had time to reach his patient horse. Luke flinched but didn't look back.

Looking puzzled, Cade whispered, "What was that all about?"

"Later," Lucy whispered back, nodding slightly in the direction of Mary's listening ears. "Time to go inside, Mary. Let's see if Cora has time for a game of cribbage before she has to leave."

CHAPTER 4

The day had gone better than he'd expected. He certainly hadn't been lying about how good Lucy's dinner had been. Eyeing the basket he held balanced on the saddle in front of him, he wondered if he really had to share the contents with Jack. He knew he would, even if tempted to do otherwise. Of course, knowing his brother, Jack might well have decided to ride out again rather than spend a quiet day at home.

He really didn't blame Jack for wanting to spend time with his friends; he only wished he knew more about the kind of men they were. Cade had already warned him that not all men had willingly put away their arms when the war ended. Some had been too restless to stay in one place or else had no home left to return to. Others wanted revenge for all that the war had cost them. But some had learned to love killing and had found other avenues for their pleasure.

Lord of mercy, don't let Jack be running with the likes of them.

Knowing there wasn't much he could do about the problem until Jack trusted him with his secrets, Luke shoved the worry to the back of his mind. There were a few things he could be happy about—the friendship of Cade and his family, for one thing. And for another, tomorrow he'd be the proud owner of a small flock of chickens. Mrs. Samuels had about talked his arm off, but she'd given him a fair price for several hens and a rooster.

How would Cade like being lumped in with a bunch of squawking hens? Knowing him, his former commander would find it funny. Luke suspected Lucy would even understand. He figured that Cade might have shared some of Luke's story with her. After prodding the idea like a sore tooth, he found that he wasn't particularly concerned about her knowing. If she'd been worried, he would have never been allowed to cross her threshold, Cade's invitation notwithstanding.

His horse shook her head and snorted, warning him that they were no longer alone. He could just make out the outline of a woman walking along the side of the road. Unfortunately, there was only one woman who had any business out this direction, and that was Cora Lawford. For a few seconds, he was tempted to take off through the woods or, better yet, head back to town on some trumped-up excuse. But that was a coward's way out, and he was through running.

He could hang back, following along behind her, to make sure she made it to the safety of her tidy little home. No, she'd wonder what he was up to once she realized she was being followed. Having discarded that idea, he toyed with riding right past her without speaking at all, but knew he wouldn't.

Rather than examine his motives too closely, he decided that his ma would have expected him to be neighborly enough to escort the girl home. He urged his mare into a quick trot before he lost his nerve.

As he drew close, Cora turned to wait for him. He'd been right not to avoid her. She'd been aware of his presence before he'd seen her. He reined in the mare a short distance back and dismounted. He looped the handle of the basket over the butt of his rifle in its scabbard.

"Miss Lawford."

"Mr. Gibson," she acknowledged as she turned and continued on her journey.

He fell into step beside her. They walked in an uneasy silence for a short distance before she spoke again.

"Is your horse too tired to carry you the rest of the way?"

Damned if he didn't like her prickly nature. He hated knowing that about himself. "Not at all."

"Then why are you walking?"

"I live out this way." He wondered how long it would take her to figure out his real purpose.

"Don't play the fool, Mr. Gibson. It doesn't become you." She paused midstep and rounded on him. "Don't tell me that you're laboring under the mistaken idea that I'm a helpless female and unable to make it home alone?" Her eyes spat fire at the very idea that someone would think she couldn't take care of herself. He didn't want to be the one to teach her different, but she obviously had no idea how dangerous the world could be.

"I wouldn't dare."

Her hands on her hips, she stood glaring up at him. "I won't have it, Luke Gibson. I was walking home by myself long before you and your brother showed up."

"Then start walking, since you're so good at it." He met her glare for glare. He didn't want to be her guardian any more than she wanted him to be. But if something happened to her when he could have prevented it, he wouldn't be able to live with himself.

Once again they marched along, with his mare tagging along at their heels. When he noticed a black snake slithering across their path, he broke the silence. "Slow up a bit."

"I'm not afraid of a snake." She started forward again.

"Not you, the mare."

Actually, his horse had more sense than that, but he clung to the excuse to share Cora's company for a few extra seconds. The snake was already almost to the tufts of grass on the far side of the road.

"Look, your pie really was delicious," he blurted out.

She seemed taken aback by his sudden change in tactics. "Well, thank you, Mr. Gibson. I'm glad you liked it because there's another one just like it in that basket."

Not knowing quite what to say to that, he started walking again. They were only a short distance from her house now. He didn't stop or speak again until they reached the point where their ways parted.

"I'll watch until you're inside."

She sniffed her frustration. "Mr. Gibson, I don't need or want anyone watching over me. I've waited too long to be on my own. Enjoy your pie."

He understood all about pride. He would allow her to cling to hers as much as possible. "Then I'll be moving on, Miss Lawford. Thank you for the pie." He swung up into the saddle, knowing he'd wait within screaming distance once he was out of her sight.

"See that you return my pie plate if you have any hope of ever having another one."

With that, she walked away without looking back. Good to his word, he set the mare off at a sedate pace until he reached the small gap in the trees that offered a clear view of Cora's house. He stood watch until she was safely inside.

When Cora had firmly shut the door behind her, he put her out of his mind except to consider the fate of the pie she'd given him. He supposed if Jack had actually caught fish for supper, he'd be obligated to share. But maybe not. Grinning, he urged the mare into a fast trot, content to be heading home.

Jack watched Luke ride in. Bored with his own company, he walked out to meet him. He took note of the basket bumping along on the side of the saddle and wondered what was in it. With luck, Cade's wife had been kind enough to send part of their Sunday dinner home with Luke. The thought had his mouth watering.

"Is that what I hope it is?"

Luke handed the basket down to him. "I haven't looked yet, although I've been told there's a whole pie in there."

Jack whistled a long note as he handled the basket with reverence. "What kind?"

"We had apple at the house, so I assume that's what this one is, too." Luke started unsaddling his horse. "Don't go running off with that basket, though. I don't want you rooting through it before I have a chance to take inventory."

Jack tried to look insulted but gave up. Luke knew him too well. "All right, but hurry. I wouldn't want the pie to go bad."

Luke snorted in derision. "It won't last us long enough to go bad." He looked at Jack over the mare's back. "Any luck fishing?"

Considering Luke seemed willing to share the pie,

Jack was glad he had a nice pair of catfish waiting to be fried up for their supper. "I threw back a couple of bluegill that were too small, but I managed to land a pair of good-sized bullhead catfish. Enough for the two of us." He lifted the basket higher. "Especially with whatever is in this basket. It's too heavy for just a pie."

Luke slapped the mare on the rump as he turned her out in the small corral with Jack's horse. He picked up the saddle and tack and carried them into the barn.

"Well, let's go see what we're having for supper."

It started the same way it always did: the screech of rusty hinges as metal scraped against metal, the jangle of keys, the sting of wrists rubbed raw from shackles, the stench of men unwashed and despairing. The shuffling walk mastered only after falling too many times to count because the chains were too short for a man of his height.

The worst were the screams that rent the darkness and the gnawing fear that if he ever joined in the nightly chorus, he'd never be able to stop. He tried to turn over and bury his head in his blankets to deaden the noise.

But the dream was a prisoner inside his own head, and no amount of twisting and turning could protect him from the misery of his memories. He spun in his blankets until they held him captive, just as the chains had for five long years.

When the iron bars slammed closed in his dream, the dead came to visit. One by one his boyhood friends, bloody and broken beyond repair, waved and nodded as they hobbled past his cell on their way to heaven or hell. They never said a word, just looked at him with mind-numbing fear in their eyes. He wanted to reach out, to say he was sorry for not going with them, but the chains on his wrists kept him from even offering them any sort of comfort. And finally, Freddy would appear, laughing and happy with a gaping hole in his gut, forcing Luke to remember things better left forgotten. His young friend didn't seem to mind that he was dead and Luke wasn't. But Luke minded. He wasn't sure he'd ever forgive the Yankees—or himself—that he was the only one still breathing.

His chest ached with the need to grieve. So much time had passed since the war ended, and still the pain of so much loss hadn't faded. The dream spun on, the uniforms changing from tattered gray and butternut to dark blue. The faces were the same. More young men, those killed by Luke and others like him, marched in wounded formation past his cell. His feeling of guilt was only slightly lessened, because he knew he'd been the one to pull the trigger.

Stop! Please, for the love of God, stop! he begged them, but he didn't know what he meant. Stop coming? Stop and talk? Stop and forgive?

The hand on his shoulder felt all too real. As much as he missed his friends and Freddy, none of them had ever reached out to him before. He tried to knock the hand away, knowing it was bloody and would leave a mark on his clothes, his skin, his soul.

"Get away from me!"

"Damn it, Luke, you're dreaming again! Wake up!"

He recognized the voice. Jack. *Oh, God, don't let Jack be in the parade.* He couldn't bear it. Not with their mother and father already dead. "Jack?" he whispered. "Tell me you're not dead."

"Hell, no, I'm not dead. I'm also not asleep anymore.

Wake up. You're dreaming." This time the hand on his shoulder wasn't quite so gentle.

Luke managed to pry his eyes open, even though he was afraid of what he might see. Jack loomed over him, his features barely recognizable in the darkness. Slowly, his dream-riddled mind started to make sense of things, sifting fragments of reality from the nightmare that hovered within reach.

"Jack? Was I screaming?" Lord, he hoped not, but he felt winded, as if he'd been running for hours. The truth was he'd been running for much longer than that. Five years, maybe more.

Jack rocked back on his heels and waited now that Luke was awake. "Not screaming, but moaning loud and thrashing around." He paused and cocked his head to one side. "Just like all the other times."

"Shit." Luke found the strength to sit up. "Go back to sleep."

"Do you want to tell me about it?"

He appreciated the offer but refused it. "Hell no."

Jack pushed himself back up to his feet. "Then I'm going back to bed." There was more than a hint of relief in his voice.

Luke didn't blame him a bit. "I'll be outside." He reached for his boots.

"See you in the morning." Jack wandered over to the corner of the room he'd staked out as his own.

Luke waited until Jack was settled and back to sleep before gathering up his own bedroll and heading out into the darkness. So far, the only cure he'd found for the nightmares that tore his nights to pieces was to sleep outside. For some reason the memories and the ghosts seemed to need four walls and a roof to find him. He didn't know why, nor did he care. At least it meant he could get some damned sleep.

Outside, he stood on the high side of the porch just to breathe some fresh air and let the sweat dry on his skin. When his hands had mostly stopped shaking, he dragged his blankets behind him out to the big sycamore tree that shaded the house in the worst heat of the day. At night, it offered him a roof over his head without the walls to close him in.

He tossed the blankets on the ground in a heap, knowing it would be awhile before he'd be able to close his eyes and sleep. For a few minutes, he walked around in the darkness, keeping to the places he knew best. It felt good to be moving, not that he could out-distance the memories or the pain.

Maybe he did need to talk to someone, but not Jack. Even if he could understand what Luke had gone through, Luke still thought of Jack as his little brother who needed protection from the ugliness in life. It was probably more of his wrongheaded thinking, but he couldn't help how he felt.

Cade, maybe. Luke had a fair idea that his friend had suffered because of the war. Hell, they all had, just in different ways. But Cade had built a fine life for himself and didn't need Luke's problems heaped on his shoulders.

He kept walking. Other than tripping on the occasional stone or root jutting up in his path, he took some pleasure in his nightly wanderings. Sometimes he ended up at the river; other nights he walked halfway to town and back. The destination didn't matter, just as long as he could move freely. He lengthened his stride because he could. The scars from the leg-irons marked him forever, but he'd worked hard to break the habit of walking in short steps.

Once again the memories had caught up with him, but not like before. The night sky arched above kept him from being caged. The stars moved in a stately dance through the dark velvet, their patterns reassuring and familiar. Orion had always been his favorite.

A yawn slipped past his guard, reminding him that it was time for all men of good sense to be asleep. He looked around, trying to gauge his location by the shapes of the trees and bushes around him. At first, he didn't recognize much of anything, but then he realized that the large shadow looming up out of the darkness in front of him was Cora Lawford's house. If he'd stayed lost in his thoughts another thirty feet, he would have run right into her front porch.

He immediately backed away. What had made him walk in this direction? What a damned fool thing to be doing! As quietly as he could, he retraced his steps without looking back. It was an accident, not intentional at all, that he'd been heading for Cora's home. Once he was safely back on Gibson land, he broke into a slow run until he reached the sheltering branches of the sycamore tree.

This time, he straightened his blankets into some semblance of order before lying down. He closed his eyes to listen to the sweet night sounds of a Missouri summer night. A few crickets sang out their love songs while the cicadas droned on in accompaniment. In the distance, the frogs added their voices to the lullaby, gradually lulling him to sleep.

This time, as he drifted off, the memory of brown eyes and apple pie invaded his dreams and made him smile.

Jack was already saddling up when Luke crawled out of his dew-dampened blankets and headed back to the cabin in hopes of finding a hot cup of coffee. He wanted to protest, but he was in no shape to face another argument with his brother. And after last night, Jack probably didn't want much to do with Luke either. Neither of them had gotten much sleep.

At least Jack had made coffee. After tossing his bedroll into the corner, Luke poured himself a cup and sat down. His head ached and his mouth felt as if a crop of tree moss had taken root. The first sip of the coffee went a long way toward scalding his mind and his mouth clean. He stretched his legs out and tried to make plans for the day.

For years someone else had made every decision for him. Now, he even appreciated the simple pleasure of being able to choose which chore to do next. He closed his eyes and considered the possibilities. First off, he needed to shore up the old chicken coop. It wouldn't take more than a few nails and cleaning out some cobwebs. Then by early afternoon, he'd have to figure out a way to bring home the chickens. Without a wagon, he'd probably have to make several trips with the unhappy birds stuffed in cages and slung over the back of his horse. They'd get over it as soon as they were set free; his horse might hold a grudge.

Maybe if he got the coop done early enough, he'd have time to start on the garden he had planned. He'd already picked up seeds in town and staked out the corners where he wanted to dig. At least some of his father's old garden tools were still usable. A few hours of digging and weeding, and he'd be ready to plant. In a couple of weeks, the first few sprouts would be poking their heads up out of the dirt. He could hardly wait.

Looking around the dim interior of the cabin, he

wished he had more time to work inside. It wasn't surprising that the whole place had gone to hell over the years. After all, the cabin had sat vacant for the better part of ten years. Although the land hadn't suffered other than to be overrun with weeds, the cabin hadn't handled the neglect at all well. The only residents had been the four-legged kind, and they hadn't done much to keep the place up.

A movement outside the dingy window caught his attention. He didn't need to see clearly to know that Jack had ridden out without saying where he was going, when he'd be back, or even good-bye. Before he even knew what he was doing, Luke was on his feet and running. He might not have the right to order his younger brother around, but, damn it, the kid could at least let him in on his plans.

By the time he reached the porch, Jack had already disappeared into the trees. For a brief second, Luke considered tracking him down and demanding that Jack put in his fair share of time around the farm. But the truth was, rebuilding was Luke's idea, not Jack's. If his brother had really been interested in farming, he would have kept the place going while Luke was away.

Luke was the one who couldn't let go of the past, who needed to see the family home as it had once been. Maybe he needed to reestablish his roots before he could look toward the future, and Jack had other needs. It was that simple.

Sighing, Luke went back inside. The day that had stretched out before him, filled with possibilities, had lost its glow. Resigned to spending more long hours alone, he headed back to scrounge something for breakfast. His mood lightened considerably when he found out that Jack had left without eating the last piece of Cora's pie.

Maybe the day wouldn't be so bad after all.

Cora wandered around her house, trying to find something useful to do. She'd already swept the floor, washed everything that would hold still, rearranged her few books, and scrubbed her windows until they gleamed. Finally, she picked up her sewing basket and the fabric she'd already cut to fit the bedroom window and went out on the porch to sew.

The day felt close, too muggy and hot for this early in the year. Her dress stuck to her like a second skin. She settled herself on the steps and did her best to ignore the heat. In less than fifteen minutes, she gave up and ripped out the row of stitches for the second time. Disgusted with herself, she made a halfhearted effort to fold the material neatly before setting it aside.

Maybe a short walk would help.

Before she could change her mind, she set off cross-country toward the river. The shortest route and the one she always took led right through Luke Gibson's front yard. He couldn't possibly object to a neighbor crossing his property.

Well, yes, he could, knowing Luke Gibson. He'd given her every reason to think he didn't appreciate her company one bit. But this was different, she argued with herself. She wasn't going out of her way to see him. Not at all. She'd made the same journey across the Gibson farm several times since moving into her house. The only difference was that the place had been deserted on the other occasions.

It wasn't deserted now.

Even from this distance she knew which Gibson

brother was hard at work attacking the ground with a hoe. She automatically looked around to see if Jack was anywhere in sight, but it appeared that Luke was home alone. Not only that, but he had his shirt off.

The sight had her heart stuttering and her feet stumbling. She tried to remember if she'd ever seen a man with his shirt off but couldn't gather up a single coherent thought. If Aunt Henrietta's teachings had taken hold, she would have either spun around and headed right back to safety or fainted dead away. However, it wasn't delicate sensibilities or the heat that was making her dizzy.

She was walking toward temptation itself.

She managed to get right up to the cabin before Luke noticed her. He took one look in her direction and deliberately kept right on working. Deciding if he could ignore her, the least she could do was return the favor. She was almost past him before allowing herself one more sinful peek, only to find him marching right toward her.

At least he'd managed to yank his shirt back over his sweaty skin. Not that he'd buttoned it up. With some effort, she managed to drag her gaze back up to his face.

"Where do you think you're going?" He planted himself directly in her path.

"To the river." She tried to go around him, but he just moved with her.

"I didn't know the road to the river ran right through my land."

Nervousness was turning to anger. "It doesn't, but I didn't think you'd mind if I went this way. It shortens my walk considerably."

"I mind."

For several seconds, they stood glaring at each other,

neither one wanting to give an inch. Finally, Luke slid to the side and waved her on.

"Go ahead this time, but I don't want you hanging around here."

That did it. She'd had enough of his rudeness. "Listen here, Mr. Luke Gibson, I had no intention of intruding on your precious privacy. I have been walking this way to the river since before my house was even finished. Forgive me, but for one moment I forgot you even existed. All I was thinking about was spending a few minutes down by the river." She drew upon the manners that Henrietta had drilled into her. "Now if you'll excuse me, Mr. Gibson, I'll take my leave of you."

Her chin took on a stubborn tilt that anyone who knew her well recognized as a signal that her temper was about to fly. She gave Luke a disdainful sniff and continued on her way. Before she'd gone three steps, he caught her by the arm and spun her back around.

"The river isn't a safe place for you to go alone."

"Afraid I'll fall in? Well, don't let it worry you. I can swim, Mr. Gibson, not that it's any of your concern."

He muttered something under his breath that sounded like "damned fool woman," but she wasn't sure. "No, I'm not afraid of you falling in. In fact, I'd be tempted to push you in myself."

She did her best to hide how much that hurt to hear. "But?"

"But there are some dangerous men in the area, the kind an innocent like you should stay away from."

Temper loosened her tongue. "Worse than you?"

She regretted the outburst the second she said it. For a brief instant she thought she saw a flicker of hurt in his eyes, but then the ice was back.

He towered over her, his body rigid with fury. "Think the worst of me because I was in prison if you want to, but don't say I didn't warn you. The woods and the river aren't safe for a woman alone."

He was gone before she could string together enough words to offer an apology. She didn't know what to do. Unable to move, she watched him rip his shirt back off and fling it to the ground before attacking the ground with the hoe again. The prudent thing to do would be to walk away until he'd worked off some of his temper.

But she wasn't feeling prudent. Even so, she approached Luke cautiously.

"Mr. Gibson?" When he didn't respond, she walked a little closer. "Mr. Gibson?"

Rather than get within striking distance of the hoe, she sidled around the edge of the garden he'd marked out and waited for him to notice her. Other than to turn away from her, he paid her no mind at all.

Gathering what courage she could muster, she reached out to touch his bare arm. "Luke, please listen."

She could feel the tension thrumming through him and the play of his muscles as he hacked at the ground. Finally, he paused midswing and glared down at her hand on his arm.

Now that she had his attention, she stepped back to avoid crowding him. "I'm sorry, Luke. I didn't know."

He slowly brought his eyes up to meet hers. Whatever he saw there must have satisfied him. "Don't worry about it. It's nothing."

But it was. "My temper sometimes gets the best of me, but I never meant to insult you."

He arched an eyebrow at that obvious lie.

"Well, not about something as serious as that,

anyway." She wanted to know more. Curiosity was another of her faults. "Why?"

He didn't pretend to not understand, but neither did he explain. "Listen, little girl, I have work to do. Go on home."

"But I . . ."

"Please, Cora. Go home."

She didn't like being called a little girl, but nothing in her experience had prepared her to deal with the likes of Luke Gibson. Whatever his story was, she knew it would break her heart just to hear it. Recognizing her own cowardice, she retreated. She walked back to her house without once looking back, her only company the sound of a hoe tearing up the ground.

Jack avoided the river. He also avoided the farm. If he could have managed to avoid his own company, he would have done so. He'd been riding cross-country since early morning with no destination in mind, just a handful of places he didn't want to be.

He wished he knew what Baxter wanted from him. If he knew the man better, maybe he would have asked him. But, hell, he didn't even know the man's real name. As far as Jack could tell, Baxter changed his name as often as most men changed shirts. The group of men who came and went from the encampment had no formal organization, other than that they all answered to Baxter.

Jack didn't know half the group by name. In the last days of the war, he'd ridden with several of them in a desperate attempt to throw off the Yankee rule once and for all. When the war ended, he'd come straight home, expecting to find Luke there. Instead, he'd found the farm deserted, looking much as it did now. It had taken him weeks to find out that his brother's reward for killing one Yankee too many was a five-year sentence in a Kansas prison.

Knowing he couldn't run the farm by himself, Jack had spent those years wandering and marking time until Luke returned. He'd turned his hand to anything that kept money in his pocket and food in his stomach. Mostly, he had herded cattle, sometimes for their owner, sometimes not. He was a fair hand with cards and even better with a gun.

Maybe the seeds of restlessness had taken root too deeply, because the long-awaited return to the family farm had left him largely unsatisfied. Luke might find some pleasure in fighting stumps to a standstill or planning where to plant turnips, but Jack hated every damned minute he spent sweating over a piece of rocky Missouri soil.

He thought about telling Luke the truth of the matter. But even though he had no use for the farm, he wasn't quite ready to turn his back on his big brother now that they were back together. Someone had to be there to jar Luke out of his nightmares. He shuddered in the bright sunshine. He had no idea what horrors were chasing through Luke's mind at night, but it spooked Jack every time it happened.

His horse snorted and stamped its foot, yanking Jack back out of his thoughts. His hand slipped down to the grip on his revolver until he knew what had disturbed his gelding. Off to the right, he could see the silver glint of sunshine on water. So he hadn't avoided the river after all. The tension drained out of his shoulders. He was a safe distance from the stretch of water that Baxter's men had claimed for their own.

He dismounted and led his sorrel through the woods

to the rocky edge of the river. His horse immediately pushed past him to drink its fill of the clear, cool water while Jack listened and watched to make sure they were alone. Other than a few dragonflies darting and hovering over the water, he seemed to be alone.

Deciding he'd ridden far enough for a while, he staked the gelding where it could graze. After one last look around, he stretched out in a patch of dappled shade, intent on catching up on some of the sleep he'd lost because of Luke. Maybe after some rest, he'd be able to make up his mind about riding with Baxter.

Helping out with some cattle of dubious ownership was one thing, but he'd never done anything worse. If he chose to ride with Baxter, his life would change for good. Or maybe for worse. Eventually, he'd have to make a decision, but not now.

CHAPTER 5

"What do you think?"

Cora didn't immediately answer for the simple reason that she didn't know enough about horses to give the stable owner an intelligent answer. The best she could say was the mare was pretty and the gelding was taller. She was fairly sure that those traits weren't the right ones to base a decision on.

"How old are they?" That seemed like a reasonable thing to ask.

"She's about five." The owner ran a practiced hand down the mare's flank before turning his attention to the gelding. "He's a little older, but not enough to make a difference."

"Do they know how to pull a buggy?" If only one of the pair knew how, her decision would be made for her.

"If not, they can learn."

Sighing, she was back to where she'd started. If only Cade or Mitch were around; she knew they'd be able to advise her. But Mitch was out at his farm, and Cade was out of town for a couple of days. She could wait until he returned, but by then, one or both horses could be already sold.

Feeling desperate, she looked up and down the street, hoping to find someone who could help her.

A familiar figure was just walking into The River Lady. How had she missed seeing Luke Gibson ride through town?

"I'll be back in five minutes, Mr. Milton."

He shook his head in disgust. "All right, Miss Lawford, but you have to make up your mind. I have other customers who'd be right glad to take both of these horses off my hands."

She figured he was exaggerating, but either way, she couldn't expect him to wait for her to make up her mind. Making her way across the street, she picked up her skirts to avoid dragging them through the dust and worse. Once she reached the sidewalk, it dawned on her that she had no way to get Luke's attention. She couldn't very well walk into The Lady without ruining her reputation for good. Nor could she stand at the door and yell his name. That might work, but there were some things a lady did not do.

Even lurking outside the door was questionable. But what other choice did she have? Perhaps she should wait down the street a short distance. Luckily, she'd gone only a few steps when the batwing doors to the saloon opened as John Horn, a local farmer, walked out into the sunshine.

"Mr. Horn?" She hurried to his side and waited for him to recognize her.

"Miss Lawford, is it?" He immediately snatched his hat off his head, his weathered face looking confused. "You shouldn't be standing around the saloon, ma'am. Is something wrong?"

Her face flushed with embarrassment, but she was determined to stand her ground. "No, everything is fine, Mr. Horn, but I need to speak to a, uh, friend who just went inside. Could you possibly ask him to meet me across the street?"

"Sure, Miss Lawford, I'll do that. Who is that you need me to fetch out for you?"

She closed her eyes and prayed that Luke wouldn't embarrass her further by refusing to come. "Luke Gibson. He's wearing a dark blue shirt and a black hat."

Satisfied that Mr. Horn would see to it that Luke came out, she hurried back across the road to wait. It didn't take long. A few seconds later, Luke looked out over the swinging doors, obviously less than pleased to have his visit to the saloon cut short.

The second he laid eyes on her, he shook his head in disgust before disappearing back into the depths of the saloon. Was he going to refuse her request? She was about to give up and return to the stable when Luke flung open the saloon doors with a bang and sauntered across the street. From a distance, he appeared calm, but one look at his face had her backing up, regretting the impulse to ask him for help. Maybe she'd be better off to apologize for disturbing him and simply choose a horse on her own.

"I'm sorry to have bothered you, Mr. Gibson."

Luke stopped short of running her down. "Are you in the habit of accosting men in saloons, Miss Lawford?"

"I did not accost you!"

"No, you had some farmer do it for you. You're damned lucky your friend didn't have to yell out my name to find me. The whole town would have been talking by nightfall." He whipped his hat off and knocked it against his leg in frustration as he looked up and down the street. For the moment, no one seemed to be taking any interest in their conversation.

"Now why did you find it necessary to haul me away from my well-deserved drink?" He knew he was growling, but he'd been planning on savoring that beer. Instead, he'd had to gulp it down. Right now, it was churning away in his gut. Helped, no doubt, by the presence of Cora Lawford.

Cora's eyes flickered in the direction of the stable down the street, where a man stood glaring in their direction. "You see, I need a horse."

"What's that got to do with me? Are you asking to borrow mine?"

"Not at all." She looked at him as if he was being unusually dense. "I'm going to start teaching school come fall, and I'll need a horse to get me there. I have the money, but I don't know the first thing about buying one."

"And you want me to . . . what?" he asked, although he already had his suspicions.

"See that gentleman waiting by the stable?" Cora was careful to keep her eyes firmly somewhere south of Luke's face and away from the stable. "He has several horses for sale, but he keeps pushing me to buy that mare or the gelding next to her. I'm not sure I trust him."

"Well, then you've already learned the most important thing about buying a horse, but that doesn't explain why you need me." He wasn't sure he wanted to know, either. The last thing he wanted was Cora Lawford needing him for anything, unless it was to scratch a mutual itch. For the breath of a second, he pictured her, naked and needy, in his bed. Damn, he had no business thinking that way.

"I need someone I trust to help me pick out the best horse for me."

Luke felt as if he'd just been hit in the gut. Did she have any idea what it meant to a man to have a woman like her say she trusted him? Every time he had himself convinced that he'd succeeded in running her off, she managed to slip past his guard again.

"If I weren't in town, who would you have gotten to help you?"

She tilted her head to the side as she considered the matter. "I guess I would have sent word to Mitch Hughes or waited until Cade came back to town. Either way, I might have missed out because Mr. Milton has other buyers interested."

She really was as innocent as she looked. And as much as he wanted—needed—to walk away from those huge, trusting eyes, he wouldn't. "Let's get this over with," he growled, more gruffly than he'd meant.

Taking her by the arm, he all but dragged her back to the impatient-looking horse trader. When they reached the corral, Cora yanked her arm free and then proceeded to make introductions. Hell, she all but suggested they all sit down around a pot of tea and a plate of cookies.

"Mr. Milton, this is my friend Luke Gibson. I would never make a purchase as important as this without consulting him. You understand." She offered the man a bright smile.

Luke ignored the whole process as he turned his attention to the two horses Mr. Milton had been trying to fob off on Cora. It didn't take him long to know that neither of the poor beasts was worth considering. Obviously, Luke wasn't the only one who recognized Cora's essential innocence and how easy it would be to take advantage of her. He probably thought it was all in a day's work, but Luke wanted to land a hard punch to the man's jaw just for thinking about it.

Luke straightened up. The look he gave the horse trader had the man stumbling backward.

"If this is the best you can do, we'll be going." He

reached for Cora's arm and led her away from the corral.

She started to protest but quit when Luke shook his head slightly. They'd gone only a few steps when Milton came hurrying after them. "Wait, mister. I have more horses to show the young lady. I'd only just gotten started."

Luke squeezed Cora's arm as a warning before he rounded on the hapless trader, his hand on his gun. "I'd hate to think that you would have sold such shoddy goods to a schoolteacher, Mr. Milton. I wouldn't take kindly to that idea at all."

Milton recognized a threat when he heard it and had the good sense to take it seriously. "I understand, sir. I do understand. I have a few other horses with me. I'm sure one of them will suit the young lady's needs." He disappeared into the stable.

As soon as he was out of sight, Cora turned on Luke. "I didn't ask you to bully the poor man, Luke Gibson. I just wanted your advice."

"If you want me to leave, say so."

"You know very well I don't want you to go, but you could act nicer."

He shrugged. "No, I couldn't. Do I stay, or can I get back to my beer?"

Cora gave him a disapproving look, but didn't pursue the matter any further. She gestured toward the mare. "What was wrong with her? I thought she looked good."

"You mean she's pretty. Looks don't mean a damned thing when it comes to horses." He walked over to the two horses. "The mare is too old, for one thing. Her feet are in bad shape, for another."

"He said the mare was only five."

Luke snorted. "That old girl has seen a lot more winters than that."

"And the gelding?"

Before he could answer, Milton was back. He was leading another pair of horses. Although Luke was careful to keep his expression strictly neutral, he had to admit that these two were promising.

Luke walked around the two horses with Cora trailing behind him like an excited puppy. The first one was a tall sorrel, handsome and obviously in the prime of life. But it was the second one that caught Luke's eye. A dark gray and ugly as sin, the horse had all the markings of strength and endurance. He wondered if Cora would insist on going with looks over quality.

He did a thorough exam of both animals, determined to give both a fair evaluation. He might not have wanted to get involved, but damned if he'd be responsible for letting Cora buy an animal that was dangerous or not up to handling Missouri winters.

After he'd checked for any obvious physical infirmities, he asked the owner to saddle up both horses. When the sorrel was ready, Luke mounted up and rode out of town. Cora wouldn't normally need to run her horse, but he wanted to make sure that the animal was sound if the occasion ever arose.

The sorrel had a hard mouth, but otherwise seemed satisfactory. He put the leggy gelding through several different gaits and even had him jump a couple of logs for the hell of it. He had to admit to a certain amount of jealousy that Cora was the one buying the horse, especially since he'd had trouble scraping together enough to buy a beer.

When he returned to the stable, Cora sensibly kept all of her questions to herself until he'd ridden both horses. He waited until he was out of her sight before urging the second one into showing its stuff. The gray moved easily into a ground-eating gallop that had Luke grinning from ear to ear. Together, they tore down the road and then veered off into the woods. After jumping several obstructions, they splashed across a creek before turning back toward Lee's Mill.

Despite the workout, the gray showed no signs of weariness, as it responded to the slightest signal from Luke. He leaned down and patted the animal on the neck as a reward for a job well done. Reluctantly, he dismounted and led the horse back to where Cora stood waiting.

Luke offered her the reins. "Do you want to try them out before I tell you what I think?"

"I don't think that's necessary." She chewed her lower lip as she studied the two horses. Nodding in the direction of the sorrel, she said, "That one sure is a good-looking horse."

He should have guessed that she'd go for handsome over solid, although why that bothered him so much, he didn't know.

"But," she continued after a bit, "I'm inclined to pick the gray. Something about him makes me think he has heart."

She took the reins from Luke's hand and reached over to stroke the big horse on the nose. The gray responded by leaning down, asking for a scratch. Cora laughed with delight.

Looking back over her shoulder, she nodded to Luke. "Definitely the gray."

"Do you have a price limit?"

"Whatever you think is reasonable."

If she smiled at him one more time, he wasn't going to be responsible for his actions. He had no desire to get involved with a decent woman, but a man could resist temptation only so long. The sight of those pretty hands stroking the horse's neck had him gritting his teeth. How could a sane man be jealous of a damned horse, and an ugly one at that?

Angry all over again, he led the sorrel back to where the horse trader stood waiting to negotiate the deal. At least Luke had a handy target for his bad mood. He tied the sorrel up at the railing and then gave Milton the kind of smile that made a wise man want to find safe cover.

"How much for the gray?"

Milton brightened right up. "The lady has an eye for good horseflesh. The man I bought the gray from sure hated to part with him."

"I asked how much."

Luke let his hand stray to his gun as he asked the question in a mild tone. He was glad to see that Milton was smart enough to understand the unspoken threat, because the man immediately stuttered out a price that was probably slightly less than the horse was worth. Luke figured he could have dickered a bit more, but it wasn't the other man's fault that Cora made him so irritable.

"She'll take him."

"I'll have the papers drawn up."

"Fine."

Figuring he'd done what he'd come for, Luke walked away. He should have known that Cora wouldn't let him go so easily.

"Mr. Gibson, wait."

He thought about ignoring her, but knowing Cora, she would have just found some other poor fool to drag him out of the saloon again. As it was, it sounded as if she was running to catch up with him. He gave up and turned around to wait for her.

"What is it this time?" He didn't bother trying to be polite.

"I wanted to thank you for your help. I don't know what I would have done without you." She gave him one of those bright smiles that had him wanting to either wring her neck or kiss her senseless, or both.

"Fine." He started to walk away, when her next words brought him to a halt.

"And I wanted to pay you for your time." She already had a handful of bills in her hand.

He didn't know whether to be insulted at the offer or ashamed because for a brief second he considered taking the money and grinding it into the dirt. "I don't want your money."

"But why?" She looked sincerely confused by his refusal.

"Would you have offered to pay Hughes or Cade?"

"No, but I only wanted . . ."

That did it. "You just don't get it, do you? I don't give a damn what you want or don't want. You've already wasted enough of my time, little girl. Now, if you'll excuse me, I have business in the saloon."

He left Cora standing there, her hand falling back to her side. The trouble was, there wasn't enough whiskey in the whole damned town to help him forget the way the light in her eyes died just before he walked away.

Cora recorded the last of the day's purchases and looked around for something else to keep herself busy. For the first time since she and her friends had founded the Luminary Society, she wasn't looking forward to attending the meeting. She'd done her best to hide her lack of enthusiasm, but unsuccessfully, she suspected, based on a couple of odd looks that Lucy had given her.

Normally, she relished the spirited discussions among the women who attended the meetings, but not tonight. Leaning against the counter, she wondered if she should make her excuses and go on home. No, that would only bring on more questions than she had answers for.

"What's the matter, Cora?"

She should have known that if Lucy thought something was wrong, she wouldn't hesitate to ask. Cora knew that Lucy's intentions were well meant, but she couldn't explain what was wrong when she wasn't sure herself.

"I have a slight headache. It's making me tired." She forced a smile. "I'm fine, really."

Lucy looked as if she wanted to argue the point. But luckily for Cora, a group of their friends picked that moment to arrive for the meeting. She took advantage of the distraction to lose herself in the crowd heading upstairs to the meeting room over the store. She took a seat in the back, hoping to remain inconspicuous for the duration of the evening.

With a few minutes, the current president of the Society, Josie Hughes, called the meeting to order with a rap of the gavel Lucy had ordered from St. Louis for that very purpose. All the women counted the days until it was their turn to wield the symbol of power.

"Thank you, ladies, for coming tonight. I know you are all looking forward to continuing last month's discussion of Miss Austen's *Emma*. Before we get to that, is there anything that you would like to add to this evening's agenda?"

A hand shot up near the front. Josie set the gavel

aside and nodded in the woman's direction. "Yes, Mrs. James?"

As the lady in question rose to her feet, Cora closed her eyes and leaned back against the wall. The very thought of listening to another of Mrs. James's rambling complaints threatened to make her imaginary headache all too real.

The rotund little woman turned to face the rows of women behind her. She first nodded in Josie's direction and then toward the rest of them. "Madame President, ladies, I would like to know what we are going to do about the low caliber of men who have taken up residence in our midst. It is bad enough that they insist on living here, but I have personally seen one of them accosting one of our own members."

Even knowing the woman's tendency toward the melodramatic, something in what she said had Cora sitting up and listening. A sick feeling settled in her stomach as Mrs. James shot her a particularly smug look.

On the other hand, Josie looked genuinely perplexed. "I'm sorry, Mrs. James. Could you be more specific?"

"Yes, indeed I can, and I will. Ladies, we have a convicted murderer living near our town."

There were a few gasps, enough to amply reward Mrs. James. She allowed the murmured comments to continue for a short time while she basked in the attention she'd drawn. Finally, though, she held up her hand to silence the crowd.

"I have it on good authority that Luke Gibson," she said as she once again turned her beady eyes in Cora's direction, "was only recently released from prison for killing a man in cold blood. I'm sure that all of you are as appalled as I am that he walks freely around our town, daring to bother innocent young women."

Cora's stomach lurched. She'd learned part of the truth from Luke himself, but somehow hearing Mrs. James announce his past in her smug little voice made it sound so much worse. Her hands itched to slap the woman or at least drag her back to her seat and gag her.

It took Josie several sharp raps with the gavel to bring the ensuing chaos back under control. She rose to her feet and stared down the remaining few women who continued to ignore the call for silence.

"Mrs. James, I know your intentions were good." Josie looked as if she'd been sucking lemons. "However, in the future I would appreciate it if you would approach a member of the board before the meeting if you have something you want added to the agenda rather than springing it on us unannounced."

Both Josie's late father and her first husband had been drunkards. As a result, Josie herself had suffered from the sharp side of Mrs. James's tongue, especially when Josie had been wrongfully accused of murdering her abusive husband. No doubt she would have been happier if the woman had not seen fit to join the Society. However, one of the primary goals of the group was to welcome any and all women who wanted to join.

Mrs. James wasn't ready to abandon the battlefield. "Fine, Mrs. Hughes. But now that the matter is before us, I don't see how we can continue to ignore the threat this man represents."

Before Cora could marshal her arguments in defense of Luke Gibson, Lucy stood up. Never slow to take a hint, Josie immediately whacked the gavel again. "Lucy Mulroney now has the floor."

Mrs. James started to protest, but she reluctantly sat back down when Josie raised the gavel, ready to force the issue.

Lucy calmly moved to the front of the room. "Mrs. James, I understand that you are concerned and that you have the welfare of us all at heart."

That was a lie, Cora decided, but Lucy was adept at handling the few members of the Society whose favorite pastime was stirring up trouble.

"But since Mr. Gibson is not here to defend himself, I feel I must speak on his behalf. My husband has known Luke Gibson since the very beginning of the late war, when they served together. According to Cade, Luke Gibson fought bravely for what he believed in. He was responsible for saving the lives of the men in his unit on numerous occasions."

Very few of the women in the room had survived the years of grim fighting without being touched by the loss of a loved one. They all understood how bad it had been, no matter which side they'd supported.

"I have had the pleasure of having Mr. Gibson join my family for dinner, as Cade counts him as one of his oldest friends. I am not aware of the exact details of Mr. Gibson's conviction, but you all know my husband well enough to know that Cade would never put his family in danger. I would like to think that the people of Lee's Mill would find it in their hearts to allow a war hero a chance to prove himself and to rebuild his life."

Her friend's impromptu speech seemed to have gone over well because no one else took up Mrs. James's cause. That didn't necessarily mean the woman would let the matter rest. From the way she pursed her lips, she did not appreciate having her personal crusade brought to such an abrupt halt.

Cora could only be glad that her name hadn't been mentioned specifically in connection with Luke's, although it was too much to hope that Mrs. James hadn't already talked to Aunt Henrietta.

At least Cora had been forewarned. If she avoided Henrietta for the next week, perhaps her only relative would forget all about the fact that she was living so close to a criminal. Knowing it was too much to hope for, she resigned herself to dealing with her aunt's efforts to control her life as best she could.

But the real victim here was Luke Gibson. No one should be tried and convicted without being able to defend himself. However, Cora had learned from Lucy and Melinda to pick her battles carefully. Not that long ago, she would have beaten Lucy to the front of the room in her rush to defend Luke. But since Lucy had managed to quiet things down already, Cora was content to bide her time and watch what happened next. However, if anyone else attacked Luke Gibson in front of her, why, she'd better be prepared for a fight.

He wouldn't appreciate her even thinking such a thing, but she believed in standing up for her friends. And despite his continued efforts to run her off, she was determined to get to know him better. They were neighbors, after all.

Josie Hughes took control of the meeting and immediately launched into a summary of the last meeting. Deciding she wasn't up to debating even the most minor of issues, Cora let the discussion ebb and flow around her as her mind once again turned to Luke Gibson. It had been a week since he'd helped her buy Falstaff. Despite his reluctance, he'd done her a huge favor.

And what did he get for his trouble? Insulted. Even now, her face flushed hot from embarrassment for being so stupid as to offer him money for his time. She'd only been trying to do the right thing, but somehow it had all gone horribly wrong. In an effort to make amends, she'd left another of her apple pies sitting on his porch when she knew for a fact he wasn't home.

So far, the only sign that he'd accepted her apology was the return of her empty pan.

The sharp rap of the gavel alerted her that the meeting was drawing to a close. Normally, she would stick around to help with the cleanup, but she wasn't sure she wanted to tonight. And now that she lived outside of town, it only made sense that she try to get home before dark. Gathering up her things, she slipped out the door using a group of women as a shield. Once she was outside, she hurried to the stable where Falstaff was waiting.

The big gray whickered softly as soon as she walked through the door. After only one week, she was deeply attached to her horse. He might not be much to look at, but everyone who'd seen him had been impressed with her choice of mounts. Mitch Hughes had insisted on trying him out, as had Cade Mulroney. Both had returned with broad grins on their faces, pleased with the lively ride he'd given them. For her, though, Falstaff had proved to be a complete gentleman. He stood quietly by a mounting block for her and obeyed her every command.

And he was good company on the long afternoons she spent by herself, following her around as she worked in her newly planted flower beds. She liked to think that he enjoyed her company, but then maybe he was as lonely as she was.

Either way, both of them were content to be on their way home.

***

Damn, he hated digging up stumps. He could see why his pa had left so many along the edges of the fields he'd hacked out of the Missouri woods. Each and every one he had gone after damned near killed him before he managed to wrench it free from the ground. On the other hand, he took his victories wherever he could.

Retrieving his shirt from the rock where he'd tossed it earlier, he used it to wipe the sweat off his face and chest. Glancing at the sun, he gauged the time to be somewhere around midday. Time for a well-deserved break. He picked up the water pail but left the rest of his tools where they lay. There was another stump right next to where the last one used to be. It made him tired just to think about it.

Wading through the tall grass, he stumbled onto a covey of quail. The rapid-fire flutter of their wings startled him into dropping the empty pail as he stumbled back out of their path. He managed to keep his feet, but just barely. He bent down to pick up the pail again when the sound of riders approaching had him ducking back down for cover.

They rode into sight along the far side of the field, too far for him to make out much detail other than they were heavily armed and rode in military precision. He kept low and moved along to his left, trying to see if he recognized any of them. Since they were headed toward the river, he had to assume they were the ones that Cade had warned him about. It wasn't the first time they'd skirted the edge of his land on their way to and from the river.

No one knew much about the leader other than that he went by the name of Baxter and that it was rumored he had fought for the Confederacy. Even less was known about the men who rode with him. So far, they hadn't caused any trouble locally, but according to Cade, the sheriff kept a wary eye in their direction.

When the last one disappeared into the woods, Luke decided to wait another minute or two before breaking cover. He had no particular reason to worry, but a little caution never hurt. Men who rode in packs wouldn't take kindly to anyone taking an interest in their business. Finally, he started back on his way to the cabin and lunch.

The first thing he noticed was that Jack was back. He'd been gone for over a week without a word, leaving Luke wondering if it ever occurred to his younger brother that he might worry. Obviously, Jack didn't give a damn about what Luke thought. Rather than risk a fight, Luke headed into the cabin while Jack saw to his horse.

When Jack came through the door, Luke already had a pot of coffee and some of last night's stew warming up on the stove. Jack tossed his gear in the corner before taking a seat at the table, exhaustion written in the lines in his face and his bloodshot eyes.

Once again, Luke held his tongue. "There's enough for two if you're hungry."

"Sounds good."

Luke shot him a wry look. "You don't even know what's in the pot."

Jack rubbed his whiskered jaw. "I've been eating trail dust for days. Anything is better than that."

"Where were you?"

As soon as the words were out of his mouth, Luke regretted saying them. Whenever he questioned Jack's comings and goings, he either sulked or exploded. This time, he did neither.

"I decided to visit a friend up near Columbia." Jack slumped wearily against the table. "We rode together for a while after you went to . . . uh . . . went away."

"You can say it, Jack. After I went to prison. Not talking about it doesn't change the fact that I lost five years of my life in that hellhole." Luke didn't like thinking about it either, but his nightmares kept the memories fresh and alive. "What's your friend's name?"

Jack immediately tensed up. "Does it matter?"

Luke was beginning to fear that it wasn't a coincidence that Jack got home at the same time that Baxter and his men rode through. Damn, he didn't want Jack hanging around with a bunch like that. Even if they hadn't committed any crimes locally, that didn't mean they hadn't somewhere else. In a week of hard riding, there was no telling where they'd gone. Next time he saw Cade, he'd ask him if there had been news of any bank robberies.

The wisest course would be to back off for now. Until he had some hard facts, there wasn't much point in aggravating Jack to the point that he took off again. Reaching for their two bowls, he dished up the stew and handed one across to Jack, who kept his eyes firmly on the table.

"Thanks."

"You might want to hold off until you taste it before you decide if you're grateful."

Jack blew on a spoonful before taking a careful sip. "Not bad. Practice has improved your cooking."

Rather than point out that he was getting so much practice because Jack wasn't around to help, he decided to change subjects. "You missed out on one of Miss Lawford's pies while you were gone."

Jack perked up enough to look around. "Did you save me a piece?"

"Would you have saved one for me?" Luke wiped up the last of his stew with a piece of bread.

"Of course. After all, you're my favorite brother." Jack managed to keep a straight face, but the twinkle in his eyes betrayed him.

"I'm touched." Luke grinned. "But need I remind you that I'm your only brother?"

"That is hardly my fault." He handed his empty bowl back to Luke. "Look, I haven't had much sleep the past few days. I'm going to stretch out for a while. I'll help you some with the chores later."

Luke hadn't been expecting anything else. He put the dishes in the sink to soak and filled his pail with water again. Jack was already snoring softly in his corner before Luke made it to the door.

Out on the porch, he automatically looked for the telltale sign of smoke rising from Cora's chimney and didn't see any. It was the only way he had of knowing if she was home or in town. Not that it was any of his business what she was doing. He'd told her often enough to stay away from him. He'd be better off if he listened to his own advice.

He wondered how she was making out with the horse she'd bought. Cade and his friend Mitch had both felt it necessary to check the gelding out for themselves. He might have felt insulted if Cade hadn't admitted that they'd only done so in order to get to put the big gray through its paces. He wondered if the two of them had enjoyed racing down the road as much as he had.

Suddenly, pulling stumps all afternoon in the hot sun lost all its appeal. There were a few things he needed at the store, and he'd like a chance to talk to Cade without Jack around. Before he could talk himself out of it, he went back inside and put on a clean shirt. He scribbled out a note for Jack in case he woke up and wondered where Luke was. Ten minutes later, he rode out.

He tied his horse up outside The River Lady. A quick shot of whiskey was a fair reward for all the hard work he'd put in that morning. With luck, Cora Lawford wouldn't find an excuse to have him hauled out of the saloon before he had a chance to savor his drink. Afterward, he'd hunt up Cade and have a long talk with him.

The same farmer who had come hunting for him last time walked through the swinging doors just as Luke was about to go in. Luke nodded in greeting. The man started to smile, then his eyes opened wide in recognition. He stumbled backward several steps and hurried off without a word.

What had gotten into him?

Maybe he figured Luke held a grudge because the man had helped Cora find him the other day. Short of chasing the man down, there wasn't much Luke could do but wait his chance to tell him any different. He pushed the doors to the saloon open and stepped inside. He paused inside the door long enough to let his eyes adjust to the darkness. There was nothing like a good saloon to make a man feel welcome.

As he walked through the clutter of tables and chairs, the scattering of customers took note of his passage. That was normal enough, but not the ripple of silence that followed along behind him. By the time he reached the bar, the only noise in the place was the sound of his own footsteps. An uneasy feeling danced up his spine. He knew what an ambush felt like, and this wasn't far off of it.

"C-can I help you, Mr. Gibson?" The bartender kept his hands busy nervously polishing the counter with a stained rag.

"Whiskey." How had the man learned his name?

"Yes, sir. Right away, sir."

Luke tossed a coin on the bar to pay for the drink. The silence stretched on. He picked up his whiskey and slowly turned to face the room. Almost immediately, men picked up their cards or suddenly found their drinks the most interesting thing in the world to look at. What the hell was going on?

Once again, he drew no pleasure from his drink. The last time, he'd had to gulp it down because of Cora. The burn of cheap whiskey sliding down his throat didn't hold much appeal when everyone in the room was either staring at him or pointedly trying not to. Maybe he'd better have that talk with Cade now. Tossing back the last of his drink, he set the glass down on the bar behind him, all the while watching for any sudden movements out of the corner of his eye.

He made it to the porch outside with no problems, but it felt good to have the flimsy protection of the swinging doors at his back. He untied his horse, figuring he wouldn't be returning to The Lady anytime soon. The only trouble was more than a few of the people outside were staring at him, too. Maybe it was all in his head, but he didn't think so. He kept his movements slow and sure, not wanting to startle anyone into doing something stupid, but he couldn't wait to reach the relative safety of Cade's office.

When he reached the newspaper office a short distance down the street, he took one last look around as he tied his horse's reins. Whatever doubt he had was erased when a pair of women caught sight of him and immediately crossed the street to avoid him.

There could be only one explanation. Someone had found out about his past.

CHAPTER 6

The knowledge that he'd been found out left him feeling vulnerable standing out on the street. He quietly slipped inside the front door of the *Clarion*. The typesetter looked up from the press. If he recognized Luke, he gave no sign of it.

"Can I help you?"

"Is Cade around?"

The man nodded in the direction of an open door behind him and went back to work. Luke walked in without bothering to knock. He found Cade leaning back in his chair with his feet up on the desk. A cloud of cigar smoke hovered above him as he stared up at the ceiling. Luke dropped into the chair facing the desk.

"If that's what it takes to edit a newspaper, I may have to apply for the job."

Cade managed to smile and puff on the cigar at the same time. "I'm thinking."

"You expect me to believe that?" He propped his own feet up on the desk.

"No, but then you know me too well." He stubbed the cigar out in a handy ashtray. When the smoke cleared a bit, he dropped his feet and leaned forward. "You look like hell. What's wrong?"

"I came into town for supplies and to see what you

know about that bunch that lives down around the river. Before coming here, though, I dropped in at The River Lady for a whiskey. Soon as I walked in the place, it got real quiet." He frowned. "I thought maybe I was imagining things, but when I walked down here from The Lady, I swear people were either staring at me or else doing their best to avoid me."

Cade muttered a string of curses under his breath. "I was afraid of this. I was going to ride out this afternoon to warn you that someone found out about you being in prison. Ever heard of a woman here in town by the name of Mrs. James?"

Luke considered the name but shook his head. "Not that I know of. Maybe I knew something of her before the war, but I don't remember the name."

"Well, apparently she knows about you. She stood up at the Luminary Society meeting last night and announced to the whole damned world that you were sent to prison for killing someone. Wanted to know what the women wanted to do about it."

If Cade hadn't looked so serious, Luke would have laughed. "What did this Mrs. James expect the others to do? They can't very well run me out of town."

"No, but they could make things mighty uncomfortable for you. You'd be surprised how much influence a bunch of determined women can have."

For a moment, the image of a lynch mob composed solely of angry women filled his mind. It was scarier than he cared to admit.

"I wonder how she found out. The only people who knew were you and Jack. He hasn't been around enough lately to do much talking." It went without saying that Cade would have kept his secret.

On the other hand, Cade looked a little guilty. "I told Lucy about it, too, but she would never have said a word, not even to her best friends, Melinda and Cora."

"She wouldn't have to tell Cora Lawford, because I already did. But all I told her was that I'd been in prison, but not why."

If Cade wondered why Luke had been talking to Cora at all, he didn't ask.

"Well, I guess it was bound to come out sooner or later. There's not much I can do but go about my business and keep a low profile."

Cade reached into his desk drawer and pulled out a bottle and two glasses. "With luck, the talk will die off in a short time. Besides, there are plenty of folks around who are willing to give a man a chance to prove himself."

He poured Luke a shot and pushed it across the desk to him. "What else did you want to talk about? Something about Baxter and his men?"

"I saw them ride across the back of my farm this morning in the direction of the river. I was wondering if you'd heard anything about where they'd been."

"Any particular reason?"

Luke sipped slowly at the whiskey, giving himself time to decide how much to tell Cade. "I don't know for sure, but I suspect Jack's been riding with them some. He'd get mad if I questioned him on it, so I thought I'd see what I could find out on my own."

Cade sipped at his own whiskey. "I've actually met Baxter in person, back when Mitch Hughes was still sheriff. We rode out to the river to see if Baxter knew anything about a murder Mitch was investigating."

"And did he?"

"He wasn't involved, if that's what you mean. He knew the victim, though."

"What was Baxter like?"

"I liked him." Cade leaned back in his chair to stare at the ceiling again. "He could have been any one of a hundred men I met during the war—a born leader, but the kind willing to take a few too many risks for my comfort."

Luke nodded. He'd served under men like that himself, especially when he rode with the irregulars. It was as if they were never truly alive unless they were leading a charge into enemy fire, screaming out their fury at the enemy with a wild grin on their faces.

"And his men?"

"I didn't really meet any of them. They kept to the shadows out of sight, but I could hazard a guess that most of them had no place to go back to after the fighting stopped. As far as the sheriff can tell, the numbers vary because they come and go."

That agreed with what Luke knew. Jack spent a day or two at home and then would disappear for a time. He wouldn't worry so much if he knew what Jack and his friends were doing. The last thing he wanted was for Jack to get involved with a gang of ruffians. One Gibson brother spending time in prison was enough.

"I guess I'll have to talk to Jack." Not that he wanted to. There was a good chance that Jack would get mad and leave again, maybe for good. It was clear Jack wasn't cut out for farm work and that he was there only because of Luke.

"Is there anything I can do?"

Luke stood up. "Not that I can think of. I'll go next door and pick up my supplies and head back to the farm. Maybe if I stay scarce for a while, people will forget about my prison record."

Cade followed him to the door. "If I run into the sheriff, I'll see if I can find out if he's learned anything new about Baxter and his men. He won't mind me asking because I'm always nosing around looking for a story."

"Thanks, I appreciate it."

He drew a deep breath and stepped through the door, half afraid that the townspeople had gathered outside to run him out of town. For the moment, though, the few people he could see seemed intent on their own business, leaving him free to slip next door and pick up enough supplies to hold him for a week or so.

A handsome woman walked out of the store just as he reached the door. He tipped his hat out of respect and stepped out of her way. She looked vaguely familiar, but he couldn't place her.

"Good afternoon, Mr. Gibson." She smiled. "I don't think we've been introduced. I'm Melinda Hayes. My husband is the pastor here in town."

Now he remembered. Cade had mentioned them by name. "Nice to meet you, ma'am."

"I've heard good things about you from Cade and Lucy."

And some things that weren't so good from someone else. The concern he saw in her eyes seemed sincere.

"David and I would love to have you join us for Sunday dinner at the parsonage whenever you would like to come."

"That's right kind of you, ma'am."

"I'll have David stop by to see you, if that would be all right." Her smile widened a bit. "I hear tell you have a bit of a sweet tooth. I'll send along a little something extra with David when he comes."

"I'd say that you shouldn't go to any bother, Mrs. Hayes, but my mama didn't raise any fools."

"I can see that." Her laughter brightened the whole

day for him. "Well, Mr. Gibson, it was a pleasure meeting you at last, but I must be going."

"Thank you, Mrs. Hayes." He liked this woman. She struck him as someone who would make up her own mind about a person.

They'd been standing in the doorway, so the bell over the door didn't chime as he came in. He wished he'd thought to ask Mrs. Hayes who was working in the store, not that it mattered. Under the circumstances, he couldn't be picky. At first glance, he didn't see anyone behind the counter, so he picked up one of the baskets that Lucy kept handy for customers to gather their purchases.

He started in the back, figuring on working his way toward the counter. It was going to take longer than he'd like because now he wanted to buy enough to last longer than a week or two at least. If Cade was right, things might settle down if he stayed out of sight for a while. He'd been buying supplies piecemeal as an excuse to go into town more often. That had to stop.

A few minutes after he got started, he heard the door open again. He decided to stay where he was until he knew who had come in. At the call of the bell, there was the sound of footsteps overhead and then hurrying down the staircase. He wanted to curse when he heard Cora Lawford's voice.

"Is there something I can help you with?"

Unless he was mistaken, there was a definite coolness in Cora's voice. He wondered why.

"I need some white thread."

"It's right over there where it always is, Mrs. James."

The name brought him up short. It had to be the woman who'd made the public announcement at that women's meeting. How had she found out about his conviction? He was tempted to step out from behind the shelves to see what she'd do. Instead, he moved to the far edge until he could see the two women standing near the counter. He had a feeling that things were about to get interesting.

Cora deliberately turned away from the older woman. She could either get her thread herself or leave. Cora didn't much care which. Considering Mrs. James's behavior at the meeting, it would be some time before she would be more than barely civil to the interfering harridan.

"Don't get snippy with me, Cora Lawford. I've already given your aunt an earful about you associating with that man." Mrs. James's voice grew more shrill with each word, as her narrow face and overly long nose turned a bright shade of red.

That did it. Cora snatched a spool of thread off the shelf and practically threw it at the woman. "Mrs. James, I am simply amazed that you find time to sew, since you spend all your time minding everyone else's business."

"Well, I never."

"Oh, yes, you did, Mrs. James. If you can't find real trouble to stir up, you make up something." Cora kept her hands clenched at her side to keep from pelting Mrs. James with a whole box full of thread.

"I didn't make up anything I said about that murderer you live by. Every word I said about him was the truth!" She pointed at Cora, her finger quivering with righteous anger. "And I did see you talking to him out on the street, right where anyone could see you. When I realized that you had no idea what kind of man he is, I did the only thing a good Christian woman could do. I told your aunt that you were in danger of losing your good reputation by consorting with a criminal."

No one was going to dictate her life for her again. It was time the busybodies of this town figured that out. She would consort with whomever she wanted to.

"Here is the truth, Mrs. James, not that you have more than a nodding acquaintance with the concept." She ticked each item off on the fingers of her hand. "Mr. Gibson's family farm happens to be near my home. His family lived there long before the war. He has friends who think well of him, which is more than you can claim. And what you saw the other day was a neighbor helping a neighbor pick out a sound horse. That is hardly a crime, Mrs. James. He was a gentleman the entire time."

She marched out from behind the counter to stand face-to-face with her opponent. "And finally, Mrs. James, if I had my choice between consorting with Luke Gibson and spending another minute in your company, it would be no contest at all. Take your thread and leave. No charge."

Mrs. James wasn't ready to concede defeat. "I'll have you know—"

"I said leave, Mrs. James. If you are not out of this store in the next minute, I will have the sheriff remove you for trespassing and threatening me." She took a step toward the door herself as a sign of her determination. "Personally, I would enjoy seeing you behind bars for a few days. Maybe you'd learn to mind your own business instead of everybody else's!"

"Your aunt will be hearing from me, missy, not to mention Lucy Mulroney. You may tell her that if she continues to employ the likes of you in her store, I will be taking my business elsewhere."

"Be my guest."

Cora flung open the door and waited for Mrs. James to depart. She immediately closed and locked the door. After a second's hesitation, she turned the sign to read "closed." Until she calmed down, she would be in no condition to wait on another customer.

Her hands shook and her knees felt weak now that the fight was over. How dare that woman continue to blacken Luke's name and call herself a good Christian! Perhaps a cup of tea would calm her nerves. After she put the kettle on to boil, she would work off the rest of her frustration by giving the storeroom floor a good scrubbing.

Turning away from the door, she bounced off a wall that hadn't been there a few seconds before. A pair of strong hands latched on to her arms to keep her from falling as she stared up into a pair of furious ice-blue eyes. Her heart stuttered and then raced out of control.

Oh, Lord, had he been there the entire time? For the first time in her life, she felt as if she would swoon. As foolish as that always seemed to her, anything was better than facing Luke after he'd heard her say she was willing to consort with him. His mouth was moving but she wasn't able to make any sense out of what he was saying. Maybe that was for the best.

He shook her almost gently. "Damn it, Cora, don't you go fainting on me. I won't stand for it."

He practically dragged her over to one of the chairs by the stove and shoved her down in it. She grabbed on to the arms of the chair and held on for dear life. A storm was coming, one that might very well leave her flattened in its wake.

The buzzing in her ears was fading, enough so that she could hear Luke walk away and then back again.

He shoved a cup of water in her face with an order to "drink it, damn it!"

She wrapped both hands around the cup and managed to get it to her mouth, only spilling a little of it. Even so, it helped her to regain her composure. With as much dignity as she could muster, she set the cup down and rose to her feet.

"Are you feeling better?"

Despite his concern for her well-being, there was no warmth at all in the question. It took a surprising amount of courage to look him in the eye, but she did her best.

"Is there something I can do for you, Mr. Gibson?" Instead of calming his temper as she'd hoped, her storekeeper act seemed only to fuel the fire.

"Yes, there is, Miss Lawford," he snarled. "You can mind your own damned business!"

"But she . . ."

"I don't care a whit about Mrs. James or anyone else in this town who has a problem with me or my past. But if they want to make something of it, I will handle it myself."

He hadn't raised his voice at all, but she winced at the controlled fury in his words. His face was all hard edges. Her hand ached to smooth away the anger and the lines.

"I was only trying to help." She hated the way her voice trembled. Tears were threatening to fall, which would only embarrass her more.

She thought she'd seen Luke upset with her before, but nothing prepared her to deal with the grim-faced man glaring down at her. He'd done everything but take an advertisement in Cade's paper to warn her off, but she hadn't taken him seriously.

An apology was in order. "I'm sorry, Luke." When he

started to interrupt her again, she held up her hand. "Please let me finish. I meant no harm, only I couldn't stand listening to that old busybody. I would have defended anyone she attacked." She'd like to think so, anyway.

Some of his anger seemed to drain away. "It is my battle to fight, Cora. I don't need you or anyone else trying to protect me from the likes of her."

"But I don't want to see you hurt any more." She knew the instant the words slipped out that she'd made another mistake.

"You just don't listen, do you?" He grabbed her arms again and pulled her up on her toes so that their faces were only inches apart. "Leave me alone. Don't talk about me; don't think about me; don't come near me."

But then his gaze dropped to her mouth. The weakness she'd felt before didn't come close to the way every joint in her body now seemed to dissolve away. Slowly, so slowly that it hurt to wait, he moved closer until she could feel the soft touch of his breath on her skin. She watched the ice in his eyes melt into the blue of a hot summer sky as his lips almost touched hers.

Her eyes drifted shut, waiting for the instant when the two of them would come together. For a fraction of a second, she thought she felt his lips brush against hers. But the sensation was lost in the shock of stumbling backward as Luke let loose a string of curses at the same time he let go of her.

She managed to catch her balance without falling. The pain that ripped through her had nothing to do with banging her knee on a wooden crate. Luke stood in front of her, wild-eyed and edgy.

"Don't you have any kin to keep you locked up?"

he snarled. His chest heaved as if he'd been running long and hard.

Frustration and grief for the opportunity lost helped her stand her ground. "My aunt tried her best to cage me, but I won't live that way. Not anymore. I don't need a keeper."

"The hell you don't, little girl! You go tempting the wrong man like that, and he'll drag you down to the floor before you can scream for help." He took another step away from her and then another.

She matched him step for step. "Don't call me a little girl, Luke Gibson. I'm an adult, in case you haven't noticed." She stood, hands on hips, and dared him to look for himself.

His eyes trailed down her body, but he jerked his gaze back up to her face with a sharp intake of breath when he realized what he was doing. He could talk all he wanted, but he'd noticed that she was all grown up all right. But now wasn't the time to force the issue. It was enough that they both knew that he was fighting a powerful attraction to her.

He started to say something but apparently changed his mind. He threw open the latch and stormed out of the store without looking back. Cora carefully locked the door behind him, staring out the window as Luke mounted up and cantered out of sight. Unable to think beyond the next few minutes, she sought the dubious comfort of the straight-backed chair that Luke had forced her to sit in earlier.

Leaning forward with her face in her hands, she didn't know which one of them had won that particular skirmish, but it had left her badly shaken and confused. In one morning, she'd succeeded in making an enemy of Mrs. James and ruining any chance she'd ever had for being friends with Luke. The first one was no great loss in her life, other than it might cause problems with her aunt. That didn't concern her. She'd had to fight for every inch of freedom she'd won and would continue to do so. No matter what Aunt Henrietta had to say about Cora's behavior, she couldn't force Cora to live with her again.

But losing Luke hurt, a pain that started in her head and ended up suspiciously close to her heart. For the moment, there wasn't anything she could do about it, but sitting and feeling sorry for herself wasn't the answer.

Finally, she found the strength to stand. The storeroom floor still needed scrubbing, and a few tears in the soapy water wouldn't be noticed.

Jack went from sound asleep to wide awake in the space of a heartbeat. His gun was in his hand before he even had time to figure out what had disturbed his sleep. He cocked his head to one side, listening and waiting. Finally, he heard the squeak of the corral gate closing.

Luke was home.

Jack put his gun back in its holster before throwing off his blanket. By the time Luke walked in the door, Jack was sitting at the table sipping a cup of bitter coffee. He didn't bother trying to look as if he'd been up any length of time. For once, though, his brother didn't bother to comment on Jack's irregular habits.

Instead, Luke walked past him, unbuckled his gunbelt, and dropped it on his bedroll. Then he peeled off his shirt tossed it in the pile of clothes in the corner. He picked up another one that had seen better days and yanked it on over his head. After picking up a small pail, he filled it at the sink with several angry pumps of the handle. Finally, he stalked back out the door, kicking a crate out of his way and shattering it into pieces against the wall.

All without saying a single word. Curious.

Jack decided it might be worth a few hours in the hot sun to find out what had his older brother so worked up. He paused long enough to scoop up what was left of the crate and toss the pieces into the kindling box.

Outside, he went into the barn to pick up an extra shovel before heading out to where Luke had been clearing stumps. Carrying the shovel back over his shoulder as he walked along the path, he whistled a song that had been one of their ma's favorites. He could already hear the ring of the ax ripping into wood. At the rate Luke was swinging it, he'd have himself worn out pretty damned fast.

That was all right with Jack, except for the likelihood that Luke would expect him to pick up where he left off. It wasn't that Jack couldn't work hard; he just didn't like to. However, if someone was making life difficult for Luke, Jack wanted to know about it. His brother had suffered enough for one lifetime.

When he reached Luke, he made sure to make his presence known. "What did that poor stump ever do to you?"

Luke stopped midswing. "If you don't like how I'm doing this, you're more than welcome to take over."

Jack surprised them both by holding his hand out for the ax. After a second's hesitation, Luke held it out. Jack gripped it with both hands and began working away at the tap root that held the stump fast in the ground. After a half a dozen or so swings, he stopped to tie a bandanna around his forehead and strip off his shirt.

For the better part of an hour, the two of them

worked in tandem, one using the ax, the other the shovel, until they had the stump loose in its hole. After they worked a chain on it, the two of them strained against the chain until the stubborn roots broke free. Satisfied with their accomplishment, Jack took a long drink from Luke's pail before handing it back to him.

The two of them sought the shade of a large oak tree, trying to catch their breath and cool off a bit. Before Jack had a chance to ask what was wrong, Luke brought the subject up himself.

"Do you know anything about a Mrs. James in town?" He didn't look at Jack, but kept his eyes trained on the hills in the distance.

"Should I?"

"Not particularly." Luke plucked a piece of grass and stuck it in the corner of his mouth. "She found out about my prison record and decided it was her Christian duty to warn all the women in town at their society meeting last night."

Jack didn't miss his brother's quick glance in the direction of their pretty neighbor's house. So that's the way the wind was blowing. No use in mincing words or letting his brother dance around the real problem.

"So did she manage to scare off Cora Lawford?"

Luke ignored the question. "I knew something was wrong when I stopped in at The River Lady for a drink. As soon as I walked through the door, everybody stopped talking and stared at me." He tossed the blade of grass down and reached for a handful of last year's acorns to toss.

"I decided to talk to Cade to see what he knew. Before I got inside, a couple of women crossed the street to keep from coming near me." He paused again, this time for a drink of water. "Cade heard all about it from Lucy. She tried to convince them all that I deserved a second chance, but I would have to say without much success, considering everything."

Jack tried again. "Did she say how Cora Lawford took the news?"

Another handful of acorns went flying. "I stopped in the store to pick up some supplies."

"And?"

"The James woman came in, bent on giving Cora an earful about consorting with the likes of me."

That brought Jack to attention. "You never told me that you've been consorting with her. Was it fun?"

"Go to hell, little brother," Luke told him without any real heat. "She was talking about when I helped Cora pick out a horse."

Disappointed, Jack leaned back against a handy rock. "So what did Cora have to say about that?"

A reluctant smile tugged at the corner of Luke's mouth. "She ripped into that old hag something fierce. Seems she doesn't take it kindly when someone tries to tell her what to do."

"You mean she defended you."

"That, too." He stared up at the sky as if he could find his answers written in the few clouds scattered overhead.

"So what has you all riled up?" Jack asked, even though he suspected he knew the answer. Luke always did have a noble streak a mile wide. He probably thought Cora Lawford was too good for him, the damned fool.

"I don't hide behind a woman's skirts. I fight my own battles."

"You don't seem all that upset that Lucy Mulroney spoke up for you." Deciding he'd said enough for one day, Jack took another long drink of water before picking up the ax. "I'll help you with another one, then I need to be going."

He waited to see how Luke would respond to that announcement, but he only reached for the shovel and followed Jack out to the next stump.

Jack was scared, plain and simple, even though his two closest friends among Baxter's men, Jeb and Isaac, didn't seem at all worried. They'd joined up with the rest of the riders about an hour ago on their way to a town up in the northwest corner of the state. No one had told Jack precisely what they were up to, but he could guess.

Baxter hadn't said a word when Jack showed up with his friends, but he had given him a long, hard look, as if taking his measure. Finally, he'd nodded and then led the group cross-country. After several hours of hard riding, they'd made camp under the cover of a thicket of pine trees near a shallow creek. Jack made himself useful, gathering firewood and drawing water for the cook.

The men broke up into small groups, smoking or talking softly. Jeb and Isaac were both on first watch, leaving Jack at loose ends. Using his saddle as a back-rest, Jack stretched out on his bedroll and dealt himself a hand of solitaire on the blanket. After a couple of hands, a shadow fell over the cards. He looked up to see Baxter standing over him.

"Walk with me."

"Yes, sir."

Jack was careful not to show his reluctance as they walked along the edge of the makeshift camp. He glanced at some of the others, trying to gauge their reaction to his being singled out again by their leader. As far as he could tell, no one gave a damn. He wasn't sure if he should be relieved or worried.

Once again, Baxter led him to the edge of the river and then stood silently listening to the soothing sound of the water. The sky to the west still had a hint of red where the sun had only recently slipped out of sight. Above their heads, the first sprinkling of stars slowly appeared.

"I guess you made your decision."

"I'm here."

"I always like to give a man one last chance to ride out, no questions asked." Baxter crossed his arms over his chest. "Come morning, it will be too late. We've got plans."

"I figured you did." Jack was proud of how calm he sounded.

"I hear your brother spent some time in prison."

The sudden change in subject surprised him. Now that all of Lee's Mill knew about Luke's past, there was no use in denying it. "Yes, sir, he did."

"They say he killed a man." Baxter started walking again.

Jack fell into step beside him. "A damn Yankee, sir. The bastard killed one of Luke's friends when he tried to surrender at the end of the war."

"He say much about prison?"

Jack figured he owed Luke enough loyalty not to tell anyone, even Baxter, about Luke's nightmares. "Not a lot."

"Like I told you, Jack, I give everyone a chance to change his mind. Be ready to ride at dawn or be gone. One or the other."

Jack needed to know what lay ahead if he stayed. "Where are we going, sir?"

"Does it matter, boy?" For the first time, there was a deadly chill in the man's voice.

Jack shook his head, afraid that if he opened his mouth he might say something else wrong.

"Get some sleep. Relieve Isaac at midnight."

Baxter walked away, leaving Jack staring after him. The man was sure enough a puzzle. Jack wondered what the man really thought about his wanting to ride with the gang, even though he'd made it clear that Jack was welcome to stay. On the other hand, he'd gone out of his way to offer Jack the chance to back out again.

Hell, maybe he should. He hadn't lied when he said that Luke didn't talk about his time behind bars. But it was clear that war and prison had left their mark, especially at night when dreams chased him out of the house. Jack had no desire to find out first-hand what Luke already knew.

On the other hand, he also didn't want to be a dirt farmer his whole life. Luke seemed to want nothing more than to plant corn and feed chickens, but Jack wanted a hell of a lot more for himself.

But big plans took big money. He'd be an old man before he'd have any cash if he stuck around the farm with Luke. His ma and pa both died trying to hang on to the place, and never had more than enough money to make it from one year to the next.

Isaac and Jeb were always bragging about how much money they'd made since they hooked up with Baxter and the others. They never said what they'd done to get it, but Jack could guess. Of course, both of them spent most of it on women and cards as fast as they got it. Jack didn't plan on being that foolish. A few jobs and he'd have enough to light out for someplace new. California, maybe, or the Oregon Territory.

So come morning, he'd be there when Baxter called out for them to mount up.

Cora was worried about Luke. As far as she could tell, he hadn't been back to the store since the day they'd argued, and that was over a week ago. It was none of her business, but he couldn't go without supplies forever. If he didn't come in soon, she'd talk to Lucy about taking some out to his house.

The clock on the wall across the room tolled the hour. Lucy would be down in a few minutes to relieve her. Normally, she would have been happy to stay all afternoon, but the freight company had delivered a shipment of books to the school. She could hardly wait to unpack them.

The second she heard Lucy coming down the steps, she took off her apron and reached for her hat. It wasn't much on looks, but it would keep the sun off her face.

Lucy smiled when she spotted Cora already waiting by the door. "In a bit of a hurry to leave, aren't you? I thought you liked working for me."

"I do, and you know it. But I want to get out to the schoolhouse before the weather changes." She pulled on her riding gloves.

"Does it look like rain?" Lucy joined her at the window. "It sure does. Those clouds look pretty dark. If it starts looking worse, you should go straight home. Those books can wait."

"Yes, Mother," Cora teased. "I promise to be careful. I'll be in tomorrow at the same time. Tell Mary good-bye for me."

She hurried down the street to the stable. Falstaff whinnied a greeting as soon as Cora came into sight. After tightening the cinch on his saddle, Cora mounted up and rode out of town.

CHAPTER 7

Falstaff picked up on Cora's good mood, dancing sideways trying to convince her to let him fly down the road. After the last few houses of Lee's Mill were behind her, she leaned down over the horse's neck and urged him forward. He immediately surged into a fast-paced canter that had Cora grinning.

The gray's long legs ate up the distance, passing by the path to Cora's house in no time. A short time later, they flew past the Gibson farm. She risked a glance to the right, hoping to catch a glimpse of Luke, but the trees and undergrowth blocked her view.

All too soon, she spotted the schoolhouse up ahead. She reined in Falstaff, slowing him to a walk. The building, not even a year old, gleamed whitely in the early-afternoon sun. In her mind, she pictured the place surrounded by children of varying ages, laughing and playing games while she watched from the window.

Although she'd never taught school before, she'd been working with Melinda Hayes, who'd retired from teaching now that she was married and expecting a child. She had already helped Cora prepare her lessons for the upcoming year. Her promise to help with any problems that should arise had gone a long way toward allaying any fears Cora had about facing her new job.

She dismounted and tethered Falstaff in the school-yard where he could graze while she worked inside. The door to the building was kept locked. She could still remember the thrill when the mayor of Lee's Mill had officially entrusted Cora with its key. She wondered if he'd had any idea how grown-up that had made her feel.

The inside of the one-room building was unbearably hot from being closed up all day. She hurried to open several of the windows and left the door open to draw a small breeze through the room. It helped some to take off her hat and roll up her sleeves before she tackled the job of unpacking the case of primers. The books had been purchased by the two towns served by the school.

One by one, she pulled the books out of the wooden crate and stacked them on the floor. Once she had them all accounted for, she carried them over to the teacher's desk—now her desk, she reminded herself. There she carefully lettered the inside cover of each one "Property of the Lee's Mill–White's Ferry School."

As she waited for the ink to dry, she stood near the window where she could check on Falstaff. Aunt Henrietta thought she was insane for having such a huge horse, but Cora already loved the animal fiercely. She knew it was partly because Luke had helped her buy him, but also because the big gray was good company for her.

As soon as she'd brought him home, the loneliness she'd been fighting had eased up considerably. Whenever she worked outside, he tagged along behind her, more like a dog than a horse. She also liked knowing that she had someone else to care for besides herself, even if that someone had four legs and didn't talk.

She was about to return to the books when she noticed that Falstaff was no longer grazing. Instead, he stood with his head up and his ears perked forward as if listening to something. Cora moved closer to the window, trying to see or hear what had caught the gelding's attention. Had the weather taken a turn for the worse? No, the clouds had moved south, and the sky overhead was a clear blue.

It was probably only someone riding past on his way to town. The school was situated halfway between Lee's Mill and White's Ferry, right on the narrow road that connected them. But until she knew who it was, she stayed inside the building, trying to decide if she should close the windows and lock the door. She crossed the room to get a clearer view of the road, her footsteps echoing hollowly in the empty room, reminding her how alone she was.

She closed her eyes, trying to listen for some clue as to what was going on outside. It didn't take long. A group of riders, maybe ten to twelve of them, came riding out of the woods a short distance down the road. From where she stood, she couldn't recognize any of them. They rode past in grim silence, headed in the direction of the river.

The river. Both Mitch Hughes and Luke had warned her about night riders in the area, specifically near the river. Not much was known about them, but there had been rumors going around for months. Perhaps she would have been wiser to pay better attention to what was being said. Certainly, the next time she saw either Mitch or Jake, the sheriff, she would ask what they knew about the men.

For now, though, they had ridden out of sight. It

would take her only a minute or two to finish putting the books away, but she was in no hurry to leave. She wanted to give those men plenty of time to be on their way before heading for home.

When the books were lined up in a neat row on the shelf, she closed and locked the windows. She was relieved to note that Falstaff stood dozing in the dappled shade under a sycamore. Satisfied that it was safe, she left the building, carefully locking the door behind her.

As usual, she needed to lead Falstaff over to a stump in order to mount him. She had just picked up his reins to do just that when three more men rode into sight, this time coming back from the river. Doing her best to ignore them and any threat they might pose, she maneuvered her horse as close to the stump as she could.

Out of the corner of her eye, she realized that the three riders had veered off the road and were headed straight for her. She put one foot in the stirrup and quickly scrambled up into the saddle. At the first sign of trouble, she would kick Falstaff into a full-out gallop and ride for town.

"Miss Lawford, how nice to see you again."

She'd only heard that voice once, but she recognized it immediately. Her smile might have been a bit ragged around the edges, but she was glad to see that she knew at least one of the men. "Good afternoon, Mr. Gibson."

Jack's smile was as friendly as ever. "I'd like you to meet my friends, Isaac and Jeb."

Both men nodded, their own smiles small while their eyes glittered brightly in the afternoon sunshine. Maybe she would have been better off to stay locked inside the school. All she could do was try to bluff her way out of the situation.

"It was nice meeting you, gentlemen, but I must be going."

"But we just got here," Jack complained. Then he winked at her.

"I'm expected in town shortly." That was a lie, but if they continued to press her, she would head straight for Lee's Mill and the sheriff's office.

"Jack never told us about you, did he, Jeb? He must have wanted you all for himself." Isaac's gap-toothed smile did little to reassure her.

"That's right, but I can't say that I blame him none. If I had me a pretty woman like you, I'd be tempted to keep her all to myself, too." Jeb yanked his shapeless brown hat off his head, revealing his lank brown hair.

All three of them had the look of men who had been living on the trail. Their beards were several days old, and their clothes had been lived in for too long. Ignoring the other two, she kept her eyes on Jack. Surely he wouldn't let any harm come to her.

She blurted out the only thing she could think of. "How is your brother?"

Jack shrugged. "Haven't seen him recently. I was headed home when we saw you."

"Well, tell him hello for me."

Jeb snickered. "Sounds like you've got some competition, Jack."

Jack shot his companion a dirty look. "Shut up, Jeb." There was no real heat in his words, but Jeb didn't seem to care one way or the other.

"But she . . ."

Jack sat up straighter in the saddle and glared at his companions. "I said shut up."

While their attention was directed away from her, she

nudged Falstaff forward. Isaac deliberately blocked her way as Jeb positioned himself behind her. Panic tasted sour as she fought to keep it at bay. She kicked Falstaff in the ribs. The gray needed no urging. In a quick maneuver that left her reeling in the saddle, her faithful mount shoved past the other three horses and cantered down the road.

The sound of masculine laughter trailed after her, a reminder that she wasn't in the clear yet. Almost immediately, they were following along right behind her. She kept her eyes firmly on the road ahead, not wanting to give them the pleasure of knowing how badly frightened she was.

With her blood pounding in her ears, it was impossible to hear if they were gaining on her. She wasn't all that far from home, but leading them straight for her empty house didn't seem all that wise of an idea. Neither was charging down the road toward Lee's Mill. Falstaff would ride his heart out for her, but the three miles to town stretched out ahead of her like an eternity.

All of a sudden, her salvation appeared out of the bushes a short distance ahead. Never in her life had she been so glad to see someone. A tug on the reins had Falstaff clattering to a stop.

Luke had been fighting his restlessness—or maybe it was loneliness—for the past two days. His nights were ugly, the dreams of the dead driving him out walking until the sky was pink to the east. After only a few hours of sleep, he'd crawl out of his blankets as tired as he had been before he'd lain down. He'd done everything he could think of to keep his hands and his mind busy, but along about noon he'd realized that he'd lost the battle. If he didn't find someone to talk to besides the chickens and his horse, he feared for his sanity.

After watering the garden, he stripped off to take a bath in his ma's old washtub. More of him hung out of the tub than fit in it, but he managed to scrub off enough dirt to feel better. He'd lathered and rinsed his hair twice under the pump outside. The cold spring water stung his hot skin, but it helped clear out his mind.

Realizing how long his hair had gotten gave him the excuse he'd been looking for to go into town. The barbershop was the only place besides the two saloons that he knew he'd be safe from the temptation of Cora Lawford. He'd been fighting off the thought of her as hard as he had the nightmares of his past.

Closing his eyes, he allowed himself to savor the memory of their confrontation in the store. The image of her standing with her hands on her hips, daring him to take note that she was a woman, filled his mind. Did she think he was blind?

He'd noticed all right. Even if he hadn't been able to figure it out for himself, his body's reaction had made damned sure he knew. Hell, he'd been hard and hurting off and on for nearly two days afterward. Every time he saw the smoke rising from her chimney, he remembered how it had felt to have his hands on her. And instead of fighting him off, those dark eyes of hers had drifted shut in invitation to kiss her.

He wished he had.

Hell, he deserved to be horsewhipped for even thinking such a thing. It wasn't just that he was a few years older than she was; it was how he had lived those years that made the difference. Somehow, despite the war, she'd managed to hang on to her innocence. If

she ever found out some of the things he'd done, she
would turn away from him in disgust.

But then, maybe not. She already knew he'd been
in prison for killing a man, and that hadn't kept her
from rushing to his defense. Although he had meant
what he'd told her about fighting his own battles, it
had felt damned good for a moment to have someone else on his side.

He led his mare out of the corral and saddled her.
He'd stop in to see Cade while he was in town, in case
he'd offer Luke some of that fine sipping whiskey he
kept in his desk drawer. Afterward, Luke would eat dinner at the hotel. Or better yet, maybe Cade would ask
him home to dinner. He wouldn't balk at the chance
to enjoy some more of Lucy Mulroney's cooking.

Lost in his plans, he almost lost his seat when his
mare suddenly shied, pawing the ground in protest.
He had to fight the horse back under control before
he could see what had startled the normally placid
animal. Cora Lawford was riding straight for him at
breakneck speed. Fear for her clutched at his gut.

At first, he thought maybe the gray was running
out of control. He didn't think the mare could catch
the long-legged gelding if he got past them. Instead,
Luke wheeled the mare around so that he could
make a grab for the gray's reins when it pelted past
him.

To his amazement, though, as soon as Cora saw him,
she started hauling back on the reins. Her horse immediately slowed, coming to a skidding halt only a few
feet away from where Luke sat. It shouldn't have surprised him that one look at Cora sitting there, her
ridiculous excuse for a hat hanging down her back,
had his temper up. It was one thing for Luke or Cade

to ride the gelding like that; Cora had no business doing something so foolish.

He was getting ready to tell her so when he took a better look at her face. She was pale, her eyes huge and frightened looking.

"What happened?" His hand automatically reached for his gun. If someone had threatened her, he'd kill the bastard.

She was gasping for breath, as if she'd been the one running instead of her horse. "I was at the school when . . ."

Her explanation broke off at the sound of another horse approaching. Luke had his revolver out of the holster before he recognized Jack. His brother held up his hands in mock surrender, his grin aimed at both of them. Luke's hold on his good mood crumbled into dust. Something was definitely wrong.

"Does one of you want to tell me what is going on?" he demanded as he shoved his gun back in its holster. He didn't miss the worried look Cora gave Jack or that she made sure that Luke was between them.

"I'm afraid that I managed to scare Miss Lawford." Jack offered her one of those smiles that never failed to charm.

For once, it didn't seem to work. Cora shot Jack a look that was definitely hostile before deliberately turning away from him. Luke waited to see what she had to say.

"I was working in the schoolhouse when I saw a group of strange men riding toward the river."

"You were out there alone." He didn't bother stating it as a question. Of course she rode out there by herself. The woman didn't have a lick of sense when it came to her own safety.

"A shipment of books was delivered. I had work to

do. That's what teachers do, you know. Work at the school."

Her chin took on that stubborn tilt that made him crazy. There was no use in telling her how foolish she'd been. She already knew and didn't care. No amount of nagging on his part was going to curb her headstrong ways.

"What happened next?" He focused his attention on her, continuing to ignore his brother for the moment.

"I waited until they'd been gone for a long time before I locked up. I had Falstaff tethered in the schoolyard where I could get to him in a hurry if I needed to." She patted her horse on the neck, in case he hadn't been able to figure out whom she was talking about. What a ridiculous name for a horse.

Meanwhile, her eyes pleaded with him to admit that she'd been careful. Nothing changed the fact that she was out there alone. He reminded her of the fact. "So you were alone in the school building, which only has one door. You would have been trapped if one of them had decided to pay you a visit."

Clearly that thought had never occurred to her. "I had the windows open."

Which meant what? She could have jumped out, he supposed, or screamed for help. Neither was much of a choice.

"Anyway, I had led Falstaff to the stump I use so I can reach the stirrup. I was about to leave when three more men came down the road." She gave Jack a reproachful look. "I didn't recognize your brother right off, so they gave me quite a start. I probably overreacted."

Somehow he doubted that. From what he knew of Cora, she didn't scare easily. If he found out that Jack and his two companions had threatened her in any way, there would be hell to pay.

"Where are your friends?" Luke looked past Jack. "I'd like to meet them."

"They headed on to where they live." He dismounted and slipped around Luke's horse to look up at Cora. "I'm sorry about what happened, Miss Lawford. We didn't mean to scare you like that. Jeb and Isaac asked me to offer their apologies."

However much Luke wanted to believe him, it was clear that Cora had her doubts. However, she managed a small smile. "Well, then, I suppose no real harm was done."

"Would you like me to see you home?" Jack asked.

Even if Cora said yes, Luke wasn't about to let that happen. Despite Jack's assurances, something had bothered her back at the school. He'd bet his last nickel on it. "No, that's all right. If Miss Lawford doesn't mind, I'll see her to her door. I'm on my way to town for a haircut anyway, so it's right on my way."

"That would be nice of you, Mr. Gibson." She already had her horse sidling away from Jack. "If you're sure that it's not an imposition."

"Not at all." He nudged his mare closer to Falstaff. "I'll be back later, Jack. I'll see you then."

His brother accepted defeat with a shrug. "I've been living in the saddle for too long. I'll probably turn in early, so don't hurry back on my account."

Luke waited until Jack disappeared down the path before speaking to Cora. "Would you feel better going into town with me? I'll only be there a short time." He paused, thinking of Mrs. James and the others. "That is, if you don't mind being seen with me."

She dismissed that particular concern with a wave of her hand. "I think I'd like that. Besides, I think I should tell Jake Whitney about what I saw."

The two of them started down the road, each lost

in thought. Luke didn't know what was on Cora's mind, but he was concerned about Jack. He'd worried all along that Jake's friends ran with that bunch who lived upriver. Having him appear so soon after Cora saw the others ride through was unlikely to be just a coincidence.

Cade had said the sheriff was convinced that they were responsible for some of the bank robberies in other parts of the state, but so far no one had been able to prove it. It made him sick to think that Jack might have taken up with the likes of them. He understood that his brother was restless and needed more than a run-down farm to make him happy. But robbing banks would net a man only one of two fates unless he was damned lucky: death or prison. As far as Luke was concerned, one wasn't a much better choice than the other one. The idea of Jack's spending a single day behind bars didn't bear thinking about.

He almost forgot he had a companion until she spoke up.

"You're looking awfully grim. Do you hate getting haircuts that much?" Her expression was serious, but the twinkle in her dark eyes gave her away.

"My pa used to read to us out of the Bible every Sunday. I guess the story of Samson always left me a little nervous around barbers."

His teasing paid off. The last of the tension in Cora's face disappeared when she started giggling. He hated to bring it back, but he had to know the truth of what had happened.

"Can you tell me what Jack and the others did that scared you so badly?"

She gave the matter some thought before speaking

again. "I think maybe I wouldn't have reacted so strongly if I hadn't just seen all those other men."

"Jack doesn't bring his friends around, so I've never met them. What were they like?"

"A little older than Jack, I'd guess. Both of them looked like pretty rough characters, but that's understandable if they've been riding a long time. I've only met your brother that first day in the store, but I recognized him right off. I wasn't as scared then." Her eyes met his only briefly before darting away.

He wondered what she was holding back. If he had to guess, something Jack and his friends had said or done had scared her even more than she was willing to admit. If she'd been reassured by his brother's presence, why had she been tearing down the road to get away from him?

"And?" he prodded.

"While we were talking, their horses blocked me in. I was afraid that they wouldn't let me leave when I wanted to go." She blushed. "I guess I overreacted."

Damn Jack anyway. He knew better than to go around scaring women. "How did you get away?" If any of them had laid a hand on her, Jack included, he'd make sure none of them was in any shape to bother anyone else for a long time.

"Falstaff knocked Jeb's horse out of the way. Or maybe it was Isaac's." She shook her head. "It doesn't matter. No real harm done." Despite her assurances, she wasn't over it yet, if Falstaff's behavior was any indication. He seemed to be picking up on her tension, because he kept tossing his head and dancing sideways.

They'd reached the outskirts of town. Luke decided for Cora's sake that he'd leave her before they reached Front Street. Although she might not be worried about

being seen in his company, the last thing either one of
them needed was to cause an uproar.

"I'm going to leave you here."

"But . . ." she started to protest. Her eyes narrowed
in suspicion. "Are you trying to avoid being seen with
me?"

There was no use in lying. "Yes." Then before she
could protest, he turned his mare away. Looking back
over his shoulder, he called back, "If you want to ride
back with me, meet me here in two hours."

He was getting damned tired of being surrounded
by silence. Who had ever heard of a barber who didn't
talk a man's arm off? But as soon as Luke walked into
the shop, the man hadn't said more than two words,
other than to ask how Luke wanted his hair cut and if
he wanted a shave.

Afterward he had dropped in to the newspaper office, where the typesetter had informed him that
Cade had gone to White's Ferry for the day. So far,
other than to make sure Cora made it to town safely,
the entire trip had been a bust. He would have had
better luck finding someone to talk to if he'd stayed
home and hung out with the chickens.

He checked the time again. He still had an hour or
so to wait. Cora's proposed visit to the sheriff worried
him some, but there wasn't much he could do about
it. She had every right to tell the lawman about the
men she'd seen riding through, especially if she'd felt
threatened by them. But he hoped like hell that
she'd left Jack's name out of her report.

The back of his neck itched. He figured it was either
because of the haircut or that someone was staring at
him. Careful not to make any sudden moves, he

studied the few houses in the immediate vicinity. At first he didn't see anything, but then he noticed a movement in the front window across the street.

It was most likely someone getting nervous because he'd been stopped outside of her house for too long. Before he could move off down the street, the front door opened and an elderly woman came marching down to the gate.

"Young man, come here."

Since he had never met the lady, he looked around to see whom else she could be talking to. The street was empty except for him. What could she be wanting? There was only one way to find out, so he dismounted and led his horse over to where the woman was waiting.

"Ma'am," he said, touching the brim of his hat. "Did you want to talk to me?"

She looked him up and down, not unlike a general inspecting the troops. "I do, if your name is Luke Gibson."

Damn, he should have ignored her summons. The last thing he wanted was to tangle with someone else over his unsavory reputation.

"I'm Gibson."

"I thought so." She opened the gate and stepped through. "I'm Henrietta Dawson, Cora Lawford's aunt."

He'd be polite as long as she was. "It's a real pleasure to meet you, ma'am."

"I sincerely doubt that, Mr. Gibson," she said somewhat tartly. "I knew both of your parents. They were decent folks." Tipping her head to one side, she studied his face. "You have your father's good looks."

"Thank you." His cheeks suddenly felt hot. Where was this conversation headed?

"Don't thank me. It was the Lord's doing, not

mine. Now, tie up your horse and come along inside. I want to talk to you." Without waiting to see if he obeyed, she headed back toward the house.

He wondered how long it had been since someone had found the courage to defy her. Well, he wasn't about to be the first. Even if he weren't curious about what she was up to, he wouldn't risk alienating Cora's relative. He walked through the gate and up to the porch. Before crossing the threshold, he stopped to check the condition of his boots.

He quickly wiped them clean on the rug lying outside the door. Once he was inside, his senses were assaulted by the combined scents of cinnamon and something flowery. Henrietta waited for him in the parlor.

"Come in and have a seat, Mr. Gibson," she said, motioning toward the sofa. "I'll be right with you."

She disappeared down the hallway. From the sound of plates and lids rattling, he had to guess she was in the kitchen. While he waited, he looked around the room. It was definitely a lady's parlor. Almost every surface in the room had a doily and some kind of fussy decoration sitting on it. Just being around it all made him feel big and clumsy.

He was relieved to hear Miss Dawson coming back. She walked in carrying a tray.

"I hope you like tea and fresh-baked cookies."

"Yes, ma'am, I do," he answered truthfully. He accepted the teacup and helped himself to a handful of the fragrant cookies. "These smell like the ones my ma used to bake."

"I'll send the rest home with you if you'd like."

"I'd like," he managed to say around a mouthful of cookie.

"I have a few questions for you, if you don't mind.

They concern my niece." She perched on the edge of a chair across from him.

"Would it make a difference if I did mind?"

She pursed her lips and shook her head. "No, it wouldn't."

"Then ask away."

"Is my niece safe living out where she does?"

"From me?"

"Don't play the fool, Mr. Gibson. It doesn't become you." She sipped at her tea. "The truth is that I've been worried about her ever since she had that house built. I was relieved to find out that you and your brother had moved back out to the farm. At least she's not quite so alone."

He thought that by now Mrs. James would have made it her business to inform Henrietta exactly what kind of man was living next to her niece. Well, he wasn't going to tell her if she hadn't already heard.

"Miss Lawford knows that she can come to me for help if she needs it." That much was true enough.

"I've heard about those men living upriver."

"As far as I've heard, they've never bothered anyone in this area."

"Well, I suppose that's as much as we can hope for." She reached for a cookie. "I hear that you helped Cora pick out that brute of a horse."

"That I did. She seems real happy with him."

"Well, I appreciate you doing that. Cora is a real bright girl, but she doesn't always know whom to trust. That horse trader could have cheated her something fierce."

He wouldn't have if he'd ever heard about her aunt, although Luke kept that particular thought to himself. "She was smart enough to ask for help.

When she found out that neither Cade Mulroney nor Mitch Hughes was around, she settled for me."

"Which brings me to the real reason I wanted to talk with you, Mr. Gibson."

He braced himself. As Cora's relative, it was only to be expected that she order him to stay away.

She set down her teacup and dusted the few crumbs from her lap. "I'm sure that you've heard all about the trouble that Mrs. James has been stirring up around here."

The bite of cookie he'd just taken turned to dust in his mouth. He swigged down the last of his tea before answering. "Yeah, I heard."

Henrietta refilled Luke's cup. "She's an interfering old busybody, but I guess you already know that, too."

Where was this conversation going? "Yes, ma'am, I do."

"Well, I've known her longer than I care to admit. While I don't doubt that she has her facts straight," Henrietta said, looking at Luke over the top of her glasses, "I don't approve of either her motives or her methods."

Since his hostess hadn't made any move to throw him out or to order him to stay clear of her niece, could she have some sympathy for his plight? "I wondered why she was so determined to cause me problems. As far as I know, I've never even met the woman before this happened."

"I already told you that you have your late father's good looks." Henrietta looked smug. "Well, years ago Mrs. James had her heart set on snaring your father. She never quite forgave him for marrying your mother instead. One look at you probably stirred up some pretty painful memories for her."

She paused to let Luke absorb that little bit of

news. "I know it's hard for young people to think of their parents ever being young themselves. But I assure you that your father had more than one girl interested in him."

Something about the way Henrietta stopped talking and stared at something only she could see made him wonder if she'd been another of his father's admirers. It was hard to imagine.

Finally she brought herself back to the present with a slight shake of her head. "Well, Mr. Gibson, I had better pack up those cookies for you." She rose to her feet. "I know that you have had some hard times, Mr. Gibson. I would hope that for your sake you will endeavor to build a life that will do honor to the memory of your dear parents."

A few minutes later he walked out of Henrietta's house with a further admonition that he should stop by occasionally to keep her apprised on his progress. He carefully tucked the cookies in his saddlebag, still trying to figure out how he'd come to spend the past half an hour with Cora's aunt.

Speaking of Cora, he wondered where she was. The time they'd agreed to meet had passed a few minutes ago, but she was nowhere in sight. If she'd come while he was inside, surely she would have noticed his horse tied up outside of Miss Dawson's place.

He couldn't stand out in the street all day waiting for her. If she wasn't going to find him, he would go looking for her. Before he swung up in the saddle, Cora came around the corner. He knew the instant she realized where he was standing. A look of shock faded into suspicion. Instead of giving her a chance to grill him, he quickly turned his mare toward home and cantered down the street. If Cora had questions to ask, she could wait until they were out of Lee's Mill.

He had a few questions of his own he wanted answered. She caught up with him before the last house disappeared into the trees behind them. For a short distance, she rode beside him without saying a word. From the way she kept glancing at him, though, he figured the silence wouldn't last long. If he let her, she'd take control of any conversation they might have. To keep that from happening, he decided to fire the first salvo.

"I met your aunt."

Cora sounded horrified. "You what?"

"I was waiting for you when she ordered me into her house." He fought the urge to laugh at the look on Cora's face.

"I'm sorry. I never thought about her living so close to where we were meeting." She urged her horse closer to his. "Was she just awful?"

He relented. "No, actually she was pretty decent to me, considering. Seems she knew my parents, especially my pa. She wanted to let me know that she didn't hold with the way Mrs. James was acting." Then he patted his saddlebag. "And she gave me cookies to take home."

"Really?" Cora shook her head. "You know, I don't think I'll ever figure out that woman. When I moved in with her, she was so strict that I could hardly breathe. She criticized me and everybody I knew, but the past couple of years, she's changed."

"How so?"

"Well, for one thing, she helped us break a friend out of jail." Her grin dared him to disbelieve her.

"You and who else?"

"Lucy Mulroney and Melinda Hayes." She stared

down the road, lost in the memory. "A friend had been unjustly accused of killing her husband. When we realized that she wasn't safe in the jail, we made plans to get her out. Lucy and Melinda hit Mitch Hughes over the head with Lucy's best cast-iron skillet and knocked him out."

Luke shuddered. "That must have hurt something fierce. They're lucky they didn't kill him." He'd yet to meet Mitch Hughes. But from what Cade had told him about the man, it wouldn't have been easy for the women to pull off such a daring raid.

"Mitch never said, but I guess so. Anyway, once they had Josie out of the jail, we hid her at Aunt Henrietta's house until it was dark."

"From what I hear, Mitch Hughes was a tough sheriff. I'm surprised they didn't end up in jail themselves." Although he couldn't quite picture Cade letting that happen.

"No, he forgave them. After all, Mitch married his prisoner once he cleared her name." She sighed, obviously taken with the whole affair. "Besides, Josie is best friends with both Lucy and Melinda."

As strange as the story was, from what he knew of all the women involved, he had to believe it all happened just as Cora described. After all, Cora certainly didn't have the good sense to keep out of Luke's problems. If all those women banded together, there was no telling what kind of trouble they could get into.

At least Cora seemed to have forgotten about her earlier scare. He'd see her home, this time right up to her door, no matter how much she protested. Once she was safely inside with her door locked, he'd ride home to check up on Jack. If he found out that his brother had done anything to deliberately frighten Cora, there would be hell to pay.

For now, he was going to savor his last few minutes with Cora. Despite the fact she'd turned to him when she was frightened, he did not want her to come to depend on him, not for protection, not for friendship. He wasn't sure he could be friends with a woman at all, much less one he wanted to bed more than he wanted to breathe.

"Well, here's where I leave you," Cora announced. "Thank you for everything."

Rather than argue with her, he simply followed along behind her. When she realized that he was tagging along at her heels, she turned in the saddle to face him.

"You don't need to see me home."

"Look, we can sit here and argue, and then I'll follow you to the house anyway. Or you can save time and just accept the fact that I'm going to do what I want, no matter what you say."

For a minute he thought she would fight him, but in the end she led the way to the small corral near her house. She dismounted and immediately set about unsaddling Falstaff. Luke toyed with the idea of doing it for her, but he'd already done more for her just by being there than either of them was happy about.

She managed to catch the heavy saddle as it slid off of Falstaff's back before it hit the ground. Luke watched her lug it around to the small shed she'd had built next to the corral. He even waited while she fed and watered the horse before she finally headed for the house. Searching his mind for the words he wanted to say, he came up empty.

If he warned her to stay away from the school unless

someone was with her, she wouldn't listen. If he told her to stay away from the river, she'd argue. And if he told her to stay away from him, she would or she wouldn't. He wasn't sure which idea scared him more.

By the time she reached the porch, he was already halfway back to the road.

CHAPTER 8

After turning his horse loose, he went inside the cabin long enough to change into his work clothes. Not that there was much difference between his good clothes and those he dug stumps in. His good shirts still had all their buttons, and the colors weren't as faded. Otherwise, they were pretty much the same.

The soft rumble of Jack's snores echoed in the dim light of the cabin. For a minute he considered dragging his brother out of his bedroll to help him with chores but decided he'd rather work alone for a while. Spending much of the day in Cora's company had left him feeling edgy. One wrong word from Jack and Luke just might work off his bad mood with his fists.

He gathered up his rifle and the tools needed to attack the stumps again. Rather than leave the rest of Henrietta's cookies in the cabin where Jack would find them, he toted them out to the pasture with him. He might decide to leave a couple for his brother, but somehow he doubted it. Cora's aunt hadn't said a single word about his having to share them with anybody.

He chose his next victim and picked up the ax. Oak stumps were about the worst, he'd decided, but there was still a great deal of satisfaction to be had from each one that he finally bested. This one was smaller than some of the others had been; after about an hour of hard work, it slumped over against the side of the hole he'd dug around the roots. Another victory in his life.

Ready for a break, he picked up the cookies and wandered over toward a small spring that bubbled up around a cluster of small boulders. The water was cold and clear and felt like heaven when he splashed it on his face and neck. He sat down, leaning against the biggest rock, and stretched his legs out in front of him.

About halfway through his second cookie, he heard a single horse approaching. He reached for his rifle and waited for the rider to come into sight. As the stranger picked his away across the pasture, Luke stayed in the shadows and watched as the man studied the ground every few feet.

He was so intent on what he was doing that he didn't notice Luke start walking toward him until they were only a few feet apart. His lack of concern meant either he was pretty damned confident of his ability with a gun or else he was a fool. Luke didn't have any real desire to find out which one.

"Can I help you, uh, Sheriff?" he asked, noticing the star pinned to the man's chest when he straightened up in the saddle.

"I don't know." He dismounted and knelt down in a patch of flattened grass. "Looks like someone has been using your land as a shortcut." He stood up and followed the trail with his eyes. "To the river, most likely."

He dropped the reins and held his hand out to Luke. "We haven't met. I'm Jake Whitney." His smile didn't quite reach his dark eyes.

"Luke Gibson." He accepted the handshake. "What brings you out this way, Sheriff?"

"Cora Lawford stopped in to see me earlier." The sheriff glanced back in the direction of Cora's place. "I wanted to see if I could tell for certain how many men she was talking about. Maybe backtrack and see where they came from."

Luke studied the ground at his feet. The thick grass was matted down, testimony to the number of horses that had ridden over it. A handful of horses wouldn't have done such a thorough job.

"She told me that there were about ten, maybe twelve, who rode by the school." There was no use in denying it. On the other hand, he didn't feel the need to tell the lawman that it wasn't the first time the night riders had chosen his farm to cross.

"Miss Lawford said you escorted her into town."

"I was already headed that way." No use in letting the man get the idea that Luke had anything more than a neighborly interest in Cora. She didn't need that getting around town any more than he did.

The sheriff raised one eyebrow, telling Luke more clearly than words that he understood all too well what Luke was thinking. He looked too young to be the only law in town, but Cade thought highly of him. It wouldn't do to underestimate the man's ability to do his job.

"Any particular reason you're so interested in this bunch?" Luke tried to sound only mildly curious. It took all he could do not to look back toward the cabin to make sure that Jack was still there.

"A marshal from upstate sent a wire that there'd been another bank robbery a few days ago. He was asking everyone to keep an eye out for an armed gang passing through."

"How do you know it's the same bunch?" *Please, God, don't let there be any eyewitnesses.* Even recognizing a horse with unusual markings could be enough to convict a man.

"I don't. The marshal suspects the gang goes to

ground someplace. They pull a job every so often and then practically disappear." He gathered up the reins. "I hear you have a brother."

Damn, what had Cora told him? He'd been a fool to think she'd keep her mouth shut about Jack and his friends scaring her earlier.

"Sure do."

"I have to say that none of us was happy when Miss Lawford insisted on building out this way. I appreciate you keeping an eye on her." He took off his hat and wiped his sleeve across his forehead. Glaring up at the sky, he shook his head. "It's only May, and already it's hotter than hell."

"There's a spring over there if you want to fill your canteen and water your horse."

"That sounds good." He followed Luke back to the shade of the trees.

Luke hung back while the sheriff knelt down to help himself to the fresh, cool water. He splashed some on his face, much as Luke had done only a short time before. After filling his canteen, Jake encouraged his horse to drink its fill. While he waited, he kept his eyes on the woods on the other side of the field. Luke waited for the man to speak his mind.

"I figure they're the same bunch that camp out upstream from here." He glanced at Luke. "Mitch Hughes and Cade Mulroney paid a call on their leader when Mitch was still sheriff. The leader calls himself by a variety of names. Jones and Baxter are the two we know for sure."

He led his horse back toward the tracks. "Have you ever met him?"

Luke shook his head. "No, I haven't. Not that I know of, anyway. I met a lot of men during the war. I can't remember all of them, not by name."

"How about your brother? Does he know Baxter and his men?" He glanced at Luke, his eyes narrowed and his mouth a grim slash across his handsome face.

"He's never said." That much was true. Up until Cora told him about the two men who'd been with Jack, he'd never even known their names.

"Right now, I've got no problem with you or your brother, Gibson. See that it stays that way." With that, he swung back up and rode out, this time heading back toward town.

"So where the hell have you been for the better part of a week?" Luke nudged Jack in the ribs with his boot.

His brother opened bleary eyes and glared up at him. "Go to hell."

"I've been there and lived to tell about it." That wasn't much of an exaggeration. "Now get your lazy backside out of bed and answer my question."

Jack sat up and stretched his arms over his head and then scratched the stubble on his face. "I need a shave."

Luke did his best to be patient while his brother slowly stood up and slipped his shirt on without bothering to button it. Jack padded across the floor in his stocking feet toward the shelf that held their food supplies. He pounced on the cookies that Luke had left there for him to find. After pouring himself a cup of coffee, he settled at the table and propped his feet up on a crate.

Luke tried again. "Where have you been for the past week?"

"Here and there." To avoid saying more, Jack stuffed his mouth full of cookies.

That was all right. There weren't that many cookies left. Eventually he would run out of excuses not to talk. If prison had taught Luke anything, it was patience. But just in case, he grabbed the last two cookies for himself.

"Hey, those were mine!" Jack protested, but without any real rancor. "Did our Miss Lawford bake them for us?"

"First of all, she's not *our* Miss Lawford. Secondly, she did not bake these. Her aunt gave them to me." Luke took the seat opposite Jack. "Now, quit dancing around the question I asked. Where were you?"

"I rode up north for a few days with Jeb and Isaac to see some friends. Why is it so important to you?" Jack's attempt to look unconcerned would have worked if Luke didn't know him so well. There was tension in the set of his shoulders and the way his fingers drummed restlessly on the table.

"I dug up another stump while you were asleep." The sun was ready to disappear over the hills. He'd been waiting for hours for Jack to wake up.

Jack blinked at the sudden change in subjects. "Good. One less for me to sweat over."

"Sheriff Whitney rode past and stopped to visit while I was taking a break."

The drumming sped up. "What did he want?"

"Seems he was tracking that bunch who live down by the river. They've been riding across the back of our pasture pretty regularly. He took a good close look at the tracks. Don't know if he was just being curious or if he was tracking a particular horse."

"Tell the bastard to stay off our property."

Luke gave his brother a disgusted look. "Now that's real smart. I'm sure the best way to convince a lawman that we've nothing to hide is to tell him that he's not welcome." He wished he could pound some sense into his brother's thick skull. "It's my guess that he has good reason to keep an eye on those men. If he can tie any of them to the robberies up north a ways, there'll be hell to pay."

Jack picked up his coffee and took a long drink. Luke pretended not to notice that his brother's hands weren't exactly steady. He couldn't ignore the possibility that Jack had gotten himself in over his head with his need for adventure.

"I guess you think it's none of my business what you've been doing with your time, but . . ." But before he could finish, Jack lurched to his feet.

"You're right, big brother. It's none of your damned business." He walked away from the table to retrieve his boots. "I'll be back later."

He stomped out of the room, stopping on the porch long enough to pull on his boots. Luke felt sick. Rather than chase after him, though, he stayed where he was. After he heard Jack ride out, he gathered up his bedroll and headed outside.

Maybe he'd made a mistake in talking to Jack about the sheriff's visit. If the men Jack was running with were outlaws, then he was probably on his way right that minute to warn them that the sheriff was sniffing around their business.

Son of a bitch! If that weren't bad enough, he couldn't let the sheriff know that his interest in Baxter and his men was no longer a secret—if indeed, it ever had been—without admitting that Jack had a connection to the group. Should he make another trip to town to talk to Cade? Hell, he didn't know.

He made one last round to check on the livestock. That made him laugh. A bunch of chickens and one horse weren't much to brag about. On the other hand, it was a hell of a lot more than he'd owned in a long time.

He tossed the chickens a handful of feed just for the fun of watching them scrabble in the dust for the grain. Their frantic search for one more seed made him laugh every time. When they'd settled back down, he paid a visit to his horse. The mare leaned her head over the fence in the hopes Luke would scratch her ears.

He did as she asked, all the time wishing he had someone other than her to talk to. The faint smell of smoke drifted past on the night air. He traced it to its source with his eyes. Just as he suspected, Cora was still up, perhaps sitting in her kitchen.

Did she get as lonely living by herself as he did? Why had she chosen to live so far from town when it made her good friends worry about her? She wasn't the type to disregard the feelings of others.

His mare wandered away, leaving him alone again. He looked up at the darkening sky. Not a cloud in sight, just a blanket of stars stretched overhead for as far as he could see. He found the thought comforting. Perhaps this would be one of the rare nights when he could sleep.

There was only one way to find out. His blankets were still piled on the porch where he'd left them. He gathered them up and headed for his usual spot. After giving the blankets a good shake, he pulled off his boots and stretched out on his back with his hands locked behind his head. Rather than try to force sleep to come, he stared up at the dark branches overhead and thought about his parents.

Henrietta Dawson had been right when she said that children had a difficult time imagining their parents as young people. Had his pa ever stared up at these same stars and wondered where his life was headed? How had his mother felt about competing with other women for pa? Maybe it had been no contest at all, despite how Mrs. James had felt about the situation.

He closed his eyes and tried to imagine his parents as newlyweds. The thought made him smile in the close cover of the night. The two of them never had much in the way of possessions, but that had never seemed to matter. They had been happy together; he knew that much was true. Memories of the four of them when times were peaceful slipped past the ugliness of the war in his mind to bring him comfort.

Sleep, when it came, kept the nightmares at bay.

Cora kicked her legs free of the blankets and sat up on the edge of the bed. She didn't the need the clock in the other room tolling out the hours to tell her that it was time to be asleep. So far, she'd been unable to do more than doze for a few minutes at a time.

Giving up for the time being, she reached for her wrapper and walked through the familiar darkness to the kitchen. It was a little lighter near the patch of moonlight that shone through the kitchen window. She stared out at the hills in the distance, their shapes only faintly visible.

Turning her head only slightly, she shifted her gaze toward the real cause of her restlessness. Her encounters with both of the Gibson brothers had jangled her nerves, leaving her confused and her mind full of unanswered questions.

Jack and his two friends had frightened her badly. Her reaction was partly due to being a woman alone with three strange men, but it was more than that. She met strangers all the time when she worked for Lucy, but that never frightened her. No, there'd been something about the way they'd looked at her, especially Jeb and Isaac, that had left her feeling exposed and vulnerable. Jack might not have been a real threat to her, but his friends were a different matter.

Falstaff was fast, but she still had her doubts that she would have made it all the way to Lee's Mill before those men caught up with her. They'd disappeared awfully quickly, making her wonder if they'd cut cross-country trying to head her off, leaving Jack to herd her along into their trap. If Luke hadn't happened to be there, she shuddered to think what might have happened. Maybe she was overreacting, but she didn't seem to be able to stop thinking about various outcomes, none of them good.

And then there was Luke himself.

His surprise at seeing her riding straight for him had been genuine. Looking back, she realized that his first thought had been that she'd lost control of her horse. He'd immediately placed his mare in a position to try to rescue her. The thought made her smile, the one bright spot in the whole affair.

Luke had his own problems; she knew that. He'd told her himself that he'd been in prison. She supposed he thought that fact alone should be enough to run her off. But his continuing efforts to hold her at arm's length only served to convince her that there was more to Luke Gibson than he let on. On the other hand, Jack's easy charm no longer seemed so innocent. His apology had not impressed her. Not one bit. Even if they'd meant her no real harm, he and his friends had enjoyed seeing her squirm.

And what had Aunt Henrietta said to Luke? He had seemed more amused than insulted at her aunt's usual high-handed behavior. Cora wouldn't put it past her to have warned Luke to stay away from her niece. Little did her aunt know that it was Cora doing the pursuing, not Luke.

His behavior was so hard to decipher. One minute he acted the hero, riding to her defense, escorting her to town when he knew she was still too rattled to stay by herself. Later, despite her claims to be self-sufficient, he'd stood silent guard over her while she'd unsaddled and fed her horse. She'd half expected him to insist on doing the chores for her. Instead, he'd watched and waited until she was almost inside the house and then ridden off as if he couldn't bear to be in her presence one minute more.

An owl swept down out of the trees. The huge bird's wings beat slowly as it returned to its perch in the treetops, carrying off a small rodent. The sudden attack, silent and deadly, gave Cora the shivers. It was time to return to the safety of her bed.

The river wasn't good company. Neither were the two men sitting with him. Jack wished like hell he had someplace else to go. He was damned sick and tired of not belonging anywhere.

Luke made lots of noise about the two of them being equal partners in the farm, but that wasn't true. He knew full well that Luke was more firmly rooted to that piece of land than the stumps he kept digging out of it. If it were up to Jack, he'd sell the damned place and leave the past behind. He wasn't sure what he'd do with his share of the money; maybe he'd head west and see the Pacific Ocean for himself.

Wouldn't that be something?

He glanced at his two companions. Jeb and Isaac

had made camp a short distance upriver from Baxter and his men. Like Jack, the two weren't part of the inner circle. If the outlaw leader needed a few extra men, then Jeb and Isaac were invited along. Otherwise, the two cousins did whatever they had to in order to keep themselves fed.

Anything, that is, except work for a living. Neither of them had much use for regular hours or taking orders from anybody except Baxter. They probably wouldn't listen to him either, except for his reputation with his guns. Jack had never seen the man draw down on anyone, but he'd heard enough stories to convince him that the man was good. Maybe better than good.

"Got any money?" Jeb nudged Jack with his boot. "We finished off our last bottle an hour ago. We're thinking of riding into town to try our luck at cards."

Jack patted his pockets. "I've got a little. Enough for a bottle and a few chips."

"Let's go. The night's wasting away." Isaac kicked some dirt over the fire while Jeb fetched the horses.

"Which way we riding?"

Jeb spat a wad of tobacco on the hot coals. It sizzled and sputtered and smelled like hell. "I don't care. The saloon in White's Ferry is bigger, but the women at The Lady are prettier. I've got my eye on that red-head." He rubbed his hands together in anticipation.

Isaac laughed and slapped his cousin on the shoulder. "That's all you're going to have on her, unless your luck at cards changes soon."

"Go to hell, Isaac."

"I probably will, but you'll be there to greet me." The two of them laughed and mounted up.

Jack wasn't in any hurry to cross paths with the sheriff in Lee's Mill. But if his friends were headed that way, he'd tag along. At the first sign of trouble, though, he'd ride for home.

The moon, full and silver bright in the sky, cast enough light to make their trip easy. Once they reached the edge of town, they hurried their pace. The combined lure of women, cards, and whiskey was more than any of them could resist.

The hitching rail outside the saloon was crowded, forcing Jack to leave his horse a short distance down the street. Once the three of them reached the sidewalk, they stopped in the glow of light from the saloon's front window to count their money. None of them had much, but it was enough to get them started.

As soon as they walked through the door, Jeb started looking around for an open seat in a card game. Of the three of them, he usually had the best luck. If he didn't start winning after a bit, then Isaac would spell him at the table. Neither of them trusted Jack to do more than break even.

Jack approached the bar. The redhead Jeb had a hankering for sidled up to him.

"Buy a girl a drink, mister?" Powder and rouge did little to disguise the signs of hard living carved in her face. She ran a practiced hand up his arm as she pressed close enough to offer him a good look down her low-cut dress. "Or maybe you'd like to go upstairs with me. I'd give you a real good time."

He wanted to be tempted and even had the money it would cost to do more than look at her plump breasts. But her smile was tired, and so was he. Rather than turn her down altogether, he signaled the bartender to bring them both a whiskey.

"My friend over there is an admirer of yours, ma'am. I wouldn't want to interfere with his plans for the night." He summoned up a smile. "He couldn't wait to see you."

"I've got time for two men, if you'd like." This time her hand drifted down, brushing across his thigh. "Your friend is plenty busy right now. Why don't you keep me from getting too lonely while I wait for him?"

She reached for the bottle the bartender had left and pressed a damp kiss against his cheek. "Let's take this upstairs."

Jack's body betrayed him. It had been a damn long time since he'd taken a woman to bed. "What's your name?"

His companion smiled coyly. "They call me Red, but I can be anybody you want me to be."

Closing his eyes, he tried to imagine the perfect woman to spend the night with. Unfortunately, the image that filled his mind looked little like the woman at his side and far more like Cora Lawford. All interest in spending the evening upstairs died quickly.

He tossed back the rest of his drink. "I'm sorry, but not tonight."

With surprising perception, Red asked, "Who is she?"

"No one I should be thinking about." That much was true. He hadn't missed the way Cora looked at Luke as her savior or that his brother was looking back.

"Well, honey, I better get back to work." Red patted him on the arm and nodded in Jeb's direction. "Tell your friend I'll be waiting for him."

Jack did as she asked on his way out the door. Once he was outside, he considered his options. He could try the other saloon in town or go home. Neither had much appeal, but at least it wouldn't cost him anything to sleep in his own cabin.

***

"Sorry I'm late." Cora scurried in the door, taking off her hat and gloves.

Lucy was already behind the counter, checking the till. "Don't worry about it. It's been quiet so far."

Cora grabbed her apron out of the storeroom and put it on. "I overslept. I never do that."

Her friend stopped counting the coins in her hand to give her a worried look. "Are you feeling all right?"

"I'm fine. For some reason I had a hard time getting to sleep last night. It must have left me feeling more tired than usual." Not wanting to discuss the reasons behind her sleeplessness, she picked up the feather duster and began giving the shelves a quick cleaning.

After a few seconds, Lucy went back to her counting. The door opened just as Lucy finished putting the last of the money back in the till. Cora stopped her dusting to see who had come in.

"Good morning, ladies." Jake Whitney took off his hat and nodded first to Lucy and then to Cora.

"Morning, Sheriff." Lucy came out from behind the counter, smiling up at their first customer of the day. "What can I get for you?"

His eyes shifted in Cora's direction. "Actually, I came in to see Miss Lawford. I'd like to talk to her for a few minutes, if that's all right. If she's busy now, I can come back later."

"Cora?" Lucy crossed the room to stand beside her, offering Cora her immediate support. "What's going on, Jake?"

The sheriff included both women in his grim smile. "I need to talk to Miss Cora more about what she saw yesterday. Or rather who."

Perhaps she'd made a mistake in reporting the

riders she'd seen to the sheriff. Certainly she hadn't wanted any of her friends to find out; they worried enough. But the deed was done. Knowing Lucy wouldn't be satisfied until she knew all the details, Cora filled her in on the important parts, leaving out the part about Jack and his friends. After all, she didn't know for certain that they had been with the other men. Not really.

Turning to face Jake, she asked, "But what about them?"

"Would you recognize any of the riders if you were to see them again?" He paused, as if considering how much he wanted to tell her. "A marshal from upstate sent me a wire saying that he's sending out wanted posters all over the state. Seems a gang of ten to twelve men robbed another bank up his way."

Lucy gasped and clutched Cora's hand.

"W-was anyone killed?" Cora had to ask but wasn't sure she wanted to know the answer.

"No, but it wasn't for lack of trying." Jake looked a little worried. "It sounds like the same bunch who have been doing this off and on for a couple of years. So far, we've been lucky. They seem to prefer to do their robbing up north of here."

"So there's no real reason to suspect those men I saw." *Much less Luke's brother,* she added to herself.

"Maybe not, Miss Cora. But I'd sure feel better if I knew that for certain. Would you mind taking a look at the posters as soon as they come in? I can bring them out to your house, if you'd like."

She couldn't very well refuse to look at the posters once they arrived. The sheriff was no fool. Since she'd made the trip into town for the sole purpose of reporting what she'd seen, he would find it suspicious if she suddenly quit cooperating.

"That will be fine." She hoped neither Jake nor Lucy picked up on her reluctance. Or if they did, they put it off to being upset that she might have seen an outlaw gang.

"Well, I'd better be going, ladies. Thank you again, Miss Cora, for coming to me. I'll rest easier once I find out for certain if we have a nest of vipers living in our midst."

As soon as he left, Lucy rounded on her. "All right, Cora, why didn't you tell me about this before?"

"Because I didn't want to worry you." She went back to her dusting. "Besides, nothing came of it. Right after I saw them, I ran into Luke Gibson. He was kind enough to escort me to town and then back home."

Lucy frowned. "Could he have been riding with the men?"

Cora forced herself to remain calm. "No, of course not."

Sounding more curious than worried, her friend gave Cora a questioning look. "How do you know?"

"The riders I saw had the look of men who'd been on the trail for a while. Luke was clean shaven. In fact, his hair was still damp from washing it. He was just leaving for town when I happened by."

Something she'd said had Lucy frowning. What could it be?

"What time of day was it?"

"Afternoon." Where was Lucy going with this? "Why?"

"Seems like a strange time of day for a farmer to stop work and get all cleaned up."

She hadn't thought of that. "He was coming into town for a haircut." And he had gotten one. She knew that for certain. The barber had done a good job, but it would take more than a neat trim to tame the edginess in Luke's appearance.

"Oh, well, that explains it."

Lucy walked back to the counter and resumed her paperwork. Cora frowned as she fought the doubts Lucy had put in her head. Had Luke just come home with the night riders? She hadn't seen either of the Gibson brothers for several days, so she had no way of knowing for certain if he'd been gone or not.

Except that part of her did not want to think Luke had been doing anything other than working on his farm. Jack was a different matter. Even though she hadn't mentioned him to the sheriff, she felt sure that Jack and his friends at least knew the other men she'd seen. If she were honest with herself, she had to admit that perhaps her defense of Luke was wishful thinking.

But he had seemed genuinely surprised to see his brother, as if the two of them had been apart. Judging by looks alone, it was obvious that Jack had been eating trail dust for several days. He'd even admitted as much.

Until the wanted posters arrived, there wasn't much more she could do. It was doubtful she'd recognize any of the men. As long as none of the posters resembled the Gibson brothers, she could do her civic duty in good conscience.

And when she saw Luke again, maybe she'd find some way to casually mention what was going on. She figured she owed him another pie for his kindness to her the day before. At least that was the excuse she was going to use to drop by his house.

Her spirits lifted at the thought.

A june bug buzzed around Luke's head, seriously interfering with his efforts to sleep in. He peeled one eye open a bit and swatted at the emerald-green pest. His hand missed it by several inches, but evidently it came close enough to warn the bug to find someone else to bother.

Knowing sleep was too far gone to be recaptured, he sat up and looked around. Would he ever be able to sleep indoors again? He hoped so, because Missouri winters could be brutal. Maybe he should get a couple of dogs to help keep him warm when it snowed. Of course, if they had a lick of sense, they'd take up residence in the cabin with Jack. His bed wasn't any more comfortable than Luke's, but at least it was inside and safe from whatever Missouri weather wanted to throw at them.

As he looked around, he noticed that Jack's horse was in the corral. He vaguely remembered hearing him ride in sometime during the night. Where had he been this time? Back with those same friends, if he had to guess. Jack probably figured Luke was in no position to question his choice of companions. But if they ever bothered Cora Lawford again, he'd make it his business.

He tugged on his boots and carried his bedroll inside the cabin. Breakfast sounded good, but he didn't want to wake up Jack. It seemed all they did lately was fight. Rousting him out at this hour would almost ensure they would start the day off at odds with each other.

Rather than sit at the table and wait for Jack to stir, Luke headed back outside. A soft breeze ruffled his hair, warning him to get some chores done before the heat set in for the day. The chickens scattered when he entered their pen but came running back as soon as he picked up the feed can. While they were busy eating, he hunted up a handful of eggs to use

for breakfast once Jack woke up. He closed the gate
to the pen and headed for the corral, deciding both
horses could use a good brushing before he threw
down feed for them as well.

An hour later, he was pumping fresh water into the
trough when he realized he was no longer alone. He
hadn't heard a horse approaching, which meant his
guest had arrived on foot. Only one person he knew
lived close enough to come visiting without riding.

Bracing himself for the impact her appearance
always had on him, he turned slowly to face his
unexpected company. Just as he expected, Cora Lawford stood a few feet away, looking as fresh as the
spring morning. Damn, he wished she'd take the hint
and stay as far from him as possible. Angry because
he wanted what he couldn't have, his welcome was
less than friendly. "What do you want? Never mind—
I don't care. Just go on home."

Without waiting for her to answer, he picked up the
bucket and carried it toward the house. She trailed
along behind him, evidently determined to ignore his
bad manners.

Once inside, he set the bucket down, not sure why
he'd even brought it to the cabin. Other than Jack,
only Cade had seen the inside of the place. The sound
of Cora's footstep on the porch warned him that was
about to change. He knew the place wasn't much, but
he'd seen where she'd been living before having her
own house built. He didn't know if he could bear seeing pity in her eyes when she saw how little he had in
the way of furnishings. If you could call empty crates
and a wobbly table furniture at all.

She hesitated in the doorway.

"You've come this far; you might as well come all
the way in." He made himself turn around and face

her. That's when he noticed what she had in her hands. "Is that one of your pies?"

She gave him a shy nod. "I wanted to thank you for what you did."

Damn, he didn't want her gratitude. The pie, however, was most welcome. He pulled one of the crates closer to the table. "Have a seat. I'll make coffee."

A rustling noise from the other side of the room startled them both. The pie pan hit the table with a clatter. He had all but forgotten that Jack was home. Cora gave him a questioning look.

"It's all right. That bundle of rags and noise over there is Jack." He crossed the room and gave his brother a none-too-gentle nudge with his foot. "Wake up, little brother, we've got company."

Jack started to mumble something, but Luke nudged him again. "Watch what you say. There's a lady present." He waited a second and added, "Not to mention a pie."

Figuring he'd done his duty, he turned back to their guest. He dropped his voice. "You shouldn't have gone to all that trouble."

Cora shrugged and smiled. "It wasn't all that much trouble."

He knew he should send her home, with or without ⌐er pie, for her sake or maybe his own. But he couldn't do it. Not yet. Maybe when Jack woke up. It would be interesting to see how she reacted to his brother. Day before yesterday, she definitely had been pretty skittish around him.

"Would you like some coffee?"

"Yes, please. I can't stay long, though. I promised Lucy and Melinda Hayes I'd come into town to plan for the next meeting of the Luminary Society." Her eyes kept flickering toward the back corner of the room.

"I hear that society has caused quite a stir around here." Using a rag, he picked up the coffeepot and poured some for each of them. All he had were three tin cups, but they'd have to do. He set the third one on the far side of the table in case Jack dragged himself out of his blankets.

Luke did his best to play host. He cut the pie and managed to find two clean forks to serve it with. When he plunked a plate down in front of Cora, he noticed she was still keeping a wary eye on Jack. Maybe she'd be more comfortable outside.

"It might be cooler on the porch."

Rather than give her any choice, he picked up the plates again and went outside. Cora trailed along behind him. He set the pie down on the stump he used as a table. He motioned toward the other two stumps.

"I can't say they're comfortable, but it's better than sitting on the ground." He offered her an apologetic shrug.

She quickly chose a seat and reached for her pie. "I don't normally eat pie for breakfast." Cocking her head to one side, she gave the matter some thought. "I'm pretty sure Aunt Henrietta wouldn't approve. Somehow that only makes it taste better, don't you think?" There was a teasing glint in her eyes.

Feeling a little too edgy to sit down, he leaned against the railing to put a little more distance between them. "I doubt if your pies ever need anything to make them taste better," he told her truthfully. "But like I said, you didn't have to go to all the trouble."

"Yes, I did."

Knowing there was no use in trying to convince her different, he concentrated on finishing his breakfast.

A second piece sounded mighty tempting, but there was lunch to think about later. The idea pleased him.

Finally, Cora put her fork down. "Well, I'd better be on my way. If I'm late, they'll worry. They always do." It was clear she didn't appreciate having her friends be so concerned about her.

He knew just how her friends felt. Hell, he'd known Cora a fraction of the time they had, and he worried about her. Too damn much. Even now, he knew that he'd see her home although she was perfectly capable of getting there on her own.

"I'll walk that way with you." He half expected an argument, knowing how hard she fought for her independence.

Instead, she gave him a shy smile. "Thank you. I'd like that."

Knowing the rickety nature of the porch step, he automatically took her arm to steady her. Big mistake. The slight touch was at once too much and not enough. He jerked his hand back to his side and set out across the yard, leaving Cora to follow as she would.

He had gone no more than a dozen steps or so when she ran to catch up. She grabbed his arm and planted her feet, spinning him around to face her.

"Look, if it's going to make you mad to walk me home, then don't." The teasing glint in her eyes had been replaced by a flare of temper. "Go back to the house and leave me alone."

"I said I'd see you home, and I will." He was being contrary, but he didn't give a damn. Being this close to her and not being able to do more than glare at her was an agony.

"And I said you don't have to, if you don't want to." She stood ramrod straight, daring him to argue.

"I never said I didn't." He tried to step back, but she wouldn't let him.

"I don't have time for your moods, Luke Gibson. Now either walk me home or don't. It makes no difference to me. But if you're going to act like a jackass, then stay here."

She was right. He was being a jackass, but it wasn't all his fault. He'd told her to stay away, and she wouldn't listen. Maybe her experience with men was limited, but surely she knew the effect she had on him. Hell, right now his body was demanding he do more than walk her home. If she didn't have enough sense to be a little wary around him, maybe he'd teach her to be.

"You have to know what you're doing when you keep waltzing over here, twitching your tail in front of me."

Shock drained the color from her face. "I do not . . ." Words seemed to fail her.

"The hell you don't. There isn't a man alive who wouldn't know what a woman's up to when she takes to baking pies for him." The heat he was feeling had nothing to do with the hot Missouri sun climbing high overhead. "Deny it if you want, little girl, but you're playing with fire."

That did it. She'd put up with his moods long enough. Whatever had his tail in a trap wasn't her fault. Her hand flashed out and smacked Luke on the cheek with a crack that startled them both. "I'm not a little girl!"

If her behavior shocked him as much as it had her, she half expected him to . . . she didn't know what. He'd never hit her; she knew that much without a doubt. One second, then another, passed, both of them frozen in the moment.

Then he spoke. "No, you're not a little girl, but you act like one. Doing whatever comes into your head without worrying about the consequences." He took a step back, putting more distance between them. "I've done my damnedest to warn you. Mind you, there's nothing I'd like better than to toss you flat on your back and take you right out here in broad daylight, but that's all it would be. I'm not a gentle man, and I'm not interested in anything other than hot, sweaty sex with no promises."

Another step back, as if he didn't trust himself any more than he did her. "Think about it, because if you keep coming around, I might just take you up on what you're offering."

If he was trying to scare her, it was working. But she also knew he was lying. There was a gentle side to his nature, the one that kept warning her how bad he was. Would he really do what he was threatening? The storm raging in his eyes convinced her that he probably would.

And, Lord help her, she was sorely tempted to let him. A powerful ache started in her breasts, making them feel swollen, and moved down through her body to pool in liquid heat between her legs.

"Luke, I . . ."

"Well, well, isn't this a cozy little scene?"

The sound of Jack's voice hit her like a bucket of cold water. Luke flinched as if he'd been slapped again.

"Did I interrupt something I shouldn't have?" Jack moved alongside the two of them, his eyes seeing more than either of them wanted him to. "Big brother, if I had to guess, it would seem as if you're thinking about doing more than walking Miss Lawford home."

Cora's face flamed bright red. She pushed past the

two men, tears of embarrassment burning her eyes. Her long skirt caught on a nearby bush. Ignoring the sound of tearing fabric, she yanked it free and ran for home.

CHAPTER 9

The burst of energy carried her as far as her front porch, where she sank down in a tearful heap. How could she have acted in such a wanton manner? It was one thing to lie awake nights and let unthinkable thoughts tempt her. It was entirely another to let a man suspect what was going on in her mind, not to mention his brother.

She closed her eyes and covered her face with her hands as she tried to gather up the tattered rags of her pride. Somehow she had to regain her composure before facing her friends, and time was slipping away. If she didn't hurry, they would be more likely to suspect that something had happened. The last thing she wanted was for Melinda and Lucy to start asking questions.

The first thing her swollen eyes saw when she opened them was a pair of worn boots standing right in front of her. She knew without looking any farther that Luke had followed her home. Just what she needed.

"Are you all right?"

The concern in his voice was almost her undoing. She wouldn't cry, not any more. She would . . . not! Pulling a handkerchief from her pocket, she swiped at her eyes and nose before answering.

"I'm fine," she lied.

"I'm sorry."

For what? she wondered. She had regrets, too, but none of them had to do with the possibilities that had been burning brightly in the air between them. Deciding she didn't want to know what he was apologizing for, she didn't respond.

"Are you still going to town?"

"I have to or they'll come hunting for me." When she started to stand, Luke offered her a hand up. There was blood on his knuckles.

She took his hand in both of hers. Then she got a good look at his face. One eye was swollen, and there was a bloody cut on his cheek. "What happened to you?"

"I had a long talk with my brother." He gave her a rueful smile and rubbed his jaw with his other hand. "He's a little harder to explain things to than when we were kids."

If he wanted to joke about it, so could she. "Did he understand what you were trying to tell him?"

"Eventually. I had to repeat myself several times." He started to laugh, but then winced. "Damn, that hurts."

"Come on inside, and let me see to that cut."

He tugged his hand free, the shared laughter evidently at an end. "No, that's all right. I'll clean it up when I get back to the cabin." Shuffling his feet, he drew a deep breath. "Look, about what I said earlier . . ."

"Don't worry about it. No need to apologize." Now that they were past the moment, she didn't want to start all over again. Both of them had said more than they should have. She kept her eyes firmly on the ground in front of the steps, wishing she were anywhere else.

"Cora, I wasn't going to apologize, at least not for

everything." He shifted from foot to foot, clearly no more comfortable with the conversation than she was. "Maybe I should have put it differently, but I meant what I said. All I want is to be left alone."

That hurt far more than it should have. He sounded so lonely, even as he claimed that solitude was what he wanted.

"Can't we be friends? After all, we're neighbors. It will be all but impossible to never speak when we live so close to each other." She dragged her gaze up to his, dreading what she might see.

The blue of his eyes darkened to the color of storm clouds gathering on a summer day. "I can't be friends with you."

"Can't or won't?" She stood up, standing on the porch step so he wasn't looking down at her anymore.

"Does it matter?" was all he said. Then he walked away.

Swinging an ax got old damned fast. Jack took two more whacks at the tree and then stopped to wipe the sweat out of his eyes. It didn't help that his fist throbbed from when he'd smashed it into Luke's jaw. He flexed his fingers, trying to relieve some of the stiffness.

On the whole, his brother had probably won the fight, but at least he had given Luke a dandy shiner. If it didn't hurt so much to smile, he would have grinned. They were a pair, him with a swollen nose and sore jaw, and Luke's black eye turning interesting colors. Their ma would have taken the strap to both of them for brawling.

At least it had eased some of the tension between

the two of them. The fight might have started over Cora Lawford, but both of them had other issues that had added heat. He glanced over to where his brother was busy splitting logs for firewood.

Luke had always taken life too seriously, and five years in prison hadn't helped. If the war had never happened, Jack figured Luke would have been married by now, maybe with a passel of children. A blind man could see that Luke was fighting some pretty strong feelings about their neighbor.

Did he think he wasn't good enough for Cora Lawford? If so, he was a damned fool, because she sure didn't think so. Hell, the air sizzled with heat whenever the two of them got near each other. He might have made a play for her himself, but he figured Luke had already staked out his territory, whether he knew it or not.

After taking a long drink of water, he picked up the ax to attack the tree again. He had taken a couple of good swings when he saw a horseman moving across the back edge of the field. The man didn't look familiar; Jack was almost certain that it wasn't one of Baxter's men.

He waved at Luke to get his attention and then pointed toward the lone rider. Frowning, Luke set his ax aside and picked up his rifle before walking over to stand by Jack.

"Who is it?" Jack asked, although he already had his suspicions.

"Sheriff Whitney." Luke shaded his eyes, trying to get a better look at what the man was up to. "Normally I wouldn't complain about anyone cutting across our property, but this is getting to be a habit with him."

A sick feeling settled in Jack's stomach. "Any idea what he's looking for?"

Luke gave him an odd look. "He thinks that the bunch down by the river might have something to do with some of the robberies we've been hearing about upstate. I think he's trying to figure out where they go when they leave the area."

Did Baxter know that the sheriff was sniffing around? Probably. There wasn't much that got past the man. Still, he'd find a way to mention it next time he spent some time down by the river. But maybe he'd be better off to stay away from the camp for a while, at least until the sheriff quit hanging around.

A few minutes later, the sheriff rode by again, this time in the direction of town. He waved, the first indication he'd given that he was aware of their scrutiny. When he turned his horse toward them, Luke took up a position right next to Jack. It was surprising how good it felt to know he was willing to stand shoulder to shoulder with Jack to face a possible threat.

When Whitney finally reached them, he immediately dismounted. He smiled, but Jack didn't see much in the way of friendliness in it. He guessed the lawman's age to be somewhere between Luke's and his own, but his lawman eyes were far older than his face. Nodding at Luke first, the sheriff turned his attention to Jack.

"You must be the other brother."

"I must be."

"Mind if I water my horse?"

"Be our guest."

Luke answered for the two of them, not sounding particularly friendly. If the sheriff noticed or even cared, he gave no sign of it. He knelt down to refill his canteen and then let the horse drink its fill. Jack thought about going back to chopping the tree, but Luke seemed to want to keep an eye on their uninvited guest.

Finally, both Whitney and his horse seemed have drunk their fill of Gibson water. "Thanks, I appreciate it."

"Anytime, Sheriff."

Up until that point Luke had kept to the shadows under the trees. When he stepped out into the sunshine, the sheriff's eyes narrowed. "Looks like you've been in a fight. How does the other guy look?"

Luke jerked his head in Jack's direction. "Judge for yourself."

For the first time, a real smile spread across the lawman's face. "My brother and I used to have those kinds of discussions pretty regular. I never can remember what would set us off, but I'll never forget how big his right fist looked coming straight at my face." He rubbed the bridge of his nose. "I've always wondered what my nose would have looked like if he hadn't broken it for me. Twice."

Jack hazarded a guess. "I take it he's your older brother."

The smile faded. "He was. He died at Gettysburg."

There wasn't anything to say to that, not even to ask which color his brother had worn. It didn't matter. They'd all known too many men who'd died at Gettysburg or a thousand other places. Saying you were sorry didn't mean a hell of a lot.

"Well, I'd better be going. Thanks for the water." He gave Luke a searching look before looking at the growing pile of stumps and downed trees. "I'm glad to see you getting so much done around the place. It's obvious you're both spending a lot of time on it. I'll be interested in watching your progress."

Neither of them spoke as they watched him ride off. Once he was out of sight, and more important, out of hearing, Jack looked at his brother. "What was that all about? Some kind of warning?"

"I don't know for certain, but I suspect we'll be seeing him ride by on a regular basis until he satisfies his curiosity about your friends down by the river."

A shiver ran down Jack's spine, as if a cold breeze had just blown through. It was one thing for Luke— not to mention the sheriff—to suspect Baxter and his men had been up to no good. It was entirely another matter for either of them to think Jack had been along for the ride. Rather than lie to his brother or protest his innocence, Jack picked up his ax and went back to work.

For now, maybe he should stick closer to home.

Cora stood at the window and watched the freight company wagon rattle off down the road. Agreeing to meet the driver at the school had seemed like a good idea yesterday. It was part of her job to oversee the delivery of supplies and to carefully record the inventory.

But now that she was alone, she wasn't so sure she wanted to be there. Memories of her last trip out to the school were having their effect. Despite the oppressive heat of the day, the windows were closed and the door was locked. She hated feeling vulnerable.

It didn't help that Sheriff Whitney had stopped by her house the day before with a sheaf of wanted posters for her to look through. At his suggestion, she'd gone through them quickly to see if any of the faces leaped out as being familiar. When that didn't net him any suspects, she'd gone through them again, this time more slowly.

She'd studied each sketch, looking for some identifying mark or familiar feature. Jake had hidden his disappointment pretty well when she'd handed them back shaking her head. The truth was that she hadn't been close enough to the mysterious riders to see much detail. At least none of the posters looked like Jack Gibson or his two friends.

She was glad of that, at least for Luke's sake. The last thing she wanted to do was accuse his brother of riding with a pack of outlaws. Even though she wasn't too happy with Jack, she didn't want to see him sent off to prison.

Deciding the books wouldn't unpack themselves, she turned away from the window. The driver had already pried off the top of the crates, so it wouldn't take her long to finish up. She resented Jack and his friends for making her feel relieved about it. Looking back, maybe she had overreacted, but she didn't think so. Maybe Jack had meant no harm; for Luke's sake, she was willing to give him the benefit of the doubt. But she still got shivers every time she thought about Jeb and Isaac because they had clearly enjoyed making her squirm.

She dug the books out of the box, making sure that she had them all. In her hurry to get done, she dribbled ink on the first book, staining it forever. After blotting it as well as she could, she picked up the pen and carefully labeled the book with the school's name. She processed the rest of the books without incident. Luckily, as hot as it was in the room, it didn't take long for the ink to dry.

The shelves were filling up nicely, she thought, as she pushed the last book in place. Stepping back, she looked at her handiwork with satisfaction. Fall couldn't come fast enough to suit her. She closed her eyes and pictured that first day of school when her students would file into the room, ready to learn what she could teach them.

A faint rumble of thunder rolled over the school-house, startling her. Where had that come from? When she'd left home that afternoon, the day had been sunny and bright. She hurried to the closest window and peeked out. A bank of dark clouds was rolling in from the southwest. It was definitely time for her to start for home. Quickly, she gathered up her purse and let herself out of the building, care-fully locking the door behind her.

Outside, Falstaff had quit grazing and stood facing the oncoming storm, his ears flicking this way and that. Obviously she wasn't the only one who thought it was time to be on the move. He followed her to the stump and allowed her to clamber up onto his broad back.

At the touch of her heels, Falstaff surged forward, breaking into a quick trot as soon as they reached the road. He didn't need to be told which way to go. Cora tried to keep him reined in, but the big horse seemed anxious to reach home. Besides being concerned about the weather, she kept a wary eye for any sign of Jack's friends.

For a second, she thought she saw a flash of move-ment in the woods off to her right. She slowed Falstaff down to a walk, waiting to see if she saw it again. Be-tween the trees and the thick undergrowth, it was difficult to make out any details. If something—or someone—was out there, she couldn't see it clearly.

That didn't make the situation any less worrisome, especially the way that Falstaff seemed to be listening to something only he could hear. When he broke into a rough trot, she fought him back to a walk again, trying to make sure they were alone on the road. This time, she was almost sure that she saw something moving through the woods some distance away.

The path to the Gibson farm was just ahead. She hadn't seen either brother for more than a week, not since the day the two had gotten into a fistfight. She supposed that Luke's various wounds were well on the way to healing by now. Never having grown up around boys or men, she found them to be a constant mystery. How could Luke and Jack do each other physical harm and then laugh about it? But then maybe throwing a punch probably didn't hurt any more than words could.

The rising wind caught her hat and almost pulled it off. The storm was getting closer. A limb snapped off to her left, hitting the road only a few feet behind them. Falstaff whinnied his protest and kicked out with his back legs, fighting to wrest control from her. Cora hauled back on the reins, demanding the big gelding listen to her. For a moment, he did, but the wind was whipping up dust and leaves, making it harder for the two of them to make headway.

She glanced at the sky and saw that the black, roiling clouds had caught up with them. The thunder was no longer a distant rumble, but a pounding drum driving them ahead of the storm. A few drops of rain hit the ground, sending up small puffs of dust.

Why hadn't she kept an eye on the weather?

She drew some comfort from knowing that the turnoff to her own home wasn't much farther down the road. Once she reached her place, she'd turn Falstaff loose in the corral and take refuge in the house. She considered letting the horse have his head, knowing they'd reach sanctuary that much faster, but she wasn't sure she'd be able to stay in the saddle if he lunged again.

Then all hell broke loose at once. A crack of lightning shattered the air, hitting an oak tree no more than thirty feet away, splitting it right down the middle. Sparks flew up in the air, hissing and spitting in the rain. To make matters worse, a buck jumped out from behind a cluster of shrubs right in front of them.

In the end, the deer bounded across the road and disappeared in the trees. Falstaff bellowed in fear, jumping up and sideways. He and Cora parted ways as he tore off cross-country. The last things Cora remembered were the ground rushing up at her, a jolt as she screamed and bounced in the dusty rocks, and then blessed darkness.

Luke paced the length of the cabin and back for the tenth time in as many minutes. Just as he made the turn, lightning lit up the sky outside. He clenched his fists and braced himself for another boom of thunder, wishing like hell that the storm would blow over soon.

At least Jack had gone to town for supplies before it all started, so he wasn't home to see his older brother sweating. It didn't matter that the war had been over for years; Luke hated storms, plain and simple. Thunder and cannon fire had become one and the same in his mind.

The narrow confines of the cabin closed in on him. More than anything he wanted to be outside under the tree, but that was nothing short of stupid when lightning bolts flashed across the sky. He settled for the porch.

There was less room to pace, but the air was fresh and he didn't feel buried alive. Sheets of rain beat the grass down, laying it out flat. When the storm played itself out, he'd check on his garden to see how much damage had been done.

He was about to try going back inside again when a sharp crack split the air, followed by a faint scream. There was only one person he knew foolish enough to be caught out in this kind of weather.

"Cora!" he hollered, as he took off running for the road. In seconds he was soaked to the skin, the rain pelting down hard enough to sting. He stopped after a bit, hoping to hear something besides the storm raging overhead to tell him where to look for her. He started forward, turning his head from side to side.

Nothing. Had he imagined it?

The logical place to look was the road. Knowing Cora, she probably thought the best time to make another trip out to that school of hers was right before the mother of all storms decided to sweep through the area. He'd gone no more than another ten feet when he heard something big crashing through the underbrush. Falstaff fought his way clear of the woods a short distance away from Luke, his sides heaving and foam dripping from his mouth.

"Son of a bitch!"

He approached the gelding cautiously, in no hurry to come within kicking range while the gelding was still spooked, but the big gray looked almost relieved to let Luke take charge. Once he had the horse by the reins, he backtracked through the brush, following a trail of broken branches to the road.

The air had a pungent smell—wood smoke mixed with rain. He traced it back to an oak tree, split to the ground and smoking, obviously the source of the loud explosion he'd heard. *Please, God, don't let Cora have been close enough to catch the backlash.* Fear clutched at his gut as he continued to search.

When he saw her sprawled and twisted, lying just off the edge of the road, he forgot how to breathe. She wasn't moving, and her color had washed away with the rain. He took off at a run, letting the horse follow as he would. Kneeling in the mud beside her, Luke reached out with a shaking hand to touch her face. He was rewarded with a soft moan. Another flash of lightning snapped and crackled overhead, leaving him no choice but to move her before he could fully assess her injuries. Praying he didn't hurt her more, he gathered her up in his arms, crushing her against his chest.

His cabin was closer, but her house would be more comfortable. She moaned again. He resettled her in his arms, wishing he had something to wrap around her. Although it was spring, the temperature had dropped dramatically with the onset of the rain. Already her skin looked blue from the cold.

He thought about putting her on Falstaff's back, so they could make better time, but decided not to. It would be difficult at best to get her up on the saddle by himself, but also the horse had obviously bolted once in the storm. Another fall might just kill her.

For weeks he'd brooded over how close her house was to his when he wanted to keep as far from her as possible. But now, with her life on the line, its proximity was a godsend. He kept his head bowed over hers, as if even that little bit of shelter might make the difference. The path to her house had never looked more welcoming than at that moment.

His arms ached and his lungs burned from the effort, but he trudged on, step after step, until he reached the porch. He staggered up the three steps, grateful to be under the cover of the porch roof.

Turning sideways, he leaned against the wall to free up his hand enough to reach for the doorknob.

It refused to turn.

Evidently all those lectures on caution had finally taken effect. She'd dutifully locked up when she'd left the house. But where would the key be now? Back in the mud where she'd fallen? Giving in to the inevitable, he gently set his unconscious burden down on the porch. If all else failed, he'd break a window to get inside.

On impulse, he closed his eyes and tried to think where Cora put her purse when she was riding Falstaff. For certain it wasn't dangling from her arm. Somewhere on the saddle? That sounded right. Falstaff had moved off closer to the corral, no doubt hoping to find shelter and something to eat. Luke braced himself to head back out into the downpour in hopes that he'd find the key somewhere on the saddle. He figured the odds were slim at best, especially knowing that in all likelihood the purse would have been torn off by grasping branches and underbrush when Falstaff had bolted.

But no, there it was, tied to the saddle with a leather thong. Rather than waste time trying to undo the wet leather, he grabbed it with both hands and yanked as hard as he could. Falstaff actually stumbled sideways a step or two from the strength of Luke's effort, but the purse broke free. Groping it, he was relieved to feel the keys inside.

"I'll see to you when I can, boy," he promised Falstaff as he ran back for the porch. He felt bad leaving the horse, but his first concern had to be Cora.

With his hands shaking with the combined effects of cold and fear, he fumbled as he tried to get the key into the lock. A few muttered curses helped steady his hand, and he was rewarded with a satisfying click as he undid the lock and opened the door.

At least she'd left the stove banked, he thought as a comforting wave of heat rolled over him. He dropped the keys on the table and opened the door to what had to be Cora's bedroom. He spread a quilt out on one side of the bed to protect the other covers from getting wet. With the path clear, he ran to get Cora. She hadn't moved at all, a fact that worried him more and more. He slid one arm under her knees and the other around her shoulders. Counting to three, he managed to lift her up in one jerky motion.

Twisting sideways, he maneuvered her feet first through the door and straight into her bedroom. After depositing his burden on the bed, he hurried back to the kitchen to close the door. It was imperative that both of them get warm and dry as quickly as possible, so he added wood to the stove and put a kettle of water on to heat before returning to her side. Once she woke up, a cup of hot tea laced with sugar would help warm her from the inside out.

Back in her bedroom, Luke hesitated, unsure where to start. All too aware that Cora was a decent woman, he had no business being in her bedroom, much less contemplating stripping her bare. Even if no one else ever found out, he would know, and so would she.

Out of options, he started with her shoes, hoping that she would regain consciousness long before he had to touch a single button on her dress. He tossed the shoes on the floor; he'd worry about drying them out later. Next, he did his best to think of God and country while he eased the hem of her skirt above her knees to reach her garters. He tugged the ribbons loose and peeled her stockings down the graceful curve of her calves. The stockings joined the shoes on the floor.

He quickly jerked her damp skirt back down again. Praying for strength, he reached for the first button on her dress. One after the other slid free, revealing the top edge of her white cotton chemise. Figuring he was already damned to hell, he quickly stripped her dress down to her waist, leaving her wearing nothing but the chemise.

It was wet, too; the white fabric clung to her skin, faithfully outlining each sweet curve. She might as well have been stark naked for all the protection it offered. The rosy tips of her breasts were beaded up, making his hand ache to test their weight in his hands. Feeling more desperate by the second, he looked around for something that would restore her modesty and his sanity.

A flannel nightgown, blessedly dry, hung on a hook by the door. He grabbed it, grateful for the heavy weight of the fabric. He gathered it up and gently slipped it over her head. Before guiding her arms into the sleeves, he slid the straps of the chemise off her shoulders. Once he had that done, he eased her arms into the sleeves and then worked the gown down the length of her body at the same time he removed the last of her wet clothing.

The whole process had taken no more than a few minutes, but it left him feeling exhausted. He tried to look on the positive side. He hadn't found any broken bones, Cora was now dry, and the blankets he pulled up to her neck were doing their job. Her color had already improved.

He ran gentle fingers around her head and neck. He found a large bump just behind one ear, no doubt the reason for her continued unconsciousness. Deciding she'd be more comfortable with her hair down, he pulled out all the pins he could find and then ran his fingers through her braids to loosen them. He grabbed a towel out of the kitchen and used it to dry her face and hair.

When he'd made her as comfortable as he could, he escaped to the kitchen. The storm raged on. He stood near the stove for a few minutes, wishing he didn't have to go back out in the rain and wind, but he had to see to Falstaff before he worried about his own needs. Bracing himself for the downpour, he jumped off the edge of the porch and ran across the yard.

The horse seemed glad to see him. The big gray stood stock-still while Luke removed his saddle and bridle. Next, Luke opened the gate to the corral, where the horse could get under cover. After putting the tack away, Luke carried an armload of hay out to Falstaff. Adding a scoop of oats to the feedbox, he patted the gelding on the rump and then headed back to the house.

He checked on his patient. She seemed to stir a bit when he called her name, a definite improvement. Despite his desire to watch over her, he was starting to shiver from the cold. He didn't have any spare clothing, which meant he needed something to cover up with while his shirt and pants hung by the stove to dry.

He set his boots near the heat. After hanging his shirt and pants over the back of a couple of chairs, he pulled them closer to the stove. He hesitated removing his drawers, but they were just as wet as the rest of his clothes. At least they would dry fairly quickly. He grabbed the quilt he'd brought from Cora's room and wrapped it around his shoulders.

Gradually, the shivers stopped. He winced as feeling

came flooding back into his fingers and toes, stinging like hell. A cup of tea was sounding better and better. Holding the quilt closed with one hand, he set out the teapot and measured out the tea leaves. While they steeped, he poured a generous dose of sugar into two cups.

A noise in the other room caught his attention. He adjusted his blanket, making sure it covered everything crucial, before hurrying into the bedroom to check on his patient. Cora moaned again, her eyes fluttering open. At first, they looked confused and unfocused, but gradually Cora began to recognize her surroundings.

And Luke.

"What happened? How did I . . . ?" Her voice trailed off. She asked all her remaining questions with a confused look.

Luke allowed himself one quick feel of her forehead, checking for fever, while he answered, "My guess is lightning struck a tree and spooked Falstaff. I found you lying in the road unconscious and brought you home. You hit your head."

She tried to sit up but immediately winced in pain.

"Don't try to move yet," Luke warned her. "I'll prop you up in a minute when the tea is ready."

Cora closed her eyes as she eased back down on her pillow. Other than dark circles under her eyes, her color was looking better and better. How soon would she notice that someone had changed her clothes for her and that someone was him?

He shuffled back into the other room, wondering how he would carry two cups of tea and keep his blanket secured at the same time. The answer was obvious. He picked up one cup and carried it back to the table beside Cora's bed and made a second trip for his. On a third run, he snagged a chair from the table and dragged it into the other room.

He sat down on the chair. "Cora, wake up. I've got your tea."

This time her eyes popped open and immediately focused on his face. He brushed her hair back from her face and then gently lifted her head up to ease another pillow behind her. When he had her arranged to his liking, he held her cup to her lips.

"Sip slowly. It's still pretty hot."

She dutifully did as he told her. Unfortunately, his blanket started to slip. He quickly set the cup down and grabbed the quilt before it embarrassed them both. Especially him.

"I'll be back." He bolted for the relative safety of the kitchen. He reached for his drawers, relieved to find that they were mostly dry, although his trousers and shirt were still too wet to put on. He settled for the blanket again.

His hope that Cora was still too dazed to really understand what had just happened died a quick death. She was waiting for him, her eyes full of questions he didn't particularly want to answer.

But Cora was Cora. She wouldn't settle for less than the truth. In the short time he'd been gone, she'd managed to sit up. "Luke, why are you wearing my grandmother's best quilt? And I distinctly remember getting dressed this morning. Why am I back in my nightgown?"

He had a horrible feeling that he was blushing. "We both got soaked to the bone in the rain. You were turning blue."

And now she was turning a bright shade of red. "And you were the one to . . . uh . . . change my . . . Oh, my."

She tugged the covers up higher on her chest as the real truth of the situation sank in.

She wanted to die right then and there. At least she hadn't been awake when he'd removed her wet clothing. If the blow on the head hadn't killed her, the humiliation of being put to bed like a small child might have. Luke seemed to read her thoughts.

"I'm sorry, Cora," he said, meaning it. "There wasn't time to get another woman in here, not with the storm and all. I was afraid you'd catch your death of pneumonia if I left you in those wet things."

There was no changing what had happened. At least it was unlikely that anyone else would find out. "I guess I'm back in your debt again. You always seem to be the one to come to my rescue."

She tried to smile, but it was hard to look at him, wrapped up in that quilt. Although she'd seen him without his shirt on before, there was something much more intimate about seeing a glimpse of his bare chest and arms while he was sitting in her bedroom. Beside her bed. Right where she'd been having all those dreams about him. Oh, Lordy!

Searching for a safe subject, she suddenly remembered her horse. "Falstaff! Is he all right?"

"He's fine. He might have a couple of scratches from running through the underbrush, but nothing serious," Luke assured her, holding out her teacup again. "Drink this and I'll get some more."

"Where is he?"

"Out in the corral. I stripped off his tack and fed him. He was shaken up when the lightning hit that tree, but it's nothing he won't get over."

Luke stopped talking and cocked his head to one side, as if listening for something. It wasn't long in coming. Thunder rolled down through the hills. His fingers, laced around his own cup for warmth, turned white. As the noise faded away, he slowly relaxed again. Of its own accord, her hand reached out to his, offering a small bit of comfort. He gave no sign of noticing, but at least he didn't brush her hand off.

"It's been a long time since we've had a storm this bad."

At first, she wondered if he'd even heard her, but then he spoke. "It always sounds just like cannons. None of us could ever sleep during storms, lying awake wondering which it was. If we were lucky, we'd get rained on. Otherwise, those damned cannon-balls would come flying over, tearing up the ground and blowing everybody and everything in their path to hell and back."

She didn't need to ask what he was talking about. It was obvious that he was lost in a memory, and not a pleasant one at that. There was pain and grief etched in the depths of his eyes. Ignoring her own pain, she slid over closer to the edge of the bed and reached out to him. He hesitated only a heartbeat before pulling her onto his lap, burying his face in her hair. She closed her eyes and held on to him for dear life.

The storm seemed to gather new strength, but it might only have been the one brewing in her bed-room. Cora knew the instant the flavor of their embrace changed. Luke nuzzled her neck, sending spicy shivers of heat dancing through her. Waves of dizziness, which had nothing at all to do with the bump on her head, made her crazy for his kiss. They'd come so close on other occasions, but this time she wasn't going to let either one of them run scared.

"Kiss me!" It wasn't a request but an order, or maybe a prayer.

Luke immediately angled his mouth to capture hers,

brushing his lips across hers twice before finally taking possession. When she sighed with the beauty of it all, he tasted her mouth with the tip of his tongue, darting in and out, tempting her to join in the dance. Her fingers tangled in his damp hair, as she drew in deep breaths of his scent: rain mixed with something that was purely male. Purely Luke.

With each passing second, everything about her became more aware of the man who held her so gently in his arms. He'd given up all hope of keeping the quilt around him, giving her restless hands free run of his bare arms and shoulders. There was such strength in him, but he used none of it against her. Instead, he held her as if she were a priceless treasure.

She ached all over, especially in her breasts. Pressing against his chest helped some, but not enough. Evidently she'd made her need clear, though, because Luke immediately cupped her breast with his hand and squeezed. She thought she'd die from the sweetness of it as he kneaded first one, then the other. The feeling was nothing like anything she'd ever imagined.

"Luke, what are you doing to me?" she wondered out loud.

She hadn't meant for him to stop, but stop he did. He immediately broke off their kiss as he lifted her in his arms and deposited her back on the edge of the bed. His eyes were wild and his breath ragged. She suspected she looked much the same.

At least he didn't bolt from the room.

"Cora . . ."

Her emotions were raw. "Don't you dare apologize, Luke Gibson! Not this time."

His mouth quirked up in a half grin as he sat back down on the chair. "I wasn't going to, but it's time to stop before things get too far out of hand. Hell, I was on the verge of crawling into the bed with you." He sounded amazed by the idea.

And she would have welcomed him with open arms, but she couldn't find the words to say so.

Then he turned serious. "Were you kissing me out of pity, Cora? Because the storm bothers me?" He flinched as a crack of lightning underscored his question.

"Pity? Of course not!" She wanted to hit him with something heavy for even thinking so. "I don't go around kissing men I feel sorry for."

"And you're not all confused because of that bump on your head?"

"No, I knew exactly what I was doing." Honesty made her add, "Well, maybe not exactly." It was strange to feel shy in front of him now. "I've never done anything like this before. Is that why you stopped?"

"Partly." He yanked the quilt back up around his shoulders. "But I also stopped because only a scoundrel of the worst type would take advantage of a woman who has been through what you have this afternoon."

She wanted to protest that she was just fine. But when she started to stand up, the sudden move left her head swimming. Closing her eyes eased the dizziness, but her entire body had evidently decided it was time to remind her that she'd been thrown from a horse and knocked unconscious. She sagged back against the pillows in defeat and exhaustion.

One eye managed to open up far enough for her to see Luke's face. The smile was gone, replaced by worry lines.

He reached out to brush her hair back from her face. "Cora, are you all right?"

She leaned into his hand, taking pleasure from the

simple touch. "I will be, but right now I hurt all over." And ached in places she couldn't bring herself to mention. She shivered.

"Are you cold? Do you need another quilt?"

"Only if it has you in it." She held her breath and waited, wondering if she'd gone too far.

His eyes matched the storm outside. "Cora, nothing has changed. I'm not looking for anything permanent."

"All I want is to be held for a while."

She was lying, and both of them knew it. Even so, he nodded.

She scooted back farther on the bed, making room for both of them. When he slid under the covers next to her, it felt like he was coming home. He turned on his side and gathered her back in his arms, right where she wanted to be.

CHAPTER 10

Sensations, new and wonderful, threatened to overwhelm her. She couldn't remember the last time that she'd been wrapped up in someone's arms. The occasional quick hug from friends certainly didn't compare to the cocoon of warmth that surrounded her now. Luke shifted a bit, tucking her in against his shoulder. She thought, but wasn't quite sure, that he pressed a quick kiss on the top of her head.

Slowly, the rhythm of Luke's heartbeat and the sound of his breathing seeped into her mind, making her drowsy. He seemed to sense it, because he brushed his fingertips across her cheek and murmured, "Go to sleep. I'll be here when you wake up."

That was all the reassurance she needed. Her mind drifted off, her dreams filled with silver blue eyes and a crooked smile.

Thunder boomed overhead, echoing off the limestone cliffs across the river. Jack pulled his collar up and wished he were any damned place but where he was. Huddled under the dubious cover of a couple of willows along the edge of the river, he felt like a target for the lightning that was ripping through the sky overhead. Why hadn't he gone back to the cabin while he could? He'd had a bad feeling about the day that had nothing to do with the black clouds that rolled in over the hills to the west. He'd grown up with the spring thunderstorms and knew all their moods. This one had already raged for hours and still had a lot of anger left in it. A few trees would go down. Farmers would fret over their crops. And by tomorrow morning, the sky would be blue and life would go on.

Maybe.

Earlier, he'd wandered down to the river to see Isaac and Jeb, but they hadn't been in their usual haunts. On the way back downstream, he'd run into a couple of Baxter's inner circle. There was no way for him to know if they'd been watching for him or not, but either way it didn't much matter. Baxter had let it be known that he wanted to see Jack. If he hadn't happened along when he did, chances were they would have come looking for him.

This way, at least, he had come of his own accord, and Luke didn't have to know anything about it. But what did Baxter want, anyway? Nothing good, he was willing to bet. Jack shivered, but this time it had little to do with the damp chill along the river's edge. It was bad enough to be summoned to meet with the outlaw, but being kept waiting for over an hour wasn't helping.

The only thing he could think of was the sheriff's frequent trips across the pasture, poking his nose where it didn't belong. Well, there wasn't a hell of a lot Jack could do about that. The lawman was doing his job as he saw fit. If Baxter had problems with Jake Whitney, he'd just have to deal with the man directly. But Jack wouldn't be the one to say so.

"Thanks for coming, Jack. Especially in weather like this."

Jack jumped about a foot. How had the man

managed to sneak up behind him like that? He turned to face Baxter, not at all liking the feeling of having his back to the man.

"A couple of the men said you wanted to see me." He stuck his hands in his hip pockets, trying his best to look only mildly curious.

"That I did."

Baxter took a minute to roll a cigarette. This time he didn't offer the makings to Jack. Did that mean anything? He hoped not. Finally, Baxter struck a match and took a deep draw off his cigarette.

"I hear the sheriff has been nosing around your place." The smoke hovered between them, preventing Jack from getting a clear look at Baxter's expression. His voice gave nothing away.

Either way, it didn't matter. There was nothing to be gained by denying it. "Yeah, he came by when Luke and I were working in the back pasture. Luke said it wasn't the first time he'd ridden through there. He seems pretty damned interested in the tracks leading across our place heading down toward the river."

"Did you speak to him?"

If Baxter knew the man had come by, he probably also knew that Whitney had stopped to talk. "Only briefly. He filled his canteen and watered his horse. Said he'd noticed how much work we've done around the place." Jack shrugged. "Then he mounted up and rode off. I haven't seen him since."

"He paid a call on that neighbor of yours. Looked like he had a handful of wanted posters."

Did the man have someone keeping watch over Luke and Cora both? If so, why?

"I don't know anything about that. If Luke does, he hasn't said anything." Or why the sheriff thought Cora might have reason to recognize anybody's picture.

"We leave again in the morning. Be ready."

"I'll need to make a trip back to the cabin to get my gear. I didn't come prepared to stay."

"Don't disappoint me, Jack. I'd really hate that."

As threats went, it wasn't much, but it was enough. Baxter walked away, leaving Jack alone with his confusion and questions. After a few minutes, he mounted up and rode for the cabin. The rain continued to pour down, gray and cold. It matched his mood perfectly.

No one challenged him as he made his way along the winding trail that led back up to the road. He wasn't foolish enough to think they weren't there, though, watching his every move. They'd still be there at first light when he returned. Baxter left little to chance.

Once the trail opened out onto the road, he urged his horse to pick up the pace, more to get away from the river than because he was in a big hurry to get back to the cabin. As soon as he started packing up for another trip, Luke would either start asking questions Jack didn't want to answer or stare at him in silence, those same questions hanging unspoken in the air between them.

He didn't much like answering to his older brother at the best of times, but especially not when he had no answers he could give. Baxter was up to something; that much was a given. But the last time he'd taken Jack on one of their trips, Jack had been left in their temporary camp with Isaac and Jeb. When the others had returned, no one had much to say about where they'd been or what they'd done, although Jack could guess.

After they'd returned to Lee's Mill, there had been a front-page story in the *Clarion* about a bank robbery less than ten miles from the makeshift camp where

Jack had waited with his friends. The money in his pocket had probably come from that same robbery, although he tried not to think about that too hard. After all, he hadn't actually been at the bank. He'd been paid for doing odd jobs for Baxter and his men. How many employees ever questioned their bosses really closely over where their money came from?

Not him, that's for certain.

The farm was only a short distance ahead. Before he got there, he had to come up with a good story of where he was going and how long he'd be gone. Luke was no fool, and it didn't take a genius to figure out that Baxter and his bunch had to have some way of making a living, one that didn't actually involve working.

A short distance from the farm, he passed a tree lying half in the mud, an obvious victim of the storm. He skirted around it before turning off the road to the farm. To his surprise, the cabin was dark. He automatically looked under the tree where Luke often slept, not that he expected to find him there. No matter how much Luke hated sleeping inside, he wasn't stupid enough to take shelter under a tree in a thunderstorm.

So Luke wasn't home. Jack dismounted and turned his horse loose in the corral. To his surprise, his brother's pinto was there, huddled under the lean-to that served as a shelter for the horses. Now that was a puzzle. Where had Luke gone that he would have walked?

That didn't take a whole lot of thinking. If he were to hazard a guess, he figured his dear brother had found an excuse to wait out the storm at their pretty neighbor's house. Not that Jack blamed him one little bit. Cora Lawford was a real looker. Hell, he had been tempted to make a play for her himself. But ever since that day at the school, she'd taken to looking at him like something she'd scraped off her shoe.

He wouldn't care, except that it rankled some that she preferred Luke over him, even though Luke was a convicted killer. What did that say about her? How dare she look down her cute little nose at him just because he and his friends had scared her a bit! They were only funning with her. And now she was entertaining a man in her house and maybe even her bed.

Maybe when he returned from wherever Baxter and his men were going, he'd stop by her house and see if he could get any of that hospitality for himself. If she'd bed down with his brother, she couldn't be all that particular about the company she kept. If she was all that worried about her reputation, what was she doing living all the way out here by herself?

He opened the door of the cabin and felt his way across the room to where they kept the lamp. A helpful bolt of lightning lit the sky up, making it easier to find. Once he lit the lamp, he stoked the fire in the stove. He didn't bother to wait for it to get warm before stripping out of his wet clothes. A clean shirt and dry pants went a long way toward making him more comfortable.

Knowing he'd need the wet ones on the trip, he spread them out to dry near the stove. When that was done, he looked around for something to eat. There was a half-eaten plate of beans on the table, making it look as if Luke had left in a hurry. Sometimes they left the dishes until after the final meal of the day, but they never left food sitting out. It only encouraged four-legged varmints to move in.

He carried the plate to the porch and scraped off the greasy mess with a knife. If the rodents wanted the beans, they could eat them outside in the rain.

Afterward, he held the plate out under the eaves, letting the water pouring off the roof wash it clean. Back inside, he added some water to the pot on the stove and stirred. The leftover beans would do for a makeshift meal after he packed up.

It didn't take long. Rather than dirty another plate, he sat at the table and ate out of the pot. Finally, he sat back, full but not satisfied. Damn, he hated living on beans and bacon. Come to think of it, he hated the cabin and the farm. If he stuck around, eventually the life of a farmer would suck the life out of him, just like it had his ma and pa. The war helped finish the job, but both of them had been old before their time, breaking their backs trying to eke a living out of the rocky soil.

He wasn't willing to settle for backbreaking poverty, no matter what Luke thought. It took money if a man wanted to make something of himself. Selling the farm was out of the question, so that meant he had to find some other way of getting enough money together to start over somewhere else.

If taking orders from the likes of Baxter would start him off, so be it. Maybe the man's luck would run out eventually, but so far he and his men had managed to evade the law. Jack leaned back against the wall, the rickety crate he sat on moaning in protest. He studied the ceiling, wondering how much money each man who rode with Baxter earned over time.

Enough to keep them in whiskey and food, obviously, but Jack wanted more out of life than a cave alongside a river. He had never stayed in a fancy hotel, but he had a hankering to. If he rode with Baxter on a few jobs, surely he'd end up with enough of a stake to enjoy a few of the pleasures to be had in places like St. Louis or Kansas City.

Or maybe he'd go west. He'd heard wild tales about what went on in places like San Francisco. Sounded like fun to him. He could always come back home if life on the road ever grew old. Luke might not cotton to Jack's plans for his future, but he'd never turn his back on him. They were brothers, after all.

It was time to get some sleep. Morning would come soon enough, and he wouldn't risk Baxter's ire by showing up late. He checked his clothes one last time and then turned in for the night. If there was time in the morning, he'd scribble a note, telling Luke that he was off to visit friends again. Luke wouldn't believe it, of course, but it would give him something to say if the sheriff came around asking questions.

Luke's right arm was asleep, but he didn't for one minute consider moving it. Not when it would mean disturbing Cora—nothing would make him do that. This might very well be the only time that he'd even have the pleasure of sharing her bed. He wasn't about to end it one minute before he had to.

The storm had moved on some time ago, leaving them surrounded by silence. She lay pressed against his side, warm and sweet, her hand resting just over his heart, her scent filling his senses. He drew another deep breath, trying to memorize the moment. It would have to be enough to carry him through all the lonely nights ahead, the ones he wouldn't be sharing with her.

Even now he couldn't quite figure out how he'd come to be in Cora's bed. If anyone ever caught wind of it, both of them would be in a world of trouble, with consequences that could affect Cora's life for a long time to come. If she thought the gossip about him was bad now, wait until the good people of Lee's Mill found out that they'd slept together.

No, no one would believe that they'd done little more than kiss and cuddle. Hell, he didn't believe it himself. Just the memory of her sitting in his lap had his blood stirring again. He couldn't imagine anything sweeter than coaxing Cora into spreading her legs for him. And from her response to his kisses, it wouldn't take all that much coaxing. But a man, even one with a tarnished reputation like his, didn't go around taking a woman's innocence if he had nothing to give her in return.

"You're thinking too hard." Cora, looking sleepy and content, reached up and traced his mouth with a fingertip. "It's too early to be frowning."

He captured her hand with his and pressed a kiss to her finger. "Good morning."

"Good morning." She gave him a shy smile but made no move to put any distance between them.

"How are you feeling?"

She tugged her hand free to feel the lump the fall had left on her head. "My headache is gone, and the bump has gone down a lot."

"That's good." He was at a loss as to what to do next. Hell, he'd never spent an entire night in a woman's bed. His body had some ideas about what should happen next, but he ignored the suggestions.

"Thank you for taking care of me." Cora raised herself up to lean on her elbow, allowing her to look down at Luke. "I could have died out there in the rain and mud."

Anger seemed a safe enough emotion to be feeling. "What in the hell were you doing out in weather like that anyway? You've lived here long enough to know how bad these storms can be."

She glared back at him. "I'm not a fool, no matter what you think, Luke Gibson. The sky was blue without a cloud in sight when I rode out to the school. As soon as I realized the weather was changing, I hightailed right for home. I would have been fine, if lightning hadn't hit that tree."

When she started to move away, he tugged her back down beside him. "I know you're not a fool, Cora, but it was pretty damned scary to find you lying there in the road unconscious."

"I'm sorry to have worried you." She watched his mouth as she spoke. Then she raised herself up to press her lips against his. As apologies went, it was a heart-stopper.

Evidently Cora had gotten over her shyness, because she gradually crawled on top of him as they kissed. It felt like heaven to have her sprawled across his chest, her breasts crushed against him. He wrapped his arms around her, trapping her there while he fought to hold on to his good intentions.

But they slipped right out of his grasp, burned out of his mind by the sweet fire of Cora's kisses. What she lacked in experience, she more than made up in her willingness to learn. Her tongue darted into his mouth, teasing and tempting him to reciprocate. One of her hands tangled in his hair while the other one kneaded his shoulder.

He allowed himself the dangerous pleasure of sliding a hand down the curve of her back to cup her bottom. Cora moaned and broke off the kiss. Her eyes were filled with heat, her lips swollen from his kiss. He let her slip off to the side, but he followed after her, pushing her back onto the mattress. This time, he was the one to start the kiss, but she welcomed him with a needy sigh.

He tugged the neck of her nightgown down and slipped his hand inside to go exploring. Cora's eyes opened wide at the gentle invasion, but then drifted shut as he nuzzled his way to her breasts. He circled the tips with his tongue until they beaded up. Then he suckled one and then the other, her skin tasting sweet and warm.

"Luke!" Cora gasped, her head tossing from side to side.

He was afraid he'd shocked her and started to move away. But she tugged him back down, making her needs known. When her legs stirred restlessly, he slid one hand down under the hem of her gown. He traced the curve of her ankle up to her calves, to her knees, all the way to the silken heat of her thighs. She was so ready for him.

But he had to ask, "Cora, are you sure? It won't change anything."

She knew what he meant, but he was wrong. If they finished what they'd started—what she'd started—nothing would ever be the same again, even if all they shared was this one morning in her bed. Was she sure? Yes, this was what she'd wanted, almost from the first time she'd met Luke. Would she have regrets? Maybe, but that wasn't going to stop her either.

She became aware of her nightgown tangled up around her waist and the power of his need pressed against her leg as Luke waited for her answer. Words weren't going to be enough to convince him. She placed her hand on his chest and pushed him away. For a moment disappointment flickered in his eyes, but the heat came flooding back when he realized that she was only asking for enough room to pull her night-gown off over her head. It took all the courage she could muster to lie there, exposed to his gaze, without pulling the blankets back up around her neck.

"Aw, honey, you're just so damned beautiful."

After pressing a quick kiss to her lips, he reached for the waistband of his drawers and tugged them down. Cora kept her eyes firmly riveted on his, not quite ready to look farther. Realizing she required a little time to grow accustomed to the obvious evidence of his need, he gave her one of his crooked smiles.

"It won't bite."

She blushed as she settled back against her pillow. "I didn't think it did."

His smile dimmed a bit. "But it might hurt some because it's your first time." He brushed her cheek with the back of his fingers. "I'll try to go slow."

"Kiss me, please."

"Yes, ma'am."

It was slow and wet and so very gentle. Even as their tongues teased and tasted, his hand trailed down to ready her for what was to come. One finger and then two slipped inside her, an invasion that shocked and thrilled her at the same time. She couldn't lie still, the need to move with the rhythm he was teaching her overwhelming.

He moved over her, pushing her legs apart with his. He rocked against her, letting her learn the feel of him, as he mimicked the same pulsing rhythm. She felt as if the world had narrowed down to the confines of her bed, and it was aflame with her desire for this man. Her hands tangled in the sheets, searching for something to hold on to. As if sensing her need, Luke's hands covered hers, sharing the comfort of his strength with her.

"Cora . . ." he moaned near her ear. Then with a single thrust, he mounted her.

The sudden joining burned as her body struggled to adjust to the blending of their two bodies. She could feel Luke trembling with the strain of holding still, trying to give her the time she needed. Finally, he began to rock against her, small thrusts that rekindled the tense heat inside her.

Her body bucked against him, making her own demands clear. He started moving harder, faster, deeper, the storm between them building with each stroke. Luke reached down to guide her legs up around his waist. The increased pressure against the heart of her sent her flying over the edge. Her body convulsed in a spasm of pleasure so intense she wanted to scream.

Luke's own release followed right behind hers as he shuddered in her arms and then collapsed, spent and satisfied.

It took a few seconds for the world to right itself again. When Luke pushed up on his elbows, she wasn't sure she wanted to see what he was thinking. But then he gave her a kiss that felt chaste, almost innocent, and she knew everything was going to be all right.

He put his forehead against hers and whispered, "How are you feeling?"

"You asked me that earlier." She smiled, loving the moment. And maybe the man—but now wasn't the time to think about that. "I'm fine. Better than fine."

"I need to be getting back to the farm." His words were laced with regret. "I don't know if Jack came home last night, but if he did, he'll be wondering where I am."

"What will you tell him?" The first tendril of worry wrapped around her heart.

Luke frowned as he gave the matter some thought. "As much of the truth as I can: that you were thrown from your horse, and I was afraid to leave you alone."

"Will he suspect anything?" Not that she was ashamed or embarrassed by what they'd done. But she wasn't ready to share the change in their relationship with anyone else, especially with Jack Gibson.

"I don't think so." He didn't sound all that sure. "I hope not."

Luke sat up, the blankets falling to his waist, preparing to leave the bed. Cora quickly averted her eyes. She'd spent the better part of the night with him. Even so, she was not accustomed to seeing a naked man in her bedroom. Or anywhere, come to think of it. She fought back the urge to giggle.

Her bedroom door opened and closed. She took advantage of the moment to search the floor for her nightgown. The sudden movement hurt, her body's way of reminding her of how much she'd been through in the past twenty-four hours. A memorable day, to be sure.

Once she had on her gown and wrapper, she started to follow Luke into the kitchen. She hesitated and finally called, "Can I come out?" through the closed door.

"Come ahead," Luke answered. If he found her sudden bout of modesty amusing, he managed to hide it. Mostly, anyway.

"Would you like some breakfast before you go?" And more important, she wanted to ask, *Will you be back soon?*

Luke sat at the table, already dressed and pulling on his boots. He didn't look up. "I can't stay. The longer I'm here, the more risk we run that someone will see me leave."

On some level she knew he was right. After all, he was only trying to protect her reputation. But it still hurt knowing that he could leave her bed and walk out the door with apparently little regret. She reminded herself that he'd warned her up front that he wasn't looking for anything permanent.

By the time he stood up, she'd wrapped her wounded pride around herself as tightly as she could. What did a woman say as her first lover walked out the door? Good-bye? Thanks?

Luke looked around the kitchen, probably making sure that he left nothing of his behind, not even a little piece of his heart. Cora followed him to the door. She'd resigned herself to his disappearing without another word. Instead, he stopped in front of her. Afraid that he'd be able to see how confused she was by her jumble of emotions, she kept her eyes cast down.

But Luke didn't let her get away with it. He lifted her chin with the side of his finger and patiently waited for her to meet his gaze.

"I'll be back later to check on you. Did you have plans to go anywhere today?"

"No. Lucy doesn't need me at the store again until day after tomorrow." And she wasn't in any hurry to face her friends until she had time to come to terms with all that had happened.

"Good. I'm sure you'll be stiff and sore for a few days."

She nodded and hoped she wasn't blushing. "I'm fine. Really."

Luke's mouth quirked up in a smile. "I was talking about you falling off Falstaff."

This time there was no doubt she was blushing furiously. "Oh."

He leaned forward, brushing a gentle kiss across

her lips, as he slipped his arms around her waist. She offered no resistance, happy to know that he still wanted at least that much from her.

He allowed them only a few seconds of remembered pleasure before moving away. "I really have to go, Cora. Neither of us can afford to have someone catch me here at this hour of the morning."

"I know." She managed a shaky smile. "You go on. I'll be fine."

He seemed to want to say more, but finally he walked out the door without looking back. When she was sure he was well and truly gone, she hurried to the window on the other side of the room to watch him walk toward the woods that separated their homes.

He couldn't know for certain that she was standing at the window, but even so he waved just before he disappeared into the trees. As soon as he was out of sight, she set about making herself something to eat, ignoring the tears that streamed down her face.

He had lied to Cora; worse yet, he'd lied to himself. There wasn't a chance in hell that things could remain unchanged between the two of them after the night he'd spent in her bed. He picked up a handful of rocks and flung one as hard as he could. It ricocheted off a nearby sycamore with a satisfying crack. He reared back and threw the entire handful, accomplishing nothing at all.

He felt her gaze following him each step of the way back to his side of the property line. It wasn't easy to ignore her, but he managed to do so right up until he reached the woods. Then, before he could stop himself, he turned and waved before he plunged into the underbrush.

What in the hell had possessed him to climb into her bed? He knew better, but he hadn't been able to resist the need to offer her comfort when she was hurting. He supposed he could blame it all on the storm. Without it, Cora would never have been thrown from her horse, and he wouldn't have been so unsettled himself.

But he had never made a habit of dodging responsibility for the choices he made, regardless of the consequences.

Consequences.

Oh, hell, he hadn't given a thought to one possible outcome of the night's events. It wouldn't matter in the least if no one saw them together if Cora turned up pregnant. An image filled his mind—Cora standing by that same kitchen window, her arms cradling a babe. Their babe. Their son . . . or a daughter. He stumbled forward, trying to outrun the need to go marching straight back to Cora.

He wondered if she had yet realized the import of their actions. He didn't want to be the one to tell her if she hadn't, but there was no one else who could. She should know in a matter of days or weeks, at the most.

"Where the hell have you been?" The question was asked casually, with only a slight hint of nastiness.

Luke had been so caught up in his thoughts that he hadn't realized how far he'd come. Jack was standing on the porch, drinking a cup of coffee. Luke brushed past him into the cabin. His brother followed right on his heels.

"If I had to guess, you spent the night at Cora Lawford's."

Luke was proud of his control. For the moment, he would let his brother live, but only for the moment.

"Shut up." He filled a bucket at the pump and used the ice-cold water to wash his face and hands. And the scent of Cora off his skin.

"Look, I know it's none of my business, but . . ."

Luke had him by the shirtfront, ready to plant his fist in Jack's face. "I said shut up."

Jack managed to hold his hands up in surrender. Luke let go abruptly, sending Jack stumbling back into the table. Luke threw some more cold water on his face, hoping it would cool his temper. He picked up the rag that served as a towel and dried off. When he thought he could speak without snarling, he turned to face his brother.

"I'm sorry. I didn't get much sleep last night." He reached for the coffeepot. "Miss Lawford was out at the school yesterday when the storm came rolling in. Lightning struck a tree just as she was riding home. Her horse threw her and then took off through the woods. The damned animal came charging out of the underbrush right over there." He gestured toward the far side of the yard. "I followed its trail back to the road to where I found her lying in the mud unconscious. After I carried her back to her house, it took a good long while for her to wake up."

Jack had the good sense to look worried. "Is she all right?"

"She will be. She had a hell of a bump on her head. Between that and the cold rain, she was in pretty sad shape." He sipped the coffee, feeling pretty good about how calm he was sounding. "I stayed close by to make sure she and her horse were all right."

He kept his eyes focused on the view outside the open door rather than risk looking Jack in the face.

He hadn't exactly lied about what had happened, but he hadn't told his brother the complete truth either.

"I've come home to do chores, but once the sun is completely up, I need to go back over to check on the horse. He seemed all right last I saw him, but the rain was coming down so hard, I might have missed something."

Jack tossed the last of his coffee out the door. "I'd offer to help, but I'm leaving for a few days."

That was when Luke noticed Jack's bedroll lying by the door. Just what he needed with the sheriff sniffing around all the time. "Where the hell are you going this time?"

Jack had his own fair share of temper. "I'll know when I get there. I'm going." He picked up his gear and stomped out the door, with Luke right on his heels.

"Damn it, Jack. You know the sheriff is keeping an eye on that bunch down by the river. If he can connect them to even one of the bank robberies, he'll have the whole damned bunch on their way to face the judge." He grabbed his brother by the arm, trying to make him listen.

Jack spun around, jerking free of Luke's grasp. "Listen, big brother. Maybe you'll be happy breaking your back on this place for the rest of your life, but I want more."

"And how are you going to get more? Robbing other people?" Luke thought about pounding some sense into him, but Jack wasn't going to listen, no matter what. Luke gave it one parting shot. "It's bad enough that one of us lost five years in prison. I can't make your choices for you, but you're one dumb son of a bitch if you think getting rich quick is worth the risk of spending one day of your life behind bars."

Having had his say, he walked away, leaving Jack to do what he wanted. Luke had enough problems of his own without trying to shoulder his brother's as well. A few minutes later, he heard Jack ride out. His stomach roiled with tension and fear for Jack. The queasiness made him glad he hadn't had more than a little coffee to drink.

He tossed another handful of feed on the ground for the chickens, and then looked up at the sky. He was a little rusty when it came to praying, but he gave it his best. "Please, God, don't let Jack be more of a fool than he has to be."

After feeding his horse, he headed back into the house to clean up and scrounge some breakfast. He'd need all his strength to confront Cora.

She needed a hot bath. It hurt too much to lift a single bucket of water, much less hauling enough to fill her washtub. At least there was enough hot water in the reservoir on the stove for her to wash up. It would have to do.

Breakfast had been a lonely affair. For months, she had enjoyed the freedom that came from living alone. But one night of sharing her bed with a man had evidently spoiled her.

She reached for a bar of her favorite scented soap and filled a basin with hot water. Feeling more daring than usual, she stripped off her gown completely and started washing up. It was slow going, though. Every muscle in her body felt bruised and sore.

When she was feeling considerably cleaner, she slipped on a fresh nightgown. She had no plans for the day, so there was no hurry to get dressed. For the first time, she risked a quick peek in the mirror.

Other than a few small scratches, her face bore few signs of her fall yesterday. The bump on her head had continued to go down, even though it still hurt, giving her a bit of a headache.

Her biggest fear was that the worst damage was to her heart.

A cup of tea would do little more than offer warm comfort. For the moment it was the most she could hope for. Once the kettle was on to heat, she looked around for something to keep her hands occupied. Finally, she picked up her sewing basket and settled into the rocker near the stove. The curtains she'd made for the kitchen window lacked only hemming. It wouldn't take long to finish those and the tablecloth to match.

The simple needlework required little in the way of concentration, leaving her mind free to wander. Which it did—through the woods to the run-down cabin on the other side. What was Luke doing this morning? Probably chores, she decided. He never complained about the hard work he did. She doubted that Jack did his fair share, but Luke had never complained about that either, at least not to her.

When would he come back? She appreciated the gesture but didn't really want him checking on her just out of a sense of duty.

One of the curtains was done. Before starting the next one, she threaded her needle and knotted the ends. She had taken no more than a few stitches when she thought she heard something out in front.

Was Luke back already? She dropped the curtain on the floor in her hurry to reach the door. To her surprise, a buggy was pulling up near the corral. Her stomach plummeted when she recognized at least one of the passengers. What was Aunt Henrietta doing here? She never paid social calls before afternoon and rarely without a specific invitation. Who had brought her?

She got her answer quickly enough. Cade Mulroney walked around the back of the buggy and held out his hand to help Henrietta step down to the ground. Lucy had been sitting between her husband and the older woman. Once Henrietta was safely down, Cade held out his arms to take his infant son from Lucy. Tucking young Roy in the crook of one arm, he helped Lucy dismount.

Although ordinarily Cora wouldn't have minded an unexpected visit from her friends, today was not the day. She stepped back from the window, only then realizing that she was wearing her nightgown and nothing else. Both Lucy and Henrietta would be shocked to find her in such disarray. Ignoring the painful twinges from moving too fast, she hastened to the bedroom, already stripping off her gown.

Oh, dear, she hadn't made the bed, either. As soon as she yanked a dress over her head, she did her best to straighten the covers. She was still buttoning her dress when one of her guests knocked on the door. There wasn't time to pull on her stockings, so she settled for putting on her slippers. Hopefully no one would notice that she wasn't completely dressed.

At least she had taken the time to braid her hair earlier. Having done the best she could with so little warning, she opened the door.

"Why, Aunt Henrietta, what a nice surprise."

"I doubt that very much, young lady." Henrietta brushed past Cora, pausing only long enough for the requisite kiss on the cheek. "Lucinda and her husband were kind enough to bring me out here to make sure that you had not blown away with the storm yesterday."

She pulled off her gloves as she glanced around the room, no doubt looking for something to criticize.

Lucy entered at a slower pace, offering Cora an apologetic smile. "Good morning, Cora. I hope you don't mind us dropping in on you this way. We won't stay long." She gave Cora a one-armed hug.

"You know you are always welcome, Lucy. Now let me have that handsome baby." Cora held her arms out to relieve Lucy of her young son. "I swear he is growing like a weed."

She looked past Lucy to see where Cade had gone. "Where is your husband?"

"He thought he'd cut through the woods to see Luke Gibson since we were out this way. Personally, I think he was afraid of being outnumbered by the three of us." Lucy smiled, knowing full well that very little frightened Cade.

"Well, come on in and sit down at the table. I'll make us some tea." She forgot to move carefully. She winced as a sharp pain shot through her side. Neither her aunt nor Lucy missed noticing.

"Cora! What's wrong?" Henrietta was by her side in an instant, looking gratifyingly concerned. "Are you sick?"

The pain was starting to fade, but Cora was afraid to move again. "I'll explain in a minute. You'd better take Roy back, Lucy, while I sit down." She sank slowly back down on her rocker, holding her breath until she was safely seated.

Both of the other women hovered over her until she waved them back. "I'm fine, or I will be. I'm just a bit sore." She bit her lip, trying to find the words to explain what had happened without worrying them. Finally, she settled on the truth.

"I had business out at the school yesterday and didn't

notice the storm approaching until too late. I was almost home when lightning struck a tree. When it fell right in front of us, it scared Falstaff, and I was thrown." She managed to dredge up a brief smile. "I'm sore, but nothing is broken."

"I'll make the tea." Henrietta filled the teapot and set out the cups. "I knew that brute of a horse was too much to handle."

Cora rolled her eyes. "Falstaff is a gentleman, Aunt Henrietta. It is hardly his fault that lightning scared him. It sounded like an explosion. Even the most docile of horses would have reacted the same."

"Did you have trouble walking home?" Lucy had pulled over one of the chairs from the table. She spread out a baby quilt for Roy to lie on down on the floor. The little boy lay on his back, kicking his feet and sucking on his fist. For a moment, all three women watched and smiled.

The pleasant moment gave Cora the time to gather her scattered thoughts. How much of the truth did she have to tell them? "No, luckily Mr. Gibson heard the tree go down and saw Falstaff running loose. He made sure that I made it home safely." By carrying her unconscious body, but they didn't need to know that part.

"Once again, I find myself in his debt." She leaned back in the rocker and waited for the inquisition to begin.

CHAPTER 11

The look Lucy gave her held a world of questions, none of which Cora wanted to answer, especially with Aunt Henrietta hanging on every word. She resigned herself to a long and painful discussion, tiptoeing around the truth.

Her aunt handed her a cup of tea laced with honey. "Drink this."

"Yes, ma'am." The hot liquid scalded her throat, but she drank it anyway. The warmth spread, settling her nervous stomach.

Her aunt wandered across the kitchen to look into Cora's empty parlor. "When are you going to get furniture so we can visit like civilized people?" Henrietta perched on the edge of the closest wooden chair, her back ramrod straight. "I'm too old to spend all my time sitting around the kitchen table. I like a little comfort."

The change in subjects had Cora's head spinning. "I've been looking at the catalogs. I thought I'd place an order sometime later this month for a nice sofa and matching chair. I'll wait until they come before I order the tables. The room isn't all that big, and I need to see how it all fits in."

"That sounds sensible. Besides, I have a table or two that I could let you have." Then Henrietta noticed the pool of fabric on the floor. "Cora Lawford, that's hardly the proper way to keep your fabric nice." She leaned down to retrieve it. After giving it a good shake, she folded the curtain and set it behind her on the table with its partner.

"I assume those are for the kitchen windows."

Cora nodded. "I thought the yellow would look nice in here. I bought enough for the curtains and a matching tablecloth. I was hemming them when I heard the buggy." Why wasn't Henrietta asking more about what had gone on yesterday? Surely, she must wonder how long Luke had stayed or how Cora had managed to take care of herself.

"Don't worry about working at the store the next few days, Cora." Lucy reached over and patted her on the hand. "I can handle it by myself or get Melinda to help me. You don't need to make the trip into town until you feel better."

Cora knew her friend was trying to be considerate, but the last thing she needed was to spend all of her time pacing the floor, alone with her thoughts. "I should be fine by tomorrow."

Lucy's eyebrow arched in obvious disbelief. "I don't think so. I can't imagine you climbing back up on that horse as slowly as you're moving. Don't deny you are hurting."

Henrietta smiled serenely. "She can always ride back to town with us and stay at my house for a few days."

Now there was an idea guaranteed to strike fear in Cora's heart. She'd waited years to get out from under Henrietta's thumb. She was grateful that her aunt had been willing to take her in, but the two of them were both too strong willed to live together under the same roof without fireworks.

There was no denying the obvious. "All right, Lucy. Give me two more days and then I'll be back to work."

She glanced in her aunt's direction. A rather smug smile flashed across Henrietta's face that left Cora wondering if she'd just walked into a neatly laid trap. Well, considering how sore she was, she was willing to concede this particular battle to her aunt. After all, anything was better than moving back in with her.

"Looks like Cade is back already, and he brought Luke Gibson with him." Lucy rose from her chair to look out the window.

Cora fought the urge to do the same. The last thing she wanted to do was show more than a casual interest in her neighbor, especially in front of her eagle-eyed aunt and Lucy.

Even so, she felt the need to explain the reason for his presence. "He said he'd be back sometime today to check over my horse. It was raining too hard last night to see if Falstaff had any injuries that needed tending."

Once again, Henrietta surprised her. "Well, let's not sit here like a bunch of old hens. Shall we join the men?" Without waiting to see their reactions, she sailed out the door, leaving them to follow as they would.

The idea was so out of character for Henrietta that Lucy and Cora could do nothing but stare at the open door. Finally, Lucy stepped around her son, who had fallen asleep on the blanket. She offered Cora a helping hand, supporting her as she pushed herself up out of the chair.

"I guess we've gotten our marching orders. Can you make it that far?"

Cora tried not to laugh. "I think I would crawl, if I

had to, just to see Aunt Henrietta chasing after Cade and Luke."

"What do you think possessed her to do such a thing?"

They'd reached the porch. Cade was standing next to Cora's aunt as they watched Luke check Falstaff's feet. From where they stood, it appeared that Henrietta found the process absolutely riveting.

"Aunt Henrietta invited him into her house the last time he was in town." Holding on to Lucy's arm, Cora paused at the top of the steps. "Then she fed him tea and cookies." Apparently she wasn't the only member of the family enamored of the man. She wasn't about to confess that particular fact to her friend, however.

"Well, I would guess that your aunt approves of your choice of suitors." Lucy started down the steps, but Cora yanked her back.

"Lucy! Don't say that!"

Her friend's smile was anything but innocent. "What's the matter? Don't you want your only relative to approve of him?"

"He's not my suitor, Lucy. He has no interest in anything permanent." She couldn't quite keep the sorrow out of her voice.

"And Cade had no intention of getting shackled to another woman. Have you forgotten everything I went through with him?" Lucy looked across the yard at her husband, her love for him so bright it hurt to look at. "We'd both been hurt. It makes a person hesitate to try again. But with the right person, it's worth the risk. You just need to convince him of that."

"But Luke wasn't hurt by another woman, at least not that I know of. It's everything else in his life."

Lucy paused midstep and gave Cora a searching

look. "I'm not saying it will be easy. But if he's important enough, you'll find a way."

By then they were too close to the others to continue the conversation, which was just as well. There was too much she couldn't say and too many questions she couldn't ask. Not yet. Especially not with Luke standing only a few feet away, pointedly not looking at her.

He could ignore her all he wanted, but that didn't mean she had to put up with it. She left the safe harbor of Lucy's side to stand by her horse. Running her hand down the gelding's neck, she asked, "How is Falstaff? Was he hurt?"

Luke didn't look up from where he was cleaning Falstaff's hoof. "Fine and no. Nothing serious, anyway. A couple of small scratches."

It took her a second to sort out his cryptic reply, but she was relieved on two counts: Falstaff was all right, and Luke would speak to her if necessary.

She rested her face against the big gray, grateful he wasn't hurt more seriously. He turned and nibbled at her hair, making her laugh. "Quit it, you beast."

Luke finished whatever he'd been doing. He patted the horse on the rump. "He should be fine. I put some salve on the scratches. His left foreleg seems a bit stiff, but that should disappear in a day or two."

Their eyes met over the broad back of the horse. Painfully aware that they had an audience, she could only say, "Thank you for everything. I don't know what I would have done without you."

Of course, they both knew exactly what she'd done with him. The knowledge hung there between the two of them, its weight almost tangible in the humid Missouri air.

"You're welcome . . . for everything."

The slight pause had Cora blushing. To hide her reaction, she hid her face in the horse's mane for a few seconds. "Would you all like to come in for some coffee?"

She avoided looking at Luke again, instead focusing on the others, who were watching the two of them with unabashed interest. Cade looked puzzled by the tension he sensed but didn't understand. Lucy stepped closer to her husband, slipping a hand through his arm. To no one's surprise, it was Henrietta who took charge.

"Coffee sounds wonderful. It will go perfectly with the cookies I brought with me."

The mention of cookies had Luke looking considerably more interested in the proceedings. "Are they the same kind as before?"

"I brought Cora a different kind." She paused for effect and then added, "But there's a plateful of the others still in the buggy. Behave yourself, young man, and I'll send them along home with you."

Luke, obviously not a fool, immediately stepped up to offer his arm to Henrietta. "If I may have the honor, ma'am?"

"Don't be foolish, Mr. Gibson. My niece is the one who needs your assistance today." She started for the house by herself, obviously confident that everyone would follow behind in good order.

Falstaff chose that moment to stomp his foot and whinny loudly, evidently tired of being ignored. Glad for the reprieve, temporary as it might be, Luke reached for the horse's reins. "I'll turn him out in the corral before we go in."

Cora kept them company, although he noted she was careful to keep the horse between them. What was she so afraid of—that he'd ravish her right there in broad daylight? He had no intentions of laying a hand on her. But he couldn't very well make a public announcement of the fact in front of her aunt and the others just to reassure Cora.

He glanced back at the house as Henrietta disappeared into the kitchen. What mischief was the old woman up to? If he didn't know better, she was playing at matchmaker.

He wanted to back her into a corner and demand to know what kind of aunt would push her niece at a convicted killer, one with no money and no likelihood of ever having any. Never mind the fact that he was fighting the urge to drag Cora behind the barn and kiss her senseless. A woman like Henrietta should know better.

He glanced back to where Cora waited outside the gate. No matter how long he lived, he doubted he'd ever forget the sweetness of her kiss or the way she'd moaned when he'd taken her hard and deep. Aw, hell, even the memory was enough to make him ache with the need to have her again. Fool that he was, he'd thought coming over while Cade was there would keep him safe from temptation. Instead, he was counting the minutes until the others went back to town so he could have Cora all to himself. Not that he'd do more than look.

If luck was with them, the only lasting effect of their lovemaking would be the loss of her innocence. He wondered if anyone besides him would notice the new knowledge lurking in the depths of her eyes or the sensuous curiosity in her smile. He hoped like hell that no one could, for both their sakes. He wasn't sure how he felt about being the one to introduce her to such things, but honored seemed to come closest to describing it.

"We'd better get moving, if you want to earn those cookies."

"Does your aunt go around baking for everybody?" He hoped so.

Cora tilted her head to one side as she considered the question. "No, not unless somebody dies or gets married or has a baby." She blinked and shook her head. "You must be special, I guess."

"I doubt that." Would Henrietta bake him cookies if Cora turned up pregnant? No, she'd be more likely to come after him with a shotgun. The realization didn't scare him as much as it should have. He came out the gate and latched it behind him. Falstaff was unlikely to wander off, but there was no use in taking the risk.

He didn't bother to look toward the house to see if anyone was watching them. They were. The back of his neck itched, as if someone had his sights trained right on him.

"Shall we, Miss Lawford?" He offered his arm.

"Indeed we shall, Mr. Gibson." She tucked her hand in the crook of his arm as they started for the house.

Along the way, he realized that something in the tone of her voice made him wonder if they were talking about the same thing at all.

It was taking every bit of concentration he could muster, but so far Jack hadn't thrown up. As accomplishments went, it wasn't much, but he was proud of it. As he sat in the middle of Baxter's men, fear churned and chugged around in Jack's stomach, making his hands sweat and his head ache something fierce.

He glanced around at the others, trying to keep his

interest casual but probably failing miserably. How had they learned to do this without shaking? Jeb and Isaac rode off to his left, bandannas tied around their throats ready to be pulled up once they reached town. Neither one of them seemed particularly concerned about what lay ahead. A youth of no more than eighteen or so rode on his right, his eyes wild with excitement, a big grin splitting his face.

Jack looked up at the sky, praying for rain or deliverance or a hole to disappear into. What would happen if the panic he couldn't quite swallow overwhelmed him? He didn't know much about Baxter, but he suspected the man didn't tolerate cowardice in any form. All of which meant that there was no way to back out now. Another mile or so down the road, his life would change forever.

If everything went well, they would ride into a town picked at random off a map, do what they'd come for, and ride out again in one piece. With guns drawn, Baxter's handpicked crew would charge into the bank to load up their saddlebags with other people's hard-earned money. The rest had the job of standing guard, making sure no one interfered with their business.

Thanks to the war, Jack had faced armed men he called enemies, but at least they'd been soldiers, not farmers and shopkeepers going about their daily business. He hoped to God he wouldn't have to take aim at some poor son of a bitch whose only mistake was being in the wrong place. He'd pull the trigger if he had to, but he'd hate having to do it. At least from what the others said, Baxter staged his raids with a minimal amount of bloodshed.

Jack tried to draw some comfort from that.

They'd picked a campsite close to town the night

before so that the horses would still be fresh when they reached town. It was unlikely the townspeople would be able to muster much of a posse on short notice, but just in case, it was important that the gang have fresh horses to ensure they could put a fair amount of distance between them and their victims before nightfall.

A short distance down the road, a couple of men rode out of the trees. One of them raised his hand over his head and waved it in a circle three times. Baxter immediately repeated the gesture. One by one, all of the others pulled their bandannas up around their faces as their horses surged forward into a ground-eating canter.

Strangely enough, the feel of riding four abreast and pounding down the dusty road left Jack little time for fearful thoughts, making him feel a part of something larger than himself. When he noticed the others checking the slide of their guns in their holsters, he did the same. The trees thinned out, revealing a town snuggled down along a narrow band of river. It looked like any other little village, lazy and slow moving in the hot sun.

That was about to change.

With guns drawn, Baxter led the charge into town, heading straight for the bank he'd scouted out weeks before. A few shots fired in the air, and it didn't take long for the people to start diving for cover. Jack's companions rode in deadly silence, but he could tell that more than one of them was laughing as women and children screamed and scattered like chickens when the fox came calling.

Baxter hit the ground running, with several of his lieutenants hot on his heels. When they reached the door of the bank, one hapless soul, a farmer by the look of him, came walking out right into the terrifying sight of half a dozen revolvers aimed right at him. It didn't take him long to raise his hands and piss his pants. Baxter brushed past him, leaving it to one of his men to shove the poor bastard stumbling down into the dirt.

Despite his own earlier fears, Jack found himself laughing at the sight.

The rest of the riders spread out, their eyes searching the windows and doorways for the first sign of armed resistance. There was movement off to the left. Jack brought up his gun, ready to fire as soon as he had a clear target, when a cat shot out of an alley, a pair of mangy dogs barking and raising hell right behind it.

Time stretched and twisted. It felt like an eternity since Baxter had disappeared into the bank, but it could only have been a few minutes later when the door opened again. One by one, the outlaws backed through the door, confident that Jack and the others had things under control on the street. Once they reached the questionable safety of the sidewalk, Baxter and the others tossed the heavily laden saddlebags to the closest riders before mounting up.

Then, riding in close formation, they headed back out of town, a hell of a lot richer than they had been minutes before. Dust and despair hung in the air behind them.

By previous agreement, they rode hard back the way they'd come, waiting until they were several miles out of town before they started splitting off into groups of two and three. Eventually, they all scattered in different directions, making their trail more difficult for anyone to follow. Jack tagged along with Jeb and Isaac until midafternoon, when they stopped to rest the horses and eat something. Despite the urgency of getting away safely, Baxter had warned all of them that a tired, hungry man made stupid decisions.

"Do you think they are after us?" Jeb studied the horizon, squinting against the bright sunlight.

Jack was glad he hadn't been the one to ask the question, but he'd give damned near anything to know the answer.

"Even if they are, what are the chances they'd be following our tracks instead of the others'?" Isaac dumped a cup of water over his head and then shook himself like a dog.

Another good question, though also unanswerable. "Do you want me to leave first or wait here until you two are out of sight?"

Isaac shrugged. "Don't matter to me none. We'll all end up in the same place eventually."

Jack thought so, too, but he suspected Isaac meant the river, not hell. "I'll go then."

He led his horse down toward the rocky shore before mounting up. It wouldn't take much of a tracker to figure that if three horses stopped by the river and only two rode off, the other one had taken to the stream for a while. On the other hand, it might take some time to figure which direction he'd gone. Jack would make use of any advantage he could.

Somehow riding on his own made him feel less of a target for a lawman's bullet. He stopped and buried his bandanna under some rocks along the river. If someone stopped him, there was nothing about him that marked him as a bank robber. If every man riding alone through the state of Missouri came under suspicion, the jails would be bursting at the seams in the next few days.

Feeling better, he headed for home, figuring to take a day or maybe two to get there. Baxter had made it clear that the men should come trickling back in over the next couple of weeks, hoping that would keep Sheriff Whitney from becoming suspicious. Jack's portion of the take would be waiting for him whenever he felt like picking it up.

He was just as happy to have Baxter hang on to it for a while. He couldn't very well open a bank account to keep it in, and Luke was likely to stumble across anything Jack tried to hide around the cabin. Jack thought about that new barn Cora Lawford had built recently. Maybe he could hide it there someplace. She only used the building to store feed for her horse, so she didn't spend much time in it.

His plans made, he started looking for a place to set up camp.

Cora checked her appearance as best she could in the small mirror on the wall. Up until recently, she'd been satisfied with knowing that her face was clean and her hair combed, but her neighbor had promised to come over to saddle up Falstaff for her. She could do it herself, but he'd insisted.

Not only that, he was going to ride into town with her. She shivered with excitement. Luke claimed he needed a few supplies, but she suspected that he wanted to make sure that her fall hadn't made her skittish around Falstaff. From anyone else she would have resented the interference, but it felt different coming from him. He never made her feel helpless, even when he yelled at her for doing something he didn't like.

The corral gate squeaked open, warning her that her escort had arrived. She adjusted the pin to keep her hat firmly in place and pinched some color into her cheeks. Drawing a deep breath, she debated whether to wait until Luke knocked at the door or if it would seem too forward to go out on the porch.

She settled on the latter, figuring it might seem more neighborly and not at all like a woman expecting a gentleman caller. Even if that's how it felt to her. After locking the door behind her, she stepped off the porch and walked over to where Luke was giving Falstaff a quick brush-down. His own mare stood dozing by the corral. Cora pulled out the treats she had for the horses.

The pinto lipped up the pieces of carrot Cora held in the palm of her hand. Falstaff snorted and sidled toward her, demanding his own fair share of the goodies. She laughed and held out a carrot for him.

"You're going to spoil the two of them." Luke gave Falstaff's cinch another tug. "They're working animals, not pets."

"No reason they can't be both. Besides, he keeps me company when I work in the garden." Cora laid her cheek against Falstaff's and cooed, "Don't you, my big pretty boy? You're my big baby, aren't you, fella?"

She kept her face turned toward the horse to keep from laughing, but finally she couldn't resist peeking at Luke. The look of pure disgust on his face did her in. A giggle slipped out, and then another. She gave up altogether and let the laughter come.

"You should see the look on your face!" She smiled up at Luke as she gave Falstaff one last piece of carrot.

A reluctant grin tugged at the corners of Luke's mouth when he realized that she'd been having fun at his expense. "Very funny."

It was amazing how much younger he looked when he smiled, giving her a glimpse of the man he'd been before the war had stolen so much away from him. She would willingly make a fool of herself more often for the sheer pleasure of watching him laugh.

"Come on, I'll give you a boost up."

He stooped down and cupped his hands for her to put her boot in. For a second, maybe two, Cora stared down into his eyes, wanting more from him than help mounting her horse. His eyes darkened, the smile gone. He slowly straightened up and stepped back.

"No."

The single word tore a hole in her heart, but she ignored the sharp pain. There was no way she could deny that he'd correctly interpreted her thoughts, but that didn't mean either of them had to act on them.

"You're right, of course. I can't be late opening the store." She gathered the reins in her hands and waited for Luke to toss her up in the saddle. She didn't wait for him to mount up, but instead started for the road. He caught up with her before she'd gone far. They rode in companionable silence for a while.

"How long are you working today?"

He might be making polite conversation, but somehow she didn't think so. "I'm not sure. Lucy was worried I wouldn't feel up to a full day, so she might have made other arrangements for this afternoon."

"I've got a couple of other errands in town. I'll do them first and then come by for my supplies. Maybe we can ride back together."

Was he thinking she couldn't find her way home alone? How did he think she'd gotten there before he came back to the farm? She pulled up and waited for him to look at her.

"Why?"

He looked puzzled. "Why what?"

"Why are you timing your errands around my

schedule?" She spoke each word distinctly, as if he were slow to understand.

Judging by the guilty flush creeping up his neck, he knew he'd been caught. "It's your first day back up on a horse. I just want to make sure everything goes all right. I promise not to hover after today."

The man was sure enough a puzzle. Only a few minutes before, he'd run scared from the possibility that she might want even a simple kiss from him. Now he was acting all protective.

"All right. I'll try to be ready when you come. But if Lucy needs me to stay longer, you have to promise not to wait around town all day for me."

He didn't like it, but he nodded. The two of them continued on their way. Once they reached town, Cora turned toward the stable where she left Falstaff when she was in town. Luke rode past her to tie his mare up at the hitching rail by The River Lady. She ignored him as best as she could.

A stable boy took charge of her horse as soon as she dismounted. Rather than wait around to see if Luke was going her way, she headed directly for the store. She didn't know whether to be aggravated or relieved to realize that Luke wasn't following after her. Of course, knowing him, he was worried about what people would think if they saw her keeping company with the likes of him. Imagine what they'd have to say if they knew the truth of the situation.

When she reached the store, she risked a look down the street to see if she could spot him. He was a block or so away, pretending to study the goods displayed in a store window. Considering it was the milliner's shop, she somehow doubted the sincerity of his interest. The silliness of the situation had her chuckling when she walked in the front door of the store.

Lucy looked up from the ledger on the counter. "Well, you're in a good mood this morning, Cora. Care to share the joke with me? I could use a laugh about now."

"The numbers not adding up?" Cora reached for her apron.

"Oh, they're adding up all right, just a bit lower than I had hoped for. That's all right, though. I know several people who are coming in later in the week to pay off their accounts." She closed the book and set it aside. "So what has you smiling so much? Could it be a certain neighbor of yours?"

Cora feigned disgust. "Ever since Luke and Aunt Henrietta have become best friends, he's taken to hovering just like she does. Right now, he's down the street studying the new hats Esther has displayed in her window so I won't know he is following me."

Lucy giggled. "I'd love to have seen that. I bet he had no idea what he was looking at. We'll have to ask him later which color of feathers he liked best."

"I think blue would bring out the color of his eyes." Cora sighed, thinking about how his eyes could go from the color of ice to the blue of a steamy, hot summer day in a heartbeat. Like when he was about to kiss her, even when he didn't want to.

"I'd be careful about having that look on your face around just anybody, Cora. People will be talking." The teasing note was gone from Lucy's voice.

"Let them talk. I don't care." She wasn't about to apologize for how she felt about Luke or try to hide it, either.

"No, but he might. Remember, he's the one trying to rebuild his life. He can't afford to have people whispering behind his back any more than they already are." Lucy kept herself busy filling orders that customers had dropped off earlier.

Cora immediately leaped to his defense. "He shouldn't have to worry about what people think. He's a good man, Lucy."

"I'm convinced of it, Cora, but not everybody has had a chance to find that out for themselves. If all they've heard is the bad stuff, then they might not be willing to hear the good." Then she changed tactics. "I should have asked earlier. How are you feeling? Do you still hurt?"

Cora let her friend get away with switching topics. "I'm doing much better. A few twinges when I was in the saddle, but for the most part, I'm all better." She started straightening the closest shelves. "Luke rode in with me to make sure I didn't have any problems with my horse since it was my first time back in the saddle."

"That was nice of him." Lucy sounded like she meant it.

"It was, as long as he doesn't make a habit of it." She'd waited too long to have some degree of independence to want to surrender it to anyone. Especially to a man who claimed to want nothing from her.

Well, something maybe, but nothing permanent.

Luke decided to treat himself to a meal at the hotel. It was too early for lunch and too late for breakfast, but he'd take whatever Belle was serving. He could read yesterday's *Clarion*, drink coffee, and wait for Cora. His footsteps faltered, debating the wisdom of that idea. Maybe he should keep walking awhile.

He had no business planning this day or any other

around her. He wanted her; he wouldn't lie to himself about that. But he couldn't have her, not even if she was willing. Hell, he barely had enough money to pay for a meal. It would be another year, maybe more, before his farm would be ready for planting. Until then, he'd be scraping by and feeling damned lucky to put food on the table for himself and Jack.

Jack. There was a separate problem, but he wasn't going to worry about that one right now. Jack was a young man and would make a young man's mistakes. Luke just hoped like hell that those mistakes didn't cost him more than a few hard lessons.

But Cora. She could cost Luke what was left of his soul.

Even now he could close his eyes and remember the scent of her hair and the taste of her skin. They'd spent one night wrapped up tight in each other's arms, a memory he'd treasure until the day he died. She'd been so damned sweet about his fidgeting during the storm.

And if he were the man he could have been, before the war, before prison, before every damned nightmare that had left him scarred and scared, he would have gotten down on his knees and thanked God for sending Cora his way. But a man, one with any pride at all, didn't try to share his life with anyone when he was too much of a coward to make it through a night under a roof.

What would she think of him if—or when—she found out that once the sun went down, he started walking and sometimes didn't stop until the sky grew light in the east? If he did manage to get to sleep, the dead came to visit, robbing him of what little rest he might have gotten.

He'd almost reached the store. Without missing a

step, he spun around and headed back toward the hotel. Yes, he'd eat, enjoy a good cup of coffee, maybe read the paper. Then he'd finish his errands and head home—after he checked on Cora, but only because he'd promised. This was the last time, though. After all, she wanted to be independent. So be it.

But damn, he wished things were different.

The lobby of the hotel was empty. It was just as well; he was in no mood for company. His luck held only long enough for him to walk into the dining room. The only other occupant was Jake Whitney. The sheriff looked up from his newspaper when Luke walked in, making it impossible for him to beat a hasty retreat without looking guilty.

Nor could he ignore the man, for the same damned reason.

"Good morning, Sheriff." He started across the room, but he never made it past the first table.

"Why don't you join me, Mr. Gibson? No need for both of us to eat alone." Whitney folded the paper and tossed it on the next table as Luke reluctantly took a seat across from him. "Won any battles against stumps lately?"

Luke had to grin. "A few. But I think they would have done well fighting with the Yankees. Every time I drag one out by the roots, there's another one right behind it."

"Well, don't give up. Eventually, sheer stubbornness will beat them down."

Belle came out of the kitchen carrying a plate heaped with eggs, biscuits, and all the trimmings. She set it down in front of the lawman and then smiled at Luke. "What can I get you?"

He eyed the sheriff's meal with an envious eye. "That looks awfully good."

"I'll get you a fresh cup of coffee in a minute. If you're not picky, I should be able to put another plate together pretty quick."

"Picky, I'm not. Anything you have will be fine, ma'am." He watched her disappear back through the swinging door before turning back to his companion. "If she brings me that much, I won't have to eat again for a week."

Whitney laughed. "I've learned it's the best time to come here. The breakfast trade has come and gone, and it's too early for lunch. She's just as happy to use up what's left before serving the next meal."

True to her word, Belle was back with coffee and another heaping plate. Luke followed Whitney's example and tucked into the food with great pleasure. Neither of them was inclined to chat until they had most of the delicious meal under their belts.

Periodically, Belle would stop by to refill their coffee cups or to see if they needed anything else. As tempting as that was, Luke begged off. "I have to think of my poor mare. Another meal like this one, and I'll have to start carrying her."

Belle seemed genuinely pleased by his backward compliment. "Stop by anytime. I need to start lunch now, so if you need anything, come knock on the kitchen door."

Both of them watched until she disappeared through the door. "Nice lady."

Whitney pushed his plate back. "That she is. In fact, most of the folks in Lee's Mill are nice people."

Luke wondered if the sheriff included him in that group. Probably not, at least until he satisfied his curiosity about the men down by the river and the Gibson brothers' connection to them. Damn Jack anyway.

"Another bank got robbed."

Luke wished like hell he'd walked right on by the hotel. Belle's excellent breakfast turned to lead in his stomach. He picked up his coffee cup, relieved to see that his hand wasn't shaking.

"That's too bad. You'd think somebody would catch the bastards one of these days."

"Somebody will."

Whitney's matter-of-fact tone sent a chill right up Luke's back. He had done nothing wrong, but he feared for his little brother. Did the sheriff know Jack was gone again? He hoped not.

"I hear Miss Lawford had another mishap."

It took a second for Luke to catch up with the sudden change in subjects. No doubt Whitney had heard about the incident from Cade or Lucy. Cora wouldn't appreciate her name being bandied about, even among friends. He also didn't want the story getting out, linking his name to hers again.

"She's fine." He didn't want to say more.

Whitney smiled, as if he knew exactly what Luke was thinking. "She told me about it this morning first thing. I'd say Miss Lawford thinks mighty highly of you."

Damn, didn't she have the sense to keep her mouth shut? Neither of them could afford the gossip.

Frustration and pure disgust had him complaining: "Miss Lawford needs to keep her opinions to herself. That woman doesn't show good sense."

"Most women don't, especially when they have their eye set on a particular man."

"Who is saying that man is me?"

CHAPTER 12

"Not me." The sheriff finished off his cup of coffee. "I was just making a general observation, not pointing fingers." He held up his hands, as if to prove his innocence.

Luke would've felt like a fool for being so defensive if it weren't for the amused gleam lurking in Whitney's eyes. He decided it wouldn't hurt to explain. "Cora was knocked out when she was thrown. If I hadn't found her when I did, she might have died. Hell, she was blue from being cold and wet." The fear in his voice was real. "I'm just afraid if the wrong people found out that I took care of her, they would think the worst. I don't give a damn in hell what anyone says about me, but I don't want Cora to suffer because of my reputation."

The amusement faded into something that looked like sympathy. "If it's of any interest to you, the talk about you has died down some. Having Cade Mulroney and his wife on your side helps. Eventually, I'd guess other people will forget about your being in prison or why."

Which probably meant that, as sheriff, he wouldn't let himself forget, not for a good long while. Whitney stood to leave, giving Luke a look full of warning.

"Unless, of course, you do something stupid that gets you sent back."

"I'm not planning on it." He'd die first.

"I'm glad to hear that." Whitney picked up his hat and walked away. He turned back as he reached the doorway. "Be sure to tell your brother I was asking after him."

Luke stared after him, wondering what the sheriff had meant by that last comment. Maybe he was just being friendly, but somehow Luke doubted it. More than likely it was the man's way of warning him that he had his eye on Jack. Hell, what was Jack thinking? Jake Whitney was no fool. It wasn't all that hard to figure out that every time Baxter and his men disappeared, a bank robbery report was sure to follow.

Luke tossed the money for his meal down on the table, seriously regretting giving in to the temptation to eat at the hotel. He knew the sheriff was doing his job as best he could. Luke didn't fault him for that, but he'd side with his brother against all comers, law or no law. If Whitney ever came after Jack, he'd be facing both of the Gibson brothers.

Damn, he didn't want to go back to prison.

Cora kept watching the door. Any minute now, Luke Gibson was due to come walking through it. She patted her hair to make sure it was still neatly braided for the third time. She'd even exchanged her first apron for a cleaner one, just in case he bothered to notice what she was wearing.

Meanwhile, she wondered which Luke Gibson would walk through the door. Did anyone else see the two different sides to him? Maybe she was the only one who had looked closely enough to notice. First, there was the warm, caring man who had held her all night with such tenderness that it made her heart ache. He was the same man who had escorted her to town after her run-in with Jack and his friends and had had tea and cookies with Aunt Henrietta.

Then there was the other Luke—the one with ice in his gaze and anger simmering just under the surface. He was the one who made no promises, ordering her to stay away from him and out of his business. She sometimes wondered who he was really mad at—her for tempting him or himself for wanting her.

Admittedly, her experience with men was limited. At best she'd only been an observer, watching the explosive courtships between Lucy and Cade and Melinda and her husband David. None of that prepared her for the confusing, complicated feelings she had for Luke.

She knew she could turn to her friends for advice, but she wasn't ready to share the depths of her feelings with anyone yet. Not even Luke himself knew for certain how she felt. Oh, he suspected, true enough, but he didn't know for certain, and she wanted to keep it that way.

She loved him, but no one needed to know that yet. If nothing came of it, it would only hurt more to see the pity in their eyes. If somehow, some way, she and Luke managed to work things out between them, there would be time enough to share the excitement with the important people in their lives.

The bell over the door chimed, reminding her that she was still on duty in Lucy's store. Pasting a bright smile on her face, in case it was Luke, she turned to face her customer. Her smile faltered and then disappeared altogether.

"Mr. Gibson, can I help you?"

"Why, yes, Miss Lawford, I believe you can."

Jack flashed his smile at her, but it left her cold. Looking back to that day when they'd first met, she'd found him charming. Now she wondered how she'd been so easily fooled.

"What do you need?"

He leaned against the counter, crossing his heels at the ankles. "Do you always try to rush your customers this way?"

She wished she'd looked busy before he'd come in. Instead she'd been caught mooning over his brother.

"Do you have a list of supplies that you need?"

"Actually, I came in here looking for you." His smile dimmed only slightly as his eyes traveled from her toes up to her eyes, lingering a bit on the trip.

She fought the urge to run behind the counter, to put its solid bulk between them. "I'm tired of asking, Jack. What do you want?"

"I want," he whispered as he straightened up and leaned toward her, "to find my dear brother. I figured if I found you, I'd find him close by."

"Why would you think that?" Why was he giving her that knowing sneer?

"Because he seems unable to stay away from you." The smile was completely gone. "It's a damned shame, really. I'm a much better catch, I have to tell you."

"I doubt that, Jack." She didn't bother to soften the comment. It was nothing short of the truth, and she didn't appreciate his trying to press his own suit at the expense of his own brother.

"I could tell you stories about him that would . . ." His voice drifted off when he happened to glance out the front window of the store. "But now isn't the time." He stepped back, putting a little more distance between them.

She wondered what had caught his attention.

Looking outside, she found her answer: Luke was crossing the street, headed right for the store.

"I told you I'd find him around you."

"If you are trying to be irritating, you're succeeding," she snapped.

The bell chimed, warning them they were no longer alone. She fought the urge to scurry to Luke's side. His eyes flicked toward her and then at Jack, a frown settling in between his eyes. He always saw more than she wanted him to. Luke stepped between them, standing slightly closer to her than to Jack. She wondered if his brother would read something into that.

He did. "I knew if I wanted to find you, I only had to track down your woman."

"What do you want?"

Despite his relaxed stance, tension was coming off Luke in waves. She held her ground, but part of her still wanted to take up refuge in the storeroom and bolt the door against both the Gibson brothers.

Jack smirked. "I just wanted to let you know that I'm back from my trip."

"And how was it?"

"Successful."

"We'll talk later." Luke didn't move, but his hands clenched in fists. "Now go on home. I'll be along presently."

"But . . ."

"Now, Jack. I have business with Miss Lawford."

The younger Gibson gave Cora a knowing look, as if he knew exactly what that business would entail. She ignored him, wishing he would disappear.

Meanwhile, Luke pulled a piece of folded paper out of his pocket. "Here is the list of supplies I need to pick up."

She followed his lead, immediately falling back on

her role of storekeeper. "It will only take a few minutes to get this packed up for you."

While she started gathering the few items he'd written down, he followed his brother to the door. She couldn't quite hear what he was saying to Jack, but whatever it was, neither of the Gibson brothers looked particularly happy. She was relieved when she heard the door open and close, but she continued to work until she felt Luke walk up behind her.

"Are you all right?"

She was now and told him so. "I'm fine. It's been a slow day, so I haven't had to work too hard. Lucy already had the shelves stocked and the floors swept. Mainly, I've just filled orders."

Luke looked frustrated and not a little angry. "That isn't what I meant. Did Jack do anything to upset you?"

He had, but she wasn't going to admit it. There was enough trouble between Luke and Jack without her adding to it. "No, it was just as he said. He came in to see if I knew where you were." She made a point of turning to look up at him, so he'd know she wasn't hiding the truth.

Luke closed the distance between them, running his hands up her arms. "Jack's going through some hard times. Sometimes he says things that he doesn't mean."

Like referring to Cora as Luke's woman? He'd sounded as if he'd meant that all right, even if he made it sound like an insult. She'd noticed that Luke hadn't corrected Jack, but maybe he knew it would only make Jack drag his heels about leaving even more.

"That's all right. He looks as if he's been on the road again. I'd guess he's pretty tired." She loved the feel of Luke's hands on her. "I know I'm always hard to be around when I don't get enough sleep."

"You're never hard to be around." His eyes were

going all smoky, just the way she liked them. "When will you be done here?"

"Well, I was almost finished, but I have one very demanding customer who insists on distracting me from my work." She felt daring, so she rose up on her toes to press a kiss against his lips. "It's difficult to keep my mind on beans and flour when he's around."

"Really? What happens if he does this?" He tugged her closer, settling his mouth over hers, doing a thorough job of kissing her back. It felt as if he was staking his claim. Maybe he was. She hoped so.

Her hands pushed his hat off to tangle in his hair. Her mind blurred around the edges, making it hard to pull together a coherent answer. When he pulled back, she blinked several times before she could speak. "When he does that, I forget whether he wanted flour or salt. Or maybe it was lace and thread."

"Well, I wouldn't want to let anyone interfere with your ability to get your job done. Maybe I should lock the door and turn the sign for you."

She managed to stammer out, "That will be fine. Lucy isn't going to reopen until after three."

Her pulse didn't slow down until he was completely across the room. Even then it took her several seconds to collect herself enough to be able to locate the rest of the items on his list. At least she had the answer to the question about which Luke was going to show up.

"I think this is everything you wanted." She quickly jotted the items down in the ledger, recording the total for Lucy.

Luke handed her the money to pay for the supplies. While she made change, he loaded everything in his saddlebags. "I'll meet you by the stable."

She'd hoped to walk with him, but obviously he wasn't ready for that. People were sure to notice if he was seen escorting her through town. She hid her disappointment as best she could. "All right, I have a couple of little things to take care of. I should be along in a few minutes."

She let him out the door and then locked it again. Rather than stay with her nose pressed against the glass to watch him walk away, she made herself stand back from the windows. He did move well, though, she had to admit. There was rangy strength in the way he was built, the kind that came from hard work.

She tugged off her apron and hung it back in the storeroom. Then she made sure the money was locked in the till for Lucy to count later. Other than that, there wasn't anything left for her to do. She didn't want to follow right on Luke's heels. She looked around for something to occupy her time when she heard a sharp rap at the door. The sudden sound made her jump. Between Jack and Luke, her nerves were feeling pretty ragged. She hurried to the door to see who was wanting in.

It was Sheriff Whitney. From the grim look on his face, he wasn't there to feed his sweet tooth or to pick up some soap. For the first time since she'd known him, she was reluctant to let him in, but she had no choice. If she avoided him now, he'd only find her later.

She unlocked the door. "Sheriff Whitney, come on in. I'm sorry the door was locked, but Lucy won't be opening again until later this afternoon. I was just on my way out."

"I won't keep you long. Someone told me they saw Gibson come in here earlier." He glanced around the store, as if expecting to find him still lurking in a corner somewhere.

"You missed him. Luke just left a few minutes ago.

He came in for supplies." And to kiss her, but Jake didn't need to know that.

"Not Luke; the other one—Jack."

"Well, yes, he was." How much should she tell him? "He was looking for his brother. Luke caught up with him here."

"Did Jack say where he'd been?"

"No, he didn't stay long enough to chat. Once Luke came in, Jack left." That much was true.

Jake nodded, as if she'd confirmed something he already suspected. "I apologize for bothering you, Miss Lawford. Tell Luke that I enjoyed our breakfast this morning."

He slipped back out the door before she could either agree to relay the message or deny that she was going to see Luke anytime soon. But she was, and as quickly as she could gather up her things. Something was going on, something that involved Jack and the sheriff. No wonder Luke seemed touchy around his brother.

She pinned her hat in place as she took one last look around the store before letting herself out and locking up. Since Jake had given her a message to relay, he obviously didn't care if she told Luke that he'd stopped by. Was that a message in itself?

Luke saw Cora to her door and then took care of her horse for her. Once he'd brushed Falstaff down, he tossed some hay over the fence for him and checked his water.

Then, as much as he wanted to follow Cora into her house, he rode for home. He couldn't decide if he wanted Jack to be there or not. All in all, it had been a confusing day, mostly because of his younger brother.

It was clear that Sheriff Whitney was sniffing around for evidence that Jack and the others down by the river had been out of town again. If he could verify they had, it would be the second or third time he knew for certain that their movements corresponded to bank robberies. Son of a bitch, did they think they could hide their activities forever?

There was smoke coming from the stove, so Jack had come home after leaving the store. Rather than confront him immediately, he'd take care of his mare first and maybe even feed the chickens. The more he acted as if nothing were wrong, the more likely the two of them would be able to have a simple conversation.

But if Luke stormed into the house, demanding answers, they'd fight for certain. The last thing he wanted was to drive Jack off, because this time he might not come back. The more Luke warned him against his choice of friends, the more Jack was going to defend them.

Hell, he even understood Jack's need for something more exciting than working the farm. He'd been young once, back before the war stole the youth of a generation. Once the possibilities had seemed endless; the world outside of Lee's Mill had been full of opportunities for a young man feeling restless. Some of those opportunities probably still existed if a man was willing to work hard. Unfortunately, Jack seemed to be more interested in earning his way with his gun rather than his strong back or his mind.

Evidently Jack had been watching for him. Luke barely had time to unsaddle his mare before his brother appeared at the corral gate. He watched in silence while Luke saw to his horse's needs.

"I put some stew on to cook."

Luke picked up his saddle. "Sounds good. It's been a long day." Jack followed him into the barn.

"So are you seriously courting our Miss Lawford?"

The question grated, just as Jack knew it would. "She's not *our* anything."

"She wants to be."

"People want things they can't have all the time." Like him. He wanted her so much it hurt.

"You're a fool, Luke. Take what she's offering, even if it's only for a few nights. Get her out of your system."

"You must want your nose broken, little brother." Luke said it without any rancor, determined to work the conversation around to Jack's problem with the sheriff without losing his temper. He scooped up a can of chicken feed and went outside to toss it to the noisy birds.

"I like my nose just fine as it is," Jack answered agreeably. "I also like the lovely Miss Lawford. If you're not interested, say so and step out of the way. Let me have a run at her."

"Go to hell, Jack."

He dumped the chicken feed in a pile, leaving them to fight over it. For a peaceful minute or so, the two of them stood side by side and watched the hens squabbling over their evening meal. It felt good to share the moment, at least to Luke. He had no idea what Jack was feeling.

"I had breakfast with Jake Whitney this morning." He didn't have to look at Jack to feel the sudden increase in tension. "I decided to splurge on a decent meal. When I walked into Belle's dining room, the sheriff was the only other customer. Short of insulting the man, there was no way to avoid him." He didn't want Jack to think he and the sheriff were becoming friends, although under other circumstances, they might have.

He risked a quick glance to see how Jack was reacting, but his face was completely expressionless. "Mostly we just ate. Hell, Belle's cooking is so good, it would have been a shame to let it get cold."

"I've eaten there once or twice. You're right about the food." Jack bent down and picked a stalk of grass to chew on. "What all did our wonderful sheriff have to say?"

"Not much. He thought the talk about me had died down some." There was no need to tell Jack what had been said about Luke's role in saving Cora. "He asked about you. Wanted me to tell you so."

"I don't suppose you think he was only being friendly." Jack sounded unconcerned one way or the other.

"Well, he didn't say more than that, but I had a feeling he suspected that you'd been gone again." He paused briefly to let that sink in before he delivered the final message. "Later, after you and I had both left the store, he stopped in to see Cora. Someone had told him that you'd been there. Whitney asked Cora if you'd said anything about where you'd been."

Jack's temper finally slipped loose. "Why won't that son of a bitch mind his own business?"

"He probably thinks it is his business as long as he suspects your friends have been up to no good." He skirted the issue of what Jack himself had been doing. For the life of him, he couldn't figure out how to ask him or if he even wanted to know.

"I'd better go check on the stew."

Jack started to walk away, but Luke reached out to grab him by the arm. Jack stopped. He glanced down at Luke's hand and then jerked free of his grasp. "Don't push it, Luke."

"Don't push what, Jack? What have you got to hide? Is Whitney right to be concerned about what you've been doing when you're gone?"

"What I've been doing is my business, big brother. You and your good friend the sheriff need to keep your noses out of it."

Luke wanted to argue, but it was hard to convince someone to pay attention when he had no intention of listening. And maybe Jack was right. It was his business, not Luke's. Besides, he'd fought too many battles in his lifetime to want to become entangled in another losing cause. The best he could hope for was that Jack would wise up in time to save himself.

After a bit, he followed Jack toward the house. He tried to tell himself that he'd done all he could for his brother by warning him that the sheriff was interested in him and the others. If Jack wasn't smart enough to get out of it on his own, then there wasn't much more Luke could do.

Before going inside, he automatically looked toward Cora's place. A thin trail of smoke showed over the treetops. He drew some comfort from knowing she was nearby; he fought the temptation to walk away from his own home to seek sanctuary in hers.

The smoke faded and disappeared as a small breeze stirred the air. What was she doing? Probably cooking herself a meal or maybe doing some of the stuff that always seemed to occupy a woman's hands—sewing, maybe. He wished he could be there to watch. He'd always loved to sit on the floor at his mother's feet while she worked a needle—her prize possession—in and out of a piece of fabric.

He'd yet to figure out how to bring up the subject

of pregnancy with Cora. He didn't want to worry her needlessly, but neither could they ignore the possibility. The amazing thing was that he wasn't all that worried. If he'd made her pregnant, he'd stand by her. If she'd let him. Somehow he knew she would fight him on it, especially when she knew he had no intentions of getting married otherwise.

And fool that he was, he found himself almost wishing . . .

"I swear, big brother, you're positively moonstruck about that woman." Jack stood leaning against the doorframe. "I have to say, it's positively pitiful to watch a grown man get all tied up in knots by a pair of pretty . . . uh . . . eyes."

"Shut up, Jack." He seemed to be saying that a lot lately. The truth was that he wished he could talk to someone about what he was feeling, but Jack wasn't that person.

He followed his brother into the cabin feeling more lonely than alone.

Jack was leaving again. Luke knew it in his gut, and this time it was unlikely he'd return anytime soon. He'd pretended not to notice when Jack repacked his saddlebags and set them where he could reach them easily. If that hadn't been obvious enough, there was the little matter of his leaving his horse saddled and ready out in the corral.

He supposed he could let Jack slip out, thinking his departure went unnoticed, but that wasn't going to happen. With Whitney on Baxter's trail—and therefore Jack's—there was a good chance it could be a long time before Luke saw his brother again.

The moon rose in the sky, its silvery glow casting the

night in a contrast of stark light and deep shadows. Luke stretched out on his bedroll and waited, wishing there were something he could do to change things. Dealing with his own problems took so much of his time and energy that he hadn't had much left over to help Jack with his.

Another regret he'd have to live with. Damn.

The sound of rusty hinges whispered in the night air. Luke stayed still as he waited for his brother to leave the cabin. Just as he expected, Jack was on the porch. He stared in Luke's direction, probably trying to decide whether or not he was asleep.

Once Jack headed for the corral, Luke kicked free of his blankets. He might have to let Jack leave, but he wouldn't let him go without saying something, even if it was only good-bye. He didn't bother with his boots, figuring his approach would go unnoticed longer without them.

Luck was with him. He caught up with Jack before he had a chance to reach the gate. "Leaving without saying good-bye, little brother?"

His voice startled Jack, but not so much that he went for his gun. "Good-bye," Jack muttered as he reached for the latch. "What are you doing up?"

"I'm up most nights."

"Well, go back to bed. I'm a big boy and can take care of myself." Jack led his horse out of the corral. After tossing his saddlebags across its back, he lifted up the stirrup to check the cinch. "If you've got something else to say, spit it out. Otherwise, I'm going."

There was so much to say, but he couldn't find the words, at least the right ones. He had to try, though. "Jack, listen. I know working the farm was my idea, not yours. I even understand that there's nothing in Lee's Mill for you, at least not right now."

Jack picked up his rifle and slid it into its scabbard and mounted up. He looked down at Luke. "And?"

"I just want you to be careful, no matter where you go or what you do. Men like Baxter have a habit of dragging others down with them. Leave if you have to, but don't—"

Jack cut him off. "Look, I've got to be going."

Luke stepped back, knowing he'd done all he could, and that it wasn't enough. "Watch your back, little brother. Keep in touch. We've already lost too much time."

"I wasn't the one in prison."

Luke bit the back the urge to yell, *But you might end up there if you aren't careful.*

Jack's bitterness burned like acid, leaving Luke sick at heart. He couldn't stand still and watch Jack disappear into the woods, possibly forever. Instead, he started pacing and wondered if he walked long enough and far enough, could he leave the past and his memories behind him.

Jack reached the road and debated which way to turn. The saloons would still be open in Lee's Mill, and a bottle of whiskey sounded damned good to him. On the other hand, chances were that the sheriff would also be running loose in town. He was in no mood to put up with the bastard's poking his nose where it didn't belong.

He looked back toward the cabin but couldn't see it. He'd already put too much distance between himself and the farm. It was no longer home to him and hadn't been for a damned long time. Maybe it was all those years he'd spent alone, wandering from place to place waiting for Luke to come back.

But neither of them was happy sharing that ramshackle cabin with the other. Luke wanted too much, and Jack had too little to give him. Despite their best intentions, they'd grown apart. Maybe it was that simple.

He passed the path to Cora Lawford's house. On a whim, he turned off the road and cut through the woods. When he reached the edge of the clearing, he stopped and waited. It took only a few minutes before his patience was rewarded.

His noble big brother emerged from the shadows off to his left. He'd suspected all along that Luke's nightly walks might lead him to Cora's porch. The only question had been if the porch was as far as he went. Knowing Luke's misguided sense of honor, he wouldn't think of crossing her threshold, no matter how badly he wanted to.

The fool.

Anybody with two eyes could see that she had some strong feelings for Luke, but apparently he was too stupid or too blind to take note. Hell, it was enough to make Jack want to pound his brother's head against a handy tree. He'd meant what he'd said earlier. If Luke wasn't interested in bedding her, he could at least get the hell out of Jack's way. He wouldn't mind spending his nights exploring all the possibilities of Cora Lawford's bed.

He wondered how that tart mouth of hers would feel . . .

Before he could complete that thought, he realized that Luke was walking in his direction. There'd be hell to pay if he caught Jack lurking outside of Cora's house. He'd never believe that Jack had only meant to see if Luke had come that way. But if he moved now, Luke would spot him for certain. Why hadn't he kept to the road?

Fortunately, Luke was too intent on Cora's house to notice much else. He stood staring at the front door. Was he thinking about paying a call on the lady at this late hour? Jack found himself hoping that Luke would take that first step forward. Maybe his brother would find some peace with Cora if he'd just give himself a chance.

Then Luke was gone in the blink of an eye, back the way he'd come. Jack shook his head in pure disgust as he waited to make sure he didn't return. That bottle of whiskey was sounding better by the minute. To hell with Sheriff Whitney; he wasn't enough of a threat to keep Jack from spending a few hours at The River Lady. After a few drinks and some poker, he'd ride for the river and throw his lot in with Baxter and his men once and for all.

Unlike Luke, the outlaw leader was honest about what he wanted—other people's money. In fact, if it had been Baxter who had caught Cora's eye, he wouldn't have hesitated more than a second or two to take what she offered. Luke's nobility was only going to keep him lonely and poor. It was enough to leave a bad taste in Jack's mouth. He urged his horse into a canter. The faster he reached town, the sooner he could wash his mouth out with whiskey.

For the second time in a week, Cora had someone pounding on her front door before she had a chance to get dressed. At least this time, it wasn't her Aunt Henrietta. That didn't mean she was exactly happy to find Luke glaring at her when she opened the door.

She'd no sooner invited him in than he was scolding her.

"Next time don't open the door until you know who is standing on the other side."

"Luke Gibson, get out of my kitchen and go home. I don't need you or anybody else to treat me like a child." She pointed to the door and waited for him to leave.

"I'm not going anywhere, not until we talk." He folded his arms across his chest, making it clear that he wasn't going to be ordered out.

"Fine. I'm willing to talk, but I won't be lectured." She slammed the door and walked past him into her bedroom. "Sit down and be quiet while I get dressed."

She took her time, partially to let him stew for a while, but also to make herself look presentable. Not that Luke had taken any trouble to clean up before pounding on her door. He looked as if he hadn't slept; certainly he hadn't shaved. The shadow of a beard gave him a rough look that had her pulse racing. How would it feel against her skin?

If they could quit fighting, maybe he'd let her find out. She unbraided her hair and ran several strokes of the brush through it. Instead of braiding it as she normally would, she left it loose to tumble down past the middle of her back. Satisfied that she'd done as much as she could in a short amount of time, she set her shoulders and walked out to face Luke.

He was still standing right where she'd left him. It didn't appear that he'd moved at all while she was out of sight. Stubborn man. Well, she hadn't had break-fast yet and figured it was likely that he hadn't either. Whatever he had to say could wait until she fixed them both a simple meal.

"You might as well sit down, because I'm not going to talk to you until I've made coffee." She gestured toward the closest chair. "If it makes you feel better, you can glare at my back while I cook."

She wasn't sure, but she thought she might have heard a muffled laugh when she bent down to add wood to the stove. When she peeked at her guest, however, he still looked grim. Fine, let him be that way. She picked up a basket and handed it to him.

"If you won't sit, at least make yourself useful. Gather the eggs and bring in a bucket of fresh water."

After a moment's hesitation, Luke took the basket and slammed out of the kitchen. She quickly pulled the curtains aside to see if he was going to do chores or leave. It was a relief to see him start toward the pump. He took the time to give Falstaff fresh water before filling a bucket to carry into the house. He set it on the porch before heading back out to the small pen where she kept a few chickens.

By the time he was finished, she had bacon sizzling in the skillet and the coffee ready to pour. It took only minutes to fry up the eggs and set a plate in front of her grumpy guest. She picked up her own meal and sat down across from him. For some reason, she felt the need to keep the expanse of wood between them.

At least he didn't refuse to eat. She wasn't sure how well the bacon and eggs would have settled in her stomach with Luke glaring at her the whole time she ate. After a bit, Luke walked over to the stove to pour himself more coffee. Before he set the pot back down he waved it at her, silently asking if she wanted more. She held out her cup in answer. If he didn't want to talk, fine.

The whole situation was starting to amuse her. How long could two adults sit at the same table without saying a word? She gathered up her dishes and carried them over to the sink. Luke was right behind her with his.

"Those can wait." He tugged her back toward the table.

She felt as if she'd won some little game by making him be the first one to speak. But the serious, almost grim, look in his eyes kept her from celebrating the petty victory.

"Luke, what's wrong? Why are you here this morning?"

He'd been about to take another sip of coffee but stopped. He set the cup down on the table. "Let's take a walk."

"Fine. Let me get my hat." She reached for the one she wore when gardening. It wasn't stylish, but it would keep the sun off her face. Judging by Luke's behavior, she had her suspicions that the walk would be a long one.

After she locked the door, they started off in the direction of the river, taking the shortcut across Luke's farm. Rather than let the silence become a burden between them, she chatted as they walked, with Luke answering in single words or even an occasional grunt. As they passed his cabin, she noticed there was only one horse in the corral.

Had Jack taken off again? If so, that might account in part for Luke's foul mood. Sometimes she'd love to shake Jack until his teeth rattled. Why couldn't he be more of a help to his brother? More of a comfort instead of just another burden?

A few minutes later, the trees gave way to the rocky shore along the river. Despite the early hour, the temperature was already climbing, especially in the woods. But along the water, a breeze stirred that felt cool and peaceful. She let Luke lead her along the edge of the river until they reached a downed log. Cora sat down and waited for Luke to make up his mind to talk.

He picked up a handful of rocks to toss into the water. A few skipped several times before sinking. Others he aimed at stumps and boulders that jutted above the surface of the river. A row of small turtles slipped off a log with a series of splashes, making Cora smile. She wasn't the only one who had noticed Luke's mood.

"Jack left last night." Another rock pinged off a stump. "I don't think he's coming back this time." This time he took aim at an innocent willow tree downstream.

She ached for him. As far as she knew, Jack was all the family Luke had. His desertion had to hurt, especially when Luke was working so hard to restore their family home. If she ran into Jack, she would tear into him for what he was doing to Luke.

"I know farming isn't for everyone"—Luke glanced over his shoulder at Cora—"so I understand that he needs to find himself. I'm more worried about who he's joining up with."

She knew without Luke's having to spell it out. Jack had taken up with the men along the river, the very ones that Sheriff Whitney was keeping a wary eye on.

"What are his plans?"

Luke dropped down on the log a short distance away from her. "I don't know. I wish I did. I tried to warn him that the sheriff is no fool. If he manages to tie any of them in with the bank robberies, he'll round up the whole bunch and send them to prison." He shuddered in the bright sunshine.

In all the times they'd talked, he'd never once

mentioned what his life had been like in prison. She was almost afraid to ask, but if she was ever to understand Luke and his moods, she needed to know.

"It was bad, wasn't it?"

Luke froze, staring out at the river, his whole body rigid with tension. She was afraid she'd presumed too much, intruding where she wasn't welcome. But to her surprise, he reached out and took her hand in his, still keeping his eyes averted.

"Bad doesn't even come close to describing what it was like." He glanced at her out of the corner of his eye but then turned away again. "We were treated little better than animals. Worse really. Most people take care of their livestock, right up until they slaughter it for food. The warden and his men didn't give a damn how many of us they carried out feet first."

"Were most of the others prisoners of war, too?" she asked when he paused again.

His laughter at her question had nothing to do with humor. "I wasn't a prisoner of war, honey. No, according to them, I was a common murderer. The only reason I didn't hang was that I got a sympathetic judge."

Tears of grief and anger for him burned her eyes. She let them slip down her face unheeded, afraid that if Luke noticed them, he'd quit talking.

"Five years they kept me in that cell, mostly in solitary confinement because the warden was a Yankee. Five years of never taking a full step because they kept me chained. Five years of eating bugs in my food. Five years gone, wasted because I killed one too many Yankees."

"Why did you?" She knew him well enough to know there had to be a reason.

His anger boiled over. "Because we were stupid enough

to try to surrender to the wrong damned man. A Union officer deliberately gut-shot my friend. Said he was a spy or some such idiocy." He turned his grief-stricken blue eyes in her direction. "Freddy was just a kid. All he wanted to do was go home. Why wouldn't they let him and the rest of us live in peace?"

She tugged her hand free from his. Desperate to help him bear the pain, she moved to sit in his lap so she could wrap him in her arms and offer a woman's comfort. There were no words she could string together that would ease the memory of his friend's wasted death. But maybe she could help him to remember past the end, back to when the young soldier had been alive.

"Tell me about him."

Slowly, he began to tell her about Freddy, how they'd met, how long they'd served together. At first, the words came slowly, increasing in speed until they almost tripped over each other as he rushed from one story to the next. As the picture he drew of his friend became clearer, she could feel some of the tension draining away.

When silence slid back in between them, it was calm and easy. The only sound was the slippery passage of water over rocks, singing the same soothing song it had sung for eternity. Cora settled her head on Luke's shoulder, enjoying the feel of his arms around her in the warmth of the morning sun.

She knew there was more he wanted to say to her. Everything was all jumbled up in Luke's mind, but somehow she didn't think he'd come to her house to talk about Jack, much less his years in prison or his poor friend Freddy. No, something else was at the root of the grim look he'd worn when he'd knocked on her door.

As much as she didn't want to spoil the moment, he would only stew about it until they talked it out, whatever it was.

"Luke, what did you want to talk to me about this morning?"

His arms tightened around her shoulders as the tension came racing back, scaring her more than she cared to admit. Whatever it was, it had to be serious.

"Cora, I want you to know that I'll stand by you if you're . . . uh . . . um . . ." His words coasted to a stop.

She leaned away from him, better to see his face, trying to understand what he was stumbling around, trying to say. "If I'm what?"

He took a deep breath and tried again. "You know that I'm not looking to complicate my life."

She nodded, frowning. Where was this conversation going?

"I just wanted you to know that I'll do the right thing by you, if it turns out that you're in a family way."

Cora gave his noble offer all the consideration it deserved. Not trusting herself to say a word, she fought herself free of his arms and walked away without looking back.

CHAPTER 13

Luke watched Cora leave, his stomach churning, unsure what to do next. Everything had seemed so clear on his way to her house that morning. How had his plan gone so wrong? There had been no mistaking the flash of pain across Cora's face before she'd turned her back on him and walked away.

He stared at the river, watching the water slip by just like the days of his life. Maybe if he sat there long enough, he might actually convince himself that letting her go without a fight had been the right thing to do. After all, he'd done his duty in offering to stand by her. Hell, most men wouldn't have done as much. He was practically a hero by some people's standards.

But not by his.

Words and emotions could be a volatile mix, especially when he added in a heavy dose of tarnished honor. Despite his grudging good intentions, he knew in his gut that Cora deserved better, much more than he could offer her. After all, she had been the innocent one; then he'd taken even that away from her. If he were the man she thought he was, the man he wished he was, he'd find it in him to regret taking her to bed. But that one night spent in her arms had been the single best moment of his life, not that he'd thought to tell her that.

But it was true. Those few hours when he'd done nothing more than hold her had gone a long way toward healing him. Hell, he'd told her the worst there was to know about him and his life. Instead of running him off, she'd clung to Luke with all her might, offering him the comfort of her words, her touch, her body.

And damned fool that he was, he'd just let her walk away.

He was up and running for the woods before he was aware that he'd made the decision to go after her. Just before he reached the sheltering shadows of the trees, a shot rang out, sending him diving for the ground.

He scrambled over rocks and roots for several feet in search of better cover, wondering who the hell was shooting at him. He got his answer quick enough as several riders splashed across the river a short distance upstream from where he'd been sitting.

An unfamiliar voice called out to him, "Gibson, is that you?"

Were they looking for him or for Jack? Considering they were armed and he wasn't, he didn't stand much of a chance if they decided they didn't like his answer. From this distance, he might pass for Jack, but not once they got a clear look at him.

"Who's doing the asking?"

"Most folks call me Baxter, Mr. Gibson. Why don't you and I go for a little walk?"

Luke rose up slowly. From what he'd heard about Baxter, if the man had wanted Luke dead, there wouldn't have been any warning shot.

The outlaw leader dismounted and handed the reins off to one of his two companions. He started downstream, leaving Luke to catch up. They walked along in silence, giving Luke a chance to study his unwanted companion. Baxter looked to be a little older than he was, but it was hard to judge. The war had aged its warriors beyond their years. As far as he could remember, he'd never met the man before. They'd fought on the same side, but that didn't mean much.

Baxter broke the silence. "I apologize for the gunshot, but it seemed like the best way to get your attention."

"You've got it now." Luke let a little of his anger show. "Of course, you could have just knocked on my door if you were that anxious to talk to me."

Baxter laughed and clapped him on the shoulder. "I suppose that's true, Mr. Gibson, but from what I hear, the sheriff already spends enough time riding across your farm. I didn't think you'd appreciate me giving him another excuse to pay you a call."

"I've got no problem with the law." Not anymore. He planned to keep it that way.

"No, I suppose not." Baxter stopped walking. He smiled at Luke. "As a former comrade in arms, I wanted to extend an invitation to you."

Luke didn't wait to hear it. "There's nothing you have to offer that I'd be interested in."

Baxter maintained a friendly smile that didn't quite match the hard glint in his eyes. "The way I figure it, we—men like you and me—lost more than just the war. Hell, you spent time in prison—five years, wasn't it? Five long years that they stole from you. I just wanted to give you the chance to get back a little of what is owed to you."

Maybe the man really thought he had all the answers, but he was wrong, at least as far as Luke was concerned. Nothing and nobody could give back one single day of those five years. And stealing another man's hard-earned money wouldn't buy him peace of mind.

"I meant what I said, Mr. Baxter. Thanks, but no thanks. I want nothing to do with whatever you and your men have planned."

Baxter gave him a quizzical look. "Does your lack of interest extend to your brother as well?"

Luke met Baxter's eyes without flinching and lied through clenched teeth. "Jack is a grown man. As such, he makes his own decisions. What he does is his own business."

Baxter's smile broadened, the first one to reach his eyes. "Younger brothers are a burden, aren't they?"

His bemused question startled Luke. He hadn't expected to like Baxter but found himself warming to him.

"That they are," he agreed without asking Baxter how he knew. Nor did the outlaw volunteer the information. They were both aware that what Luke didn't know, he didn't have to hide from Jake Whitney.

They started back upstream to where Baxter's two men waited. "I don't know how much longer we'll be in the area. I'm afraid that Sheriff Whitney has become a little too interested in our affairs."

When Luke didn't say anything, he added, "For what it's worth, I'll keep a careful eye on Jack."

For some reason, Luke believed him. "Why?"

Baxter looked toward the hills, staring at a memory he didn't bother to share. Judging from the grim look that settled around his eyes, it wasn't a pleasant one. "Let's just say that he reminds me of someone I used to know."

When they reached the others, Baxter took back the reins to his horse. Before mounting up, he extended a hand to Luke. "It was a pleasure to finally meet you, Mr. Gibson. I assume the sheriff won't hear of this little visit."

"Not from me." He could promise Baxter that much.

He turned away before they rode off, not wanting to show any interest in which direction they went. Besides, he had his own pressing business to see to. He kept to a slow pace, not wanting to be seen running away. The outlaw hadn't avoided capture by being careless. Luke had little doubt that he was being watched even now by another of Baxter's men positioned just for that purpose.

He stumbled to a brief stop. If Baxter was having him watched, the last thing he wanted to do was lead them straight to Cora's door. He had no way of knowing if they'd been there before she had run off. If not, it could look suspicious to them if he made a beeline for her door after leaving the river. Either way, he wasn't going to take any chances, not when her safety was at stake.

No, he'd go about his daily chores. That would go a long way toward reassuring Baxter that Luke wasn't going to go running to the law. He also knew Baxter's offer to keep an eye on Jack was two-edged. Maybe he meant just what he said—that he'd keep a watchful eye on him. But it also served as a subtle threat to keep Luke in line. Either way, it worked.

He picked up his ax and shovel. There was another stump waiting to be cleared by the back field, giving him a good target for his temper. He just wished he could get word to Cora that he wanted—needed—to talk to her. The more time passed without their getting matters resolved, the harder it was going to be for him to convince her to give him another chance.

Especially when he couldn't tell her what caused the delay.

Was nothing in this life ever easy?

The rest of the morning passed slowly enough to fan his frustration. When the sun was directly overhead and hot enough to melt rock, he decided to take a break. Instead of sitting in the shade by the spring as he usually did, he walked back to the cabin. He didn't want to risk running into the sheriff on one of his increasingly frequent trips across Luke's farm on his way to the river.

The damp heat left him thirsty, but not hungry. He knew he'd regret not eating something, so he choked down two thick slices of stale bread smeared with butter. It didn't do anything to fill up the hole he'd felt inside since Cora had left the river. He wondered if it was too early yet to risk a trip over to her house.

Was Baxter's man still watching the house? He mustered enough willpower to keep from looking over his shoulder. Maybe he was being too careful, but maybe not. Glancing up at the sun again, he decided to put in another hour, maybe two, and then call it quits. After a quick trip back to the river to clean up, he'd take a leisurely stroll over to Cora's place.

And he'd stay there until she listened to him. If he could figure out what it was that he wanted to say.

The door was locked and the corral was empty. Hellfire and damnation, where had she gone this time? She hadn't mentioned going into town, but obviously she had. He could follow her, but he'd feel like a fool wandering from one end of Lee's Mill to the other trying to find her.

Where would she most likely go if she was upset?

Lucy's house? The store? Maybe to see the pastor or his wife? No, not there. She couldn't discuss something so private with the pastor swithout running the risk of his insisting that she and Luke get married, child or no child.

He thought about Henrietta Dawson. Would Cora go to ground at her house? Hell, he didn't know. Her aunt had a certain fondness for Luke because of his father, but how long would that last if she found out that he'd bedded her niece?

If he hadn't been so damned cautious earlier, he might have caught her before she left. Now he had no choice but to go home and saddle up his own horse. He hadn't planned on a trip into Lee's Mill. What excuse could he give if anyone asked him why he was in town? If it were a weekend, no one would question his taking some time off from the farm, but it wasn't.

He didn't need another haircut yet. A bottle of whiskey sounded damned good, but he didn't have the money to throw away on liquor. Besides, he wouldn't find Cora by hanging around The River Lady. He hoped he'd think of something before he reached Front Street.

Rather than follow his usual route, he circled around and entered town from the far end by the stage office. He rode slowly, keeping an eye out for any sign of Cora or any of her friends. Unfortunately, it took him only a few minutes to ride the entire length of the street. When he saw the stable, he wanted to kick himself. Cora always left Falstaff there when she was in town. If the horse was in the corral, then Cora was in town.

The big gray was nowhere to be seen. Son of a bitch, where should he look next? He turned back up

the street. A glass of Cade's best whiskey sounded
pretty damned good. Deciding that was the best idea
he'd had all day, he dismounted and led his horse up
to the hitching rail outside the newspaper office.

Inside he found Cade and his typesetter standing by
the printing press and frowning. His friend glanced up
from the paper in his hand at the sound of the door
opening and nodded.

"Go on in my office. I'll be with you in a few minutes." He turned his attention back to the paper. "This
looks fine. Run a few extra copies for me to send out
on the stage."

Luke decided not to wait on Cade to offer him a
drink. He yanked open the desk drawer and reached
for the bottle and two glasses. After pouring each of
them a drink, he started to put the whiskey back in
the drawer but changed his mind. One shot wouldn't
be enough. He set the bottle on his side of the desk
and sat down to brood.

The sound of his desk drawer opening and closing
in the other room registered in the back of Cade's
mind as he read over the still-damp newspaper in his
hand. Luke, never exactly cheery looking, had looked
decidedly grim when he'd come through the door. It
was worth the cost of a glass or two of good whiskey if
it would loosen his friend's tongue enough to tell Cade
what had him all tied up in knots.

If Cade had to guess, he'd guess Luke either had
woman trouble or problems with his younger brother or
both. There wasn't much Cade could do but listen if it
was Jack, but Cora Lawford was another matter. Not
more than an hour ago, she'd come through town with
much the same look on her face. Cade was no expert on

affairs of the heart, but he knew from firsthand experience that sometimes if two people walked around looking as if their guts were tied in knots, chances were they were in love. If that was indeed true, Luke and Cora had it bad. That didn't mean they had a smooth road in front of them.

Cade liked Cora, but she was headstrong and didn't always use good common sense. Her fight for independence had been hard fought and he respected that, but he didn't agree with her choice of homes. She'd bought a prime piece of land, all right, but her living out there alone worried her friends. And he was against anything that worried Lucy.

"Before you start the run, Will, take a break." Cade started to walk away before adding, "A short one. And make sure you eat something before you stop in at The Lady."

He ignored whatever his employee muttered under his breath on his way out the door, knowing that if Will wasn't complaining, he wasn't happy. Besides, he'd enjoy his third beer more if he thought he was fooling Cade. Both of them knew the rules of the game they played.

Forgetting about Will for the moment, Cade wandered into his office. Just as he expected, Luke occupied one of the two chairs that faced his desk, his long legs stretched out, his hands wrapped around a glass with a little whiskey left in it. Cade had little doubt that the glass had been full only a few minutes before. In fact, he suspected that Luke was well into his second glass.

Cade picked up the one Luke had poured for him and took a healthy swig. "Want a cigar to go with that?" he asked, nodding in the direction of the bottle, which sat closer to Luke than Cade.

"No."

"Can I put the bottle away?" Cade started to reach for it but stilled his hand when Luke frowned.

"You'd better, if you want any of it left."

Cade didn't give a damn about how much whiskey he had left. He was more worried about his friend, but he kept that thought to himself. Figuring Luke would talk in his own good time, he took his own seat and propped his feet up on the desk. After a minute or two, Luke looked around as if wondering how he'd come to be there.

"I hadn't planned on coming into town today." He leaned back in the chair, trying to look relaxed and failing miserably.

Maybe Cade could prod him along. "How is Jack doing these days?"

Luke flinched. "Last time I saw him, he was fine. He's decided farming isn't for him." There was real grief in his voice.

"Damn, I'm sorry to hear that. I was hoping he'd help you make a go of the place." Cade reached for a cigar. After biting the tip off, he struck a match and puffed several times. When he had a satisfying amount of smoke hovering in the air, he spoke again. "What's he going to do?"

Luke's eyes shifted to the side. "I didn't want to ask too many questions he wouldn't answer."

Which meant Jack might well be walking on the shady side of the law. Damn, no wonder Luke looked sick. It didn't matter that Jack was an adult; as the elder brother, Luke would still feel responsible for him. For Luke's sake, he hoped like hell that if Jack did mess up, it wasn't anywhere close to Lee's Mill. Sheriff Whitney would throw him in jail, no matter whose brother he was. People were slowly starting to accept Luke, prison record and all. But if another one of the Gibsons got in trouble with the law, it could go hard on both of them.

"I'm sorry."

"It's his life." Luke shrugged and tossed back the last of his whiskey.

"Want a refill?"

"No, I'd better be going. Since I was in town, I wanted to stop by." He set his glass on the desk and stood up.

Cade did the same, figuring he'd have to go after Will if he didn't return in another few minutes. "Lucy told me to invite you for dinner again. Do you want to come this Sunday?"

Luke immediately shook his head. "I'd better not, but thank her for me. Maybe in a week or two."

Damn, Cade hated seeing his friend looking so hangdog. Maybe Lucy could do something with him. "Tell her yourself. She's next door at the store. She'll be mad if you don't stop by to see her. Besides, you need to see how big our son is getting, and Mary has been after me to see when you'll play chess with her again."

"All right, I'll stop by, but then I'd better get back out to the farm."

When the bell chimed, Lucy looked up from her ledger to see Luke Gibson standing in the open doorway, as if unsure of his welcome. She wondered if he'd be any more forthcoming about what had happened than Cora was when she'd been in earlier. Lucy's instincts told her that Luke was behind Cora's bad mood and restlessness. Whatever it was, Cora hadn't wanted to talk about it, and Lucy hadn't tried to force the issue. Her friend was more than a little stubborn. If she thought Lucy was interfering too much, she'd take it badly.

Sometimes it was hard to remember that Cora was a woman full grown. It didn't seem all that long ago that she'd been a young girl chafing under the rigid control of her aunt. As much as they would all like to wrap her in cotton to protect her from the bumps and bruises of life, she had to make her own way in the world. And right now it appeared that Luke Gibson might be one of those bumps.

Deciding she couldn't very well choose sides when she didn't know what the problem was, Lucy pasted a smile on her face. "Well, come on in, Luke. It's been a long time since I've seen you."

He took the final step into the store and closed the door behind him. "I won't stay if you're busy." He gestured toward her ledger. "Cade wanted me to stop in. He was doing some bragging on that son of yours and said I should see how handsome he was for myself."

"You're not interrupting anything that can't wait. Roy is upstairs asleep." She came out from behind the counter and took Luke by the arm before he could use that as an excuse to leave. "I need to check on him anyway. Mary will be mad that she missed you. She went over to see Melinda Hayes for a while."

"Tell her I'm sorry I missed her."

At the top of the stairs, Lucy led the way to a small bedroom. Roy was lying quietly in his cradle, sucking on his fist in his sleep. The two adults watched him in silence. At one time Lucy had been convinced that she'd never risk the dangers of marriage again in order to have children. Now she had a loving husband, a sweet stepdaughter, and a son they all three adored. Life was a constant source of surprises.

She happened to glance up at Luke. The stark pain on his face as he looked down at Roy cut right through to her heart. What could he be thinking about that would make him hurt so much? And what did it have to do with Cora?

"I'd better be getting back downstairs," she said, in case Luke wanted to leave.

His relief in leaving the baby's room was almost palpable. She didn't take offense; rather, she was more concerned about him than ever. Maybe he'd said something to Cade. Luke followed her down the stairs. She half expected him to head right for the door, but instead he started wandering around the store, picking up things at random and then setting them back down.

Enough was enough. The only way he and Cora were going to settle their differences was by talking. If Cora wasn't going to seek out Luke, then Lucy was going to point him in the right direction and pray she was doing the right thing.

"I'm surprised you and Cora didn't ride into town together."

Luke dropped a hammer, barely missing his foot. Lucy bit back a laugh. Had she and Cade ever been at such cross-purposes? Yes, they most certainly had, she had to admit.

"When was she here?" He returned to the counter, still carrying the hammer he probably didn't really want.

Lucy pretended to study the clock. "Oh, I'd say she left about an hour and a half ago." She picked up her ledger, pretending an interest she didn't feel. "She kept pacing the floor and muttering. Finally, she left."

"Did she say where she was going?"

"Not exactly."

He looked so disappointed, Lucy took mercy on

him. "But I know that another shipment of books was delivered out to the schoolhouse yesterday. By the way, Luke, would you like to come to dinner this Sunday or next?"

Luke didn't answer because he was already halfway out the door. She doubted he'd heard a word after she said *schoolhouse*. Once Roy woke from his nap, she'd track down her husband and see if he'd had any better luck finding out what was wrong.

It was her third trip walking around the inside of the room, but it hadn't helped settle her. Every other time she'd come to the school to put away supplies or just to spend time enjoying the feel of the place, she'd come away feeling energized and focused. Well, except for the time she'd run into Jack and his friends. And then there was the storm, but she didn't want to think about that.

But all the other times had felt good.

And now even her precious textbooks held little appeal for her. She'd managed to unpack almost half of them. She glanced over to where they lined up like good little soldiers in neat rows on the shelf, but she drew no pleasure from the sight. Giving up all pretense of working, she paused by the bookshelf and ran her fingertip along the titles.

How could she hope to teach her students all that they would need to know when she had so few answers for herself? With one sentence, Luke had taken a night she thought was special and beautiful and turned it into something ugly, all in the name of duty.

She blushed to think that she hadn't even thought of the possibility of a pregnancy resulting from sharing her bed with Luke. It wasn't that she hadn't known how babies were made, maybe not in great detail, but at least the basics. There just hadn't been time for her to think that far ahead. Her hand slipped down to her waist the same way she'd watched her two friends do when they'd suspected they were with child.

Could she be carrying Luke's baby? She knew she should be worried, maybe even terrified, but she couldn't find it in her heart to feel that way. Perhaps it was just too early for the reality of it to hit home. People would talk, but she didn't care. A child should be considered a miracle, not a punishment for loving someone too much.

Oh, she wasn't naïve enough to think that it would be easy, but she knew as well as she knew anything that her friends in the Luminary Society would stand by her. And despite their past differences, she knew her Aunt Henrietta would be shocked, but she'd get over it. In private, Henrietta might lecture Cora about her folly, but no one would dare criticize her niece, not to her face.

The only person she dreaded facing was Luke himself. Her feelings for him hadn't changed, but right now she was so angry she wanted to shake him. No matter what the circumstances, she had no intentions of marrying him or anybody else for anything less than love. Her parents had died when she was still pretty young, but she remembered how they were together. Their marriage had been happy, and that happiness had spilled over to their relationship with their daughter.

She'd also seen how bad a marriage could be. Her friend Josie had been married to a vicious man, both a drunk and a wife beater. Josie was now married to Mitch Hughes, the former sheriff of Lee's

Mill; she'd blossomed since finding happiness with her new husband.

If Luke were to bring up the subject again, what would she tell him? Thanks, but no thanks? Or should she walk away again, leaving him to stew in his own juices? Somehow she didn't think he'd let her get away with that again. His graceless offer had stunned her into silence, and it had hurt something fierce when he'd let her walk away without a word.

Next time—if there was a next time—she would give him a piece of her mind. She knew he wasn't looking to . . . what was it he'd said? Oh yes, he wasn't looking to complicate his life. Well, that was too bad. He'd certainly managed to complicate hers rather handily. It was only fair that she return the favor.

As embarrassing as it was to admit, despite his prickly nature, the man only had to look in her direction to have her aching all over with the need to touch him again. The feelings had been bad enough before the night they'd spent together. Now that he'd taught her the joys of passion, she wanted to experience it again. Soon. Even often.

It was time to finish up before heading back home. After she'd left Luke, she'd ridden into town in order to avoid him for a while. She'd headed right for Lucy, but once she got to the store, she'd been reluctant to share her problems. Never one to miss the obvious, Lucy had picked up on Cora's distress, but she hadn't pressed her for details. It might have been a relief to unburden herself, but Cora wasn't ready to talk about the situation between her and Luke, not until she understood it better herself.

Her feelings for Luke were too raw. As mad as she was, she also didn't want any more rumors slipping around town that would hurt his reputation. She smiled. He wouldn't appreciate knowing that she was trying to protect him again, especially after he told her specifically not to. That little bit of defiance pleased her greatly.

Having poked and prodded the situation from every direction she could think of, she decided it was time to get back home. She grabbed up the last few books and arranged them next to the others on the shelf. Her hands felt dusty, so she wiped them on her skirt after shoving the now-empty crate over to the side of the room with several others. Sometime before school started, she'd have to get someone to break the crates apart and stack the wood somewhere out of the way. When the weather changed in the late fall, she'd use it for kindling.

She hadn't gone more than two steps toward the door before she realized that she was not alone. The shock of facing three men standing inside the doorway had her backtracking, wondering how they'd managed to come in without her noticing. In the heavy silence, she could even hear her heart pounding in fear. If Jack or one of his friends would say something, it wouldn't be quite so unnerving. But all three of them silently stared at her, letting their pawing eyes say it all for them.

What would Aunt Henrietta do if confronted by three such unsavory characters? For one thing, she wouldn't give an inch, nor would she let them see how frightened she was. Perhaps Cora wasn't as strong as Henrietta, but she'd give it her best. Drawing herself up to her full height, she did her best to stare them down.

"Was there something you wanted, Jack?" His leering smile made her regret her choice of words, but there was nothing she could do if he chose to misinterpret her meaning.

Jack flashed her one of his best smiles. "Well, Miss Lawford, we were just riding by and saw your horse. We thought we would stop to see if we could do anything to help you."

She didn't believe him, not for one second. It didn't take much to see that they were up to no good. Trying to hide her uneasiness, she answered brusquely, "No, there isn't. I've already finished unpacking the books." She forced herself to add, "But thank you anyway."

The man on his right, Jeb if she remembered correctly, spat a stream of tobacco juice out of the corner of his mouth. It landed on the floor with a sickening splat. If he'd done so just to be disgusting, he'd succeeded.

"Well, I must be going, gentlemen. As I said, I'm already finished with my work, so there's no reason for you to tarry any longer."

"We'll see you to your door, Miss Lawford," his friend drawled. "There are some mighty unsavory characters in these parts."

The first real frisson of fear settled in her stomach as the three men laughed. "That won't be necessary. I assure you I am not in need of an escort." She sidled across the room, hoping to reach the stairs to make a run for her horse, although she figured her chances of reaching Falstaff and making a clean getaway were pretty slim.

"We insist on seeing her home, don't we, Jack?"

For a moment, she thought he was going to help her, but then he smiled at his friends. "You see, Miss Lawford, I was just telling my big brother the other day that I'd like a little of that hospitality you've been showing him."

He started across the room toward her, stopping only inches away. She backed up, unable to stop herself, but there was nowhere to go. "Jack, you don't want to do this. You know you'll regret it."

Jack tilted his head to the side, as if to consider the matter. Then his grin turned a little nasty. "No, actually I don't think I will." He ran his fingers down her arm and then back up to cup the back of her head. She whimpered, wishing she could have shown no fear. The strong smell of liquor on his breath only added to the nausea she was fighting.

"We'll start with a kiss and then see where it takes us."

"It will take you straight to hell, little brother, if you so much as touch her again."

CHAPTER 14

Luke stood in the doorway, the bright sunshine behind him making it impossible to see the expression on his face. It didn't matter. The cold fury in his voice was enough to convince everyone in the room that death had just walked in the door. Jeb and Isaac both froze, well aware that they were at a disadvantage with their backs to Luke's rifle.

Jack, on the other hand, had no such fear of his brother. He did let his hand fall away from Cora, though, freeing her to move away. She wanted to run screaming across the small room right into Luke's arms, but she knew better than to get between him and the other three. He might have caught them unaware, but the two of them were not out of this yet.

Instead, she edged to the side, working her way around the room until she'd joined Luke by the door. Not for one instant did he take his eyes off the three men lined up in front of him.

"Did they hurt you?"

"I'm a little scared, but that's all." So much so that her hands were shaking, and she wasn't sure her legs would continue to support her, but none of that mattered right then.

"Good, maybe I won't have to kill them after all."

This was a side of Luke she'd never seen before, one

she wasn't sure she liked, even if he had rescued her from his brother's clutches. He'd tried to warn her that he wasn't the kind of man she thought he was. Maybe he'd been right.

"Gentlemen, drop your guns on the floor and then kick them toward the corner."

"Aw, come on, Luke. We were just having a little fun." Jack started toward his brother, his hands held out away from his revolver.

"Don't come another step closer." Luke's gun came up, aimed right for Jack's chest. "I said drop the guns."

All three men complied but only grudgingly. When the last gunbelt slid across the floor toward Cora, she gathered them up.

"Cora, why don't you take those on outside and hang them on the nearest horse? Then mount up and ride out. My brother and his friends will wait here with me while you get on your way."

She stopped long enough to retrieve her purse before lugging the heavy gunbelts outside. The silence in the room was heavy with threat, her footsteps the only sound that disturbed the unnatural quiet. She looped the gunbelts over Jack's saddle, all the while wondering how Luke would get away without turning his back on the three of them. She knew he wouldn't appreciate her asking, so she did as she was told. It took her two tries to scramble up on Falstaff's broad back. As soon as she was settled on the saddle, she urged him into a fast trot. When she was out of sight from the school, she pulled up to wait for Luke. He'd yell at her for doing so, but she had to know that he managed to get away from those three without mishap.

Three shots rang out, all fired in quick succession, followed by silence. Cora stuffed her fist against her mouth to muffle a scream, fearing Luke had killed

Jack and his friends. Or worse yet, three against one, they'd managed to get the drop on him. Only the fear that she'd be riding right back into gunfire kept her waiting where she was. If Luke didn't come around that corner in another thirty seconds, she'd ride for town and Sheriff Whitney.

One . . . two . . . three . . . she counted the time off in her head. Each additional number only served to convince her that Luke was dead or wounded. Was she sitting in the middle of the road like a ninny while the man she loved lay bleeding to death on the schoolhouse steps?

That thought was enough to have her yanking Falstaff's head around to ride back. Before they'd gone more than a handful of steps, though, Luke came tearing down the road. He barely slowed down when he reached her side.

"Get the hell back to your house, Cora! Do you want to face them again?"

Falstaff didn't need to be told twice to follow him. Cora's relief at seeing Luke alive and unharmed was short-lived. Had he actually had to shoot his own brother? Not that she was worried about Jack—at least not much. No, her real concern was the effect that it would have on Luke. He'd only started getting over the war and his time spent in prison. He didn't need Jack on his conscience.

She risked a peek back down the road before cutting off through the woods to her house. For the moment, there was no one following them. Even so, she urged Falstaff to go as fast as he could. Right now, all she wanted was to reach the house and lock her stout door behind her. And Luke.

He was already off his horse and waiting for her. He grabbed Falstaff's reins while she dismounted. He ran toward the small corral and turned the horses loose after yanking off their saddles. Cora figured she'd only be in his way while he dealt with the animals. She waited on the porch for him to join her.

Finally, he was walking toward her, the grim look in his eyes unchanged from when she'd left him at the school. Unlike his brother, though, she knew she was in no danger from this man.

"What happened after I left? I heard gunshots." She braced herself for the worst.

"I scattered their horses." He pushed past her into the house, leaving her to follow as she would.

Inside, he positioned himself by the front window, watching the narrow road to her house. The hardness she'd seen for the first time at the school was still there, both in his stance and in the grim set to his jaw. She hardly recognized him as the same man she'd taken to her bed. For a short time, she hovered by the door, unsure what to do next. The burst of energy that had carried her out of the schoolhouse all the way to her kitchen had burned out, leaving her unable to move. She reached out a hand to the back of the nearest chair, hoping it would support her.

Before she could inch her way closer to the table, Luke was beside her, lending her his strength. Ignoring the chair he pulled out for her, she went right into the safe harbor of his arms and let the tears come.

"Go ahead," she managed to say between sniffles. "I know you want to."

His voice rumbled through his chest. "And what exactly am I wanting to do?"

She leaned back to look up into his face. His eyes weren't ice cold, but instead were filled with concern. "Yell at me. For going out to the school again by myself."

He tugged her back against his chest. "Maybe later.

Right now I'm too busy being glad that I happened to get there in time."

"What happened after I left?" She didn't care about Isaac and Jeb. They didn't matter, but Jack did.

"I waited until you rode out and then I ran their horses off. I figure by the time they catch them, the alcohol will have worn off enough to keep them from doing something else just as stupid." He drew a deep breath. "I'm sorry that my brother was part of that."

"You don't need to apologize for his behavior, Luke. He's the one who acted like a fool. You can tell him I said so when you see him later."

Luke gently stepped back from her. "Remember, he moved out of the cabin. I don't know when—or if—I'll be seeing him again."

She allowed him the small distance between them, sensing he needed it. "I'd forgotten. I guess I've had other things on my mind." Most of them had to do with the man standing in front of her.

"I'm going to take a look around outside."

"Fine. While you're out doing that, I'll fix us both something to eat. I know it's early for supper, but I missed lunch." She crossed her fingers that he wouldn't refuse.

"Lock the door behind me. I'll knock when I come back." He picked up his rifle and left.

As she washed some greens she'd picked earlier, it occurred to her to wonder why he had happened to show up at the school. No one except Lucy had known that she had planned to unpack the latest shipment. Had she sent him to look for her? She hoped not. Not that she wasn't grateful for his unexpected arrival, but she hated to think he'd come only because Lucy had forced him to.

Once she had the table set, she stood at the window

and watched him walking around outside. Despite everything that had happened, she still wanted him. Did he realize that he was so determined to hold her at arm's length because he was a good man, not wanting to taint her good name with the problems of his past? Probably not.

He made the last turn around the yard to head back toward the porch. She hurried back to the stove, not wanting to be caught watching him. When he rapped on the door, she wiped her hands on a towel and crossed the room to let him in.

"Why were you at the school this afternoon?" The question popped out, surprising both of them.

Luke didn't immediately answer. He took care of locking the door and leaned his rifle against the wall where he could get to it in a hurry.

"Did Lucy send you out to check on me?"

"Are you sorry I was there?" he asked, avoiding her questions altogether.

She wasn't going to let him slide out of answering, because his reasons were important to her. She laid her hand on his arm, an unspoken sign that she wasn't going to back down on this. "Answer me, Luke. Why were you there?"

He studied her hand on his arm. "I went into town looking for you. Lucy didn't ask me to check up on you, if that's what you're asking. When she happened to mention a shipment of books had been delivered, I drew my own conclusions."

Lucy never "happened" to do anything. If she'd told Luke about the books, she'd had her own reasons for doing so. Maybe Cora hadn't been as successful hiding her turmoil from Lucy as she'd thought. If Luke had shown up looking for her, Lucy probably had drawn her own conclusions and acted accordingly.

"Why were you looking for me?"

Luke raked his hand through his hair, clearly frustrated with his part in this conversation. "Because I handled everything badly this morning. I wanted to make sure that you were all right."

"Why should you care? You've already made it perfectly clear that you're willing to do your duty, as you call it." She crossed her arms across her chest and glared up at him. "Tell me, Luke, how do you think that makes me feel? Grateful? Honored? Well, I don't—not one bit."

"Why the hell not?" His eyes snapped in fury. "I'm offering to do the right thing."

"What's right about it, Luke? Why would you want to shackle yourself to me when that's the last thing you want to do? You've made that perfectly clear from the beginning."

She moved back and wished that he wouldn't let her. When he didn't stop her, she turned away, pretending an interest in the pots on the stove. For the life of her, she couldn't remember what she was cooking or even why.

"But, Cora . . ."

"Forget it, Luke. I don't want to discuss it anymore. Besides, we don't even know if I'm . . . uh, you know." She blushed and resented it.

"But we can't ignore the very real possibility that you might be . . . uh, you know," he argued, echoing her own words.

She could hear the smile in his voice as his arms slipped around her waist. He rested his head on top of hers. At first, she ignored him as best she could. But the warm lure of his body called to hers. She eased back against him, wishing the real distance between the two of them were as easily closed.

The simple meal was ready, but she wasn't hungry, not for food anyway. She turned in Luke's arms, feeling more at home there than she had any place since her parents had died. She wasn't blind to his faults. She even understood his reluctance to complicate his life with what they shared between them.

But she also knew that she'd waited her whole life to find a man who made her feel this way. She wasn't going to give up easily, but she didn't want to trap him into marriage. No matter how much she loved him, it wouldn't be enough if he spent the rest of their lives resenting her.

Would he kiss her if she asked him to?

As soon as the thought crossed her mind, his eyes turned all smoky blue and hot. She tipped her face up, making it easier for his lips to find hers. The way she was feeling, a kiss wasn't going to be enough, but it was a good start.

Jack felt sick. He wanted to blame it on the cheap whiskey he'd been drinking since before noon, but that wasn't the real reason. He'd never realized that shame could make a man feel as if he'd been poisoned. Ever since Luke had burst into the schoolroom, Jack had wanted to crawl under the nearest rock and hide. And he might just have to do that the next time Luke set eyes on him.

He'd hardly recognized his own brother staring at him down the long barrel of Luke's rifle. The bitter chill in Luke's eyes would probably haunt Jack's nightmares for years to come. Would he have really pulled the trigger? Maybe. Probably. Dear God, he hoped he never had to find out.

There was some comfort from knowing that Luke

would have made sure that Cora got home safely. Jealousy added to his discomfort. If he hadn't been such a damned fool, maybe he could have been the one to escort Cora home. He was willing to bet that his dear, noble brother wasn't standing guard on her front porch.

A cup of hot coffee sounded good, but he didn't want to approach Baxter's campfire unless he had to. The outlaw had ordered all of them to keep a low profile until he decided when they'd break camp, this time for good. If he found out that the three of them had been messing with a local woman, there was no telling what he'd do.

Isaac and Jeb had made themselves scarce as soon as they'd caught up with their horses. Considering what a disaster the day had been, he couldn't find it in him to care where they were. They hadn't been the ones to corner Cora in that room full of desks and books, but they'd only been waiting their turn.

His stomach cramped at the thought. If the expression in Luke's eyes had frightened him, the one in Cora's had surprised him. She had looked up at him with fear and anger, but worst of all, recognition that he was less of a man than his brother.

There were times he almost hated Luke. How had he managed to live through the war and five years in prison and still seem so damned noble? The first few weeks after Jack had found him outside the prison, Luke had been content to drift along from one town to another, one saloon to the next. But it hadn't taken long for Luke to get restless, anxious to return home.

Jack had figured that once Luke got a good look at the hopeless condition of the family farm, the two of them would turn and ride away. It sure hadn't worked out that way. Somehow, Luke had seen past the overgrown pastures, the holes in the roof, and the weed-choked garden to the memories of how it used to be. And maybe, with enough hard work, it could be again.

Perhaps things would have been different if they hadn't stopped in Lee's Mill to buy supplies that first day. One look at Cora Lawford and Luke had swallowed the bait, hook and all, even if he was too stubborn to admit it. But just like those bluegill and catfish they'd grown up fishing for, eventually he would run out of the strength to fight, and she would reel him in.

Jack wished them the best. Hell, he'd even dance at their wedding if he thought either one of them would let him in the door.

Several of Baxter's men stood up and walked away from the campfire. The outlaw leader himself was nowhere in sight. Still feeling in need of a cup of coffee, Jack decided this was the best chance he was going to have. He stood up and brushed the sand off the back of his pants before digging his cup out of his saddlebag. When he was sure that the men were going to keep walking away from him, he wandered over toward the fire. Using his handkerchief to protect his hand from the hot coffeepot, he poured himself a cup. Even though he got the dregs, it felt good going down.

Unfortunately, his stomach was feeling pretty unsettled. The strong coffee mixed uneasily with the whiskey he'd had earlier. Damn, if he wasn't careful, he might just humiliate himself in front of everyone. Maybe he'd be better off finding a quiet spot to lie down.

After tossing out the last of his coffee, he started back to where he'd left his gear. He found a shady spot under a nearby willow tree, its drooping limbs offering him a little bit of privacy. His blanket wouldn't offer much padding against rocks, but he lucked out and found a patch of sand. It felt damned good to stretch out, shading his face from the sun with his hat.

He shut his eyes, in hopes that he'd be able to sleep off the sick feeling in his stomach. But he still couldn't stop thinking about the events of the past few days. He didn't regret turning his back on farming, but he knew his decision was a disappointment to Luke. His choice of friends didn't set well with his brother, either. Too damned bad. At least they weren't willing to settle for digging rocks and stumps out of the ground for the rest of their lives.

Then there was the little matter of Cora Lawford. Son of a bitch, he wished they'd ridden right by the schoolhouse instead of pestering her. Hell, the woman was probably going to end up being his sister-in-law, and she had looked at him as if he were vermin. The more he thought about it, the madder he got. After all, he wasn't the one who'd been in prison.

Well, Cora and Luke could both go to hell. He had friends who had bigger plans than dirt farming. Once he pocketed his share of the last job and maybe helped Baxter out on a couple more like it, he'd head west and find a new place to live. One where he didn't have people watching his every move.

He flopped over on his side and tried to find a comfortable position. Finally, as the heat of the day continued to climb, he dozed off.

Luke forced himself to concentrate on eating the simple meal that Cora had prepared for the two of them. Everything tasted good, but he couldn't help but feel disappointed. If the pot on the stove hadn't decided to boil over a few minutes ago, hissing and spitting and raising a ruckus, he might have been in

Cora's bedroom right then, satisfying an entirely different appetite.

He had no business thinking about such things, but it was damned difficult to keep his mind on collard greens under the circumstances.

"Is the food all right?" Cora sounded worried. "I know it wasn't anything fancy."

Realizing that he'd been frowning, he forced a smile. "Everything is fine. I was just thinking." About her. About her bed. About . . . damn, he had to quit this.

"What would you like to do after we're through eating?"

He choked on a bite of cornbread as he considered what he could say other than the obvious answer to that particular question. His body's immediate reaction made him glad that he was sitting at the table. He took a drink of water to clear his throat and to give himself time to think of an answer.

"I, uh, need to check on my chickens." Not much of an idea, but more sensible than what he really wanted to do.

"Let me clear the table and then we can walk over to your place."

He had his horse right outside in the corral. If he had a lick of sense, he'd saddle up his pinto and ride out. If Jack and his friends wanted to cause more trouble, they would have by now. With any luck, Luke had put the fear of God into his brother. Even now, he wished he could lay him and his two friends out flat for frightening Cora. Maybe those other two didn't know any better, but Jack sure as hell knew how to treat a lady. Their mother had raised them up right.

And considering everything, he wasn't much better than Jack when it came to Cora. Maybe he was worse.

After all, he'd done far more than try to steal a kiss from an unwilling woman.

He watched Cora as she made quick work of the few dishes they'd used. There was something that just plain felt right about sitting in her kitchen, watching her do such homey things. A man could do far worse than share his days—and nights—with a woman like Cora. But not him. Until he could sleep nights without hiding under a tree, he had no business trifling with her.

And he wanted to do a lot more than trifle. He remembered all too clearly the sweet taste of her skin and how it had felt to join his body to hers. If he could shove his conscience back into the dark recesses of his mind, he'd drag Cora into the next room and toss her on the bed. Once he had her naked and under him, her legs wrapped high around his waist, maybe he could forget all the reasons he shouldn't be thinking about such things.

A shot of fury surged through him as he shoved back from the table. He picked up his rifle on his way out the door. Cora wasn't far behind him.

"Luke, where are you going?"

He owed it to her to say something. "I've got chores to do."

"What's going on?" She sounded puzzled. "I thought we were going to walk over together."

He lashed out in frustration. "It doesn't take two to feed a bunch of damned chickens."

His words sent her staggering back a step, as if he'd hit her. But then she dug in her heels and stood her ground. "Luke Gibson, I have about had it with you. One minute you're sitting at my table, pleasant as can be. The next you blow up for no reason at all as far as

I can tell." She stomped her foot in frustration. "I swear, I have no idea what you want."

That did it. If she wasn't careful, he'd show her what he wanted right there on her front porch, consequences and conscience be damned. In just a few strides, he stood in front of her wishing like hell he dared take what she was offering.

"I'll tell you what I want. I want my parents back, alive and well. I want the war to never have happened, and while I'm at it, I want my dead friends to quit haunting every minute I sleep and most of the time I'm awake. It would be damned nice if I could stand to sleep inside instead of under the tree in the front yard. Hell, I even want the five years back that were stolen from me." He ran his fingers through his hair in frustration. "If I can't have any of that, I'd be happy if my brother wasn't about to ride off with Baxter and his bunch for God knows where." He stepped back farther from temptation. "I figure none of that's going to happen."

Then, before he gave in to the urge to kiss her, he spun around and damned near ran all the way back to his farm. He was almost to the cabin before he remembered he'd left his horse at Cora's. He kept going anyway. There'd be time later when he could slip back to bring his mare home. He had a feeling he'd be up most of the night anyway.

Cora sank down onto the top porch step and watched Luke's retreat. He'd told her more in that one angry burst than in all the other times they had talked. She tried to weed through it all, trying to understand what demons were driving Luke so hard.

Based on her recent encounters with Jack, she thought Luke was right to worry about the direction

Jack was headed. Other than the rumors everyone had heard, she didn't know much about Baxter. But from what she'd seen the day he and his men had ridden past the school, they were a rough-looking lot. It was easy to believe that there was something to Jake Whitney's suspicions about their possible involvement in a series of bank robberies scattered around the state.

She leaned back against the railing and drew her knees up. There wasn't much she could do about Jack, any more than she could bring back their mother and father. She understood all too well the pain of losing both parents before their time. There wasn't a day that went by that she didn't think of her own mother and father and miss them. The pain of their loss had gradually faded over the years, but she doubted it would ever leave her completely. There was so much in her life that she would have loved to share with them. Would they have been able to help her know what to do about this complex man who held her heart in his hands?

She suspected Luke had never had a chance to grieve over the loss of his family because he'd been too busy fighting a war. Their deaths had gotten lost among all those he saw on a daily basis.

Which brought her to the final part of his pain. Considering the horrors he had witnessed, she wasn't surprised that he was having nightmares from the war. But if he saw his dead friends every night, no wonder he had trouble sleeping. But what did that have to do with his spending his nights outside under a tree?

When he had time to think about what he'd said, she had a feeling he'd regret letting that last bit slip out. He would probably think his problem was a sign of weakness. She already knew he was bothered by the sound of thunder. Wasn't the night they'd spent together enough to convince him that she didn't think less of him for it? But she wasn't going to conveniently forget about what he'd told her. Not when she sensed that it was at the heart of the reason that Luke didn't allow himself to reach out to her.

She glanced up at the sun, trying to gauge the time. It would be another few hours before nightfall, giving her plenty of time for a long nap. Once the sun went down, she would stand watch in the woods bordering Luke's cabin. Maybe then she'd get some answers.

Cora woke up slowly, feeling confused and groggy. She stumbled out of the room to the kitchen, where she splashed water on her face and hands, trying to wash away the cobwebs in her mind. The clinging heat had made it difficult for her to fall asleep. She'd finally dozed off, but it hadn't been particularly restful. Maybe she would have been better off to spend the late afternoon and evening hours working in her garden or reading.

Another splash of water helped make her feel marginally better. A cup of coffee might make more of a difference, but she couldn't stand the thought of stoking up the fire. The house was already hot enough.

An hour later, she left her house, wearing the darkest dress she owned. She hadn't had much experience in skulking around at night but figured her brown calico would make it more difficult for Luke to see her.

The moon was almost full, giving her enough light to make her way through the trees. A small animal bolted across the path just ahead of her, before diving into the thick undergrowth. She managed to stifle a small shriek of surprise. It wouldn't take much to alert Luke to her presence.

Finally, after almost tripping over a knotted root, she reached the final few trees near Luke's cabin. The night was far enough gone that she thought he might well be asleep. But in case he was still up and about, she leaned against a large tree several yards away from the path she'd been following, hoping to disguise her presence by sharing its shadow.

Time passed slowly as she stared into the darkness, trying to locate Luke in the shifting shadows. There was no light coming from the cabin, but maybe he'd already gone to bed. If so, he was sleeping inside, contrary to what he'd told her earlier. Finally, the door of the cabin opened. She eased back farther into the shadows as she watched Luke walk out onto the sagging porch.

He stayed where he was for a minute or two, but then he stepped down from the porch and started off toward the woods, directly toward her. She fought the urge to retreat, deciding it was highly unlikely that he'd been able to detect her presence in that short amount of time. Instead, she froze and waited to see where he was going, even though the only logical destination was her place.

What was he up to? What would he think if he knocked on her door and she wasn't there to answer? Considering he was well on his way along the path, she had little choice but to wait and find out. Following him now would cause more problems than it would settle. He'd never believe that she'd been out for a stroll and happened to end up at his place at such a late hour.

It also seemed unlikely that he'd wait this late to pay her a visit. There had to be another reason. As she looked around, she noticed the empty corral, giving her the obvious answer to her question. Luke had gone to fetch home his mare, figuring Cora would likely be asleep. If he looked around, he'd see what he expected to—a dark house and a locked door. He'd have no reason to think she was anywhere but tucked into her bed.

Alone.

The minutes dragged by while she waited for him to return. Finally, she thought she heard a rider approaching from the road. Perhaps it was Jack coming home for some reason, but she doubted it. Luke wouldn't have wanted to risk his horse coming through the woods at night. It only made sense that he'd take the safer, although longer, route.

Sure enough, he rode into sight a couple of minutes later, heading straight for the corral. She could hear him talking to the mare, which made her smile. So she wasn't the only one who found a horse to be good company during the lonely hours of the night. Once he had the animal settled for the night, Luke headed straight for a big sycamore tree.

She leaned forward, straining to see what he was doing in the black velvet shadows under the tree. From where she stood, it appeared as if he was shaking out a blanket. When she realized that he was indeed preparing to sleep under the spreading branches of the tree, her heart hurt for him. After he sat down, she heard a couple of soft thumps, most probably his boots hitting the ground.

After he stretched out on the ground, she wished she could leave, because the longer she stayed, the more she risked discovery. Luke would not easily forgive her intrusion on his privacy. But until she was sure that he was indeed asleep, she was reluctant to move, even in the protective shadows of the trees. To rest her weary legs, she slowly eased down to sit on the ground. With her legs drawn up, she leaned back against the tree to wait.

"No! Please, God, no!"

Luke's agonized words ripped through the night, shattering the silence. Cora's eyes popped open as she tried to make sense of her surroundings. How had she come to be sleeping on the ground?

"Get down, damn it! Do you want to get blown to hell, too?"

With this outburst, she realized that it had been Luke's voice that had awakened her.

"I didn't mean for you all to go on without me. I'm so damned sorry."

He sounded hoarse, as if his soul were being ripped in two. Even from a distance, she could feel his pain and grief. Staggering to her feet, she ran across the clearing to where he still lay under the tree. Even in the dim light of the fading moon, it was obvious that he was caught up in the throes of a nightmare. Dropping to her knees beside the twisted pile of blankets, she reached out to touch his shoulder.

His muscles felt rigid with tension as he fought the enemies in his dreams and grieved for the friends he'd lost. She tried to shake him awake, to bring him back from wherever he was trapped in his sleep.

"Luke, wake up. It's just a dream."

She used both hands when he didn't respond. "Luke, the war is over. You're dreaming. Wake up. I'm here."

He knocked her hand away and turned away. "Cora? You can't be here. Don't you know people are dying?"

She pulled him back. "Luke, I need you to wake up. I'm not a dream; I'm really here."

This time he seemed to hear her, as he struggled to wake up. When his eyes opened, it took several seconds for them to focus on her face. "Cora?" he whispered, even as his arms snaked out of the blankets to grab on to her shoulders. Just that quickly, he had her pinned to the ground, his mouth plundering hers.

His dreams always had a grim taste of realism to them—the sights and sounds so damned vivid. Blood oozed and screams almost broke his heart. But he couldn't remember ever tasting anything as sweet as Cora's kiss in the long hours of the night. Nor was touch ever part of his nightmares, one reason he always woke up feeling so damned alone.

So if he was tasting Cora and he was touching Cora, he must not be asleep. With recognition came anger. He shoved himself up to look down at her. How much had she seen and heard?

"What are you doing here?" He warned her, "And this is no time for lies or excuses."

She reached up to touch his face. "I needed to know, so I came."

He released her as he sat up. "So now you know. Go home."

"No. I'm through letting you push me away, Luke Gibson." She softened her words with a gentle hand on his arm. "Talk to me. Let me help."

"It's too ugly for you to deal with, little girl," he said with no real heat in his words. Even as he said it, he already knew he would tell her if she insisted. Maybe it would help to share, and he was so damned tired of trying to be noble.

"Lie here beside me and tell me what you can. I'm in no hurry, and I'm not going anywhere."

So he did. The words came slowly at first, but then they sped up. His memories gave him nightmares, and now Cora would likely have a few, too. But it felt as if a wound, long festering inside him, had been finally lanced and cleaned. His tears mingled with hers, to grieve for all that he'd lost. Then, when the words slowed to a trickle, she kissed him, a benediction that made him feel blessed by her sweet acceptance.

Just that quickly, he had his arms around her, pulling her up high against his chest. The feel of her breasts crushed against him felt like heaven. He was dimly aware of her hands tangling in his hair, as he began to kiss her back, loving her sweet sounds of pleasure that drove him crazy.

He broke off the kiss long enough to pant, "Cora, you know where this is headed? And what can happen if we do this again?"

Her eyes, dark and heavy-lidded with passion, stared up at him. Slowly she nodded.

"And this is what you want?"

A smile, slow and full of a woman's power, was his answer. He felt the heat of that smile as if he were standing next to a fire that raged out of control. Fingers fumbled with buttons as they each tried to fight their way through the frustration of fabric to the skin beneath. Finally, Luke felt the sweet silk of Cora's back as it curved down to her waist and then flared out again. Some of the fierce urgency died away, allowing him to savor each new sensation as he took great care to satisfy Cora's wants and needs first.

Somehow it felt right to seek the pleasure of each other's bodies in the night air, with nothing to shelter them but the simplicity of nature herself. And when they lay spent in each other's arms, he felt as if peace had come at last.

CHAPTER 15

The day dawned bright and clear. The air was fresh and cooler than it had been in weeks. Cora felt a bit wicked for having slept out under the stars in her lover's arms. Although she'd gotten very little sleep, she awoke feeling energized. In fact, she'd felt daring enough to show Luke just how much energy she had. Judging by the look on his face when she'd left for town, he'd been impressed.

For the first time since she'd met him, she walked away. In fact, he'd only reluctantly let her go to town alone. If Lucy weren't depending on her to work for her, Cora would have cheerfully spent the day exploring this new turn of events. While Luke hadn't hinted at anything as permanent as marriage, he had agreed to come for dinner after she got back from town.

It was a start.

Footsteps on the stairs reminded her that she was not alone in the store. Lucy had gone upstairs to take care of some paperwork, but it sounded as if she might have finished. Cora schooled her features into a more businesslike expression rather than the silly grin she'd been fighting all morning long. Eventually, she'd share with her friends, but not until she and

Luke had time to reach some sort of agreement on what their relationship would be.

Cora knew when Lucy reached the last step without having to look, thanks to a handy squeak in the wood.

"Well, I'm glad to have all that done." Lucy joined Cora at the counter. "I love owning the store, but I surely do grow tired of all the paperwork that goes along with it." She looked around the store, a satisfied look on her face. "It appears that you have everything down here under control, so I think I'll head on home. Cade will be relieved to have me take over watching the baby from him. He doesn't think much of changing diapers, you know."

Cora laughed. "Can't say as I blame him. I'm not fond of it myself."

"You'll change your mind when you have a baby of your own."

Luckily Lucy was too busy admiring the new display of yard goods to notice Cora's reaction to her words. Her hand automatically went to her waist, as if to protect a new life, one that might not exist. But if she and Luke had indeed created a child, her whole life would be different. She could only hope that she was prepared to face those changes.

Then she realized she'd been wrong. Lucy had noticed all right, judging by the frown on her face as she stared at Cora's hand. Then the frown was gone as Lucy did her best to look merely curious.

"So, tell me. Has there been any progress between you and Luke Gibson?" She trailed a finger along a row of canned goods, all the while watching Cora out of the corner of her eye.

"I'd have to say that things are about the same as they have been. We're still figuring out how to be friendly neighbors." So, that was a bit of a stretch. They were way past just being friendly.

Finally, Lucy stepped close enough to take Cora by the hands. "Don't get me wrong, Cora. I like Luke, but I worry about the hunger in your eyes when you look at him."

"I don't . . ." Cora tried to protest.

Lucy shook her head. "Don't lie to me, Cora, but also don't lie to yourself. You took one look at him the first day he walked through the door, and you haven't looked at any other man since. I think you need to be careful."

It was far too late for her to be careful with her heart, but she wasn't going to admit that. "I thought you liked Luke."

"I do, Cora, but he's not an easy man to know. He has a past that has some people worried. Everyone knows that those men the sheriff has been keeping an eye on ride across Luke's farm. Now I know he hasn't had anything to do with all the bank robberies, but some folks don't know him like we do. If there's ever any trouble in the area, it could go hard on him. I wouldn't want you to get caught in the middle."

"He's a good man, Lucy. He'd never let me get hurt." She knew that as well as she knew her own name.

"I hope you're right, Cora." Lucy gave Cora a quick hug. Then she looked at the clock. "Oops, I need to be going." She picked up her purse. "Thank you again for working for me, Cora. I don't know what I'll do come fall when you start teaching school. It's been a real blessing for me to have you in my life."

"That road runs both ways, Lucy. If it hadn't been for you and Melinda taking me under your wings, I don't know what I would have done. Aunt Henrietta and I get along better these days, but it was a long time coming." Cora followed Lucy to the door. "I'll lock up when I leave."

"I appreciate it. You can either drop the key by the house or leave it with Cade next door at the paper. He said he'd be working later than normal today to make up for staying home this morning."

"All right. Give Mary and Roy each a hug for me."

"I will."

Lucy hurried out the door, no doubt anxious to get home to her family. Once she was gone, Cora wandered around the store, making sure everything was in good order. There didn't appear to be anything that needed doing, so she picked up the book the Luminary Society was going to discuss at the next meeting. She sat down on the staircase and started to read, knowing she would hear the bell above the front door if a customer came in.

Luke had some hard thinking to do and some decisions to make. After Cora had left for town, he walked out to the spring and sat down at the base of a tree and stretched his legs out in front of him. He stared at the rippling water and thought about the future and how he felt about it.

It took him several minutes to come to any conclusions. But if he had to sum it all up, he would have to say for the first time in years, he felt good about what was happening in his life. He had a home, one that he was willing to spend the rest of his life taking care of. He had friends in town, ones who didn't hold his past against him.

And he had Cora.

She'd heard all there was to know about him, the

good and the bad, and hadn't flinched. In his wildest dreams, he'd never thought to find a woman with her strength of character. Maybe that same spirit that made her fight to stand on her own had made her that way.

Could he risk asking her to share his life? He'd almost blurted out a proposal earlier, before she rode away on Falstaff. He still meant to ask her to marry him, but he wanted more time to get the words right. Maybe he'd be able to string the right ones together before she came home from town.

He tried some out.

"Cora Lawford, would you be willing to take a chance on an ex-Confederate soldier?" No, he'd done his best to be a good soldier, but that was over.

"Cora Lawford, would you marry me and help me learn to sleep indoors again?" No, too pitiful. Besides, the one night he'd spent in her bed, the nightmares had stayed away.

"Cora Lawford, I don't have much to offer, but I'm a hard worker, and I promise to do right by you." Better, but not perfect.

Before he tried again, he heard someone hollering. He stood up and listened again. It sounded like Jack calling his name. What could he be wanting? Fearing the worst, Luke took off at a lope for the cabin. Each step of the way, his stomach clenched in fear, thinking of all the things that could have gone wrong in the short time Jack had been gone.

He was relieved to see his brother wandering around the barn, still calling out Luke's name every so often. Evidently he gave up on finding him at the farm, because he turned and headed for the woods that led to Cora's house. If he'd come looking a couple of hours later, that's exactly where Jack would have found him. Luke slowed up and waited for Jack to notice him.

"Oh, there you are. I need to talk to you."

Once again Jack looked as if he'd been putting in some long hours in the saddle. Where had he been this time? Would the sheriff pay another visit in a day or two, asking where Jack had been? The idea worried him considerably, so his words came out sounding angry.

"So talk. I'm right here." He crossed his arms over his chest and waited to see what Jack had to say.

"I was wondering if we could trade horses for a while." Jack rocked from foot to foot, as if he was having trouble staying in one place. Or was afraid to?

"Why? You've always liked that gelding." He glanced over to where the horse was tied up by the corral. Its head hung down, as if it was close to exhaustion.

"He's pulled up lame. He should be fine in a few days, but I can't ride him like he is."

Luke decided to check the horse over for himself. Jack trailed along behind him without saying any more. Either he didn't have a good reason for the horse's condition or else he figured Luke wouldn't want to know what happened.

After running his hand down each of the horse's legs, checking for wounds and swelling, Luke untied the reins and led the sorrel around the yard a couple of times, watching it walk. Sure enough, the animal favored its right front leg. The limp was obvious but didn't appear to be serious.

"What have you been up to that you've been riding him so hard?"

Jack immediately bristled. "We've had this discussion before. What I do is my own business."

"You don't want my advice on anything, but you

want me to clean up your messes." He started stripping off the horse's tack. There was no use in letting the animal suffer because its owner was an idiot. "Take the pinto, but I want her back in a few days and in good shape. She doesn't deserve to be treated like this. If the gelding's leg doesn't mend, you'll have to find yourself another horse."

"Fine." Jack picked up his tack and started transferring it to Luke's horse. "I appreciate this."

"Not enough." Luke closed his eyes and tried to find some words of wisdom that would help steer his brother off the path he'd chosen. Finally, all he could find to say was "Watch your back."

Jack was already mounting up. "I will. Thanks again."

Luke turned his back, unwilling to watch Jack ride away again. Each time he disappeared from sight seemed more and more final. Luke understood Jack's need to find his own way in the world, but he'd feel better if Jack had chosen a better class of friends to run with. Baxter himself seemed to have a gift for leadership. If he was behind the bank robberies, he'd done a fair job of covering his tracks.

But both times Cora had been frightened at the school, Jack's other two friends were involved. Luke wouldn't mind it at all if Jake found some way to lock Isaac and Jeb up for a good long time, as long as it didn't involve Jack. If something happened that separated Jack from the others, maybe he'd come around. But maybe not. He seemed pretty damned determined to make his own choices, no matter where they led him.

Thanks to the visit from Jack, Luke felt too restless to sit back down by the spring and think anymore. Suddenly, he didn't want to wait until dinnertime to see Cora. Riding Jack's horse wasn't an option, but the walk to town would give Luke more time to work out exactly what he wanted to say to Cora.

He'd be covered with dust by the time he walked all the way to Lee's Mill, but there wasn't much he could do about that. Once Cora was done at the store, they could ride back double on Falstaff. The horse might not appreciate the extra load, but Luke would enjoy the trip if he could hold Cora in his arms the entire way. He didn't think she'd object, either.

Pleased with his plans, he headed for the house to pick up a clean shirt to change into once he reached the edge of town.

Even with the windows open, the air hung heavy, hot, and still in the store. Cora fanned herself with a piece of paper, but it did nothing except stir the heat around a little. The temperature continued to creep up, until it leeched away all her energy. She had to guess it was affecting everyone else the same way, because she'd had but one customer in the past two hours. Unless it got busier, she was going to close up early and head home.

To Luke.

A happy grin spread over her face, sending new energy tingling through her veins. If only she could turn the clock ahead. With nothing to keep her mind or hands busy, it felt as if the time would never pass. She looked around the store, considering her options. It was still too hot to do anything inside, but the front porch of the store could use a good sweeping. As dusty as the road was, she could sweep once an hour and not keep up with the grime.

After fetching the broom from the storeroom, she headed outside, relieved to at least breathe some fresh air and move around a bit. Keeping her strokes short, she began gently brushing the dust toward the front edge of the porch. If she worked at it too hard, it would only serve to send the dirt flying up into the air before it settled right back down where it had been.

When a small breeze stirred, she stopped and enjoyed the feel of it cooling her overheated skin. Since no one was around, she unfastened the top two buttons of her dress, wishing she dared remove her petticoat and kick off her shoes. Maybe later, Luke would be interested in a walk along the river. If they waited until the sun started its descent behind the hills, the two of them could sit on that same log and watch the sky turn colors. Then as the lightning bugs started flickering in the woods, he could walk her home and maybe stay the night.

She frowned. Last night, she had seen firsthand what Luke went through in the dark hours of the night. Her stomach knotted up just remembering his agonized cries from the depths of his dreams. At least he'd let himself accept the comfort of her body. A flash of heat rolled through her that had nothing to do with the summer sun beating down from overhead.

Older women often referred to the marriage bed as part of a wife's duty, if they spoke of it at all. Only rarely did any of them even so much as hint that a man could pleasure a woman every bit as much as she could him. Maybe it wasn't true for everyone, but there was no way for her to find out for certain. She didn't dare ask anyone, not even Lucy or Melinda.

All she knew was that when she lay with Luke, he completed her.

She worked her way to the far end of the porch and stopped. Leaning against the railing, she stared down the street, not really seeing anything but the memories in her mind. It took several seconds for her to notice the commotion at the far end of town. A group of horsemen had just come into sight, riding full out. As they passed, the few people on the street started running for cover through the closest doorways. One even dove to the ground to wiggle under a convenient porch. His feet disappeared with one last push.

The riders ignored him as they continued relentlessly down Front Street. There was something unusual about their appearance, although she couldn't see them clearly through the cloud of dust their horses threw up. Growing more uneasy, she backed toward the doorway, wanting something more solid between her and the riders than the porch railing.

Once she was inside, she stood next to the front window, where she could peek out without being seen. As the horses pounded by, she noticed two things that had her heart pounding. She reached out to lean against the wall as her knees began to shake. The men had bandannas hiding their faces and guns gripped in their hands.

And the last horse in line was Luke's pinto. There was no mistaking those markings.

She dropped the broom to grab on to the nearest shelf for support as her mind tried to find a way to make sense of what she'd just seen. What did a group of armed men want in Lee's Mill? Before her mind could come up with a reasonable answer, a burst of gunfire exploded down the street. As best she could tell, it came from the direction of the bank.

After the first rounds, there was a brief silence before the shooting started up again. She dropped to the floor, knowing full well how little protection wooden walls and glass windows offered against stray bullets. She crawled across the room to hide behind the counter, hoping that everyone in town had been able to make it to cover safely.

She wanted to cover her ears against the terrifying noise, but it sounded as if it was getting closer. Tilting her head one way and then the other, she couldn't really tell. If she was right, then maybe she'd been wrong about the bank. It could be just a bunch of fools raising a ruckus just because they could, but that didn't seem likely. Rowdies didn't bother to cover their faces when they rode through town.

No, those men hadn't been having fun; there was grim determination in the way they rode. If she had to guess, they were the bunch she'd seen that day by the school. The memory made her shiver in the heat of the day.

She closed her eyes and prayed for the safety of her friends and neighbors, especially Jake Whitney and his deputy. Both of them were good at their jobs, but the odds were against them, two men against those hard-looking ruffians.

This time she could hear someone hollering, but she couldn't make out what was being said. But the gunfire was getting closer. She risked a look over the counter, not sure what she hoped to see. A riderless horse galloped past followed by another horse with its owner slumped over the saddle, a splash of bright red staining his shirt.

Oh, Lord, people were dying, maybe people she knew. Tears blurred her vision as she dropped back down to the floor. Maybe if she weren't alone, she wouldn't be so frightened, but the noise combined with the tension made her shake like a leaf. She squeezed her eyes shut, praying it would all go away.

Someone ran past the window on the side of the store. Without knowing who it was, she could only hope that he would keep right on running. She had no idea what she'd do if one of the gang tried to take refuge in the store. Had she locked the door? She couldn't remember. Rather than risk another look, she tried to recall each detail from the second she first noticed the riders coming toward her.

She remembered backing through the door while still watching the street. Next, she'd watched at the window until the gunfire had sent her ducking for cover behind the counter. All of which meant the door probably was not locked, not that it mattered since the windows were also wide open. And, from the sound of things, someone was climbing in through the one in the storeroom.

Her throat closed up as she frantically tried to figure out what to do. She might make it to the bottom of the stairs, but it was doubtful that she'd make it to the top without being seen or heard. The front door was closer, but she could still hear gunshots coming from the street. Finally, she clambered to her feet to look for a place to hide. Leaning against the counter for support, she decided her best choice was the cluttered corner where Lucy kept the fabrics and sewing notions.

She'd gone no more than a few steps when a loud thump followed by several curse words warned her that she was no longer alone in the store. The need to run threatened to send her into a complete panic. She stumbled forward, losing her balance as she caught her heel on the hem of her skirt. Before she could right herself, the sound of a gun being cocked robbed her of her breath and her last chance to escape.

Luke shrugged out of his dirty shirt and tossed it over the lowest branch of a nearby oak, planning on retrieving it on his way back home with Cora. Knowing her, she'd think leaving his laundry hanging in a tree was funny. That was all right. He liked the sound of her laughter.

He continued on his way as he buttoned his good blue shirt. Knowing he was only a few blocks away from Cora had him picking up the pace as he considered how much his life had changed. Only a few days ago, he'd figured on living out his life alone. Now he could hardly stand to be parted from Cora. That he was almost running down a dusty road served as one more sign that he had it bad. The thought didn't worry him as much as he thought it should.

The first few houses in town were just coming into sight. He took off his hat long enough to run his fingers through his hair. As he adjusted his hat to shade his eyes from the sun, he heard a series of popping noises, a sound all too familiar to him: gunfire. His hand automatically reached to check the ease of movement of his revolver in its holster. He had no quarrel with a few rowdies having a little fun, but he didn't want to walk into the middle of an unsettled situation unprepared to protect himself.

He glanced up at the sun's position in the sky. It was a tad early for somebody to be raising hell. Normally, it was several hours after sunset before any trouble started. When the gunfire continued, he wondered where the hell Jake Whitney was. He hoped the lawman wasn't out in the countryside, checking up on Baxter and his men, including Jack. The townsfolk wouldn't much appreciate having Front Street shot up while the sheriff satisfied his curiosity.

More gunfire. By now, Luke had reached the outskirts of town, although there was no one in sight, which didn't surprise him. Anyone with good sense took to cover when shooting started. Although the sound rattled around and echoed through the houses, he could tell that most of the shots were coming from the near end of town. What was there besides the saloon? The stable, the hotel, and the bank. As soon as the thought crossed his mind, he froze.

His gut told him that the bank was being robbed. He started walking again, hoping like hell that he was wrong. If Baxter and his men had decided to move on, it made sense that they might finance their plans with an illegal withdrawal. While Luke didn't have any money in the bank, he knew others who did. It was unlikely that they'd let Baxter ride in and ride out without fighting to keep their money right where it belonged.

Not that he gave a damn what happened to Baxter or the men who chose to follow him, with one important exception—Jack. The sick feeling he'd been fighting since Jack had left, determined to seek his fortune with his friends, roiled through Luke's stomach. If his younger brother was embroiled in the shootout, Luke would do whatever it took to get him out.

For now, he had to plan his approach. He wouldn't be of much help to anybody if he stumbled in front of a barrage of gunfire. When the shots slowed to a stop he worked his way down the street. The final two blocks to Front Street offered little in the way of cover, so he cut over to a narrow alley that ran along the far side of the hotel. Hugging the side of the building, he drew his gun and kept moving forward, stopping every few feet to listen. Other than sporadic shots, it didn't sound as if the fight was moving. If he had to guess, he figured that both sides had taken cover and were now trying to wait each other out.

Finally, he reached the front porch of the hotel. He took off his hat and knelt down to take a peek around the corner. He kept his movements slow and deliberate, figuring any sudden motion would be more likely to draw fire. Once he had a clear view of the street, he wanted to curse. From what he could tell, the sheriff and his deputy had managed to pin down Baxter and a few of his men in the bank.

Several windows of the bank were shattered, but there was no telling whose bullets had done the damage. It seemed more likely to be the work of the would-be bank robbers. If there were citizens of Lee's Mill trapped inside with Baxter's men, Sheriff Whitney would be hesitant to risk hitting them.

Luke studied the street. He could pick out several more familiar faces backing up the sheriff and his deputy, Cade among them. Unless he was mistaken, the man crouched down beside Cade was his typesetter, Will.

From the looks of things, Baxter had picked the wrong town to rob, but he'd probably figured that out for himself by now. Luke didn't give a damn what happened to him, as long as he didn't take Jack down with him. The only way Luke was going to be able to help was to throw his lot in with the sheriff. Luke waited until Cade glanced toward the hotel before waving his gun over his head to catch his eye.

Cade nodded in his direction before turning his attention back to the bank. In the time it had taken for Cade to notice Luke, the sheriff had disappeared. Was he going to try to work his way up behind the bank? Before Luke could check out that theory, the click of a hammer sent a chill up his spine. Raising his hands slowly, he turned to find Jake Whitney staring down the barrel of his rifle right at him.

"How did you get out of the bank?" Ice had nothing on the chill in Whitney's voice.

"I was never in it."

"I warned you, Gibson. People around here might forget about you killing that Yankee after the war, but they won't take kindly to you and your friends trying to rob their bank."

What had he done to make the sheriff think he was involved in this mess? "I don't know what you're talking about. I walked here from my farm to meet Cora Lawford. I heard the shots as I came into town."

The rifle didn't waver an inch. "If that's true, why is your horse tied up outside the bank?"

"How the hell should I know?" His bluff wasn't convincing. If his mare had been stolen, he would have reported it, and the sheriff knew it. "Check my gun. It hasn't been fired recently." He tossed his revolver on the ground and then stepped back. Whitney knelt down slowly, careful not to give Luke a chance to run.

He sniffed the gun and checked the cylinder to see that the gun was fully loaded. "So what are you doing slipping around back here?" he asked, as he lowered his rifle and held the gun out for Luke to take.

"It's just like I said. I walked into town to meet Cora when I heard shots."

The sheriff's eyes narrowed in suspicion. "If you walked, why is your horse here? There's no mistaking those markings, so don't lie."

"I don't know." That much was true. He didn't know why Jack had gotten mixed up in such a mess. On the other hand, the sheriff hadn't asked him who had his horse. He might be stretching the truth a bit, but he hadn't actually lied.

"Has anybody gotten hurt?"

"A couple of Baxter's men—one's dead. I shot him

and another as they tried to make a break for it. From the look of the second one, he won't last long either. His horse tore out of town with him barely hanging on. Once we get this mess cleaned up, I'll worry about him." Whitney looked more grim than ever. "We don't know what's happened inside the bank. We're guessing there weren't many people inside when Baxter made his move. The banker and his tellers were still there, but that's all we know for sure."

Luke mentally counted the number of horses he could remember seeing out in the street. "Did anyone get an accurate count of how many of them there were?"

"Best guess is at least ten, maybe twelve, rode into town. Someone saw about five of them go into the bank."

"There are more horses than that out there. How many others got away?"

"Good question." Whitney started back the way he'd come. "You stick with me until I sort out this business about your horse. We'll circle around and see if we can tell."

Luke supposed he couldn't blame Whitney for not taking him at his word. There was no denying that his mare was tied up outside the bank. Unless he wanted to openly accuse his own brother of stealing her, the sheriff had to know Luke was hiding something.

The two men gave the bank a wide berth before poking their heads out to do another count of the horses. There were only five still tied up near the bank. Three others were milling around loose a short distance up the street. Added to the two Whitney had already mentioned, that left at least three men unaccounted for. While he'd like to think that they'd been lucky enough to make good their escape, Luke had his doubts. A new sense of urgency had him feeling edgy.

"Has anyone checked to make sure they haven't taken cover somewhere close by?"

Whitney shook his head. "There hasn't been time."

A new volley of shots came pouring out of the bank window and had the deputy and the others ducking their heads. As soon as they did, the door of the bank burst open as a handful of men came pouring out, their guns spitting bullets.

Both Luke and the sheriff returned fire. The first outlaw out the door screamed and fell to the ground as a splash of blood bloomed on his chest. The one behind him took one in the leg. He took another step or two before collapsing in the street. Immediately, the others dove back into the dubious safety of the bank and started shooting. As the sheriff started shouting orders, Luke slipped away. Whitney wouldn't like it, but he'd deal with that problem later. Right now he was more worried about Cora and Jack.

Zigzagging between buildings, Luke studied the ground, not sure what he was looking for. Thomas Mercantile was only a short distance up the street from the bank. Anyone who had spent time in Lee's Mill knew that the store was owned and operated by a woman. If any of Baxter's men had made it away from the bank on foot, they'd be looking for a place to hole up until things down the street settled down.

They also might be needing more ammunition or even medical supplies. The more he thought about it, the more certain he was that he was on the right track. He considered going back for more help, but for Jack's sake, he couldn't risk it. Whitney wouldn't hesitate to shoot. Cade would kill anyone who threatened his wife and child without a second thought.

All of which left it up to Luke to make sure the women were safe and to rescue Jack if possible. And if it turned out that anyone had hurt Cora, Luke would give no quarter, brother or no brother. He turned down the street that ran alongside the newspaper office to Cade's house. Before he reached the front yard, he caught sight of Lucy in the upstairs window. She looked worried but not scared.

One worry off his mind. He veered back toward the store. At the mouth of the narrow alley that ran between the newspaper office and the store, he knelt down to study the dusty ground. Three sets of heel prints led up the alley. They looked undisturbed and fresh, but he had no way of knowing if they'd been there ten minutes or ten hours.

He kept looking, turning his eyes from side to side until he spotted something that brought him to an abrupt halt. If he'd been moving any faster he would have missed it—four or five small spots of wetness on the ground. Dreading what he'd find out, he touched the first couple and then looked at his finger. The small bit of mud stained his skin red.

Blood.

CHAPTER 16

Fear for his woman coupled with fury toward anyone who would threaten her made him want to burst into the store, gun blazing. He drew on the skills he'd honed back in the war, doing his damnedest to ignore his concern for Cora long enough to come up with a plan. It wasn't all that different than when he'd had to leave his wounded friends to bleed on the ground while he fought to push the enemy back. Only then could he go back and try to ease their pain and get them to safety.

If it was too late, then he had used his grief to keep fighting.

The windows in the back of the store were all open, no doubt the way the outlaws would have entered the store. They could be watching to make sure no one else used the same route.

That left the front door, which would make him an easy target. He wouldn't be much use to Cora by getting killed on the front porch of the store. There had to be another way into the store. Cade would not have built a place where his wife could be trapped.

Luke backed up to take a better look at the second floor. There were windows along the back. How could he reach them? A ladder would be the obvious answer, but there wasn't time to fetch one. He wouldn't leave

Cora trapped inside a minute longer than absolutely necessary. He looked at the newspaper office behind him and then back at the store. The two buildings were of a height and little more than six feet or so apart.

He could jump that far. Turning his attention to the newspaper office, he ran around to the far side before approaching the front door. Before coming around onto the porch, he leaned around the corner to make sure no one was watching from the store. It appeared that he had a clear path to the front door. He sidled along the wall until he reached the door. Luckily, Cade had left in a hurry, so the office wasn't locked up.

Luke slipped in the door and then locked the door behind him to slow down anyone who might be following him. He took the steps two at a time up to the second floor. Although he looked out onto the alley below, he decided to climb to the roof from the back window to cut down on the chances of being seen.

Once he was upstairs, he holstered his gun before sticking his head out of the window. There wasn't much to hold on to, but he'd find some way to climb onto the roof. Turning around, he sat down on the windowsill with his upper body outside and his feet still on the floor. With a long stretch he could reach the edge of the roof. As he got a good grip on it, he pulled himself through the window until he was standing on the sill.

It took every bit of strength he could muster to pull himself up onto Cade's roof. Luckily, the pitch of the roof was fairly shallow, so he didn't have much trouble standing up on it. Crouching low to keep a low profile, he worked his way across the roof to the edge next to the store. He studied the situation and finally decided to just back up and take a running leap.

At the very worst, he'd hit the ground below and break his neck, he decided with a grim smile.

He counted off the steps as he ran—one, two, three, and then he was flying through the air. The impact when he landed knocked the breath out of him. Ignoring his body's demand for air, he rolled over onto his back and sat up. He remained motionless for several long seconds, waiting to see if anyone in the store below had heard him land.

He wasn't sure that silence translated into safety, but at least no one was shooting through the ceiling at him. Using the window across the alley as a guide, he tried to judge how far he was from the corresponding one below him. When he figured he was close, he lay down on his stomach and worked his way toward the edge. As he groped for a handhold, he picked up a splinter that hurt like hell. He pulled it out with his teeth, ignoring the small ooze of blood as he swung his legs down off the edge. His fingers ached with the strain of supporting his weight until he could get his foot on the sill below.

The window wasn't open far enough for him to climb through. Using his foot, he raised the sash up a few inches at a time until he couldn't move it any more. Then, with a wordless prayer, he let go of the roof with one hand to grip the window with his fingers. Figuring it wouldn't get any easier, he went for broke. With some quick scrambling, he managed to get his feet through the window far enough to keep from tumbling backward down to the ground below.

Each noise seemed to echo like cannon fire, but so far if anyone had noticed, they chose to ignore him. Once inside the window, he tried to get his bearings. The room was filled with a few rows of benches and a couple of long tables across the front. As he looked around, he remembered Cora's telling him that the Luminary Society had a meeting room above the store.

Deciding he'd make less of a racket without his boots, he slipped them off before walking across the floor. Everything seemed to be taking way too much time. His heart pounded as he gently turned the doorknob and eased the door open to listen. For the first time, he could hear an angry mumble of voices coming from down the stairs.

He wished like hell he knew who was there and where they stood. Once he started down the steps, he'd be visible to anyone who happened to look in his direction. Why hadn't he thought to get someone to raise a ruckus outside while he attacked from above? It was too late to worry about it.

Bracing himself for the worst, he slipped through the door and crossed the short distance to the top of the stairs. Each step took him that much closer to Cora—and Jack. He drew a deep breath and prayed that she was unharmed. On the third step, he paused to listen.

"Get out of the way, Gibson!"

At first Luke thought they'd spotted him, but then he heard his brother. Another two steps brought the room into view.

"Like hell I will. The two of you stand a chance of getting away if you go back out the way you came in. The longer you wait, the more likely that sheriff is going to decide to come looking for us."

"She's going with us when we leave. That lawman won't be as likely to shoot if he might hit her." This came from a different speaker.

"Only if you go through me."

"That won't be a problem for us." Ugly laughter followed the threat.

"Which one of you wants to die first?" Jack smiled, sounding more calm than his former partners. "Baxter doesn't think much of cowards. What do you think he'll do when he finds out you were hiding behind a woman's skirts?"

"He's not going to know. Besides, Baxter has his hands full with the sheriff and his deputy right now."

Jeb, or maybe it was Isaac, took another step forward. Jack's voice sounded a little breathless. Was the blood in the alley his? How badly was he hurt? Luke came down two more steps. He hunched down to see better. The scene came straight out of one of his nightmares. Cora was pinned in the corner, surrounded by a tumbled mess of fabric and other notions. Jack stood between her and his two companions, his gun in hand. His other arm hung limply at his side; blood ran down his sleeve to drip into a small pool on the floor.

Sheer determination seemed to be the only thing keeping him on his feet. He swayed forward but managed to catch himself. The only question now was if the two men would run out of time before Jack lost consciousness. He might take out one of them, but it was doubtful that he'd get off a second shot in time. Cora had a large pair of scissors in her hand, ready to defend herself if necessary. She looked scared but not helpless.

Luke needed to draw their attention before Jack collapsed. If he could make it all the way down the stairs, he'd stand a better chance of taking control of the situation. Jack's eyes flickered in his direction and then back to the two outlaws. Unfortunately, Cora wasn't as adept at hiding her emotions. As soon as she saw Luke, her face lit up with hope.

All hell broke loose in a short, vicious burst of gunfire.

"Get down!" Luke screamed as he plunged down the last two steps, gun blazing.

For once, Cora did as he ordered without arguing. She dove behind a table and disappeared from sight. Jack's first shot tore into Isaac, sending him reeling backward, blood gushing from his chest. Luke's bullet spun him back around, finishing what Jack had started. The man was dead before he hit the ground. Luke took aim where Jeb had been, but the outlaw managed to take cover behind the counter as he sent a spray of bullets across the room.

Luke hit the floor rolling. He ignored the sudden burning in his upper arm. Experience told him it was a flesh wound, the kind that hurt like hell but didn't kill.

He could hear Jeb scrambling across the floor toward the storeroom, no doubt intent on escaping through the window. He didn't give a damn where the bastard went as long as he kept going. The silence didn't last long. Someone was shouting "Hands up!"

A couple of shots rang out, followed by the sound of running feet. Luke recognized the next voice. "He's dead." Cade didn't sound particularly upset by the fact.

Luke crawled across the floor to his brother. He ripped open Jack's shirt. Cora had already started tearing strips of fabric off a bolt to use for bandages.

While she did that, he lifted Jack up against his chest. Fear for his brother's life tasted bitter. "Jack, you hold on. We'll have the doctor here in a few minutes."

Cora knelt down beside them. She shoved a wad of fabric on Jack's arm and then quickly wound another strip around it to hold it in place. Blood bubbled out of a hole on his right side. She put a makeshift bandage over it and pressed down. Jack moaned in pain.

His eyes fluttered open briefly. A faint smile stained his lips.

"Nice timing, Luke." Then he sank back into unconsciousness.

"Jack, damn you, hold on." Luke held on with as much strength as he could muster.

The front door slammed open with Sheriff Whitney leading the charge. He took two steps into the room. It didn't take him long to assess the situation. He ran back out long enough to start yelling for the doctor. When he returned, he'd holstered his gun.

"Can he be moved?" His voice was surprisingly gentle.

Cade came up behind him. "Let's take him to my house."

The two men found a wide board to use as a makeshift stretcher. With Luke's help they carefully lifted Jack and carried him to Cade's house. Lucy saw them coming and threw open the door.

"Put him on the table. Doc will have an easier time seeing to him there." She led the way. As soon as the doctor arrived, Lucy shooed everyone out of the room, including Luke.

"We'll take good care of him, Luke. Right now all you'll do is be in the way." Lucy gave him a gentle hug. "Doc will do his best for him."

Cora stood beside him, still covered with his brother's blood. Luke gathered enough of his wits to hold out his arms to her. Thanks be to God, she didn't even hesitate.

Two hours later, Cora ached with weariness. The doctor's report had been guarded at best. He'd managed to stop the bleeding, but Jack had lost a lot of blood. All they could do was watch and wait. Lucy and Cade had insisted on Jack's being left in their care until he was strong enough to be moved.

If he lived through the night.

Luke hadn't been able to do more than nod. His eyes glittered with the same terror that filled his nightmares. Cora drew some comfort from the way he seemed to need her touch, his fingers intertwined with hers. Maybe together they would get through this.

A knock at the door disturbed her thoughts. She tore her eyes away from Luke long enough to see who'd come in. Her aunt swept into the room. Henrietta immediately headed right for the two of them.

"Cora, my dear, are you all right? I would be upset that you didn't send for me immediately, but I understand that other things had to take priority." She nodded in Luke's direction. "How is your young man?" She spoke as if he were across the room rather than right beside Cora.

"He's worried about his brother." She gave Luke's hand a squeeze.

"Understandably so, from what I hear." Henrietta stepped in front of Luke. "Young man, look at me." It took a second or two, but finally he did as she asked.

"I want you and Cora to come with me. There's nothing you can do for your brother right now but pray. You can do that from my house. Both of you need to get cleaned up and eat something. I won't brook any arguments from either of you. If there's a change, Mr. Mulroney will send word." Rather than give either of them a chance to object to her high-handed demands, she turned her back on them. "Now come along."

Cora wanted to hug the woman. She stood up and tugged Luke to his feet. "You won't be any help to Jack if you don't take care of yourself. Aunt Henrietta's right about that."

The three of them walked the few blocks to Henrietta's house. They drew stares from those they passed because of the dried blood on their clothes and the stories already making their way through town. Once they were inside Henrietta's house, she started bossing them again. For once, Cora let her. In only minutes, they were washed up and in clean clothes. Sometime she'd have to ask Henrietta how she happened to have a shirt and pants for Luke. Right now, she was too tired to be curious.

"Now, Mr. Gibson, you sit down at the table and tuck into that bowl of stew. I pride myself on my cooking, and I won't see it go to waste." Her tart words didn't change the concern on her face.

Luke managed a small smile. "Yes, ma'am."

For the first time since the outlaws had cornered her in the store, Cora felt like things might work out. She took a seat across from Luke so that she could keep an eye on him. When he'd done justice to the simple meal, she decided it was time to talk about a few things.

"Jack had your horse, didn't he?"

Luke nodded. "His gelding had come up lame. We traded horses for a few days."

"I knew there was a good explanation." She smiled, happy that her instincts hadn't played her false.

Henrietta joined the discussion. "I'd like to know how you came to be in the store right when you were most needed."

Luke kept his eyes on Cora as he answered Henrietta. "I had something I wanted to say to Cora that couldn't wait, so I walked to town. The sheriff and others already had Baxter and his men pinned down in the bank when I reached the edge of town."

He seemed to get lost in the memory, but neither of the women tried to rush him. Cora appreciated her aunt's tact.

"I saw my mare tied up outside of the bank, so I knew Jack was involved. When the outlaws tried to fight their way out, I saw he wasn't with them and neither were those two . . ." He paused. "Uh, those two fools that he's been riding with. I knew Cora was at the store, and I had to make sure she was safe. I found blood in the alley next to the store, so I knew they were in there." He shuddered and reached across the table to take Cora's hand again.

"How did you get to the second floor?"

His smile was getting stronger. "I jumped from the roof of the newspaper office and climbed down into a window."

"You what? You could have died!" Henrietta sounded horrified. Cora didn't blame her.

"I couldn't think of any other way to get in without them knowing. And like I said, I had something I wanted to say to you. I just wish Jack hadn't been there. That's the last time he scares you, Cora. I promise."

She shook her head, the fear still fluttering in her chest. "He tried his best to hold them off long enough for me to get out. Jack protected me from those two men, Luke. I mean to thank him as soon as he wakes up."

"If he wakes up." The blue in Luke's eyes dimmed to a dull gray.

"Now, Luke Gibson, don't go doubting that the good Lord can work miracles. Your brother did the right thing there at the end, and God knows that." Henrietta started clearing the table. "As soon as I get these dishes in the sink, I'll go in the other room. You probably would like a little privacy when you ask my niece to marry you."

Cora gasped in outrage. This was too much, even coming from her aunt. Her face turned bright pink in embarrassment. It took all her courage to face Luke, but to her amazement he was grinning. Henrietta sailed out of the room, leaving the two of them alone.

"Luke, I'm sorry. Sometimes she gets these wild ideas in her head."

"And sometimes she's right, Cora. That's exactly what I was going to talk to you about."

He walked around to her side of the table and tugged her to her feet. "I rehearsed what I wanted to say all the way to town, but I couldn't get the words right. Then with all that went on, all I could think about was keeping you safe. I don't have much to offer you, Cora Lawford, but if you'll have me, I promise I'll spend the rest of my life doing just that."

She knew what he felt for her—it was there in his eyes and in the way he'd been holding on to her. But she still wanted the words, so she asked a simple question. "Why?"

He frowned, clearly not understanding what she wanted, so she explained. "Why do you want to marry me, Luke? Sheriff Whitney gets paid to keep people safe, but he doesn't go around marrying them."

The words didn't come easily, but finally he put the right ones together. "I want to marry you because for the first time since before the war, I've got something to live for, something that brings me peace." He brushed a kiss across her lips. "And that something is you. You've made me happy, you've made me furious, and somehow, you've made me love you."

The next kiss was much more serious. He stole

her breath away. Finally, though, he let her answer. "I will be proud to be your wife, Luke Gibson."

"It took you long enough, Luke Gibson!" Henrietta stood in the doorway. "I know young people don't think they need anyone's blessing anymore, but if anyone asks, you have mine."

Luke left Cora's side long enough to pick up her aunt and twirl her around the room, finally setting her down next to Cora. Then he kissed Henrietta on the cheek. "Of course we want your blessing."

To Cora's amazement, Henrietta giggled and blushed. "Now, you stop that, Luke Gibson!"

A knock at the door brought an abrupt halt to the celebrating. Henrietta hurried to see who had come calling. Cora slipped her arm around Luke's waist, letting him know without words that she would be by his side, no matter what the news was. Just that simple gesture helped keep despair at bay.

Sheriff Whitney joined them in the kitchen. Lines of exhaustion bracketed his mouth, but his eyes were alert. He acknowledged with a nod the united front that Cora and Luke presented.

"We need to talk, Gibson."

Cora started to protest, but Luke hushed her with a quick squeeze. "I'm sure Miss Dawson won't mind us sitting down at her table, Sheriff. We've all had a long day." Luke pulled out a chair for Cora and then sat down next to her.

"I want to know what happened after you left me by the bank."

Luke told him what had happened, wishing like hell he could leave his brother's name out of it. To his surprise, Whitney actually laughed when he described climbing down from the roof. "That's a heck of a story."

Luke had a few questions of his own. "What happened to that bunch at the bank?"

"Well, no one from Lee's Mill was hurt. That Baxter fellow had locked them all in Cletus Bradford's office and told them to keep down. We managed to take Baxter and two of his men alive, although one was shot in the leg. After Doc took care of your brother, he came down to the jail to check him over. He should pull through."

The mention of Jack's name had Luke feeling sick. "What about Jack?"

The sheriff leaned back in his chair and stretched his legs out in front of him. "The way I figure it, your brother stumbled into a situation in the store. He did his best to keep Miss Cora here out of the clutches of those two men until help arrived."

"And?"

"And according to Baxter, he never saw Jack anywhere near the bank today." If Whitney doubted the outlaw, he didn't say. "Well, I'd better be going. I hope your brother pulls through." They followed him to the door. Just before he walked out, he turned back to Luke. "With everything that's happened, I almost forgot. Baxter had a message for you, Luke. He said that his brother's name was Freddy. Any idea what he was talking about?"

Luke felt as if he'd been punched in the stomach. "Yes, I do."

"You sure you want to do this?"

"I'm sure." Luke pushed his brother out of the way to look at himself in the mirror. "You're just jealous."

"Not me. That aunt of Cora's scares me." Jack

shuddered. "She says I have to walk her to church next Sunday."

Luke met his brother's gaze in the mirror. "She's not as fierce as she thinks she is."

Jack didn't look convinced. "She knew our parents. It's sure strange to hear tales about Ma and Pa when they were little more than kids themselves."

"I know, but I like hearing her stories. Somehow it makes it seem like Ma and Pa are still with us."

"We'd better be going. Cora won't appreciate you being late for the wedding. Not to mention Miss Dawson." Jack clapped him on the shoulder.

Lucy had insisted that the two of them use her house to get ready rather than riding in from the farm. Jack's strength was returning, but slowly. Even the short walk to the church was a strain. The time he'd spent flat on his back recuperating had given him the chance to re-think what he wanted to do with his life. Although he still didn't want anything to do with farming, he had no intention of repeating his mistakes. Luke drew great comfort from that.

But now he had more important things on his mind. Cade was waiting for them on the church steps. "About time you got here. I think Miss Dawson was about to send Jake Whitney to haul you in."

Luke ignored the teasing as he took his position at the front of the church. Jack stood beside him as they waited for Cora. Henrietta had kept her busy for the past few days, allowing Luke to see her only a few minutes here and there.

But finally there she was, walking down the aisle, a serene smile lighting her beautiful face, her dark eyes full of promises. When Cora tucked her hand into the crook of his arm, he felt as if he'd been made complete.

Experience the Romance of
Rosanne Bittner